I0788457

ACKNOWLEDGEMENTS

This has been a long journey getting here! Now the book has come to fruition and has finally made its way onto bookshelves! The last ten years have been a roller coaster of a life, and there were many times I wondered if I was ever going to publish. Times I wondered if giving up would be better than saying it took me ten years to write. Yet, with the encouragement of so many loved ones, I pressed on.

I want to first acknowledge my Savior and Lord Jesus Christ for being the main inspiration behind the story. He gave me my imagination from the time I was young, and allowed it to grow and blossom into what would turn into a novel! I only pray my efforts would bring Him glory and help further advance the Kingdom of God. I give any glory and praise to Him who allowed for this amazing opportunity!

I then want to acknowledge my husband, who though I met later on in my book journey, was my greatest accountability partner and encourager in the hardest stages of my editing process.

Then also, to all those who have been patiently awaiting the launch of Kingdoms Quest. You have been one of my main motivators. I only pray it was worth your wait!

Thank you to my family who never gave up on me, my sisters for giving me loving feedback, and my editors who also endured the wait as well.

UNITED HOUSE Publishing
Waterford, Michigan
info@unitedhousepublishing.com
www.unitedhousepublishing.com

Cover Design:

Cover Layout and Interior Design:
Matt Russell, In The Light Creative, matt@inthelightcreative.com

Printed in the United States of America
2025—First Edition

SPECIAL SALES
Most UNITED HOUSE books are available at special quantity discounts when purchased in bulk by corporations, organizations, and special-interest groups. For information, please e-mail orders@unitedhousepublishing.com

To my mother, who nurtured my imagination and never told me my dreams were too big. And to my father, who placed the first fantasy books in my hands and sparked my desire to write a story of my own.

And to you, the reader, may this story inspire you to seek the Kingdom of God, for there is no greater or more rewarding quest in this life.

PROLOGUE

The cold wind whipped Alaina's dark hair across her face, momentarily covering her electric blue eyes. An arrow would fly into the soldier at the bell tower any moment now, and he would drop. Alaina was to climb the wall to meet her rescue team as soon as that happened. Together, they would find the hidden dungeon where she would read the faces of every prisoner to find her father. He should be easy to find, given his eye color and the fact that she could see the gift in him.

The woods were quiet, just as before she left on this journey with Koen and her brother. In this moment of silence, the memories came back to her.

When Alaina was young, her grandmother told her she had inherited two special things from her father. The first thing that stood out was the color of her eyes: they were just like her father's, but unique from anyone else. Her twin brother had also inherited the eye color. They were an electric blue that was both beautiful and soul-piercing simultaneously. The second thing was "the gift"—the ability to read people like an open book. She could tell if the man in front of her was an enemy or a friend; she could tell the personality from a simple glance. She knew who she could trust and whom she could not; she could tell a thief from an honest man. Sometimes, though, Alaina wasn't sure if it was a gift. She saw the anger, the sadness, the evil, and the hatred in every face she looked at. It was hard for a young girl, but she had grown strong, and with God's help, she carried the gift when it was a burden.

Alaina sighed. So much had happened. She just hoped it wouldn't be for nothing.

She looked up when she heard a thud. The arrow had found its mark, and the soldier was down. It was time to move.

"Lord, help us," she prayed, sprinting towards the wall.

ONE

For not in my bow do I trust, nor can my sword
save me. But you have saved us from our foes
and have put to shame those who hate us.
Psalm 44:6-7, ESV

A warm breeze set the green leaves of the forest trees dancing, while birds sang joyful songs in the dense canopy. All was well in the land of Azgalia . . . or so it seemed.

Eighteen-year-old Alaina breathed in and slowly raised her bow. Her midnight black hair lay on her shoulders as her electric blue eyes followed the buck. The buck was truly a stunning sight, and his beauty almost made her reconsider the need for dinner that night. Her family, however, needed the food. She raised her bow and aimed while holding her breath. Just before she let the arrow loose, the buck took off at lightning speed, and Alaina froze.

She knew the buck had not sensed her.

Her eyes darted around for the thickest tree to hide in. Her grandmother had taught her how to hunt, fight, and hide from any animal without being sensed. Her grandmother's resourcefulness had always inspired her. Many women in their area were not skilled in what her grandmother was skilled in. With quiet agility, she tucked herself behind a tree and waited.

Her grandmother always told her to be careful of these forests because they were known for drawing strange things from faraway places. Alaina knew her grandmother was mostly teasing because of the stories she used to read, but she also knew her grandmother truly wanted her to be cautious. She searched the area to see what had scared the buck. It could've been anything, but the forest seemed strangely quiet.

Just then, she heard a twig snap under what must have been something heavier than a wolf, but lighter than a bear. She lowered herself to the ground so she could better understand what was coming toward her. Then she saw it . . . or . . . him—a tall young man, maybe a couple of years older than Alaina, with a strongly built frame. He walked past where she had been standing, nervously checking his surroundings. Alaina could not see his face because of the shadow a tree was casting upon him. His clothing said he was a simple peasant, but his posture said otherwise. Alaina finally saw what she had been looking for. The symbol of her kingdom's greatest adversary, Mizcriea, was on the sword's pommel.

Alaina was familiar with the numerous stories of King Malikai of Azgalia's attempts to forge peace with the recalcitrant King Cleatus of Mizcriea. Why would this man be wandering in her forest?

The man was a few feet away when Alaina jumped out from behind the tree, and with skilled precision, lifted her bow and pulled the arrow back. She caught the man off guard, but he still matched her speed as he drew his sword. The shadow still covered him so that Alaina couldn't see his face.

"Who are you, and what are you doing here? Don't bother lying," Alaina spoke with a stern voice.

Sword still drawn and with a ready stance, the young man answered, "My name is Koen, and I am simply taking a morning stroll in the woods. Who might you be, and what is a young girl like you doing in the forest alone?" His tone sounded humorous.

Alaina hated being considered young, but her grandmother was always wise enough to point out what the scriptures taught about youth in the book of 1st Timothy.

Wait . . . did he say, Koen? She couldn't breathe for a few moments after she heard his name.

Koen was her father's name.

Out of all the names this stranger could have, it was that one. Her stomach didn't feel so good.

Alaina gathered herself and focused. His voice was smooth, but there was a slight sound of a Mizcriean accent.

"Step into the light, and I will answer your questions," Alaina said calmly.

Koen slowly stepped into the light, and Alaina immediately read his face.

Fear. Kindness. Uncertainty. Honesty.

Sometimes, she read more than she cared to know about a person, and sometimes, she read only their characteristics and what kind of person they were. She couldn't control her gift like her grandmother said her father could. With Koen, she saw a lot, but she knew there was more to learn. He was burying it within himself.

By the looks of it, his face showed he was a young man, older than adolescent years, but young enough that he'd just come out of them. He had short, dark blonde hair and deep-set, sea-green eyes. He looked kind and had a meaningful gaze.

Alaina lowered her bow and answered softly, "You hide your accent well, Koen. My name is Alaina. I was out here hunting a buck, which you just so happened to have scared away. Also, I told you not to bother lying. Now tell me, why are you here?"

Koen looked a bit startled that Alaina could hear his accent and that she could tell he had lied. "Very observant. It's quite nice to meet you. Where I come from, there are no girls with your color eyes," He smirked. " I am from Mizcriea, and as to what I am doing, that is a very long story. However, I can assure you I am on your side," he put his hand over his heart, "and I am sorry about the buck. I will help you catch him, if you'll let me."

Alaina smiled at his comment about her eyes. "Mizcriea . . . " she started, and Koen waited for her to do something.

Alaina thought for a moment. "Where are you staying?"

Koen sheathed his sword and squinted with suspicion. "I have nowhere to stay. I've traveled far from home and have only stayed uncomfortably on stick beds with rock pillows."

Alaina motioned toward her home, which was two miles away. "We have an extra room in our cottage, if you would like."

Koen looked skeptical. "Excuse me for seeming so suspicious. You've only just met me, not to mention, I am from your kingdom's greatest adversary, yet, you trust me?"

"I'm just good at reading people," Alaina said with a shrug. She'd told this to people plenty of times, and since it was such a common phrase, no one ever questioned it.

However, even though she trusted Koen was good, she was still unsure about sharing her secret with others, especially people she didn't know very well. Her grandmother advised her it was best to keep the gift hidden, because if an enemy were to get hold of it, it would be disastrous.

Koen looked confused.

"So, Koen of Mizcriea, will you help me catch the buck in exchange for dinner and rest in our cottage?" Alaina raised her eyebrow.

"Of course," Koen said, still sounding a bit uncertain.

"Fine, and make sure you keep that sword sheathed. You don't want to be discovered." Alaina started walking the way the buck went.

"I will. Unfortunately, since I've been trying to put as much distance as possible between my kingdom and myself, I'm not quite sure where I am in Azgalia." Koen looked for tracks in the dirt.

"You are in the southern region of Azgalia, and unfortunately for you, the southern people are much less tolerant of your people than any other region of Azgalia." Alaina looked over at Koen and saw something she hadn't seen before. There was a scar stretching from behind his right ear to the top of his spine. She assumed it was from a sword fight.

"I see." Koen paused to look for more tracks. "My Kingdom is all the same. Depending on the Azgalian, they will either throw them to the blood lizards, hang them, or burn them alive," Koen said rather bluntly and bent down to observe some more tracks, and looked at Alaina when she didn't respond. "What's wrong?"

Alaina shook her head. "It's nothing. I would rather not talk about it."

Koen nodded in understanding and stood to point the way the buck had gone. "Do you know how to track?"

"Of course." Alaina rolled her eyes with a teasing smile and bent down to examine the forest floor. "See how the branch broke over there? And there, where the rock looks like it was dragged in the dirt? The branch broke because when the buck darted away, it stepped on it. The noise spooked it more, causing it to hit the rock, which made it trip." Alaina looked back up at Koen.

"Yeah, I know how to track. I was just wondering if you knew," Koen laughed.

"Oh." Alaina blushed. She then followed Koen as he continued the search for the buck. He began to say something else about tracking, but her mind went elsewhere. "Koen, why are you here? In Azgalia, I mean. I trust you for good reason, but the others won't be so easily persuaded." Alaina stopped and looked him in the eyes.

"The main reason is my father." Koen stood. "He ordered me to do something that confused, hurt, and made me question myself." Alaina could sense that this was the secret he'd buried deep within himself. It must have been something horrible. "My father has always been hard-hearted, but I could have never imagined him being capable of asking me to do what he wanted. After he asked me to do it, I was shocked and confused. He threatened to hurt me if I said no." Anger started to rise in him. "And to think I had even the slightest thought to do it!" Koen shook his head with sadness and regret.

"What did he ask you to do?" Alaina asked softly.

"He . . . he asked me to murder my mother." Koen's eyes met the ground in shame.

Anger. Hurt. Fear. Hate. Sadness.

Alaina stepped back, afraid he would punch the nearest thing to him.

"Oh, Koen, I am so sorry," Alaina said with sympathy.

How could a father order his own son to do that? She knew there were evil people in the world. Her grandmother had told them stories of men who did terrible things, but she had never met someone like that. She hoped never to read a gaze which decried those things.

"You know what's worst of all?" Koen flashed his green at her, and she just shook her head.

"He killed her himself, and I was too cowardly to stop him. So, I ran away. That's how . . . " Koen reached up to rub the scar on his neck.

Alaina looked down and whispered, "I'm so sorry." She looked up. "My mother died at my birth. A few weeks later, my father had to leave for a work matter. My father's name was Koen as well." Alaina looked at him and saw his eyes widen with surprise.

"How interesting." Koen nodded for her to go on.

"Indeed. Well, my father would occasionally go on work trips. This one, though, he left and never came back. There was never any word of him. People reported Mizcriean activity at the border during that time. We believe the Mizcrieans found him and killed him." Alaina looked at the ground in sadness.

"I'm sorry, Alaina." Koen looked at her. "For a time, though, I saw the hatred slowly show itself in my father. I didn't notice it when I was young, but as I grew older, it became clear that he was evil. When I ran away, I was glad to be away from him, but I was devastated when I heard he had carried out his own request." He shook his head. "I should have stayed and fought."

"I can't imagine anyone would be themselves in that situation." She paused to think. "Do you know why he wanted her .

. . gone?" Alaina was careful with what she said.

Koen blinked at her. "I honestly can't say why I'm sharing this with you. Do people normally trust you so much?"

Alaina smiled knowingly, "Only if I trust them in return."

Koen nodded and continued the conversation, "He wanted her gone because she was the only good thing in the way of his hatred. Whenever he felt like destroying something, she would bring hope, which he hated. Not only did I leave my mother, but I also left my brother with him. My father always favored my brother, Cronin, more than me. Although Cronin looked up to Father, he was a good brother to me. I just wish I had taken my mother with me," Koen said as he continued looking for tracks.

"Will you ever go back?" Alaina asked.

"I'm not sure, I was . . . "

"Shh!" Alaina held up a finger and slowly pointed ahead of them. The buck was a couple of hundred feet away. She motioned for them to sink to the ground. They crawled over to the nearest tree. The buck raised its head and looked around. When nothing seemed to be wrong, it returned to eating the grass.

Alaina quietly raised her bow and once again aimed. She found her mark and took a deep breath, as her eyes took in the buck. Her heart sped at the anticipation of her shot. Buck hunting was both peaceful and exhilarating at the same time.

Sorry, bud, but we need the food, Alaina thought.

She let out her breath and let the arrow fly swiftly to its mark. The buck fell, and Koen readied his knife.

Soon, they were on their way to Alaina's cottage. "You said 'we' when you were talking about your cottage. Who stays with you?" Koen asked.

"Ah, so you're a good listener?" Alaina smiled, "I have a twin brother." Then, her smile faded. "And a grandmother who is very ill."

"Twin brother?" Koen asked curiously.

"Yes. If we were both girls, we'd be mistaken for each other. Or boys, I guess." Alaina shrugged.

"I see. Since you say you two look so much alike, he must be a very pretty boy," Koen laughed at his own joke as Alaina shook her head and blushed. "Tell me, is your eye color common in Azgalia?" Koen asked.

"No, as far as I know, they are unique. Only my father's family has them. We call them lightning blue," Alaina said.

"Very interesting. So, what was the other thing you inherited from your father?" Koen asked.

Alaina hesitated to answer.

To her relief, her twin brother David chose that moment to jump out from behind a tree.

Startled, Koen and David unsheathed their swords. They stared at each other, waiting to see what the other would do. Alaina laughed, and they both looked at her, bewildered. Koen then realized this was her twin and sheathed his sword while keeping an eye on David.

David was a head taller than Alaina and stood an inch or two shorter than Koen. He was strong from outside work and sword practice, but had a more petite frame than Koens. Their grandmother told him countless times, "You've got a good head on those shoulders, young man. Be sure not to lose it."

"Oh, David, I know you want to have a real sword fight, but don't go attacking my guest," Alaina said, stopping laughing but continuing to smile.

David rolled his eyes. While eyeing Koen, he said, "Well, sister, maybe I wouldn't attack him if you weren't bringing a Mizcriean here!" He still had his sword unsheathed but lowered.

"He is good, David." Alaina looked seriously into David's eyes, which were much like hers, and he nodded in understanding.

"Tell me, do all Azgalians surprise their enemy by jumping from behind trees? Because I'm noticing a pattern." Koen smiled.

Alaina laughed, but David stood solemn.

"Dinner?" David asked, nodding toward the buck. Alaina nodded, and they headed toward the cottage.

♕

"How is Grandmother?" Alaina asked.

"The same," David said. He stared at the buck cooking over the fire outside the cottage. He turned his head to look at Koen. "Koen, tell me, how are you with the sword?"

Koen was glad to have engaged in conversation with a fellow man. "I was once told I was the best in my region. As I see it, I'm good as long as I can survive a fight."

David nodded. "Have you ever been in a real fight?"

Koen hesitated to answer but finally did. "I have fought against robbers who would come and steal from my city."

"I know it's not as common in Mizcriea as it is here, but would you happen to know the Greenlands sword dance?" David leaned forward.

"I have heard of it, but I'm afraid I do not. I'm a fast learner, though." Koen smiled.

"Excellent!" David stood and unsheathed his sword. "This dance has been performed in Azgalia since the second generation of rule," David explained.

Koen nodded and unsheathed his sword. It was beautiful. She would have thought he stole it if Alaina hadn't trusted Koen. The beauty of the sword, plus his masterful sword stance, showed he was more than a simple merchant's son. Alaina was determined to figure out just who Koen really was.

David and Koen started the dance, and after a few tries, Koen had it down. The swords danced along with their feet as both young men moved in fluid motions. Alaina was mesmerized. Both of them were skilled swordsmen and performed with excellence. She was delighted to have a front-row seat to such talent.

Then, unexpectedly, Koen delivered a volley of cuts and slices with class. When he saw an opening, he thrust David's chest, but pulled back just in time. Koen smirked as David fell back two steps. David remained focused and recovered quickly. He made his sword fly faster with a combination of his own making. Koen was momentarily surprised but recovered and retreated to memorize David's tactics. "Fancy sword and fancy feet," David said in between breaths.

Alaina watched with excitement as she realized this was no longer a sword dance but a competition for who wielded the sword better. She thought about stepping in and making them stop the fight, but then she remembered her grandmother once telling her, "When it comes to men and competition for dominance, it's their own fight." Since this wouldn't cause any physical harm to either of them, she decided to sit back and enjoy the show. She also chose to study each of their styles.

Koen had the skill from years of practice, but David was born for the sword. Koen had powerful cuts, while David was speedy and quick on his feet. Alaina read each of their faces and could tell Koen was having more fun than he should be having. He laughed as David made him stumble backward. Koen recovered and unleashed the skill he had been holding back. Wide-eyed and sword-flying, David was in retreat and doing his best to defend himself. Alaina saw Koen as the better swordsman, but David would be the better with a little more practice.

"Come on now, David, is that all you got?" Koen challenged him with a smirk.

Alaina saw the humor in Koen, but only determination in David. David gave it his all, yet it still wasn't enough.

Koen saw his opportunity and knocked the sword out of David's hand. Both stood still, heavy breathing, with sweat dripping from their foreheads. David appeared shocked, while Koen smirked. Alaina started clapping, and both the boys' heads whipped around to look at her. She could tell they both had forgotten she was there, and she erupted in laughter. Koen's smile widened, and David shook his head and hid a smile as he turned to pick up his sword.

"I've got to say, David, you are very good." Koen gave a meaningful smile, and David squinted, questioning whether to believe the compliment. "Just not as good as me." It was Koen's turn to laugh as he fell back onto a log by the fire.

"Don't worry, David. With a few more dances, you'll beat Koen for sure!" Alaina and Koen fell back laughing while David just shook his head.

"So hilarious." David rolled his eyes and smiled.

A noise in the house brought their laughter to an abrupt halt. Alaina and David exchanged looks of concern as they thought about what might have happened. They leaped to their feet and sprinted towards the house. David unsheathed his sword as Alaina grabbed her own, resting by the door. David was the first to open the door and rush inside, nearly knocking over a chair. Alaina's heart was racing as she thought about what could've happened. They both froze as they heard a creaking sound coming from their grandmother's room. David turned to look at Alaina and nodded towards the room. They bolted and swung open the door to find their grandmother reaching to get a bowl of water that had spilled. The room was small, with two windows that usually remained shut. There was a desk beside the head of the bed where the bowl had been, and a chest at the end of the bed. Two candles made up for the light that the windows did not provide. The walls throughout the cottage were made from stone and wood panels.

"Grandmother, are you alright?" Alaina asked in a worried tone.

Her grandmother looked up. "Of course, my dear. Why wouldn't I be?" she smiled.

"We heard something loud from outside," David said.

"Oh, yes." She stopped talking as if she had forgotten what had caused the sound. Her wrinkled face revealed her illness, and Alaina's heart ached for her.

"Grandmother?" Alaina stepped forward and put her hand on her grandmother's shoulder.

"Oh, hello, sweet Alaina." Her grandmother smiled.

"Grandmother, what happened here that was so loud?" Alaina asked.

"Oh yes! I tried to get a drink of water, but, in my reach, I knocked over the bowl. I then went to try to pick it up, and that's when you two came in." Their grandmother smiled from her place on the bed. She hadn't left the bed in a week due to weakness; however, that didn't stop her from trying.

Alaina sighed and sat down in the chair by the bed. David sheathed his sword and went to pick up the bowl and water. All three heads turned at the sound of the wood flooring creaking across the room. It was Koen standing in the doorway.

"Is everything okay?" Koen asked awkwardly, looking at their grandmother and then at Alaina.

"Yes, she seems to be fine." Alaina tried calming her nerves.

Before Alaina rose to tend to the meat still outside, David interjected that he would take care of it. Alaina knew he offered to do it to get away from Koen. She wasn't sure, though, if it was because Koen had beaten him at the sword fight or because he was a Mizcriean. Maybe both.

Alaina motioned toward their grandmother, "Koen, this is my grandmother, Maryann. Grandmother, this is Koen. I met him this morning while hunting."

Maryann smiled at Koen as she looked at him, but her smile slowly disappeared. "What is it, Grandmother?" Alaina asked.

"It's . . . it's nothing, my dear. I haven't seen a Mizcriean for quite some time." Maryann looked sad, and Alaina read that the sight of Koen pained her. It wasn't Koen himself, but it reminded her of someone. Her father, she guessed. Alaina's father was Maryann's son, and when Alaina's father went missing, Maryann was heartbroken.

"He is good." Alaina met her grandmother's eyes, and Maryann seemed to understand. Alaina looked at Koen and saw pain in his eyes. Being in a foreign land and being perceived as an enemy must be awful.

"It's nice to meet you, Maryann," Koen said with a smile.

Maryann smiled, "Same goes for you, young man."

He nodded and excused himself to help David with the meat.

Alaina turned to look at her grandmother, only to find she was staring at her.

Pain. Guilt. Sadness. And . . . hope?

Sometimes, Alaina wished she couldn't read people.

"Alaina, my dear child. You are a beautiful young lady who bears a striking resemblance to your father and mother. I don't have to read faces to see you will do great things in the days ahead, but always remember that you are a daughter of a King. Always glorify His Kingdom and not your own," Maryann said.

"Yes, of course. Though I have to ask, why are you telling me this?" Alaina asked.

"Because I'm afraid I won't be with you much longer, and the trials you'll face, you'll have to face without me." Maryann looked deep into Alaina's eyes. "And about Koen . . . "

Alaina looked up. "What about him?" she asked.

"He's more important than you think." Maryann slowly closed her eyes and drifted off to sleep.

Alaina wondered at her grandmother's words. Maryann had a secret, and so did Koen. She'd find out what they were in time. If her grandmother could see something great in Koen without the gift, then he really was something extraordinary.

Alaina closed the door behind her and turned to look at the portrait of her parents. It was the only way she knew what they looked like. For a moment, Alaina studied them. She and David shared their father's striking eyes and dark hair, but their mother gave each of their faces a loving and soft touch. Her father was very handsome, and her mother very beautiful. Oh, how she wished to have known them. She then walked down the hall toward the kitchen. Koen was seasoning the stew while David sat in a chair, running his hand down the blade of his sword.

"David, why aren't you helping Koen?" she asked.

"He said he wanted to do it, so I encouraged it. " David grinned, "Right, Koen?"

Koen turned around and put the meat on the table. "You said I could exchange help with dinner for a bed, so I'm doing that."

Alaina nodded and sat down with them. Koen went to scoop out his portion of stew when Alaina cleared her throat to get his attention. She folded her hands and said kindly, "We pray before eating." She smiled and closed her eyes. After praying, they all dug in. David was quiet throughout the meal, as usual around people.

Later that night, she showed Koen to the spare room.

"Alaina?" Koen asked.

"Yes?" She answered.

"Thank you for letting me stay here. I'm not sure why you trust me, but I'm glad you do," Koen said.

"You're welcome." She smiled.

"I plan to leave in the morning," Koen said as he leaned against the wall.

"Where will you go?" She asked, and when he hesitated,

she said, "Well, before you leave, at least let me draw you a map."

"Thank you again." Koen smiled before walking into the room and shutting the door behind him.

Alaina turned to see David looking at her from the end of the hall, worry in his face. "What's worrying you?"

"Can't I hide anything from you?" David tried to smile, but failed. When she waited for him to continue, he motioned for her to come closer. When she was close enough for only her to hear his words, he said, "Grandmother is getting worse. When she . . . " he struggled to continue, "When she passes, what will we do?"

Alaina understood his worry because she had thought about this often. "I don't know."

"Sister, you deserve a good future. You could marry one of Cedric's sons. Either would make a suitable husband and take good care of you," David said.

Cedric was a wealthy merchant in the city with five sons. Alaina thought most of the sons were greedy, except for one. The one she knew was good had already asked her to court, but Alaina had declined.

"No, David, you know that's the last thing I want," she said.

"Well, maybe it's not what you want, but what you need," David pushed.

"Say I do marry one of them. What will become of you?" Alaina asked.

"I will stay here and take care of the cottage," he said.

"You couldn't stay here forever," Alaina said.

"Why not?" he asked, and Alaina looked at him. "Well, then, I will move into town and work for Cedric. I could watch over you and check in on the cottage now and then," David reasoned.

Alaina shook her head. "Surely this isn't what we are to do with our lives. You are a skilled swordsman, and I have the gift; are we to waste our God-given talents?"

"I don't know. All we can do is pray." David looked down.

Alaina nodded and was quiet for a moment. "You are tired and need rest," Alaina stated.

"Yes, and so do you. Goodnight, Alaina." David turned and went to his room, the closest room to their grandmother.

Alaina had taken up the chore of hunting instead of caring for her grandmother because David was better at medicine than she was. Secretly, though, she enjoyed hunting. The girls her age who lived in the city would never step into the woods alone. Her father had built their house in the forest to protect his children from the city folk, especially when he knew one would inherit his gift. He encouraged them to go into town and be involved when they could, but for the most part, it had kept Alaina safe as she grew into her gift.

Alaina walked into her bedroom and crawled into bed. Sleep slowly welcomed her, and she fell into a deep dream.

TWO

"Father?" Alaina asked.

"Yes, I'm here, my dear girl." His deep, comforting voice welcomed her.

"Is that you?" she asked again.

"Yes, Alaina," he said. She ran to him, but just before she reached him, his eyes grew wide, and she read pain on his face.

"Father!" Alaina screamed. Her father collapsed to the ground, and she saw Koen recover his sword from her father's back. "Koen, how could you?" Alaina cried.

"I'm a Mizcrien." He gave an evil grin and walked away.

She ran to her father and burst into tears.

"Alaina, why did you trust him?" her father asked weakly.

"Father, I . . . I thought," Alaina cried all the more. She heard someone yelling her name. *David*? she thought. "David!" she cried out.

"Alaina!" came his voice.

Alaina's eyes shot open, and light from the day burned her tired eyes. She saw her twin brother and was relieved it had been a dream, but horrified by what it could mean. She then realized David's face was one of panic and urgency. "What is it, David?" Her thoughts flew to those of Koen. *What now*? Her mind screamed.

"It's Grandmother! She's slipping away fast!" David pulled her out of bed. Every other thought left her mind, and all her attention was on her grandmother. Brother and sister raced to their grandmother's room.

"David, what's wrong?" Alaina felt tears coming as she gazed upon Maryann's face.

"I checked on her a few times during the night and noticed her breathing was quite fast. I gave her some of the medicine the healer in the city gave us, and it helped." David placed his hand on Maryann's forehead, and his face showed great concern.

"She has a fever," David said.

"What do we do?" Alaina asked.

"Go to town. Get a healer . . . fast!" David gave Maryann more medicine and put a cold rag on her forehead. Alaina sprinted out the door and ran for her horse.

"Alaina, what's going on?" Koen shouted from a bench by the cottage.

Alaina thought it would be wiser to bring company. "Koen, come with me!" She reached the barn and grabbed her dappled grey horse, Ophelia. She clipped the lead rope on the halter and led her out of the stall.

"What's wrong?" Koen reached the barn swiftly. Alaina could see genuine worry on his face.

"My grandmother is much worse," Alaina said while she put the bridle on. "Grab the bay horse." Alaina pointed to David's horse.

Koen was quiet as they rode out to the city.

It would take nine minutes to get to the city, and she guessed they would spend, at most, five minutes there. Once they left, it would take another nine minutes to get back.

They urged the horses out of the property. They flew past

trees and jumped over logs. Lines of worry were etched across Alaina's face. She hoped her grandmother would still be alive when she got back.

Precisely nine minutes later, she spotted the city gates. While they rushed past people, she read face after face.

Greed. Anger. Deceitfulness.

The entire city wasn't bad, though. People were sinful, Alaina knew. Yet, she also knew many Azgalian people were faithful to God. There was plenty of good in Azgalia.

Kindness. Love. Gratitude.

The faces overwhelmed her so much that she wished she could close her eyes.

When they arrived at the healer's house, Alaina jumped off her horse and threw the reins to Koen. She all but sprinted to the door and pounded on it to make sure the elderly man would hear her.

"Yes, I'm coming!" The old man called from inside. Alaina grew anxious when he didn't come immediately and banged the door again. The man opened the door.

Annoyance. Exhaustion. Frustration.

Aside from these, though, she could see the man's kindness. "Rodney, I am truly sorry to have awakened you, but my grandmother is very ill and dying. I need you to come with me right away," Alaina urged.

"Come with me and help me collect my things," Rodney said as he quickly spun around toward the back of his house. Alaina turned to ensure Koen was okay, and at his nod, she followed Rodney inside. His home was simple, but his yard was a giant garden. Plants covered every inch. She watched him step over roots from pots and plants growing out of the ground. She would have laughed as the older man hopped over his plants if it weren't for her current situation.

"Now tell me, dear, what symptoms is Maryann having?" Rodney picked up a sack and waited for Alaina to answer.

"Rapid breathing, fever, chest pain, and a bluish tint to her skin and nails," Alaina said with a waver in her voice.

"Any coughing?" Rodney asked while picking certain herbs.

Alaina thought for a second and answered, "Only after drinking."

"I think I know the problem," Rodney said.

"Can you help her?" Alaina asked with a sliver of hope.

"It depends, my dear," he said when he finally picked the last herb.

"Depends on what?" she asked.

"If it's as bad as I fear." Rodney looked sad.

Alaina let a tear slip but quickly brushed it away. She needed to stay strong. She fixed a determined expression and met Rodney's eyes. "The horses are out front."

"I'll ride with the boy, if you don't mind," Rodney said.

Alaina looked at Koen, wondering if she should let Rodney ride with him. He mouthed the words, "It's okay," and smiled. She nodded and let out a sigh.

Then, they were off again. They pushed the horses and passed people who yelled at them for loping through the streets. The hoofs pounded to the cottage in the woods. When they arrived, Alaina swung off again and helped Rodney to the ground. She ran inside with the healer while Koen took care of the horses.

"David?" Alaina called as she opened the door. David came

into the kitchen with a look of worry and fear.

"She's getting worse, please hurry." David escorted Rodney to the room.

Alaina stood back and watched the healer work on his herbs; that was all she could do. He helped Maryann drink the concoction, listened to her heart, and checked a few more things.

"I will watch her for the next hour and call you if there are any changes. If there is anything that needs to be done today, go finish it," Rodney said with a kind smile.

"Thank you, Rodney." Alaina nodded and left the room. Though part of her wanted to stay, she knew if her grandmother could speak, she'd remind her to feed the horses.

On her way out of the cottage, Alaina spotted Koen out by the barn cleaning a horse trough. "You don't have to do that," Alaina said as she walked over to where he was.

Koen looked up at the sound of her voice. "I know, but I asked David what I could do to help, and he said I could clean a horse trough." Koen shrugged.

"Wow, what great hosts we are." Alaina rolled her eyes at the thought of her brother.

"I was joking," David said humorously from behind her.

"Oh, I'm sure," Alaina said, clearly not believing him.

"Hey, I'll even help." David smiled as he bent down to pick up a brush off the ground.

Alaina laughed and walked over to the hay bales to feed the horses.

Soon after they had finished the chores, Rodney called them into the cottage. As they entered the room where Maryann lay, Rodney turned around with a look that sent Alaina's heart sinking. She felt like running out and going as far away as possible.

"It's as I feared. If I had seen her sooner, I might have been able to help more, but I'm afraid it's too late. Her lungs are filling with fluid, and she won't last long. I'm so sorry." Rodney turned to pack his things and stepped out of the room.

Alaina's mind screamed at what she could have done differently to help. She could have left Koen and arrived there faster. She could have helped David with the night checks on Maryann. She could have read her face and known that it was worse. Why hadn't she thought of that?

Then, a deep, comforting voice came from behind her. "Alaina, I know what you're thinking. You're thinking of how you could have done something different. It won't help, I assure you. Sure, you could have, but you didn't. It is what it is, and I'm sure there's a reason," Koen said as he gently laid a hand on her shoulder.

Maryann was sweating, but could move her hand just enough for Alaina to see it. Alaina moved to her side in an instant.

Maryann motioned for her to come closer. "David."

Alaina was momentarily confused and then called David to her side as well. They leaned in and listened intently to their beloved grandmother's last words. "Children," she began, using all her strength to continue. "I have kept this from you all these years. I was selfish; forgive me. I feared you would leave me," she paused to breathe. Her body shook, and her wrinkled face showed great pain.

Alaina saw that whatever she was about to say was her secret. It pained her to say it, but she also saw something else: hope.

"We would never leave you, Grandmother," David whispered, and Alaina saw he was holding back tears.

"Please, don't be angry with me." Maryann continued, "I see now my mistake." She looked straight into their bright blue eyes, her own green ones meeting them. Maryann struggled to continue, for she was slipping away. "Your father . . . " she coughed once, "is still . . . " She shut her eyes in pain.

"Grandmother!" Alaina cried.

Maryann held her hand, eyes still closed, and said, "Your father is still alive."

Alaina's eyes grew wide. She looked at David and found he was also confused.

Maryann gathered all her strength for her last words. "I received a letter a year after he was taken, saying he was still alive. He said he was being treated well in Mizcriea and asked that no one come for him."

Alaina couldn't believe it.

"One thing was in the letter, however, that said otherwise. He told me to tell Marie hello for him," Maryann said. Marie was the mother of David and Alaina. It didn't make sense; she had died the night of their birth. "I believe he was trying to tell me something. Children, you must go." She coughed and looked toward Koen. "He is here for this reason. Go, find your father, and restore the Kingdom." Maryann's eyes shut, she squeezed their hands, and her last breath escaped her lips.

The dam holding back Alaina's tears crumbled, and she let the tears flow. Her heart felt like it could split in two. Maryann had been there all her life. She was the only mother Alaina had ever known, and now she was gone. And now her thought-to-have-been-dead father could be alive. Eventually, the tears stopped, and Alaina sat in shock, thinking about everything.

"She's gone," she whispered as she looked at David. He was just staring at the floor.

Sadness. Anger. Disbelief.

"She was telling the truth, David," Alaina whispered through a wavering voice.

"Why did she wait so long to tell us? He could be dead by now," David said, trying not to sound angry.

Alaina understood why he was angry. He had lived without a father figure his whole life, which was hard for a young man. Then there was the fact that she may have never told them the truth if she hadn't passed today. Maybe it was by God's providence, but it was still frustrating. It would be hard to leave home and travel across two kingdoms. Also, what did she mean by "restore the kingdom?"

"What do we do now?" Alaina asked cautiously.

"How am I supposed to know? Do we risk it all for our could-be-dead father?" David's voice rose a little.

"He could be dead, but he could also be alive. There could still be a chance he's there, alive and waiting for rescue. They kept him alive for a year after his capture. Surely, they needed something from him. Maybe they still need it. We could still have a father." Alaina wasn't sure whether she was trying to convince herself or David.

David was silent for a few moments. "I just don't know." He put his head in his hands.

"If you decide to go, I can be a guide," Koen carefully suggested.

"Thank you, Koen." Alaina thanked him, and the room fell quiet again. No one said a thing. Alaina heard her horse whinny from outside. She sighed and closed her eyes.

Suddenly, David stood up and looked towards the door. "Fine. We leave tomorrow morning. Start packing, and I'll plan the route with Koen." He walked out without another word.

Alaina sighed again and stood up to find Koen looking at her.

Sympathy. Shock. Understanding.

"I'm terribly sorry, Alaina," he said.

"It's not your fault. Are you sure you want to come with us if we go?" she asked, just to make sure.

"Absolutely," Koen reassured her and waited a moment. With a nod, he walked out to help David.

Alaina knew he wasn't as sure as he wanted to sound. Uncertainty was all over his face. He was worried about going back home and facing his father.

"I am deeply sorry for your loss, miss. I wish there were something more I could've done." Rodney appeared in the doorway.

"It's not your fault. Thank you very much for your help, " Alaina said with a smile.

"I, ah, I was hoping your friend here could take me back to Norwest?" Rodney looked at Koen and smiled kindly.

"Yes, sir, I will take you back. May I borrow your horse again?" Koen asked Alaina.

"Of course. Thank you," Alaina nodded. The older and younger man walked out the door and were on their way. If Rodney knew a Mizcrian was taking him back, he'd go crazy. *Better that he didn't know*, she thought.

Alaina made her way to her room to start packing. She packed clothes for both cold and warm weather. She had never been outside Norwest and her woods, so this would be a first.

She wasn't sure if she was prepared to read all the faces she would encounter, but she also knew it would be helpful. Alaina silently prayed for safety on the upcoming journey.

♔

David was leaning over the map, wondering if bringing Koen was still a good idea. He'd just have to pack up some weapons . . . and not just for Koen.

"I think we should head to Norwest first and get the supplies we need," Koen suggested.

"I don't know; people know we don't come out of our home often. They'll ask questions, and we don't want to tell them," David said.

"True, but you two don't look like the others of Azgalia. You'll stand out no matter what and constantly be questioned," Koen reasoned.

"I suppose. After Norwest, maybe we should go down to the coast?" David pointed at Chessinton, a city near the coast.

"What for? It's just out of the way," Koen said.

"We can take a ship. It would be faster, right?" David said.

"It would also be more dangerous. It's safer on foot. On the water, Mizcrieas' fleet of ships are ruthless. Not to mention, they're everywhere. We couldn't pass, even with the best ship in Azgalia. At least by foot, we could hide better," Koen suggested.

"Okay, so say we get to the border . . . how do you suggest we get them to let us into Mizcriea?" David crossed his arms.

"I thought the only possible way to cross the river to the other side was guarded by Mizcriean patrol?"

"It is, but I happen to know some people." Koen stood up straight. "My uncle works the border, so I know I can find a way to get him to let us pass."

"Your uncle works the border?" David squinted.

"Yes. My uncle." Koen crossed his arms and stared at David. "You know . . . brother of my father, husband to my aunt . . ."

"Yes, I know what an uncle is," David rolled his eyes. "I'm just curious to know why your uncle works the border. After all, you are just a merchant's son, are you not?"

Koen cleared his throat, "Well . . . I, uh . . . the king favors my uncle. He was a guard in the castle and helped save the king's life, so the king trusts him to watch over the border."

"Ah, I see." David nodded with a hint of suspicion in his tone. "So, he'll let you pass. What about us?"

"Well, I can say I'm bringing you both over as slaves." Koen shrugged.

"Okay." David looked back down at the map. He realized how foolish he had been to agree to that plan, considering Koen was a stranger. Yet, Alaina trusted Koen, and David trusted Alaina to know Koen's true motives. "We need to pack." With that, he walked out of the room.

Alaina put her saddlebag over a stool and stuffed it with small packages of food and bottles filled with water that they had in the cottage. She added some bandages for the wounds that were sure to come. Alaina looked up at her horse in the stall. "Ophelia, this is a good idea, right?" she asked her horse, not expecting an answer. When no answer came, she smiled and walked over to Ophelia to hug her around the neck. "It has to be." She thought momentarily, "So what do you think about Koen? Do you think he's keeping a secret, too?" After a few seconds, Ophelia blew through her nostrils. "Was that a yes or a no?" Alaina laughed.

"A yes?" a voice said from behind Alaina, making her jump. It was Koen.

"Ah, how much of our conversation did you hear?" Alaina did her best to look innocent.

"Not much, sadly. I only heard you ask your horse if it said yes or no," Koen laughed.

"Oh, okay, good." Alaina smiled, bent over to pick up a bucket, and started to walk toward the well.

"So, uh, how are you doing?" Koen asked her.

Alaina looked at his face to see what he was implying. Sympathy.

"I'm doing better than I thought. I suppose the news about my father left me in a small state of shock."

"True. I am surprised by how well you and your brother have taken it. You two seem pretty . . . " He paused to search for a word. " . . . tough." Koen smiled.

"Well, I am, but I don't know about David. He acts tough, but he's really a big softy." Alaina smiled, trying to lighten the mood.

"I can see that," Koen laughed. "So, what's for supper to-night?"

"You're hungry already?" Alaina pretended to be mad.

"I can't help it! I'm a growing boy!" Koen said in defense, and Alaina shook her head, smiling.

"Well, maybe you and David should go hunting so you guys can gain more trust in each other," Alaina suggested.

"I'm all for it if he is," Koen said.

After filling the bucket with water and bringing it back to the barn with Koen, Alaina told him she would check on David. She headed inside and found David sitting on the floor of Maryann's room.

"We should bury her by Mother's grave," he said without turning to face her.

"Yes, we should," Alaina agreed as she knelt beside him. "Are you okay?"

"Not really." David shook his head.

"Do you want to talk about it?" Alaina asked.

"No," David said without looking at her.

"Alright. Will our cottage be okay? I mean, we'll be gone for a long time." Alaina tried to get him to talk, even if it was about nothing important.

"Yes, it will be fine," David answered.

Alaina sighed. "David, I know you're in shock and sad, but so am I. We can't just shut off. We have a big journey ahead of us, and I will need your help every step of the way. In return, I will help you, too."

"I know. It's a lot to take in. Have you ever stopped to think about how dangerous this journey will be? We could only make it halfway and be killed by wild animals. We have no clue what's out there," David said, still not looking at her.

"Yes, of course, I thought about it. I've thought about all the wild animals, the dangerous people, the poisonous plants, and everything else . . . but the fact that our father could still be alive? It's worth the risk to me. What else do we have to do? If we die and never find our father, we can say we at least dared to try in the first place. I would rather we die being courageous than waste our lives wondering. Also, I'm sure Koen saw many things on his way from the Mizcriean border. All of us are skilled with a weapon, and I'm sure we can take care of ourselves." Alaina searched her brother's face. She hoped he would feel peace again.

"Yeah, perhaps you're right." David nodded his head.

Alaina sighed and stood up. "Koen wants to go hunting, and I think you should go with him," she said, and David nodded. Then she turned toward the door.

"Alaina?" David called before she exited the room.

"Yes?" she answered.

David now turned to face her. "If we are in a life-or-death situation, leave me behind. It's my job to protect you, and I will not watch my sister die."

"David—" Alaina started, but read his face.

Determination. Courage. Strength.

"I understand, but hopefully, it won't come to that." Alaina smiled briefly, and David nodded.

She walked out of the room and heard Koen come inside.

"Is he okay?" Koen mouthed with his lips.

"Yes, and I think he agreed to go hunting with you," Alaina smiled.

"You think?" Koen looked worried, but he headed towards David's room anyway.

Alaina waited by the door to see if David would go hunting with Koen. After a small conversation she could hardly hear, two pairs of footsteps came down the hall.

"Going out then?" Alaina asked with her hands on her hips.

"Yes, we are." Koen smiled and glanced at David, who nodded.

"Great! I'll get everything ready for dinner. Be back soon, and don't go far," Alaina told them.

"Yes, mother," David teased.

"Yes, ma'am. We'll be back soon, ma'am." Koen saluted and started toward the door.

"Okay, okay, I get it!" Alaina laughed. "Now go, I'm getting hungry."

Koen stepped outside, David following close behind him. Alaina stopped David. "When will we bury Grandmother?"

"After dinner," David said.

"Okay. Be nice." Alaina waved them out.

"So, are you as good a hunter as your sister?" Koen asked.

"Yes. Our Grandmother taught Alaina and me together. Neither of us was allowed to go hunting alone until we were experienced enough. When Grandmother fell ill, I took up caring for her instead of hunting," David said while he looked at the ground for tracks. He and Alaina agreed that he was more capable of helping Grandmother. David was stronger and understood medicine better than Alaina, making him more capable of lifting his grandmother in and out of bed and providing home remedies.

"I see," Koen nodded and paused. "So, would you prefer a

squirrel," he pointed to a squirrel on a branch above them, "or deer?" He pointed in another direction towards a deer.

"I prefer deer, but if Mizcrieans prefer squirrels, you go ahead." David started slowly in the direction of the buck.

"Oh no, we usually eat cow, pig, or bison." Koen laughed when David rolled his eyes. "It's true!"

"Right," David said as he sank into a squatting position.

They sat in silence while they waited for a buck to appear. David didn't care if silence hung between them; in fact, he preferred it. Koen, however, looked as though it made him highly uncomfortable. David looked into the forest to hide his face, which showed his amusement.

Soon, a buck appeared. Not far off, the buck roamed through the forest a few steps at a time while eating the grass. His ear shook whenever a small insect buzzed near. The antlers looked strong, showcasing the buck's might. It was truly a breathtaking sight.

A low rumble sounded and broke David's stare. He looked around and then realized it had been the growl of his own stomach. He inhaled and drew back his bow. He aimed, and as soon as he exhaled, he let the arrow fly into the buck. It struck the heart, and the buck went down immediately.

"Nice shot!" Koen stood up, grinning.

David had forgotten his presence, so Koen's sudden excitement had startled him. "Uh, thanks." David stood and approached the buck to see if it had died instantly, as he hoped. When he confirmed his hope, he bent down and pulled a sharp knife to start the field dressing.

"Why don't I do that? After all, it's been a while since you've done it, right? I wouldn't want you to puncture anything and ruin the meat." Koen had a point.

David thought for a moment. Not wanting to admit he wasn't very qualified for the job, but also unwilling to ruin a meal, he answered, "Yeah, that's probably best." Standing up, he handed the knife to Koen.

"I know you wanted to do the shooting, so do you want to head back and catch the squirrel?" David asked jokingly.

"You sure you don't just want to get rid of me?" Koen looked up and laughed.

"I wouldn't dream of it." David smiled. After the dressing was done, they were soon on their way back to the cottage.

They walked halfway there without talking when David broke the silence. "Koen, I want to warn you," he started.

"Warn me? You mean you *actually* care about me?" Koen smirked.

"No," David said in a serious tone. Koen's face turned serious as well. "I care about Alaina. You are only coming on this quest with us for guidance, nothing more. Alaina is off-limits. If you dare try anything rash, don't be surprised if you wake up with a sword in your stomach." David stopped and faced Koen. "Understood?"

Koen looked at David for a moment before replying. "I understand completely. You have every right not to trust me. Your sister seems to, though. If I could ask that you could give me the benefit of the doubt, I'd like to think of each other as friends eventually," Koen said.

"Thank you. Since you have agreed to my terms, I will do my best to be optimistic about your presence. Although a friendship is highly unlikely." David turned toward the cottage.

They continued their walk back in silence, and David took

this as an opportunity to dwell on thoughts of his Grandmother. He let his feelings settle and tried to make sense of them. His life was about to undergo a drastic change. He may never see these forests again, or he may never come home, or he may return home with a father. Either way, he had to prepare himself for the worst.

When they finally reached the cottage property, David went to fetch Alaina, while Koen prepared the buck for dinner.

"Was your trip a successful one?" Alaina spun around when she heard David come in.

"Yes, it was, my sister. Dinner is going to be fantastic." David smiled.

"I wasn't talking about dinner. I was talking about getting along with Koen. After all, we'll spend a lot of time with him."

David's smile faded. "Yes, we agreed on some things, and I think I'll be able to tolerate him much better now."

"Funny. Well, you can get the water, and I'll get the side dish," Alaina said as she walked over to stir a steaming pot.

"Sure thing," David said.

♕

After dinner, David and Alaina buried their grandmother next to their mother's grave. Koen stood by and paid his respects. "I am really, very sorry. She seemed like a wonderful lady," Koen said as he passed the twins on his way down to the barn.

"Where are you going?" Alaina turned to ask him before he got too far.

"I was going to feed the animals before the sun sets, if that's alright?" Koen asked.

"Yes, thank you." Alaina nodded and wiped a tear that was lingering on her cheek. Koen gave a subtle nod and headed down the hill.

"Are you going to be ready for the morning?" David walked up beside her.

Alaina managed a smile. "Are you?"

He shook his head. "Probably not, but we should try to get some sleep either way."

"Not just yet," Alaina said, looking at the horizon beyond the trees. The sky was darkening, and the sun was beginning to set behind the distant mountains. She took a deep breath of the fresh air and slowly let it out.

"Sunsets were her favorite," David said, barely loud enough for Alaina to hear.

Alaina looked at David's face and almost cried again. He was broken over their loss, and she completely understood. Their eyes met, and he managed a soft smile through his tears. He wanted to be strong for her, but she tried to be strong for him as well. After all, she could see beyond what he portrayed.

David then offered his arm to Alaina, and she locked hers in his. Together, they walked down the hill.

Upon entering the kitchen, they found Koen reading a book at the table. "That's one of my favorites," Alaina motioned toward the book.

"I found it on the bookshelf." Koen smiled and closed the book.

"Well, you should get some sleep; we have a big day tomorrow," Alaina stated as she unlocked her arm from David's.

"Yes, mother." Koen smiled and spun on his heel as he headed to his room.

"Do I need to go to bed too, Mom?" David asked with a smirk.

"You know what, David?" she said with a fake, angry voice, giving him a playful punch.

He rubbed his shoulder and quietly laughed. "Goodnight."

"Goodnight," Alaina said, shaking her head.

THREE

*For God gave us a spirit not of fear but
of power and love and self-control.*
2 Timothy 1:7, ESV

Loud. Annoying.

One. Two. Three. Alaina's eyes shot open.

"Hey, lightning eyes, you up? We have to head out soon." Koen's voice came from the other side of the door.

Alaina moaned and rubbed her eyes. She blinked a few times, then stared at the ceiling, letting her thoughts sink in. Koen had said something . . . lightning eyes?

"You sure you still want to do this?" His voice came again.

This time, Alaina answered to let him know she wasn't backing down. "Yes, I'm up. Is David?"

"I'm up!" David shouted from somewhere in the cottage.

"Mmkay, be out in a sec." Alaina rolled out of bed and looked around the room. It was still dark outside.

She grabbed her brush and went to the small mirror to comb her hair. She hurried the brush through the tangles and threw on her clothes. After braiding two parts of her hair, she picked up her packed bag and walked to the door. She turned around to say goodbye, committing every detail to memory: the bed quilt her grandma made, the dark wooden desk where she wrote all her stories, the window where she knelt to pray every night, and the mirror that had belonged to her mother. Each item made her heart ache. So many memories. She knew this could very well be her last time here. She took a deep breath, put her hand on the handle, twisted it, and opened the door.

"Ready?" David peeked his head in the hall.

"Pretty much. What about breakfast?" Alaina walked toward him.

"I'm making eggs," he answered.

"Okay, I'll start on the horses then." Alaina put her bag on a chair in the kitchen.

"Nope, they're ready, too," David said.

"What? How long have you two been up?" Alaina asked, surprised.

"Well, I never really fell asleep. I couldn't stop thinking. So after I decided to stop trying to fall asleep, I started to get things ready." He shrugged.

"And David woke me up with all his noisy walking, so I got up and decided to join him," Koen said.

"Oh, I see." Alaina nodded slowly, still trying to wake up. She hadn't slept much last night; today would be a long day. "Is there anything that's not ready to go?"

"Um, no, I think we got it all. Eggs are ready." David set the eggs on the table. "Dig in."

Alaina scooped eggs into her bowl and then passed the spoon to Koen. He cleared his throat and said, "So, while you two are eating, I thought now would be a good time to tell you . . ."

"Tell us what?" Alaina leaned forward. She could tell he was nervous about whatever he would say to them.

"I . . . I, uh . . . I . . . " She saw his eyes shift. "I'm just happy you guys trust me enough to let me help you," Koen said with a weird smile.

He lied.

Alaina knew he wanted to say something else, but wasn't quite ready to tell them. She would ask him about it tonight. Secrets wouldn't make their trip easy or safe; they must be revealed today before they head out for good. She decided to tell him her secret tonight, too.

"Yeah, well, thank Alaina. I'm still warming up to you," David said rather thoughtfully.

"Thanks," Koen gave her a weary smile.

Alaina smiled. "Of course. So, where are we headed first?"

"Norwest, to gather some supplies. After that, we'll head north and probably end up sleeping in the forest," David answered her.

She nodded. "So, which horse is Koen riding? Blade, Oasis, or Wayne?" she asked. Blade was David's horse, Oasis had belonged to their grandmother, and Wayne was Oasis's four-year-old colt.

"Why not Ophelia?" David asked, teasing her.

"No one rides her but me," Alaina said and raised her eyebrows, waiting for an answer.

"Not Blade. I had him saddle Wayne because he didn't want to ride an old mare. Koen here says he's a good rider, so we'll see about that." David smirked.

"I promise I'm a good rider. I was riding before I could walk," Koen said proudly.

"Well, Wayne's been throwing people off since before he could walk," Alaina laughed while the two boys stared at her, confused. She rolled her eyes and waved it off, "Never mind."

"Why Wayne?" Koen pushed his plate away and sat back

in his seat. "Doesn't seem like a normal horse name."

"We named Wayne after my grandfather. That's only half Wayne's name, though. His full name is Wild Wayne, and I'm sure you'll find out why soon enough," Alaina smiled.

"Ah, very interesting," Koen said, and it went quiet.

"Ready?" David broke the awkward silence.

"Yep, let's go." Koen stood up with his plate in hand, eager to go outside.

All three stepped through the door and headed towards the barn in silence. While walking, Alaina suddenly felt a hand on her shoulder.

"Grandmother would be proud of us," David said before entering the barn.

"I know she would. This is what she wanted, after all," Alaina said. She headed toward her horse and stroked her mane. "David, are you leading Oasis, or am I?" They had to bring Oasis into town to find someone to care for her since there wouldn't be anyone at the cottage to do so.

"She gets along better with Ophelia, so you should lead her," he answered back while adjusting something on his saddle.

"Okay." All three walked the horses outside so they could mount. Alaina handed David Oasis' lead rope while she mounted Ophelia. After she was settled in, David gave her the lead rope.

After David and Alaina were in the saddle, they looked back to where Koen was, and sure enough, he was having trouble with Wayne. Wayne wouldn't hold still, so Koen couldn't get his foot in the stirrup. David smirked, and Alaina shook her head. "Told you so."

"Yeah, yeah." Koen made Wayne run in a few circles before he had him stop. Wayne's nostrils flared, and he threw his head up. "Hey!" Koen shouted, and Wayne immediately dropped his head. Koen looked back at the twins and smiled proudly. "That's how you do it." He then put his foot in the left stirrup slowly and carefully, keeping an eye on Wayne. When it was in, he tugged on it a little. Nothing.

He tried a tug one more time, but Wayne stayed still. Deciding all was fine, Koen jumped off his right foot. Wayne bolted forward as soon as it was in the air, throwing Koen back towards the ground. Koen landed with a thud. For a second, he lay on the ground, accepting his defeat.

David was busting up laughing. While she tried to hold it back, Alaina couldn't help but laugh with him.

"Yup, that's how you do it!" Alaina laughed through her words.

Koen moaned as he sat upright. "Whatever." He hid his smile while he stood up.

"Sure you don't want to ride Oasis?" David called out. His face was red from laughing.

"Nope. I'm getting on that horse if it's the last thing I do." Koen walked toward Wayne, determined to mount the crazy horse.

"I might have forgotten to mention that my grandmother and I were the only people ever to ride him. He sorta prefers women," Alaina said with amusement in her eyes.

"Well, that probably would have been helpful to know." Koen folded his arms. "I'm still riding him, though."

"Okay, but only if you're sure," Alaina said.

"I'm sure. Would you mind holding him for me, though?

Maybe he'll stay still long enough for me to swing my leg over this time," Koen suggested.

"Sure," Alaina nodded and dismounted Ophelia, still holding onto Oasis' lead rope. She ground-tied Ophelia and approached David to hand him Oasis' rope. "I'll take her back when we're done," Alaina told David.

"Maybe you should try jumping on instead of the proper way," David suggested as he took the rope from Alaina.

"What makes you say that?" Koen raised an eyebrow.

"Well, isn't that how you mounted him the first time you rode him?" David asked Alaina.

"You're right. I did. It couldn't hurt to try," Alaina agreed. Putting her two fingers in her mouth, she let out a high-pitched whistle. Wayne's head came up from eating the grass. With his ears pinned up, he found where she stood, and after one more whistle, he came trotting straight past Koen toward Alaina. Koen spun around on one heel and watched the crazy horse trot up to Alaina like he was her pet dog.

"Unbelievable," Koen shook his head in disbelief.

"Ready?" She stood an arm's length away from Wayne's head to give him room, but still close enough to step in if she needed. She motioned for Koen to take the reins. "Whenever you're ready."

Koen positioned his right foot in front of his left, took a deep breath, and stepped out with his left foot. He pushed off, grabbed the front of the saddle, and swung his right leg over. When he landed in the saddle, Wayne snorted and sidestepped. "Whoa, boy. Easy, easy," Koen tried to calm the horse.

Alaina rubbed back and forth on Wayne's forehead. "Hey, bud. It's alright. Easy." Wayne threw his head, stomped his foot, and after a few more fits, he finally gave up. She waited until he stood still for a few seconds before finally stepping away. "Be careful with him," Alaina said.

"You were talking to the horse, right?" Koen gave a nervous smile.

Alaina mounted and took Oasis from David. "I'll bring up the back, just in case you need my help," she told Koen, and he nodded in return. David led in front of Blade.

They took the trail Koen and Alaina rode on their way to the healer. Her mood dropped slightly at the thought. It had all happened so fast.

Everything was happening so fast.

FOUR

"Hey, how are you holding up back there?" Koen called behind him.

"I'm okay, how about you?" Alaina called back.

"I'm doing great." Koen gave a toothy grin. She could see he was trying to lift her mood. She knew he saw her face and assumed something was bothering her. *That's sweet*, she thought.

Alaina forced a smile back, and her smile faded when he turned his head away. She was going to have to tell him her secret tonight.

After four long miles, the city gates came into view, and Alaina saw Koen hide his sword under his clothing. They entered the gates, and, at first, it seemed like no one noticed them. Not far into the city, however, people began to recognize them. Alaina listened as her horse's hooves tapped on the cobblestone streets. The sound calmed her nerves and made her momentarily forget about the people around her.

Her grandmother would often take her and David into the town and buy them small toys or treats. She always loved riding her horse into town and listening to her horse's hooves hit the cobblestones. Her grandmother told her that Norwest was one of the smallest and safest cities in Azgalia, which was one reason her father had chosen to live close to it. However, rumors spread faster in small towns. Alaina had learned that the hard way.

She looked up to take in the sights around her and tried to return to her seven-year-old self, but all she received in return were faces.

Kindness. Generosity. Peace. Love.

Alaina felt at ease when she read goodness in people. It gave her hope. Even the kindest people, though, can whisper. Alaina looked down at the cobblestone street and listened to the people around her. She heard whispers like, "Those are Maryann's grandchildren," "Mizcriens killed their father," and "They live out in the forest." Other people wondered about Koen and gave him strange looks. Some mentioned seeing her ride in and out of town the other day with the healer.

No one had heard of their grandmother's death, and no one needed to know.

Alaina rode up next to David. "Where to first?"

"Rodney's is first on the list," David answered.

"Why do we need to go to Rodney's?" Alaina asked.

"We need to pick up some medicine for future wounds or sickness," David said.

Alaina nodded in understanding. That was David, always planning, thinking clearly, and being smart. She wouldn't have thought to get medicine until they needed it. When they arrived at Rodney's house, Alaina decided to stay with the horses while Koen and David figured out the medicine with Rodney.

"Excuse me, young lady!" A woman's voice called from behind.

Alaina turned around to see who had called her.

Curious. Nosy. Smug. Afraid.

Alaina squinted, trying to figure out the woman's motive

for talking to her. She was older than Alaina but younger than her grandmother. She looked about the age her mother would be. She had hazel eyes and dark, red hair. Her nose was rather pointy, and her face was very round. She looked familiar.

"Hi, how can I help you?" Alaina answered.

"Hi, dear, would you mind reminding me of your name?" the woman asked.

"My name is Alaina, and who might you be?" Alaina asked.

"Ah, yes, Alaina. I am Cedric's wife. I have five sons, and one of them asked to court you. Surely you remember me?" The woman smiled.

"Oh yes, I remember." Alaina gave an uneasy smile.

"Oh, good! If you do not remember, my name is Fiona. Well, my dear, I was just on my way to pick up some pots for my flowers when I saw you here. I also saw you ride into town yesterday on your dappled horse with a young man and leave in a hurry with that healer, Rodney. Well, I was just wondering what might have caused all this. You've never come into town two days in a row. I'm sure you understand my curiosity?" Fiona gave a rather fake smile and laughed.

"My grandmother had been very ill, and yesterday morning, she took a turn for the worse. So we came to get Rodney to help." Alana looked down and blinked away the tears that begged to be let loose. "But there was nothing he could do."

"Oh my, I am so sorry for your loss. Your grandmother was a. . . ah . . . a very unique woman," Fiona said, tilting her head. Alaina knew she meant well, but she could also see through her. Her sympathy wasn't heartfelt.

"Thank you, ma'am," Alaina said with a nod.

"So, since you're here in town, I thought I might invite you and your company to dinner? My eldest son was talking about you the other day. I think it would just make his day if you were to come for a visit," Fiona said.

Ha, she thought. Fiona's eldest had been known to be very intimidating and harsh. That is what was causing her fear. Alaina was putting pieces together now. He probably told her to come out and talk to Alaina. She noticed smugness because she took pride in her plan to invite Alaina to dinner. She thought it was rather sneaky and clever. Curiousness and nosiness were just part of her personality; she was one of the top gossipers in the city.

"Oh no, thank you for the offer, though. My brother, friend, and I had better be on our way. We have some things to take care of," Alaina declined politely.

"So, will you be leaving the cottage then? Since your grandmother has passed?" Fiona ignored her decline and continued the conversation.

"Um, well," Alaina stuttered and looked behind her when she heard the door shut. "Oh, thank goodness," she said under her breath. Koen stepped out, followed by David, who had a sack full of emergency medicine, as he called it.

"Oh, well, hello there, David. It is good to see you," Fiona said.

"Hello, Mrs. Fiona," David nodded kindly.

"You look more handsome every time I see ya. Maybe more than my boys. Too bad you all never got along," Fiona said, trying to get him to talk.

"Yes, too bad." He shrugged and stuffed the sack in his saddlebags.

"Hello, young man. What might your name be?" Fiona put

her hand on her hip while she stared down Koen.

"Hello, ma'am, my name is, ah–" He stopped short and glanced at Alaina to see if she thought it was okay to tell Fiona his name. Alaina nodded slightly, and he continued, "Ah . . . my name is . . . it's Shander," Koen said with a playful grin.

"What an unusual name. You must not be from around here, so where are you from?" Fiona crossed her arms with a raised eyebrow.

Goodness, she is so nosy, Alaina thought. "It was good to see you, ma'am, but I'm afraid we must be on our way," Alaina interrupted and mounted her horse. With a farewell wave, they rode away from the odd woman.

Alaina nudged her horse forward to catch up with Koen. "Shander, huh? Where in the world did you get that from?" Alaina laughed.

"Um, I may have made it up in a rush." Koen gave a sheepish grin.

"Right. Maybe next time, we can come up with something more convincing?" Alaina laughed.

"Well, what would you have in mind?" Koen asked.

"How about . . . William?" Alaina suggested.

"You're kidding, right?" Koen shook his head.

"Better than Shander," Alaina laughed. "Where to next, David?" she called ahead.

"I need to get a warmer tunic, and then, I think that will be all for now. The next city isn't too far. If we need anything, we'll just have to wait until we get there," David called back.

Alaina nodded in agreement, even though David couldn't see her. She hoped the next stop would be quick and they wouldn't run into any old acquaintances again. She looked up into the sky and studied the clouds. Oh, how she wondered what it would be like to float up there, carefree, and without worry.

Her grandmother always told her that imagination is very important, even when you are older. She held onto so many of her grandmother's words and teachings.

Alaina looked back down and focused on the ground beneath her horse's hooves. One thing in particular caught her eye: a doll made of cloth with painted blue eyes and brown hair looked up at her from the street. Alaina halted her horse and looked for a little girl who might have dropped it.

When she saw no one who could have owned the doll, she dismounted her horse to retrieve it. It had been run over by a wagon, no doubt. The doll's dress had black dirt smudged on its pink color, so Alaina wiped it off.

"What are you doing, Alaina?" David's voice sounded a few yards away.

"Nothing!" Alana called back to him. She stuffed the doll in her saddlebags and mounted her horse again. She wasn't sure what to do with it, but she hated leaving such a pretty doll in the street. After all, she had always wanted one as a little girl.

She caught up to her companions again; soon enough, they were at another shop. David dismounted his horse and walked into the clothing shop while Alaina held his horse.

She glanced at Koen and saw him staring at the pommel of his sword in deep thought. Without realizing it, she was leaning forward to see his face better.

Anxiety. Worry. Despair.

Alaina thought he must be thinking about his mother. She couldn't imagine being in his situation. She wondered at Koen's past. Was it common for fathers in Mizcriea to be cruel? She had heard rumors of the cruelty in Mizcriea, but she had never imagined cruelty of that kind.

Koen broke his concentration on the pommel of his sword and glanced up at Alaina. Alaina had forgotten she was staring and blushed when he caught her. "Um, are you okay?"

"Yeah, just thinking about home," Koen said with a sad expression.

"Do you miss it?" Alaina asked carefully, not wanting to worsen his mood.

"Not at all. I'm quite enjoying my vacation." Koen tried for a smile.

Alaina nodded and looked toward the shop's entrance. "Then, why go back so easily?"

"Good question," Koen shook his head. "I guess I saw you and David's quest as an opportunity for redemption. I did nothing to save my mother, so maybe I can help you save your father," Koen said.

Alaina saw only honesty and regret in his eyes. "Thank you, Koen."

He nodded.

"What in the world is taking David so long?" she said while looking back at the shop. *He is usually in and out. He knows which tunic he wants and what size he wears unless. . . maybe he saw something he wanted to try on . . . No, David doesn't shop like that*, Alaina thought to herself.

A few minutes passed, and David finally walked out with a new white tunic, shiny leather vest, and new trousers.

"Thank you very much. I really appreciate it, but I should be on my way now. Thank you again," David walked backward out the door while still talking to someone inside. He turned around to see Alaina and Koen looking at him in confusion.

He shut the door behind him and gave a sheepish grin. "I was going to pick out the normal tunic I usually get, but the seamstress insisted on these," he said as he motioned towards his new clothing. "I told her I couldn't afford it, and I would be happy with the usual. She told me she would only charge for the tunic; the rest was a gift. I have no idea why she would do such a nice thing," David said, looking baffled.

"Seamstress, you say?" Alaina asked, and David nodded. "Then, I'm sure I know why," she said, amused.

"Come on now, David, couldn't you go back in there, work your magic, and get me new clothing as well?" Koen smirked.

Then, it dawned on David why the seamstress had been so kind. His eyes went wide, and his face turned red. "Oh." He walked over to Blade and mounted his horse. Without another word, he pointed Blade toward the end of the city and headed off.

Koen eyed Alaina with an amused smile. "He doesn't do well with those things, does he?"

Alaina laughed and followed David. They still had a little way to go before exiting the city. "Koen, keep that sword hidden," Alaina told him before she reached David.

"What about Oasis?" she asked David.

"I was thinking of my grandmother's friend. She always loved Oasis when she came over," David said.

"Oh! Mrs. Bennett? She would do well with Oasis!" Alaina smiled at the thought. Mrs. Bennett was the opposite of her grandmother in many ways, which made it all the more surprising that they had remained friends. Her grandmother was a very kind woman, but she only had a few friends she truly loved. Mrs. Bennett had been one of them.

Mrs. Bennett occasionally visited the cottage, and Alaina and David always looked forward to it. She always told the best stories, most of which were made up, making them even more fun to hear.

Finally, they arrived at a tiny house just big enough for two. David dismounted and walked up to the door. After a few knocks, the door opened.

Mr. Bennett smiled as soon as he saw David. "Oh, David, my boy. It's been some time, has it not?" he laughed and pulled David in for a hug. If there was one man David looked up to in his life, it was Mr. Bennett. He was one of the kindest men Alaina had ever met. "To what do I owe this pleasure?" He looked up at Alaina.

"We were wondering if Mrs. Bennett would like to take ownership of Oasis?" Alaina dismounted and dropped the reins to the ground.

"Oasis? Your grandmother's horse?" Mr. Bennett asked when his eyes fell on Oasis. "She does not want her anymore?"

"Actually, we also bring sad news. Our grandmother passed away yesterday morning. There was nothing we could do." David's expression showed sadness.

"Oh, my dear children. I am truly sorry. Maryann was such a wonderful lady and a dear friend to my wife." Mr. Bennett hugged the twins. "Unfortunately, my wife is out of the house right now. Although if I may speak for her, I know she would be honored to take Oasis as her own," he smiled.

"Wonderful! We wouldn't want anyone else to have her. Thank you very much," Alaina said, grabbing Oasis's lead rope and handing it to Mr. Bennett.

"So, you are off then? On an adventure?" Mr. Bennett motioned toward their saddlebags.

"Yes, sir," David nodded.

"Well, I'll be praying for safe journeys. You all take care of yourselves, you hear?" Mr. Bennett said, hugging them one last time.

Soon, they were off again.

Koen went back to thinking about home. He felt horrible for leaving his brother with his father. Hopefully, his father would take ownership of the murder of his mother, but he doubted it. Most likely, he would pin the blame on Koen.

Suddenly, a young boy ran in front of him, causing Wild Wayne to throw his head up in surprise. The horse danced sideways with uneasiness while Koen tried to calm him. "Whoa, boy." He pulled the reins up tight to grab the crazy horse's attention. When he settled back down, Koen kicked him after the others. "It's okay, buddy. That one was on the kid."

"How's Wayne holding up?" Koen heard David ask Alaina. She looked back at him, and Koen made a face that made her laugh.

Alaina's laugh reminded him of how his mother used to laugh at the faces he would make. His mother would tell him what a silly boy he was and remind him never to lose his playfulness.

However, Koen knew that sometimes he used humor to

hide certain feelings. He'd never forget being caught stealing from a merchant. Even though his uncle handled the situation, word got back to his father, who beat him mercilessly.

Afterward, when his mother saw the effects of what her husband had done to Koen, she cried. But Koen avoided the seriousness of the bruises and joked about how tough he'll look when he tells all his friends he fought a dragon.

Koen's thoughts were interrupted by a familiar sound coming from nearby. He searched for the source of the sound, a soft melody from a favored instrument his mother played. What had she called it again? A gittern? His mother had taught him to play a few songs on it, and he always loved singing them together.

He looked all around, but couldn't find anyone holding a gittern. He trotted forward. Finally, he saw a tiny little shop with an old man rocking back and forth on his heels, strumming the gittern. Koen slowed to a walk and ignored Alaina's and David's questioning glances. The older man caught sight of Koen watching him and gave a toothless grin. His mouth was missing many teeth, yet he smiled as though he was proud of it. He looked happy, but it was more than that. His eyes smiled along with his mouth, and Koen recognized it as pure joy.

"Hello there, young man. How are ya farin' this fine day?" he asked Koen.

"Just fine, sir," Koen smiled back. "Could you give me a second?" He asked the twins, and when they nodded, he jumped off his horse and handed the reins to David. "Thanks."

He approached the old man and asked, "May I buy a gittern, sir?"

"Of course ya can!" The old man rose out of his chair and slapped his knee in excitement. "Which would ya like?" he asked.

"The finest one you have," Koen smiled.

"Oh, but of course! Only, I would like to warn ye of the price. It may be a bit higher than my others," he winked and led Koen into the tiny shop. It was all made of wooden planks and was smaller than the room he had stayed in at Alaina's cottage. A little desk was positioned in the corner with a chair behind it, and gitterns covered the walls. If you could fit a gittern in any spot, it was there. No space was wasted. They were all so cramped together that he worried about removing one from the wall, fearing the others would fall right after it.

The old man walked over to his desk and pushed it into a corner of the shop that didn't have gitterns in the way. On the floor where the desk had just been, there were a few pieces of loose wooden planks with a handle on them. The old man pulled on the handle, and the planks released. He put them aside and reached into the floor to pull out a large brown chest. He smiled at Koen and unlocked it with the key around his neck.

He pulled out a dark maple wooden gittern. It was polished to perfection, and the strings looked brand new. "This would be me finest." He stood up and handed the gittern to him. "I clean it every day and every week, and I put new strings on it. I've been waitin' for just the right person to sell it to. Why, I've even declined an offer much higher than it's worth because I did not feel right about the man."

"Though you would allow me to purchase it?" Koen raised his eyebrow.

"As soon as I saw ye, ye looked like a good young lad. Ye two friends out there, I've known them since they were just as tall as my hip," he said while he pointed to his hip. "Any friend of theirs is a friend of mine." He smiled again, showing his missing teeth.

"Well, sir, I am honored. How much?" And when the older man told him the price, he said, "Not a problem!" Koen smiled and reached into his pocket. He pulled out several gold coins. "These are for the gittern, and these are for your kindness."

The old man's eyes went wide, and his face lit up. "Thank ye so much, young lad!" Koen nodded and tied a strap onto the gittern. He put it around his back to hold it and walked out of the shop.

After Koen mounted his horse and waved goodbye, the old man called out, "God bless ya, kids!"

The sun was setting when they reached the end of the city and headed into the forest. It was getting darker, and soon, they would need to set up camp. The forest was filled with all kinds of strange, unnerving sounds. Koen had grown accustomed to it over the past few weeks, though. The sky was dark blue, and a black sky would soon fill the vast expanse. For a moment, Koen was glad dragons didn't live in southern Azgalia. He had heard of the terrible monsters as a kid. His father had seen some on a trip to the southern coast of Mizcriea. They were said to live on the sides of mountains and breathe fire hot enough to make a single man evaporate. "Terrible, horrible beasts, those dragons are," he had heard his uncle say once.

A sound came from behind, and Wayne twitched his ears. When it seemed of no importance, he refocused his attention forward. The trip had been mostly silent, with little conversation. Koen used that time to practice telling the twins his secret. Hopefully, it would sound better aloud.

A breeze picked up and rushed the leaves all around them. He closed his eyes and breathed in the fresh air. The Azgalian forests were beautiful; much more appealing than those of Mizcriea. The trees were greener, the air fresher, and there were many more animals.

"We should stop for the night and make some food," David suggested.

"Agreed," Koen nodded and pulled back on his reins for Wayne to stop. He dismounted and walked over to tie Wayne to a tree. He unpacked his blanket, gittern, and a water sack.

"Koen, why don't you go hunt while Alaina and I finish up camp here?" David said.

"Okay. I'll be back soon," Koen nodded and set his things down. "May I borrow your bow?" he asked Alaina. She hesitated, but finally agreed. "I'll be careful with it," Koen winked. He had used a bow many times in his life. It was his favorite weapon aside from the sword. He had a good aim, but his swing and performance with the sword were always better.

Koen left camp quietly, hoping not to scare away any nearby animals. He marked a tree every few yards so he wouldn't get lost. He made sure to stop and listen. Wind rustled leaves, and animals sounded in the distance. It would get dark fast, so he would have to hurry. He walked a bit faster until he heard a noise. Looking over to his left, yards away, he saw a deer.

Koen sank low to the ground and studied the animal. It was a good size and would do well for supper. He crawled over to a bush and slowly rose. He lifted the bow and drew an arrow back to his chin. He adjusted his grip on the arrow and breathed in. With a swoosh, the arrow sank into the deer, making it fall to the forest floor. Koen looked around and then ran over to it. He pulled out the arrow carefully and scanned it with his eyes. It was clean, so Koen lifted it over his shoulder and grunted under its weight. He returned to camp by following the marks he had made. Finally, he saw a light a few yards from him. He headed forward and entered the camp. Alaina and David looked up at him and then at the deer.

"Oh, what a blessing!" Alaina said with a smile.

"He looks very clean and full," David nodded in agreement.

"Yes, indeed," Koen smiled and set it down. The group then prepared it and cooked it over the fire. They took what they could off and divided it among themselves. "Are we praying here as well?" Koen asked. He wasn't familiar with the type of prayer they did. He was raised to pray only to the many gods his people believed in. Every day, he and his mother would enter a special room, kneel before the gods, and ask for their blessings. He never really cared about spiritual beliefs, but he wasn't against them either.

"Yes, we'll pray here." Alaina nodded and bowed her head.

"Dear Father in Heaven, we would like to come before you and thank you for this meal you so graciously blessed us with. I pray that you give us safety over the next few weeks as we journey north into Mizcriea." A shiver ran up Koen's spine as he contemplated returning to Mizcriea.

"Amen," David finished. Koen wondered at the fact that

they only prayed to one God. He took note to ask them about it later. He would rather avoid any possible conflict until after he had told his secret.

After swallowing her first bite, Alaina laughed, saying, "I didn't realize how hungry I was."

"Azgalian deer meat is so much better than Mizcriea," Koen said while he closed his eyes and savored the flavor. It was soft, chewy, and tasty meat.

"Is it really? That's interesting to know," Alaina said thoughtfully.

"Since there is so much we don't know about Mizcriea, would you mind sharing some things so we can better understand it?" David asked.

Koen couldn't believe it. It was a perfect way to share his secret with them. "Of course. It's funny you bring that up. I have actually wanted to tell you guys something." Koen looked up to see Alaina lean forward and nod for him to go on. "Well, you see, there's really no way of saying this simply, no way of really sugarcoating it. It's probably going to be kind of a shock. You're—"

"Koen," Alaina interrupted him.

He looked up nervously, and she encouraged him to continue. "I—I um—" Koen looked from Alaina to David. "I'm the prince of Mizcriea."

FIVE

Alaina heard what Koen had said, but her mind refused to tell her mouth to speak.

So, this was his secret. She didn't know what she had been expecting, but it sure wasn't this. She had read him and thought he was good. No, wait—he was still good. He just came from an evil royal family.

Alaina heard her brother speak.

"You're a what?" David's brows furrowed in confusion.

"A prince. The prince of Mizcriea," Koen said again with a sheepish smile. David went silent, trying to search his head for answers, and the look of confusion didn't leave his face.

"Alaina?" Koen turned his gaze toward Alaina to see how she was responding. His expression showed hope, hope she would still accept him.

Alaina could only stare at him. She could only stare, unsure of what to say. She read him through and through, seeing if there was anything she could've missed.

Honesty. Hope. Fear. And more . . .

"Are you okay?" Koen tried again.

Alaina managed a simple nod. "I—I just don't know what to say, that's all."

"I understand if you don't trust me anymore. You have every right not to," Koen said.

"No, that's not it. I'm just taking it all in. In fact, it's all starting to make sense; your father, your mother, your brother, your story, and your sword," Alaina said, motioning toward his sword beside him.

"Alaina? How do we know he's even telling the truth? I mean, what in the world would the prince of Mizcriea be doing down here? He probably already knows about our father, too! Don't you?" David stood up in accusation. "This was all your plan, wasn't it?" David was heating up.

"David!" Alaina said rather loudly and grabbed David's arm. "He is telling the truth! Why would he have told us his secret if he were planning against us? Think reasonably, David," Alaina said, turning her head toward David.

Koen looked at Alaina, confused. "How do you know? How did you know to trust me? Why do you believe me? I don't understand why you're so calm about this." He shook his head in disbelief.

"I have a secret of my own," Alaina said, instantly grabbing Koen's attention.

"Alaina, I don't think—" David started to warn Alaina.

"If he trusts us enough to tell us his secret, then I see no reason not to trust him," Alaina stated, and David reluctantly sat down. Koen just looked confused. "Koen, do you remember when I told you that my blue eyes weren't the only thing I inherited from my father?"

"Yes, I remember," Koen nodded.

"The other thing I inherited is what we call a gift. It's only passed down through the bloodline, and so far, my family has it. It gives me the ability to read someone in just one glance. Their secrets, their fears, their true character, and more," Alaina said, watching his response. At first, he only held a look of confusion; then, his face slowly started to show understanding.

"Wow. Just . . . wow. That's amazing. You make so much more sense now!" Koen shook his head and laughed. "So, that's why you trusted me so easily. That's why you were calm when I told you my true identity." He paused so he could think some more. Koen looked up at Alaina. "You probably already knew I had a secret then, right? You didn't know my secret, though?"

"I knew you had a secret, and it had to do with who you were. Yet, I can't read thoughts, so what it was exactly was still hidden from me," Alaina said.

"Amazing. What do you read about me now?" Koen asked with fascination. He turned so his body was fully facing her.

"Well, I can read a lot. What do you want to know?" Alaina asked uneasily.

"Everything. Well, that might take too long. Just go until I say stop," Koen smiled with anticipation.

"Are you sure? I see the good and the bad," Alaina hesitated.

"I'm positive," Koen said.

"Okay, then . . . I see kindness, humor, confidence, strength, honesty, bravery, loyalty, intelligence, compassion." Alaina loved to make others happy. She loved seeing Koen's face light up and blush when she told him his positive traits.

"Wow, you see all of that in me?" Koen hid his blush.

"Yes," Alaina smiled.

"What about the negative things?" he asked curiously.

Alaina grew serious and nodded. "I see pride, impatience, ignorance, fear, uncertainty, stubbornness, anger, hatred, impulsiveness, and discontentment," Alaina said, watching

Koen's face go from joy to shame. "I'm sorry—"

"Please don't apologize. I needed to hear that. Of course, it's not what I would want to hear, but I need to know those things. Sometimes I don't even see the wrong in myself because my pride and selfishness so blind me," Koen said seriously. Alaina nodded, staying quiet. "So, David, you've been awfully quiet. Have you got any secrets?" Koen asked him.

"No, I don't think so. None that would concern you," David said, looking up from deep thought.

"Alaina, is he telling the truth?" Koen smirked.

"Yes," Alaina laughed after looking at David's unamused expression.

"Good. I imagine your gift can sometimes be overwhelming, but I'm sure glad you have it. It will come in handy on our trip," Koen said while throwing more wood into the fire.

"Yes, I agree. It can be hard to bear, but I know God gave it to me for a reason, and I intend to use it," Alaina said while looking into the orange flames. Koen looked up at the mention of God.

"You say God as though you are only speaking of one. Do you not pray to more than one god?" he asked.

"No, we believe in the only one true God," Alaina stated, seeing curiosity grow in his expression.

"Ah, yes. I think I have heard of your religion. The Christians, right?" Koen smiled.

"Yes, we are Christians," David popped in.

"Interesting. There aren't many Christians in Mizcriea. In fact, we usually refer to your people as the Faithful," Koen said. "You must share more about your faith with me sometime. I would be very interested in hearing about it," Koen said thoughtfully.

"We would love to share with you," Alaina smiled.

"Great!" Koen clapped his hands on his knees.

"Okay, so, just to make sure, we aren't keeping any more secrets, right?" David raised an eyebrow at his sister and Koen. Alaina shook her head and then looked at Koen.

Koen's smile grew, "I have one more."

"What is it?" Alaina saw playfulness in his eyes.

"I can sing and play the gittern." Koen shrugged, trying to hide his grin.

Alaina sat back in wonder. "You sing and play the gittern? And you're the prince of Mizcriea?"

"Yes, ma'am!" Koen said joyfully.

"Impressive," David said from the corner, and the two looked at him with odd expressions. "Well, I imagine it is difficult to learn an art such as music while being a prince," David shrugged.

"Mmhmm," Alaina nodded with amusement.

"It was. I was able to learn it while acquiring many other skills, thanks to my mother. Her voice was angelic, gentle, and beautiful. And the way she strummed the strings on her instrument was intriguing. The moment I was old enough to understand how to play, my mother taught me. She also taught me how to sing. Turns out, I had a hidden talent." Koen smiled at the memories.

"Didn't you buy a gittern today?" Alaina asked.

"I did! Would you like to hear me play?" Koen answered.

"I'd love to!" Alaina leaned forward with her elbows propped up on her knees.

Koen got up and pulled out the gittern from the saddle bag

he had placed it in. He brought it back to the fire and began to tune it. Once tuned, he looked up to ensure the others were paying attention. He smiled to himself. "I know just the song. This song was the first song my mother ever taught me to play. It helped me stay strong in hard times while growing up. Not always because of the lyrics, but just because I could hear my mother singing it in my mind, which brought me comfort."

He skillfully plucked the strings, creating a soft and beautiful melody. Koen began to hum softly along to the tune. After a few moments, he started singing the lyrics; they seemed to flow out effortlessly.

"Put courage in your heart, run swiftly to the start.

Filling your soul with hope.

Search for inner strength and feel, and make with life a lovely deal

Look deep within yourself, placing burdens to the shelves.

Trust the whisper in your mind, and listen for the chime.

Put courage in your heart, run swiftly to the start.

Filling your soul with hope."

He continued to strum for a few minutes after the lyrics ended. Alaina saw that he was deeply thinking about his mother, and the song brought back many memories for him.

"That was beautiful. The lyrics and your voice make a perfect pair," Alaina complimented.

Koen looked up and smiled at her, "Thank you."

"Indeed," David offered a compliment.

Koen nodded, "Thank you." He paused to enjoy the sweetness of the moment before slowly standing up. "I'll go get some more firewood before we sleep."

"I'll check on the horses," Alaina said and got up.

"I'll keep watch." David nodded at the two of them before they split ways.

After finishing their chores, they lay down in peaceful silence after a long day. Alaina stared into the fire, letting her thoughts of the day play through her mind. Her eyes soon grew tired, and she finally gave in to sleep.

"Alaina?" A voice sounded from somewhere. "Alaina?" It came again, but this time louder.

Alaina suddenly—although still half asleep—became aware of her surroundings. There was grass and dirt below her. The air was cold and smelled of pine. Where was she? She squeezed her eyes in hopes of clearing her thoughts. She opened them only to be met by the bright sunlight. Her back ached from the hard ground, so she let out a small groan. She was in the middle of the forest, searching for her father, who might still be alive after eighteen years, with her brother and the prince of Mizcriea.

"Oh," Alaina said aloud.

"Oh?" David asked, confused. Alaina just shook her head, dismissing his question, and he laughed. "We'd better head out soon. We want to reach Linencrest before the sun goes down tonight."

"Okay," Alaina nodded and sat up. She looked around and saw their horses eating grass nearby. The trees seemed so much greener and bigger from where she sat on the ground. The sun shone through the trees, casting a glow over them.

"It's so beautiful."

"Indeed," Koen said from off to her left. He was cleaning where their fire had been the night before. "I awoke with that same thought. I have a good feeling about today," he said while smiling.

"Let's hope. The weather is quite beautiful today, but that doesn't mean we won't have troubles," David reasoned.

"Thank you, David, for being realistic," Koen said sarcastically.

"I'm only stating facts," David crossed his arms in defense.

"Like you will be doing the rest of our quest, I'm sure?" Koen stood up straight with an amused look. He was enjoying David's irritation.

"Well, someone has to keep a level head around here," David said in frustration. Alaina looked from one man to the other. Hopefully, they won't do this the whole time. She knew it would slowly be worked out. Right now, though, she had to step in.

"Hey!" Alaina said loud enough to grab their attention. "We haven't even started yet, and you two are already bickering. Today is indeed beautiful. That doesn't mean it will be a perfect day, but that also doesn't mean we shouldn't try to make it a good one. Now stop arguing, and let's get breakfast going," Alaina finished with a satisfied huff.

"She's right," they said simultaneously. David rolled his eyes.

"Eggs?" Koen asked, looking towards Alaina.

"What do you mean, eggs?" Alaina asked, confused.

"Eggs. Do you want eggs for breakfast?" Koen smiled.

"Well, I would love eggs, except we don't have any," Alaina

said, wondering why he had mentioned it.

"Who said we don't have any?" Koen smirked and jogged a few steps to his saddle, which was lying on the ground. He opened the sack and pulled out five eggs.

"What? How do you have eggs?" Alaina asked, astonished.

"I packed it before we headed out. I wasn't sure if they'd make the trip, but if they did, I figured they'd do well for our first breakfast out." Koen smiled with satisfaction as he scanned the eggs for any cracks.

"Well, I'm glad you thought of it." Alaina smiled. "I'll start the fire."

Alaina gathered wood around their campsite and returned to start the fire. She thought about the journey ahead of them for the day. They would be riding through a lot of forest. Linencrest was on the west coast side of Azgalia. She had never been to the coast before. Her grandmother told her wonderful things about the ocean. She explained how there was water as far as the eye could see. And it was all blue. Alaina loved the idea of it. She wondered what it would be like to see that much water.

"What are you thinking?" David knelt beside her with a pan in hand.

"The ocean. Linencrest is on the coast, and I was just thinking about what it would be like to see the ocean," Alaina replied.

"I would love to see it. I must admit, I am rather excited to see the coast," David smiled.

Alaina remembered David's obsession with the idea of the ocean when he was younger. He wanted to be a merchant to sail the seas. He'd drawn pictures of boats and given them names. Alaina found it amusing that David wanted to do that, as he didn't seem adventurous. Once he found a passion, though, he ran straight for it, no matter what. After he picked up a sword, his grandmother began teaching him, and he decided to become a knight for the king. He worked hard every day since then to become a better swordsman. The hard work had paid off. Alaina wasn't sure he still planned to be a knight, though. She hadn't heard him mention the idea for a while.

"You two ready yet?" Koen walked up behind them.

"Yes, we are." Alaina cracked the eggs onto the pan and hung it over the fire. Soon, they all had eaten, and they began saddling the horses. They headed off towards their next destination.

For a while, it was silent. Alaina let her mind wander as she stroked the neck of her mare. The air was cool, and the sun still shone. Hours later, Alaina focused on the horse's walk before her. She memorized the seconds between each step until she became bored.

"Hello!"

Alaina's heart dropped at the sudden sound. She turned her head at the unfamiliar voice. Her eyes caught Koen's for a split second before Koen reigned in his horse and looked behind him.

"Hello, fellow travelers!"

Alaina caught a glimpse of a small, middle-aged man riding his horse.

"Hello, sir! Can we help you?" Koen asked, quickly ensuring his sword was covered.

"Actually, yes. I was hoping you could point me toward the city of Linencrest. I'm coming from Chessington and am afraid I have lost my way," the man said, nudging his horse a bit closer to them.

"Why, yes. It is that way." David pointed in the direction they had been riding. "We are headed there now."

"Oh, wonderful! Would you happen to know how far it is from here?" the man asked.

"My group here had planned to arrive before sundown," David answered.

"Oh, that is good news! Thank you! Would you mind if I rode along with your group? Since we are headed the same way, of course," the man said.

"Uh, yes, I suppose that'll be fine," David said hesitantly.

"Oh, wonderful. Wonderful. I hear the road to Linencrest can sometimes be dangerous and that it is best to stay with a group," the man said as he moved his horse next to Koen's.

"Dangerous? How?" Koen asked from behind Alaina.

The man craned his neck to look behind Alaina for Koen. "Oh, haven't you heard? There are these insects called stinging sticks that have an excruciating bite. If enough bite you, they can be fatal."

"Stinging sticks?" Koen raised his eyebrows.

"Yes, they are camouflaged, looking like sticks or plants, and when they bite you, it stings like fire. They are the length of my two fingers put together." The man held up both hands and touched the tips of his two index fingers.

"How many bites does it take to be fatal?" David asked.

"I'm not quite sure. You see, no one has lived to tell," the man laughed, and Koen shot Alaina a questioning look.

"I see . . . is there anything else we should know?" Alaina asked the man.

"I think the only other thing you would need to know is they also live in trees," he smiled.

"Oh, wonderful," David said under his breath.

"What was your name, sir?" Alaina asked.

"Oh, forgive my manners! My name is Arthur!"

"So, now we have to worry about tree-dwelling stinging sticks. I also assume they jump on their prey?" Koen said sarcastically.

"In fact, they do!" The man grinned, and Koen gave him a *you-are-a-crazy-man* look.

"Well, I think we should hurry then. Let's go," David said, turning his horse and starting forward again.

"This is horrible," Koen shook his head at the thought of the situation.

"You don't have any animals like that in 'you-know-where'?" Alaina glanced toward Arthur, then turned toward Koen.

"Not any insects like that. At least none that I've heard of," Koen said.

"Interesting," Alaina said as she looked ahead. Just then, she realized she hadn't noticed Arthur's face yet. She turned her head to look at him and caught a glimpse of his face before their eyes met. Her heart sank.

Deceitfulness. His intentions were not pure, and his character was very flawed.

She quickly smiled and turned away. Deceitfulness stood out the most. That usually meant that it was the most present character trait or motive. Alaina slowly moved up next to David. "I read Arthur's face," she whispered.

"And?" David looked at her with a raised brow.

"He's . . . ," Alaina hesitated, "I do not trust him."

David grunted, "Mhmm, just as I feared. Was he telling the truth about the stick things?"

"He was, and he is headed toward Lindencrest, but with ill intention," Alaina continued to whisper.

David looked at Alaina, "What do you mean?"

"Ill intentioned toward us. I believe he may try to rob us," Alaina said.

"Okay. Keep anything valuable you've brought close to you and hidden. Deceitful usually means a thief and a liar," David stated, and Alaina nodded. "Tell Koen as soon as Arthur isn't within hearing distance."

"Okay," Alaina quickly glanced toward Arthur to ensure he wasn't listening. They were in the clear. She let her horse fall behind the rest so she could be alone in her thoughts again. This trip still seemed unreal to her.

"Hello, dear, how are you faring on this lovely day?" Arthur pulled his horse back to slow for Alaina.

Alaina looked up and did her best to hide that she didn't believe his kindness to be true. "I'm doing well." She tried to smile.

"Well, that's wonderful. Where are you all coming from?" Arthur asked while he scratched his stomach.

"Norwest, sir," Alaina said, getting annoyed at his over-friendly attitude.

"Oh, what a wonderful little town that is. I haven't been there in ages." Arthur smiled and looked down at her horse. "She's a beauty."

Alaina perked up at the comment on her horse. "Why, thank you. I completely agree."

"What's her name?" He asked.

"Ophelia," Alaina smiled as she said the name.

"Oh, how lovely!" Arthur said. "My horse here doesn't have a name," Arthur said, looking up and smiling with pride. "But he's a beauty and probably deserves one."

"He is a good-looking horse. Why haven't you named him?" Alaina asked, looking down at the man's tall sorrel horse.

"Well, you see, I just got him and haven't been able to decide on a name," Arthur said.

"Well, you'll know it when you hear it," Alaina said. Arthur nodded and then continued to ride further up. She was glad the conversation had come to an end.

The rest of the ride was slow-moving, long, and exhausting. There were hills they had to climb and descend continually. All the roads there were dusty, making their eyes sting. The sun was setting when Arthur suggested they stop for the night.

"I know we had wished to reach Linencrest before sundown, but I'm afraid we still have a few hours left until we reach our destination," Arthur said for the group to hear.

"We'll go a little more until the bottom of the sun reaches the tree line," David said while he rubbed an eye.

The group nodded in agreement and continued.

Alaina ran her fingers through her hair out of habit. When she returned her hand and looked at her fingers, she discovered they were dust-filled. She groaned and thought a bath would be excellent at that moment. Unfortunately, she would have to wait until tomorrow when they reached Linencrest. It wasn't helping that she had chosen to stay behind the other riders.

She'd have to braid her hair tomorrow.

"I think my eyes are going to glue shut pretty soon," Koen squeezed his eyes and opened them, trying to focus despite the dust in them.

"We'll stop here," David said, pulling Blade into the forest. "I think we should go further into the forest to avoid robbers, though." He shot a knowing glance at Alaina.

"Good idea!" Arthur said rather cheerfully. They rode half a mile into the forest when they finally decided to camp for the night. They all dismounted, and Arthur left to fetch wood for a fire.

"Here, pour this over your eyes and then wipe them with this rag," Koen said, handing Alaina a can of water and a towel.

"Thank you," Alaina tilted her head back and poured water over her eyes. She quickly brought the rag up and wiped away the dust. "This feels so much better," she smiled and held the items out to David.

"Thanks," he said, continuing with Alaina's motions. "I don't know about you guys, but we should skip the campfire conversation and head straight to bed."

"Agreed," Alaina and Koen said in unison.

Arthur came back and went to bed sooner than the rest. He looked tired after the day's journey. He didn't own a blanket, so Alaina took an extra one and laid it over him. She remembered what she had read in his face earlier that day and realized she had forgotten to tell Koen. She called him over and walked him out of Arthur's hearing distance, just in case.

"Make sure to keep your stuff close tonight. I'm quite certain he plans to rob us," Alaina said.

"What? Really?" Koen almost blurted out loud enough for Arthur to hear.

"Yes!" Alaina said. "Keep it down, though, " she whispered, shaking her head at him.

"Sorry," he said sheepishly. "Really, though? Why would you give him one of our blankets? He'll probably steal it." Koen shot the sleeping man a glare.

"Well . . ." Alaina thought about why she had done that. "I suppose because the Bible tells us to love our enemies."

Koen looked at her, confused. "I could never."

"Neither could I, at least, without God working in my heart," Alaina replied.

"Right." Koen squinted. "Well, I'm going to try to pretend to sleep while I await the robbery of our goods."

Alaina shook her head, secretly amused, watching him walk away. Then, she turned to gather her things out of the saddlebags along with her bow and arrows. She laid them by her resting place and lay down. After thanking God for safe travels that day, she drifted off to sleep.

The following day, Alaina was the first to wake. She sat up and looked around. Her eyes felt better than last night, but she could still feel the sting from the dust.

Something wasn't right. She looked from David to Koen, but both were still asleep and looked fine. Turning her gaze to the horses, she squinted her eyes to try to figure out what was wrong.

Then, it hit her.

Arthur was gone. And so were the saddlebags.

"David!" Alaina jumped up and ran over to him. He sat up with his sword in his hand in an instant. He looked at Alaina, a confused and worried expression on his face.

"What's wrong?" David asked.

"Arthur is gone, and he stole our saddlebags!" Alaina dropped to her knees beside David.

"What? He did?" Koen's voice arose. "You were right," he said as he looked at Alaina while rubbing his eye.

"What are we going to do? We won't reach Linencrest until noon, and the road is so dry. What will we do without water? Without saddlebags for our belongings?" Alaina looked from one man to the other with a worried expression.

"We'll just have to go and fight through it," David said, "and we'll have to tie what we can onto the saddles. The rest we'll have to carry ourselves while we ride."

"And if we can't make it? What then?" Alaina asked.

"We just have to have faith that we will," David reasoned and stood up. "Come on, let's go. We don't have food, so there will be no breakfast." Koen, Alaina, and David gathered the things they had set beside them the night before. They mounted their horses and headed back towards the road.

Once they reached the road and exited the forest, the sun came into view, and they could immediately feel the heat.

"Out of all the days, today had to be hot," Koen said in disgust.

"Maybe we should ride through the forest?" Alaina looked at David.

"We could, but then we would risk being bitten by the Stinging Sticks," David raised an eyebrow.

"He was probably just lying about those, too," Koen rolled his eyes.

"No, he was telling the truth. You're right, David; I had forgotten about those," Alaina watched Ophelia's hooves for a few seconds. "So, do we just continue on the road?"

"I say we go as far as we can. If we can't take the heat anymore, we'll ride in the trees," Koen suggested.

"Sounds good," David nodded, so they continued to ride on the road. Their mouths became thirsty and dry. Their eyes grew tired of the sun's relentless heat and the dust that swirled in the air. They weren't much farther from Linencrest, but it was still far enough to be a dread.

Alaina licked her lips and blinked three times. She would never take water for granted again. She looked down at her saddle and wiped a finger across it, picking up dust along the way.

She remembered her hair and how terrible it must look. She wiped the dust off her dress and did her best to fix it. "That'll have to do," she said, blowing a piece of hair off her nose.

"Hey, look there!" Koen's voice interrupted her thoughts. She looked up and followed his eyes to where they were looking. A man was lying on the side of the road up ahead. He wasn't moving, and it looked like his belongings had been scattered on the ground.

They all picked up the pace and approached the man.

"Well, what do you know?" Koen shook his head at the sight. Alaina's eyes went wide, and she gasped. Motionless, robbed, beaten, and lying in the dirt. There, Arthur lied.

"What happened?" Alaina dismounted and walked up closer. "Arthur?"

"He's gone, Alaina," David said as he dismounted his horse. "Looks as though he was robbed himself."

"And look, our saddlebags are right there. Why didn't the

robbers take them?" Koen picked up a saddlebag. "There's still water in here!" He opened the water can and drank some.

"I'm not sure. His horse is gone, though," David said, looking around.

"If you look at the tracks, it looks as though they took the horse. Whoever it was didn't just run off," Koen said, handing the water to Alaina.

"Arthur must have stolen that horse, and whoever did this was probably taking back what was theirs," Alaina thought aloud. She drank the water and felt the liquid go all the way down. "Oh my, it tastes so good," she said, handing it to David, "What do we do with him?" Alaina motioned toward Arthur.

After taking a sip, David said, "Well, I suppose we could drag him into the forest away from the road."

They all agreed.

David and Koen dragged Arthur's body into the forest so it was hidden from the road. They covered him with leaves, sticks, and dirt.

"That should be fine," David said, and they walked back to Alaina. "Let's go."

Once again, they were on their way. Linencrest was in view a few minutes later.

"So, I have a question," Koen said, and Alaina nodded for him to go on. "Arthur was a thief, right? He's considered a bad man to you, right?"

Alaina and David nodded. "Yes," Alaina said.

"So, do you think there is any hope for him in the afterlife? I've heard of the faithful believing in the redemption of bad men and how they can become good. So, do you think Arthur deserved to die?" Koen asked.

"Good question," David smiled, and Alaina knew he wanted to answer. He loved engaging in in-depth and thought-provoking conversations. "Arthur was a bad guy, yes. Was redemption possible for him? Possibly, yes. You see, we are technically all considered bad. Romans chapter three, verses ten through twelve, says no man is good. As sinners, we all fall short of the glory of God, and the penalty for sin is death. Yet, God had mercy on us and sent his son to earth as a baby to live a perfect life so that when older, he would die for us on the cross. He paid the ultimate penalty for our sins so we wouldn't have to." David smiled. "And because of his sacrifice, we were cleansed of our sin, and his righteousness was imputed onto us, now making redemption possible for all given to him by the Father. This is said in John chapter six. So, to answer your question, Koen, yes, I think Aurther was a bad man, but so am I without Christ. I think God was ultimately in control of Arthur's life, and he saw fit for Arthur to die when he did. Now, whether Arthur became right with God before or not, I cannot say."

"So, with Christ's goodness imputed onto you, you are saved from your sin?" Koen asked.

"Yes, that's right." David nodded.

"So then, what does the afterlife look like for someone who is saved versus someone who is not?" Koen asked.

"Well, the scriptures tell us they end up in hell. It's heaven or hell. Eternal life with God in heaven, or eternal punishment in hell," David explained.

"Wow, you guys really believe that?" Koen asked genuinely.

"We do."

"Thank you for answering my questions," Koen said

thoughtfully.

"Anytime."

Alaina could tell Koen was thinking deeply. She realized what they believed was new to Koen, and the explanation of heaven and hell was tough for him to hear. Alaina knew part of the reason for that was because of his mother.

Soon, a sign appeared that indicated they were nearing the city.

"So, I say we just race there?" Koen shot David a challenging grin.

"That's not even tempting. Besides, my horse would win anyway," David said, slightly smirking.

"Oh, you think so? Well, I'll bet money that Wild Wayne here is the fastest," Koen said, patting his horse's neck.

"Careful, Koen, Blade is quite fast." Alaina grinned. "But Ophelia can smoke both of them."

"Is that a challenge?" Koen's eyes widened with excitement.

"You bet," Alaina smirked. "You in, David?"

David shook his head, "If one of us gets hurt, it's not my fault."

"Yes!" Koen and Alaina shouted in unison.

"I can't believe this," David said, still shaking his head.

"Alaina calls it!" Koen tightened his reins.

Alaina nodded and adjusted her feet in the stirrups. As her excitement grew, she felt adrenaline rush through her body. "Ready . . . " She breathed in and out. "Set . . . " Ophelia blew through her nose and stamped her foot. "Go!" They were off.

Alaina felt the power of Ophelia's hindquarters as they launched forward. Off to her left, Koen let out a holler of joy mixed with adrenaline. She quickly glanced in David's direction. She was sure the sides of his smile could reach his ears. David looked over at Alaina and laughed when Blade sped up, making Alaina give a teasing frown.

"I'll catch you!" Alaina yelled over the hoof beats. Dust flew behind them, and the wind whipped her hair behind her ears. The road dipped down slightly, and just up ahead, the city of Linencrest grew bigger as they closed the distance between.

Koen kicked Wayne harder and reached David in the lead. Alaina kept up but saved Ophelia's energy for the end. Thankfully, there was no one on their road to worry about. The forest trees on both sides blurred in her vision as they galloped. The city entrance was now in view, and Alaina urged her mount forward. "Alright, let's go!" One step at a time, Ophelia gained the lead on the two boys.

"Not fair!" Koen called out. He gave David a challenging grin and looked toward the finish. "Stop at the two trees!"

Two trees on the right side of the road bent toward each other. They knew which trees he was talking about, so they urged their mounts on, each wanting to gain the lead. Just seconds after, Alaina raced past the trees with a victory cry, followed by David and Koen.

"It's a tie!" David called out while he slowed his horse. "Whoa, boy." They pulled their horses to a slow walk and broke out into laughter.

"We should do that again sometime," Koen said.

"You just want another chance to try to beat me," Alaina laughed.

"Correction. I want to race again so I *can* beat you," Koen said smugly.

"So, this is Linencrest," David interrupted them while looking into the city. It was lively and full of color. Flags flew in the air, and people scrambled about with excitement. Little boys held wooden toy swords and fought playfully while fathers celebrated with drinks. Mothers decorated their homes, and daughters helped sew new clothes for the upcoming festivities. Something was brewing in the city. Amidst the bright colors and seemingly cheerful citizens, Alaina felt a wave of uneasiness. She didn't feel ready to take on the big city.

Alaina took in a deep breath. *Lord, please guide us.*

SIX

He sat silently, reading his favorite book. This was the most exciting part—the part where Jesus overcame death after being crucified. In this chapter, the women entered the tomb after seeing the stone rolled away from the entrance. They thought Jesus' body had been stolen, but instead, he had risen from the dead. The King smiled to himself.

Suddenly, a knock came at the door. "You may come in," King Malikai said, looking up.

"Sir . . . " a soldier started.

The King sighed, "Please don't tell me another man is missing. I don't think I can take another loss." Malikai sat in his quarters on a chair with a book in hand. He had seen that look on a soldier's face before. They all came with the same news. All his good men, his captains, generals, and good friends, were all going missing. He had searched for every single one of them. He made sure not to take any disappearance lightly. Those men had families. Those men were an essential part of the Azgalian kingdom.

"My King. Sir Dierks is nowhere to be found. We have searched . . . "

Malikai cut off the soldier.

"You have searched the whole castle. Yes, I know. Please, gather the rest of your men and set out immediately. We must find out what is happening and who is taking my men!" He gave the order and shut his book.

"Yes, sir, right away, sir." And with that, the soldier was gone, just like all the other faithful men who had worked for the King.

At first, the King thought they had decided to quit working for him, because they had something against him, but then it became clear that there was more to it. They were being taken. Powerful, strong men just up and gone. No trace left behind—just gone. It was beyond frustrating to be unable to do anything about it. If capturing some of the best fighters in Azgalia was so easy, why didn't they just take the King? He didn't understand it.

Malikai had prayed over this matter countless times. He continued to pray for the safety of his family. One member of his family had already been taken. Clearly, whoever was doing this had something against the King.

The rest of his family could very well be next. He had even brought the matters to Cleatus, the King of Mizcriea. He told him that even though he despised him, he wouldn't do something so odd. King Malikai wasn't sure he believed him. He also didn't have any evidence to show he was guilty.

It was infuriating.

"Father!" Malikai looked up from his intense stare at the book in his lap. His eldest son ran into the room. "Father, I heard that Sir Dierks is missing. Is it true?" Gavin's brow furrowed with worry.

"I'm afraid so, son," Malikai's face drooped.

"No! We have to find him! Why, I saw him just this morning. He gave me a lesson with the sword. He said I was almost as good as he was! We have another lesson scheduled for tomorrow!" Gavin stepped toward his father. "We have to find him."

"Son, I am doing my best." Malikai stood and looked into his son's eyes. They were now practically the same height. With his handsome features and strong build, Gavin closely resembled his father. He made most of the knights look small in comparison. Gavin had grown into a fine young man who would make an excellent king when his time came.

Sometimes, though, when Malikai looked at Gavin, he couldn't help but wonder what his other son would have looked like. His youngest son and second child had been the first taken from the castle. He had been only a baby, too young to talk or walk. He could barely crawl. He had never been returned or found. Malikai's wife, Laura, had been devastated.

"Father! Gavin!" His daughter, Evelyn, rushed into the room, interrupting his thought. "I heard—oh no. Is it true? Sir Dierks is gone?" Evelyn asked as tears began to run down her cheeks. "Why is this happening?" Two years after their child was taken, they were blessed with a baby girl, Evelyn. Something about her presence brought peace to those who were around her. Malikai and Evelyn had a special father-daughter connection.

"I know, my children. It's unfair. It's wrong. I don't understand why or who, but I know that even though we don't see the whole picture, God does. He knows what's happening and'll intervene as He sees fit." His children nodded, and a moment of silence followed.

"I'm going to go join the search for Sir Dierks," Gavin said as more of a statement, but he still waited for his father's approval. When Malikai nodded, Gavin didn't hesitate to leave the room.

Malikai then turned to Evelyn. His daughter carried her mother's beautiful brown eyes and her father's dark blonde hair. "Does your mother know?"

"I'm not sure. The servants are talking, but I can't imagine they would tell her without your approval," Evelyn said softly. She had a kind heart and hated seeing good men kidnapped. She was tough, though, and she had a strong, unwavering faith that helped keep her firm.

"I suppose you should be the one to tell her," Malikai told his daughter. She nodded and quietly left his room.

He sighed and sat back in his chair. He should join the search. But first, he would pray.

♕

"It is finished then?" King Cleatus of Mizcriea sat on his throne. His very presence gripped the hearts of his people with fear. Those who served him in the castle had become too accustomed to notice.

"Last we heard, they were entering the castle. They have never failed, so I would assume that it is finished by now," the commander of the knights answered the King.

"You assume? I told you that you would not see me until it was done. Was I not clear enough?" Cleatus' voice rose with controlled anger.

"Yes, sire. I only assumed you would want—" The commander stopped talking when the King rose out of his chair. "Your Majesty—"

"You know what your problem is? You assume. If you assume one more time, I will have you hanged!" Cleatus took a step forward, making the commander step back. "Is that understood?" Cleatus shouted.

"Yes, Your Majesty, of course," the commander nodded and tried to avoid running out of the room.

"Get out, and when you return, make sure you know! Go!" Cleatus shouted once more before the commander scurried out of the room like a rabbit with a dog on its tail. The commander was feared by all who were under his command, but even the most feared were nothing compared to King Cleatus.

Cleatus settled back into his throne and tapped his fingers one by one on the arm of the chair. He stared at the golden rings his fingers wore and raised his chin with pride.

Each ring represented a victory in his power plans. Every time a plan succeeded, he would make another. He wore eight rings on his hands—only two more to go.

He planned to wear the ninth ring in only a few days. Cleatus smiled to himself when he thought of his future plans. They were absolutely perfect. He would have the King taken, only to leave his son in command of Azgalia. Then, while the young ruler was figuring out his role and his father's absence, he would follow through with his final plans. Once those were finished, he would wear the tenth ring.

"Father, where is Mother? She wasn't in her quarters, the garden, or usual places." Cleatus' eldest son walked through the main doors.

"Honestly, Cronin, must you always ruin my alone time?" Cleatus rolled his eyes, ignoring Cronin's question.

"I am sorry, Father. Do you know where Mother is?" he

asked again.

"I think she said she was headed out into the city to explore the area." Cleatus turned his head to face his son. "Why must you know?"

"I was just looking for her and became worried when I couldn't find her," Cronin said.

"Alright, I answered you. Now, be on your way and do something productive." Cleatus waved him off.

"Any word of Koen?" Cronin asked before leaving the room.

At the sound of his other son's name, Cleatus froze. He slowly looked at Cronin and squinted to see if he was implying more than a question.

"I'm afraid not," he said as Cronin looked down at the floor. Clearly, he was worried about his brother. He would get over it, though, just as he would get over it when he finds out about his mother.

Cronin looked up and blew a piece of his dark, long hair out of his face. He searched his father's eyes with his own. "I do hope we find him soon. He wasn't in the best state of mind when he left," Cronin said with worry in his voice.

Cleatus gave a false, sad expression and nodded. He waited until his son left to smile. His plans were going perfectly. Except, he would need Koen to return soon if he wanted to follow through with his final plans. But he wouldn't worry. Everything would fall into place.

"All good things come to those who wait," he whispered, smirking.

Not long after arriving in Linencrest, the twins, accompanied by Mizcriea's youngest prince, found an inn to stay the night. After a good night's rest, Alaina sat up and glanced around the room. David was off to her left, sleeping on the floor. He insisted she take the bed to herself; the floor was comfortable enough. She hadn't believed him, but was thankful to have the bed to herself. Koen stayed in his own room next door.

There was a knock at the door, and Alaina jumped up to answer it. "Hello?" Alaina opened the

door to find a kind old woman standing behind it.

"Hello, dear. I was wondering when you expect to be out? I am to clean the room once you leave," the woman said kindly.

"Um . . . " Alaina glanced back at David, still sleeping on the floor. "How soon would you like us out?"

"Within the hour, if that's okay with you." The woman shifted the broom she was holding into her other hand.

"That will do. I will let you know when we leave," Alaina answered.

"Thank you, dear. And may I just say, what beautiful eyes you have." The woman smiled and nodded after Alaina thanked her.

After the woman left, Alaina closed the door and turned toward a still-sleeping David. She rolled her eyes when he snored in response. "David! Wake up!"

David shifted and groaned. "You make breakfast," He moaned aloud with eyes still closed.

After realizing he had spoken in his sleep, she rolled her eyes again and laughed. She walked over to him and shoved him softly with her foot. "David, wake up. I'm not making breakfast."

"Well, I'd hope not. You're a terrible cook," David said with a raspy morning voice. Alaina leaned forward to see if he had spoken in his sleep again, but instead, she found he was indeed awake.

"Oh, please, I'm not that bad." Alaina crossed her arms.

"You burn oatmeal. Who burns oatmeal?" David rolled over and smirked.

"That was one time," Alaina argued, and David raised an eyebrow.

"Okay, maybe more than once. Forget it. At least I don't talk in my sleep." Alaina turned around and gathered her things.

"Who talks in their sleep?" David sat up and leaned on his elbows.

"You do." Alaina hid the grin on her face.

"I do? Since when?" David asked in bewilderment.

"Since you were little. Grandmother and I used to stand in the hall and listen to you talk. We laughed for a good hour once." Alaina shook her head as she remembered that wonderful hour of joy.

"What? How come you never told me?" David asked, almost frustrated that he hadn't known.

"That would be no fun!" Alaina grinned when David lay back down with a groan.

"All this time." David shook his head.

"Hey, you two! I can hear you laughing from the other room," Koen's voice sounded behind the door.

Laughing, Alaina stood up and opened the door. "Sorry, we'll be out in just a second." Koen nodded, and before the door closed, Alaina saw him smile. Their laughing must have been contagious.

"I'm ready to go. You can just meet us outside when you're done," David said as he stood up. He bent over and shook his hair. He ran his fingers through his dark hair until it wasn't ragged-looking.

"Okay, I won't be long," Alaina answered while digging through her bag. When the door closed behind David, Alaina stood and quickly changed into a clean dress. This particular gown was simple, yet still pleasant to the eye. The colors of dark pink, beige, and brown complement each other nicely. It was suitable for both traveling and occasional city visits, such as today. It was one of her favorites, not only for those reasons, but also because it had belonged to her mother. Alaina looked down and smoothed out the fabric with her hands. She twirled once and then looked up to check if anyone had seen, but laughed at herself after realizing she was alone.

"Well, I guess I'm ready." She looked around the room and caught a glimpse of her shoes by the bed. "I can't believe I almost forgot to wear shoes," she laughed at herself and skipped over to the boots on the ground. After putting them on, she reached down for her bag. Alaina walked out of the room and closed the door behind her. She turned and continued down the hall toward the front room.

On her way, she saw the kind old woman from earlier. She told her they were leaving and that she could clean the room. "I made sure to pick up my brother's blanket before leaving. I couldn't let you do all the work," Alaina smiled.

"Oh, thank you, dear. It is my job, you know," the kind woman winked with a smile.

Alaina smiled back and, with a nod, continued on her way. She finally entered the front room and took in the sight for a moment. Everyone was smiling, their faces filled with anticipation for an event. She wasn't sure what kind yet, but she would find out soon.

Hoping no one would stop to talk to her on her way out, Alaina ducked her head down and quickly walked toward the door that led outside.

"Excuse me, miss!" a voice called behind her, and she turned around. "I didn't want you to go to your room without your key!" the inn owner told another woman.

Alaina sighed with relief. "Okay," she whispered to herself. When she reached the door, she pushed it open, and the sunlight made her go blind for a few seconds. "Wow, that's bright," she said, raising a hand to shield her eyes from the sun.

"Sure is," Koen smiled. "Here," Koen offered, helping her down the front steps.

"Thank you," she nodded and accepted his help. "Have you found out what all the excitement is about yet?" Alaina asked, looking between her brother and her friend.

"No, we were waiting for you. I was going to ask the innkeeper, but she looked busy. We did pick up some clues, though." Koen pointed toward the road. Many people stood on the sides of the streets cheering as an armored knight rode on horseback down the road. He was surrounded by a few other men who appeared to be escorting him into the city.

"Must have something to do with him?" Alaina asked while watching the knight on horseback ride down the road. She couldn't read his face because he was looking in the opposite direction.

"I'm sure, but he's not the only knight who has entered. We saw two others pass by, and I'm sure they weren't the first because the people were already celebrating when we walked out," David told her.

"Okay, so it's something to do with knights." Alaina tilted her head when the knight finally faced her.

Courage. Strength. Humility. Kindness. Honesty.

"Huh," Alaina said in a sort of wonder.

"What is it?" Koen asked as he stepped up beside her to look at what she saw. "You can read his face from here?"

"Yes. I guess I didn't expect to see good qualities in a knight surrounded by praise. I guess I was expecting mostly pride." Alaina then smiled. "It's nice to see good in people."

"I wonder if the others are like him." Koen squinted against the sun.

"Maybe," Alaina nodded. She continued to watch the knight ride down the road until he was out of sight.

"Hey, why don't we go get something to eat? I heard there is a tavern not far from here," David suggested.

"Sounds like a good plan, " Koen grinned and clapped a hand on David's shoulder, making him roll his eyes.

"Maybe we can ask around and find out what all the fuss is about, too," Alaina said as they made their way to the stables nearby.

"Yeah," David nodded and grabbed Blade's halter. Once mounted, they headed in the direction the knight had taken. No one spoke, but instead took time to observe all their surroundings. People looked busy and excited.

Alaina had known Linencrest to be a populous city in Azgalia, but she would never have expected this many people to be here.

Almost as if he read her mind, Koen spoke quietly, "So many people." He shook his head in wonder.

"You're a prince, surely you've seen this many people at least once in your life," Alaina said.

"Well, I have, but only in a wide open space or a large area that was made to fit many people. I have never witnessed this many people on the streets. This city is big, but still not made for so many people," Koen answered.

"It's there," David broke into the conversation. Alaina looked up toward the tavern and spotted a man speaking to a crowd of other men. They rode closer to hear what was being said.

"I am sorry for the inconvenience, but due to so many customers, I am afraid I have run out of ale! I am only accepting customers here to eat!" the man, who must be the tavern owner, told the crowd.

Immediately following his words, the men became angry. Some yelled, while some kicked the dirt in anger. "What kind of tavern runs out of ale!" a man shouted toward the owner, who ignored the comment.

"There are other taverns! Go find your own ale!" the owner shouted to the men before he fled inside to manage his tavern.

Soon, the crowd of ale-thirsty men dispersed, and David, Alaina, and Koen could enter the tavern without trouble.

"Sit wherever!" The owner called out to them.

The young people made their way to a table and took a seat. The tavern was indeed crowded with all kinds of people. It was loud and full of conversation, which they tried to discern from where they sat. One particular crowd of people caught Alaina's eye. Her eyes widened for a moment as she realized the knight she had seen on the street was sitting amid the crowd.

"Look! Over there!" Alaina tugged at David's tunic and pointed toward the knight.

"That's the knight from the street, isn't it?" Koen looked over as well.

"Yes! Do you think he could tell us what is happening in the city?" Alaina looked from her brother to her friend.

"Alaina, he's a knight, and he's clearly busy. Why don't we just ask the owner?" David suggested.

"Oh, because he's not busy," Koen snorted.

"Well, I'm suggesting the knight because he's the only one I trust right now," Alaina said. She looked back toward the knight to find him looking her way. Her heart dropped as she realized he had seen her. He smiled, and Alaina managed a nod back. She turned toward Koen and David. "I'll be right back." Alaina stood up, pushed her chair in, and made her way toward the knight.

Koen and David looked at each other and then at Alaina.

"Should we go with her?" Koen asked.

"I think she'll be fine." David looked after Alaina. "Let's just get the food."

Alaina felt people staring at her as she made her way past them through the crowded room to the table that held the courageous knight. She kept her chin up, despite the slight desire to hide from their sight.

"Excuse me, sir," she tapped a large man's shoulder to get through.

The man turned around with three large steps and looked down at her. His face slowly rose into an unsettling smirk. "Yes, my lady?" he asked, looking down his nose at her.

"If you don't mind, sir, I'd like to go around you." Alaina tried to smile against the sickening feeling in her stomach. This man was no good.

"Well, of course." He let out a chuckle that seemed to shake the earth beneath them. Alaina sighed with relief when he stepped out of the way.

"Oh, thank—" Alaina started to thank the man, but was cut off by him stepping back in the way, making her run into his ample stomach. He grabbed her wrists, and Alaina did her best not to scream.

"Wait, just a second. What is a young girl doing in a tavern all alone?" The large man raised the left side of his unibrow.

"Who said she was alone?" an accented voice came from behind the giant of a man.

Letting go of one of Alaina's wrists, the large man whirled around to face the man who had spoken. Alaina spotted her rescuer, and her eyes went wide.

"Let her go, you foul beast!" the knight yelled.

"What on earth?" The large man looked at the knight as if he were insane.

"Isn't that what all the knights say when they are rescuing a fair maiden from the hands of a beast?" The knight laughed and put his hand on the pommel of his sheathed sword. "Now, don't make me use this if I don't have to. Let her go, sir. Please." The knight tilted his head and raised an eyebrow.

The large man grunted and eyed the knight's sword. With a roll of his eyes and a scowl toward the knight, the large man shoved Alaina toward him and stormed out of the tavern.

"Are you alright, miss?" the knight asked as he helped Alaina up from the ground.

"Yes, all thanks to you," Alaina said while rubbing dirt off her gown.

"Well, I'm glad to be of service," the knight answered. Alaina finally looked up into his face. He looked a bit older than she was, but still considered young. The knight had brown hair matched with bright brown eyes, a kind face, and a friendly smile. He wore an expensive tunic decorated in bright colors.

"I'm glad you could be, too," Alaina smiled and paused, trying to remember her purpose for wanting to meet him in the first place. "Oh!"

"Oh?" The knight raised an eyebrow in confusion.

"My name is Alaina. I was wondering if you could tell me what all the fuss is about in the city? And why are there so many people? Oh, and pardon my manners! First, what is your name?" Alaina asked. She started to feel nervous talking to him.

The knight laughed, making Alaina ease down. "Well, first, my name is Maximillionous. Second, my friends call me Max, and you're welcome to do the same. And third," Max tilted his head, smiled, and said, "You look so much like your father."

SEVEN

"I'm sorry, what?" Alaina blinked.

"You heard me." Max smiled wider when he saw her confusion.

"You know my father?" Alaina was sure her heart was beating ten times faster now.

"Correction. I knew your father. A long time ago. When I was young," Max said. Alaina's expression went from confusion to excitement, then right back to confusion.

"How did you know him?" Alaina asked.

"He trained me in exchange for my help. I was twelve when I met your father," Max said.

"Trained you? When? When were you twelve? So, how do you know who I am?" Alaina couldn't hold back the questions.

"Why don't we sit and talk?" Max continued to smile and motioned toward a table.

"Yes, but first, let me go get my brother. He'll need to hear this, too," Alaina said. "Follow me." She grabbed Max's arm and led him toward where David and Koen sat.

"David and Koen, this is Maximillionous. We can call him Max, though. Max, Koen is our friend and David is—"

"Your twin brother," Max nodded knowingly. Alaina squinted her eyes at him.

"You know who David is, too?" Alaina asked.

"Yes. You two were born on the same day. If I heard about

one of you, you can be sure I heard about the other," Max laughed.

"Alaina, what is he talking about?" David eyed Max suspiciously.

"David, he knew our father." Alaina let go of Max's arm now that she was sure he wouldn't run away without explaining himself. "Tell us." She sat down between Koen and David, across from Max.

Max looked around at the young people. Alaina secretly already admired Max. That was the thing about her gift: sometimes she just trusted people immediately. People weren't used to that, so they were usually uncomfortable or suspicious of her. Then, occasionally, you have someone like Max. She could tell he was one of those who always seemed to be in a good mood.

"Well, I first met your father when I was twelve. I was finishing my years as a page for your father and about to become a squire. I planned to train in knighthood for the King's royal army as soon as I became a squire." Max shifted his weight in the chair to get more comfortable.

"What do you mean you were a page for our father? What does our father have to do with the royal army?" Alaina asked, confused.

Max held up a finger. "Questions after the story, miss." Alaina huffed and sat back, making Koen laugh. "Now, what was I saying? Oh yes, I would start training for the royal army. There was a problem with my plan, though. No one wanted me as their squire because no one wanted to take the time to train me. They saw me as an unfocused, scrawny little boy with wild hair. I was just excited, though. I would sit in a class all day, every day, if it meant I could become a knight. I wanted it more than any other kid there. Your father didn't care to have a squire because his job didn't require one. No one wanted to hire me, but your father took me in and gave me a chance. He told me he saw greatness in me, and though he had never been a knight, he could fight like one. So, he taught me how to wield a sword like a master. It was a dream come true for a kid like me. Your dad was the King's favorite man, so when he requested me to be his squire, the King did not hesitate to approve his request." Max paused to take a sip of water.

"Your dad returned to his house in Norwest every so often to visit his family. He still made time to train me when he came back. Then, you guys were born, so he left for a longer period to be with his family. It had been a few weeks since his last visit to the castle, and the time finally came for him to return. When he came back, he did his job and trained me. He told me during our training session that his beloved wife had died at his children's birth. He told me how much it hurt him. I was young, but also his friend, and wanted to be there for him. He told me about the twins his wife had delivered with joy in his eyes, unlike anything I'd ever seen before. He told me of his little Alaina and how she had inherited his gift. He said he could see it in her tiny face. He told me about baby David and how he saw strength and wisdom in his eyes. He was so proud of you two, even from the day you were born. Then, he left and never came back. We asked your grandmother if she had heard anything, but she hadn't. He was gone. There was word that Mizcrieans had been in the area, so we could only assume they took him. I am truly sorry he couldn't be a father for you two, but I can tell you that he was a great man and wouldn't have let you down." Max looked at the twins with sympathetic eyes.

There was silence for a few minutes before Alaina asked, "How did you know I was his daughter?"

"Your face and your eyes. I've only met one other person with your kind of eyes, and that was your father. Your face is like his in the way that there is something special about you. I only noticed it because I saw it in your father." Max looked into her eyes.

"Our father worked for the King of Azgalia? What was his job?" David leaned forward with folded hands.

"Your father helped the King discern the good from the bad, honest people from the dishonest. With his gift, of course," Max answered.

"After he disappeared, what happened to your training?" David asked curiously.

"I became a knight!" Max grinned. "The King saw me one day practicing in the garden with his son, Prince Gavin. He noticed my skill with the sword and complimented me on it. Soon after, he had me placed as the squire to the master of the knights. So, I continued training. I served in the royal army countless times. When the headmaster allows it, he will let some of us knights go out and explore the kingdom. I choose to practice swordsmanship on my vacations by entering knight tournaments. This time, I am entering the Linencrest championship tournament. Only the best make it in, and thanks to your father, I am one of the best," Max said with a grin. "I say humbly, of course." He winked at Alaina, which made her blush.

"I should've guessed! I can't believe I didn't guess sooner! It's a knight tournament!" Koen slapped the table in excitement.

"Yes, lad. That's what I just said." Max shook his head in amusement.

"Earlier, we were trying to figure out what was happening in the city. All the festivities and such. So, it's a knight tournament. I've never been to one." Alaina looked between Koen and Max. "So, you're entering it?"

"I sure am," Max smiled.

Koen looked at Max. "How good would you say you are?"

"Pretty good. I won the champion title a few years ago, but couldn't defend the title the next year due to duties with the king," Max said.

"I assume you plan to reclaim your title then?" Koen asked curiously.

"But of course," Max grinned.

"When do you compete?" Alaina asked Max.

"The tournament starts tomorrow morning. I am competing in the one-on-one sword fight, as are many other knights, so it will end up being an all-day event," Max answered.

"Could we come watch?" Alaina asked with excitement.

"I'd love that! I assume you use the sword?" Max turned toward David.

"I do," David nodded.

"That's great! I imagine you are good," Max smiled. "It will be good for you to come. You will be able to pick up some techniques."

"I think I'd enjoy that," David agreed.

"Great! Now, where are you all staying tonight?" Max wondered.

Alaina looked from Koen to David to see if they had an answer. "I'm not sure we had planned on anything," Alaina said.

"We could just stay at the inn again," David suggested.

"What? That old inn down the street?" Max sat back in his chair.

"Yes. The Ladies Inn. We stayed there last night," David answered.

"Oh no. That just won't do. While you're in my presence and cheering for me, you will be treated as honored guests at my party." Max crossed his arms with a grin. "I have a place you all can stay tonight."

"Oh, that's very generous of you. Although we don't want to intrude," Alaina said politely.

"Oh, please. It would be an honor!" Max said.

"Well then, thank you. We'd love to stay!" Alaina smiled.

"Now, I have one more question before I head back to my table and leave you to your lunch." Max looked between the three young people. "What brings you to Linencrest?"

Alaina realized they hadn't told him about their quest and her father. "Well . . . " Alaina started, "Our grandmother died a few days ago . . . "

"I'm terribly sorry to hear that." Max's face grew solemn.

Alaina nodded her thanks and continued, "And on the day she died, she told us a few years ago, she received a letter from our father," Alaina said, watching Max's reaction.

Surprise. Shock. Disbelief. Hope. Joy. Excitement. Worry.

Alaina fully understood those emotions. That's precisely how she had been feeling the last few days.

"Your father is . . . alive?" Max said, almost afraid to ask.

"We believe so. We're unsure, but because of the letter, we believe he is alive and in trouble." Alaina saw concern on his face.

"What kind of trouble?" Max's brow furrowed in worry.

"In the letter, he told us he was fine and treated well. However, one thing in the letter contradicted this. He asked us to tell our mother hello for him, but our mother died a year before the letter was sent," Alaina said.

"So, you three have set out to look for him where?" Max leaned forward in interest.

"To Mizcriea," David answered him.

"Mizcriea? Where in Mizcriea?" Max asked.

"Anywhere and everywhere," David said.

"That's an awful lot of ground to cover. What makes you think he is in Mizcriea?" Max asked.

"He said so in the letter," Alaina replied.

Max looked at the table for a moment in thought. "You know, ever since the year your father was taken, important men throughout the King's castle have disappeared. We search for them for months after each disappearance, but to no avail. The King thought it was King Cleatus' doing, but King Cleatus, of course, denied the accusation. He told the King that even though they were enemies, he would never do something so immature and unreasonable. I don't believe a word he says. Then again, I'm not the King," Max shrugged.

"So, what are you saying?" Alaina squinted in question.

"I'm saying that the King of Mizcriea probably has your father," Max said seriously.

"That can't be true. I mean, it could, but you'd think I would've known," Koen shook his head in confusion.

"And what makes you think you should've known?" Max raised an eyebrow at Koen.

Koen's eyes widened as he realized he probably just blew his secret. He glanced at Alaina and David for help.

"He, uh," Alaina looked at Koen and exchanged a knowing glance. She nodded and turned back to Max. "Koen is Cleatus's son, the prince of Mizcriea," Alaina said. She realized it was a risk to tell Max; however, her gift always overruled her natural instincts. She knew she could tell him.

"Prince, you say?" Max leaned to the side to examine Koen's clothing and held back a laugh. "You're kidding, right?"

"No." Alaina turned toward Koen. "Show him your sword."

Koen looked around to ensure no one was looking their way and reached down for his scabbard. He gently unsheathed the sword just enough for Max to see the pommel's design.

"Well, what do you know? That sure is a Micriean sword, and a mighty fancy one at that," Max shook his head in amazement. "What brought you down here? And how on earth did you meet these two blue-eyed look-alikes?" Max asked as he motioned toward the twins.

"Long story," Koen said with a small laugh.

"Alright. Well, I want to hear it later then." He thought for a moment. "I'll leave you three for now, but I'll meet you later. I'll have my squire fetch you." Max stood from his chair. "It was a great pleasure meeting you and talking to you three. Until later, my friends." Max bowed slightly and walked away toward his other table, which was surrounded by laughter.

"What are the odds?" Koen shook his head in wonder as he watched Max walk away. "And David, that was not a question. I do not care to know the exact odds, even though I am sure you can give them to me," Koen teased, and David rolled his eyes.

"I wouldn't tell you anyway. Your brain wouldn't be able to understand it." It was David's turn to laugh when Koen scowled.

"Oh, please," Alaina shook her head in amusement. "I don't know about you two, but I'm hungry," Alaina said as she picked up her spoon to dig into the soup before her.

David sat on a bench outside a small shop, where Alaina wanted to browse. He agreed since it was close enough to the tavern that they could leave their horses tied up. Koen wandered off somewhere alone, following the urge to explore one of Azgalia's largest cities.

He sat and watched people as they passed by the shop. Everyone was either in a hurry or busy with some task to help prepare for tomorrow's tournament. David had to admit he was pretty excited about the tournament. He'd never seen an actual fight before, and he imagined it would be exciting to witness one.

He couldn't stop thinking about what Max had said about his father. The story had left him both excited and confused. Had his father really worked for the King? Had his grandmother known? Surely, she had, but why had she never told them? He wondered what else he didn't know about his father.

Then, there was Max. David was surprised by how much he had taken a liking to Max. Usually, David disliked witty men who showed any sign of pride, but Max was different. He was witty, but he was also kind and friendly. He was proud but humble. He knew he was the best, yet he remained humble first. David found it fascinating that Max had trained with his father and couldn't help but hope Max would take an interest in assisting David with some skills. He looked forward to meeting up with Max later that night.

Suddenly, there was a noise that grew louder with every second. It took David back to the present and turned his gaze toward the street. Two other knights paraded down the street on horses, surrounded by crowds of people. He noticed one wore armor with gold designs and a saddle that must have cost a fortune.

"Probably last year's champion," Alaina's voice spoke from behind him.

David nodded in agreement with her observation.

"He sure has the character of a proud champion knight," she said.

"Not a good one, I'm guessing?" David asked.

"Nope," Alaina laughed and sat beside him to watch the crowd pass. "Do you know where Koen went?" Alaina asked.

"Not sure." David shrugged. "He wandered off in that direction," he pointed toward the east, "after telling me he wanted to explore the city some more,"

"Alone? Does he realize this is one of the largest cities in Azgalia? Does he expect us to find him? Or just wait until he gets back? Assuming he knows his way back, that is." Alaina shook her head.

"Honestly, I don't know what he was thinking. Nor do I really care," David said.

"I guess we'll just have to wait for him," Alaina said. "So, what did you think of Max?"

"I liked him," David said. When she didn't respond, he turned to face Alaina. She was looking at him with an amused expression. "What?"

"It's just so funny that you never really express how you truly feel about things. It's a good thing I can read right through you; otherwise, no one would ever understand you. I guess that's one good reason I have the gift," Alaina laughed.

"Exactly. Why overexpress myself when I have you?" David laughed along with her.

"What's so funny?" A voice interrupted their laughter. David and Alaina turned toward the newcomer, smiling when they saw it was Max.

"Nothing important," David said as he subtly smiled at Alaina.

"Well then, I just came to get you to see if you still wanted to stay at my place tonight. I don't mind at all," Max smiled.

"If it's still okay with you, then yes. We'd love to," Alaina said.

"Great. Where is your Mizcriean friend?" Max looked around to see if he could spot Koen.

"We're not quite sure. You see, he wandered off to explore the city," Alaina said.

"The city? Alone?" Max raised his eyebrow.

"That's what I said!" Alaina laughed.

"So, are you two just waiting here for him then?" Max asked.

"I suppose so," David said. Something on Max's arm caught David's eye in brief silence. It was a marking with three lines of different lengths stacked on each other. The top was longer than the second, and the bottom was shorter than the second.

"Max, is there any significance to that marking?" David pointed to the marking on his arm.

Max looked down at his arm where the marking was. It
was right below his wrist on his right arm. "Actually, yes,"
Max smiled. "It's a marking only the knights of the royal army
possess, and it has a symbolic meaning. I'll tell you about it
another time," Max smiled. "Now, as for your friend, should I
send my squire to look for him? He's a rather fast rider and has
a great eye for spotting people in crowds," Max said.

"I don't think that will be needed," Koen said as he rode up
on Wild Wayne and swung off onto the ground below just as
he reached them.

"Wonderful." Max smiled and clapped at Koen's entrance.
"Now we can be on our way."

"Maximillion!" A deep voice called out, and David saw
Max tense for a moment. Max squeezed his eyes shut.

"Maximillion, my friend!"

When the man called again, Max slowly opened his eyes
and mouthed the words to the young people, "He's not my
friend." He turned slowly on his heel to face the man with the
deep voice. Only then were they able to see who had called
him. It was the proud tournament champion.

"Nicholas! How are you?" Max managed a friendly welcome despite his apparent dislike of the man.

"I am well, and champion!" Nicholas gave a deep laugh.
He strode up to the group and cast an odd glance toward Koen.

"So, I've heard. Congratulations." Max shook hands with
Nicholas.

"Thank you, Maximillion," Nicholas grinned. Despite the
scars on his face from sword fights, he was a well-groomed

man. His dark green eyes bore a fierce gaze that anyone who looked into them would see. David observed his manners and glanced toward Alaina to see if she was reading his face. She was, and by her expression, she wasn't impressed.

"Actually, it's Maxamillionous," Max said with a fake laugh.

Nicholas squinted at him, but then looked again toward Koen. His gaze quickly dropped toward Koen's sheathed sword. "And what might your name be?" Nicholas reached out to shake Koen's hand.

After hesitating, Koen took it. "My name is Koen."

"Ah, good to meet you, Koen. Tell me, where are you from?" Nicholas asked, clearly making Koen uneasy.

"Um, I'm from Norwest," Koen smiled wearily.

"Interesting," Nicholas said as he squinted and rubbed his chin.

"Interesting? How so?" Koen gave an uneasy laugh.

"Oh, no reason really. Just that earlier today, when you passed by my cheering crowd on your horse, your sword fell out of your sheath when he reared up." Koen's eyes grew wider. "My servant happened to see that it was a Mizcrian sword!" Nicholas unsheathed his sword in marvelous speed and, using its tip, hooked it onto the pommel of Koen's sword and pulled it out of its sheath.

However, before it could hit the ground, Koen caught it. David shot up from his seat along with Alaina and put his hand on the pommel of his sword in a ready stance. Everyone froze.

"Now, now, Nicholas. No need to worry—" Max started.

"No need to worry? He's a Mizcriean! I know that sword! Only high-ranking knights have swords with those designs! He must be a spy sent from the enemy King!" Nicholas's eyes showed fury, and his gaze never left Koen.

"I know that, Nicholas. He's with me, though," Max tried to calm him.

"Out of all people, you being a knight of the King's special army, I would have expected you to understand." Nicholas then, for a moment, turned his gaze toward Max.

"Give me one good reason why I shouldn't run this sword through him right now," Nicholas threatened.

And before anyone could speak up for him, Koen said, "Because then you won't get to accept my challenge."

"And what challenge would that be?" Nicholas sneered.

"I challenge you to a duel tomorrow in the tournament ring. I win, I leave the city with my friends unharmed and free to go. You win, well, you decide," Koen said with a determined look. David watched as the scene unfolded before him. He recognized the bravery in Koen. He also recognized what a terrible idea this was.

"I win, I get to run my sword right through you," Nicholas said.

"Well, that's not what I was thinking," Koen laughed nervously, "but a deal's a deal."

"Challenge accepted," Nicholas agreed and lowered his sword.

"Koen–" Alaina tried to speak up.

Nicholas raised his sword again and put the tip against Koen's chest. "And don't even think about running off before tomorrow's tournament. I will find you," Nicholas threatened. Koen gulped before nodding.

"See you all tomorrow then." Nicholas resumed his friendly

expression almost instantly. "Maximillion." Nicholas nodded in Max's direction and returned to where he had come from.

"It's Maximillionous," Max said while glaring toward him when he had gotten out of hearing range.

"Koen! What were you thinking?" Alaina asked in a panicked tone.

"He wasn't just going to let me go, Alaina," Koen said.

"He's right, Alaina," Max nodded.

"But he's the tournament champion! Does Koen even have a chance at beating him?" Alaina looked at Max.

"That depends," Max tilted his head.

"On what?" They all said in union.

"On how good he is," Max said. "What do you think, David?" Max looked at David.

David thought momentarily, "I'd have to see Nicholas fight to tell who has more of an advantage. From what I've seen, Koen is very advanced with swordsmanship skills."

"Well then, I say we head to my place. There is a small training arena there. I will test out your skill for myself and help you beat Nicholas." Max smiled and clasped his hands together. "This is going to be exciting."

Alaina didn't have the words to express how impressed she was with Maxamillionous' place. The size was quite impressive, and they thought the same thing by looking at Koen's and David's faces.

"It looks like a small castle!" Koen said in wonder.

"You could say that, I guess," Max laughed.

"That is the training arena, right?" David asked, pointing to a large, gated area with stone-like steps to accommodate a small crowd.

"That is correct. It also serves as a horse arena," Max said.

"And this is all yours?" Alaina asked while she glanced around the landscape.

"Well, the king arranged this place for all the knights of the king's army who compete in the tournaments to stay. However, another fellow and I are the only ones from the King's army fighting this year. Other knights from the royal army compete in the tournament; however, they are to stay in smaller houses or inns," Max explained.

"And where is this other fellow in the King's army?" Alaina asked.

"His family lives here in Linencrest, so he plans to stay with them for now," Max said.

"Nice. So, you've got the whole place to yourself," Koen said.

"Yeah, pretty much," Max smiled. Alaina watched as two boys a few years younger than her came to hold their horses while they dismounted. She nodded, thanked them, and asked their names.

"My name is Gunther, and over there is Pax," Gunther said as he ran his hand along Ophelia's face. He was small for his age, but Alaina could see his outgoing personality made up for it. His bright green eyes lit up when Alaina asked his name. "We work here whenever there is a visitor from the King's army, or someone else important," Gunther explained.

"Max is our favorite visitor, though," Pax whispered as he

passed by them with Max's and David's horses. Gunther nodded in agreement with his blonde-haired friend.

"Well, it was nice to meet you." Alaina smiled and waved as Gunther went to follow Pax.

"And you, Miss Alaina." Gunther smiled and walked on, leading Alaina's and Koen's horses.

"Fine young lads they are," Max said while standing beside her. "Well, follow me. We still have to show you to your rooms and train Koen. Dinner will come after that," Max said as he motioned for the rest of them to follow him.

♕

Sweat dripped from the foreheads of both opponents while they breathed heavily. The day had grown warmer, making the training harder. Koen held up a hand to let Max know he needed a second. "Sorry, I haven't trained like this in a while."

"Been gone from home for too long, have we?" Max smiled.

"Sure have," Koen nodded and lowered his sword to catch his breath.

"You're good. They train aggressively in Mizcriea?" Max asked.

"I suppose. It's the only kind of training I've ever known," Koen said.

"How am I doing?" Max smirked.

"You're doing just fine," Koen laughed.

"You want to go a few more times?" Max asked.

"Sure, why not?" Koen raised his sword and stood in a ready position. Max advanced first and quickly had Koen on the defense. Koen decided to wait until Max grew weary before unleashing his offensive movements.

"Don't wait it out," Max said. "They'll know what you're doing and use your trickery against you."

Koen nodded and tried to think of a different approach. Instead of holding back, he made his sword fly a little faster to keep the fight even. He memorized the speed and strength of Max's maneuvers. Then he found a weak spot. He didn't hesitate to take the opportunity. In a flash, Koen thrust his sword forward, which made Max stumble back to avoid the blade. After the stumble, Max was thrown off rhythm, so Koen transferred into offense. He released techniques he had learned from watching the knights fight back home. He paid attention to his feet and kept an even speed. He was careful not to tire out.

Soon, Max couldn't keep up and made a retreat. He held up a hand, and both men stopped.

"Nice job, Koen," Max said through heavy breathing, "Quick thinking matched with powerful movements."

"Thanks. Good enough to win tomorrow?" Koen asked.

"Possibly. I don't believe any of those men have fought a Mizcriean in a tournament. Battle and tournament fighting are two different things. Tournaments last much longer and take more thinking and strategy," Max said. "I think we've done enough. We can do some training in the morning." They sheathed their blades and walked out of the training arena to meet up with Alaina and David, who were waiting outside the gate.

"You guys looked great in there! Think he'll be okay?" Alaina asked Max.

"I think he'll stay alive," Max said jokingly, making David

snort.

"Hilarious," Koen said, rolling his eyes.

"Dinner should be ready soon. I heard our cook is making her best dish tonight, so why don't you all go clean up and meet me in the dining hall when you're finished?" Max said. The rest nodded in agreement.

Koen followed David and Alaina inside the castle. Despite being a castle, it was very cozy and inviting. The inside was even more impressive than the outside. The detail in the flooring and on the walls was incredible. Max gave them a tour of it when they first arrived and explained that the wallpaper illustrated Mizcriea and Azgalia's history. Their rooms were each decorated in different colors and styles, all with the finest linens and furniture. It was fancy, yet comfortable. The colors raised their spirits and put them in a good mood.

Koen had to admit he liked it much better than the castles back home. The colors there were dark and made him feel uneasy. Even though Koen had grown used to it, his father's castle had always felt strange.

"We'll see you down there," Alaina said to Max as David and Alaina split into their rooms. Their rooms were right across from each other, with Alaina's on the right and David's on the left. Alaina's was decorated with light violets and yellow roses. David's was green linens and cream-colored furniture. Koen smiled and walked into his room, which wasn't much farther down. He turned left and opened the large door that led into his room. His room here was much different than his back in Mizcriea. This room was smaller and brighter. He didn't mind it at all, though. Being in this room now made him not want to go back to having a large, dark room. He imagined it would feel lonely after sleeping in this inviting environment. His room held shades of blue that matched the sky outside and colors of coral that reminded him of the sea. When they were young, his uncle took him fishing with his brother on a boat. He thoroughly enjoyed the ocean and the peacefulness it brought him.

After changing into another pair of clothes Max provided, Koen went down the hall. Since Alaina and David hadn't made it out yet, he pretended to study the wall's design while he thought about the tournament tomorrow. He wondered what his parents would say about him fighting in an Azgalian tournament. His mother, like all mothers, would be worried about his safety. She would also do her best to encourage him. She never mentioned not liking the Azgalians. She was always kind to the Azgalian servants his father had taken.

His father would have either ensured Koen's victory and destruction of every opponent, or he would have banished him for involvement in Azgalian activities. Honestly, he didn't care much about what his father thought anymore. When he was younger, he always wanted to prove himself, but now, he had no respect for his father because he was incapable of respecting anyone.

"Are you okay?" Alaina's voice cut off his thoughts.

"Um, yeah." Koen blinked to clear his thoughts.

"Great, I'm starving." David came out of his room.

"You could eat all day if you wanted to, David," Alaina said.

"True." David gave a goofy grin.

They turned down the hall and headed toward the dining room. While they walked, Koen thought about how amazing it was that he had run into Alaina in the woods. His first thought had been how strange it was to come across a girl hunting alone in the woods. He never would have thought this is where he would end up when he first left home. He left home only to meet two twins with a crazy back story that needed to be guided back to where he had run from. Not to mention, he was exactly what they needed to get their father back. He was the prince of Mizcriea. Who better to help you in a foreign country than its own prince?

"Wow, that smells amazing," David sighed.

"Why, thank you, young man," A short elderly woman said with a cheery smile. She placed a large roasted turkey in the middle of the table.

"I'm assuming you're the cook?" Koen asked with a smile.

"Yes, I am." She smiled again.

"It's lovely to meet you, what might your name be?" Koen asked.

"My name is Catherine, and what about you three?" Catherine asked.

"This is David, Alaina, and my name is Koen," he answered.

"Oh, what lovely names!" Catherine said. "I'll be right back; I must fetch the rest of the food. You go ahead and take a seat. Sir Max will be down soon." She smiled and walked back to the kitchen.

"Sir Max," Alaina raised her eyebrows.

"Well, he is a knight," Koen said sarcastically.

"Yes, I know," Alaina laughed. "It just felt necessary to repeat it. It's so impressive," she smiled.

Koen was surprised when a spark of jealousy ignited in him. He blushed in embarrassment but turned his face away so Alaina wouldn't see.

"Well, Sir Max surely isn't as impressive as Prince Koen," Max said as he entered the room.

"That's true. I did have to repeat that in my mind more than once," Alaina laughed.

Koen wasn't sure how to respond, so he just laughed with her. Max pulled up a seat next to Koen, across from David. "Mrs. Catherine! Young David is about to start drooling if you don't hurry and bring the rest of the food so we can say grace!" he called out for Catherine to hear. Soon, Catherine served the food onto the table. The young people's eyes widened at the sight of the feast.

"Wow," they all said in unison.

"Indeed," Max agreed. After saying grace and praying for protection over Koen in the tournament the next day, they all made sure to leave nothing on their plates.

"Koen, tell me," Max tilted his head and lowered his fork beside his plate, "being that you are the prince of Mizcriea, do you share our faith?"

"I do not, although I have heard of it. Alaina and David said they are Christians. Is that what you hold to as well?" Koen asked.

"I do," Max smiled.

"Interesting. I have heard of Christians in Mizcriea, but very rarely. I don't imagine there are many, as most worship numerous gods," Koen said.

"Polytheists," Max nodded, "And what about yourself?"

"I was raised to pray to the gods of Mizcriea; however, I only did it out of practice and because my mother encouraged it. Is Christianity a popular belief in Azgalia?" Koen asked Max.

"I wouldn't say popular, but it is the founding belief throughout most of the kingdom. I assume this for two reasons: our King holds to the same belief and makes a point to share it with others. Another, I would say, is that the faith has been passed down through many generations in many families. Azgalia maintains many of the founders' teachings," Max explained.

"By founders, do you mean the men who discovered these kingdoms?" Koen asked with interest.

"Exactly. They were brothers, you know. They were both raised as Christians. However, one brother never truly held to the Christian faith, so he turned against his brother in jealousy and hatred. Even though the older brother died, his legacy was carried down through his son, down to King Malikai. In fact, I do believe Mizcriea once had many more Christians than it does now. The King, before your father, killed many for their faith," Max told Koen.

"I never knew that. My father had only mentioned the Christian faith once around me, and I remember how he talked. It couldn't have been anything good. My mother never talked about it since she was so faithful to the gods of Mizcriea. That's all she's ever known," Koen said. He then looked at the twins. They both seemed very interested in the conversation that was taking place.

"But so far, I've gathered that you all believe in one God. You call Him the one true God. Those I've met with the same faith as you have been kind and merciful, which has stood out to me, especially since I am the prince of Mizcriea. In my kingdom, if I were the prince of Azgalia and had crossed borders, they would have me sentenced to death," Koen said.

"You are certainly observant. It's good to know that you are open to learning more. The fact that you were able to tell me those things means you listen. And when you listen, that tells me you want to learn," Max smiled.

"I do want to learn more about your beliefs. If you are willing to tell me," Koen said honestly.

"Of course! Well, like you said, we believe in one God. The one and true God. We believe that, in the beginning, before the universe was created, He was there. We believe He spoke the universe into existence, like His word says," Max explained.

"By His word, do you mean the Holy Bible?" Koen asked.

"Yes. It was written by men whom God chose, and God inspired it. After creating the world and all things in it, He created Adam and Eve. They were the first people ever to walk the earth. They were without sin and were pure. Two special trees were in the Garden of Eden, a place God had created for them to live. One of those trees was forbidden, called the Tree of Knowledge of Good and Evil. The Lord told Adam and Eve that if they ate the fruit of it, they would surely die. Sadly, one day, Satan in the form of a serpent tempted and tricked Eve into eating the fruit. She then shared the fruit with her husband, Adam, which was the first sin."

"Who is Satan?" Koen asked.

"Satan is a fallen angel who was cast out of heaven along with other fallen angels. They were created as holy angels but rebelled against God and rejected him as their all-satisfying King. They wanted to be their own rulers. They don't want to be sent by God to serve others. They want to have final authority over themselves. And they want to exalt themselves above God." Max paused to think. "Which is quite interesting if you think about it. When we sin, we are essentially doing as the fallen angels did. We choose to be our own rulers and don't want to answer to God. Of course, by Christ we can be forgiven, unlike them. Just puts our own sin in perspective," Max said.

"Okay." Koen nodded as he took it all in. "And what happened with Adam and Eve?" he asked.

"They corrupted the human race. Every human after them is now affected by the curse. So even now, you, me, us—we are all affected by their sin, and sin daily. Because we sin, we require a savior." Max smiled. "One day, God sent His son Jesus Christ to earth in the form of a man. He lived the life of a human and felt the pain we do. He worked and walked our streets. Yet, he lived a perfect life. He never sinned. He was sent to earth to die for our sins. He was beaten and crucified on a cross so that we would not have to be. Our sins were wiped away, and we were made pure in His eyes. He paid the ultimate sacrifice. Then, after his death on the cross, He rose from the dead three days later. Our Savior lives. He ascended into Heaven and now lives in glory once again. So, we can have hope now that we are saved." As he explained, Max watched as Koen pondered the words.

"So, whoever believes in Him is saved? Saved from what?" Koen squinted while he tried to understand.

David spoke up, "Those who repent from their sins and trust in Jesus Christ are saved. Those who obey His word and live their life to the glory of God are saved. Salvation isn't earned, however. No sacrifices are made, and no good deeds can secure you a spot in heaven. Christ died for His children and those who love him and are given to Christ by the Father.

He became the ultimate sacrifice. We sin against a righteous God every day. We have offended a holy and powerful God. He had mercy on us, though, and extended His grace on those who fear Him and sent His son Jesus to die in our place."

"Oh, okay, I get it. So, those who do not believe in Him are not saved. They go to what you call hell, right?" Koen asked.

"After they die, they go to Hell and forever have to endure the weeping and gnashing of teeth, as the Bible puts it," Max said.

"They die because of their sin, but those who believe are saved. So, what happens to those who are saved? You said heaven, but what does that mean?" Koen asked with growing curiosity.

"Heaven is where believers go when they die to live in glory with God for eternity. There will be no more sadness or hurt. It's a perfect paradise in heaven," Max smiled.

"I see. Honestly, I don't see why this makes people so angry. So many worship many gods, but then get angry when Christians worship only one." Koen shrugged. "I don't get it."

"It contradicts their beliefs, for one. I think for most of them, they simply cannot believe that one God, and not thousands created us and everything around us. Plus, worshiping their many gods allows them to continue in sin without truly being held responsible. Their gods are gods that require only a sacrifice of an animal or a few prayers to make up for something bad they did, then the next day, they can do the same thing. Whereas, worshiping God does not allow for that. Just because he forgives us doesn't mean we can go on sinning. You are to live according to God's law. Christians should long to obey God's law, because it honors him and because we love him. It's not a burden to obey him. The thing is, people love their sin. It can be pleasurable, but it also condemns you to death without a savior," Alaina chimed in.

"Well, you certainly have my mind spinning. If you don't mind, I would like to ponder what you have told me a little more. I can assure you, though, I am truly compelled by this new information you've told me. I look forward to learning more," Koen smiled.

"I'm glad! I agree, we all need to get rest. We, especially Koen here, have a big day tomorrow and will surely need our sleep. Catherine and the servants will clean up. See you in the morning, my friends." Max stood and shook hands with each of them.

"Goodnight, Max. Thank you so much for all you've done for us today. It's been wonderful meeting you," Alaina said before leaving for her room. David nodded and headed off to his room. Koen thanked Max again for sharing with him and was soon off to bed as well.

They would need the rest, for tomorrow was the Linencrest Knight Tournament.

EIGHT

The night is far gone; the day is at hand.
So then let us cast off the works of
darkness and put on the armor of light.
Romans 13:12, ESV

By noon the next day, they had arrived at the tournament registration. As they approached the registration table, an elderly man smiled at Max. "Ah, Max, good to see you back, lad. You be careful out there today. I hear they have some pretty tough ones out there this time around."

"Good to see you too, Scotty. Glad to be back, and thank you for the advice. I'm already registered, but my friend here needs to sign up." Max motioned toward Koen.

"Oh! That's great. What was your name, boy?" Scotty raised his brows and gave the group a friendly wave.

"It's Koen, sir," he said.

"And which city do you represent?" Scotty asked.

"Um . . . Norwest." Koen glanced at Alaina and winked, making her laugh.

"Norwest, huh? Well, you're the only one from there. Congratulations." Scotty patted Koen on the shoulder. "Now, just wait with the other tournament fighters, and we'll call you in when it's your turn." He motioned for Koen and the rest of the group to continue forward.

Max took the lead and led them to where Scotty had motioned. The tournament arena was vast. The one back home in Mizcriea was a bit larger; however, it was not as decorated as this one. The architectural design was stunning.

Alaina noticed his wonder and smiled. "I was thinking the same thing. Amazing."

Koen nodded in response, and soon, they approached an opening in the wall that led out into the arena. Max waved for them to follow him to the opening.

"Think it's amazing here? Look at this." Max pointed out into the arena.

Koen, David, and Alaina turned to see where Max had pointed.

"Wow!" The three said in unison.

"So many people!" Alaina said aloud, her voice drowned out by the bustling crowd.

"So many colors," David said as a smile of excitement pulled at his lips.

"Incredible!" Koen said. The arena seemed large from inside, but the actual fighting arena was even more magnificent.

"Do you know when I start?" Koen turned to ask Max.

"Well, we entered you into the same level as Nicholas, so you can fight him. You'll be the last level to compete. Although don't get too comfortable, because the beginners don't last very long," Max said.

"Oh, okay." Suddenly, Koen got a funny feeling in his stomach. He swallowed when he felt it start to crawl up his throat.

"You okay?" Alaina asked.

"Yeah, you look kinda . . . nervous." David tilted his head.

"Yeah, I am, just a bit. Weird, though, it doesn't happen often." Koen gave an uneasy smile.

"Yeah, strange that you're nervous to fight in a knight tournament against Azgalian knights in front of thousands of people. So strange," Max said sarcastically.

"True," Koen shrugged and laughed.

"This way." Max continued toward the rest of the knights. As soon as they reached the other knights, they began to recognize Max, drawing the attention of their group.

"Max!" a man from a far corner called out.

"Hey Matthew! Been a long time, my friend!" Max's smile widened at the sight of his old friend. He made his way over to Matthew and embraced him in a hug.

"Are you back in the ring again?" Matthew asked Max.

"Sure am!" Max smiled.

"Glad to hear that! I'm excited to see you compete again, friend." Matthew patted Max's shoulder.

"Well, don't get your hopes up. I hear there is tough competition out there today," Max said.

"Well, you'd be hearing right; although, we're pretty tough ourselves, eh, Max?" Matthew threw his arm around Max. "And who might these youngsters be?" Matthew nodded toward the twins and Koen.

"These people are a few friends I picked up and decided to take with me for some encouragement. One even managed to get himself a challenge in the tournament," Max said.

"Oh really? And which one would that be?" Matthew looked over the three.

"This man right here." Max clapped a hand on Koen's shoulder, causing Koen to fall forward before catching himself.

Matthew laughed, "And whom might you be challenging?"

"Nicholas, sir," Koen answered a bit nervously.

Matthew's humor suddenly changed to one of concern. "Nicholas?" He looked over at Max.

"Max, are you sure he's up for it?"

"He may not look like much, but wait until you see him in the arena." Max smiled. "He's good enough."

"I sure hope so," Matthew said, eyeing Koen.

"Well, we'd better be going. See you around, Matthew!" Max gave Matthew one last embrace before walking away.

"Nicholas sure is a well-known name, isn't he?" Alaina walked up between Koen and Max.

"He is. He's one of the best, but so am I. Koen gave me a run for my money this morning, so I have no doubt he'll do the same for Nicholas," Max said confidently.

Koen noticed Alaina's worry. "Don't worry. I'll be fine," he said.

Alaina nodded and smiled, "I pray so."

Soon, they found their spot to rest while they waited for the sword fights to start. The jousting was ending, so they were cleaning up the arena. From where they sat, they could see the whole place. Max said it was the best spot to watch the fights because you could easily see both knights.

"Will I be fighting you?" Koen asked Max.

"Only if we continue to win. If you beat Nicholas and I beat my opponent, then yes. But if either of us falls out before then, then no," Max explained.

The first knights were called out to the arena. As they watched the fight progress, Max explained the rules to them. "Whoever gets five hits first will win the fight. Five hits, or one fatal blow."

"Fatal?" Alaina looked up at him.

"Sometimes, yes. Or just one hard enough to knock them down," Max shrugged.

"Oh," Alaina nodded and turned back to watch the knights in the arena.

"The judges watch you compete and decide the winner," Max said.

The fight ended once a knight completed five hits. The winner helped his opponent up and then celebrated with the cheering crowd.

"It's so loud!" David yelled over the crowd.

"Wait until my level! It gets better!" Max yelled back. Alaina could tell he was in his happy place. He wasn't kidding. The lower levels ended quickly as they started to compete against more experienced knights. The crowd seemed only to grow louder and more excited with each fight.

"Maximillionous?" A large man called from behind them.

"Yes, sir?" Max turned around.

"You're up," the man said.

"See you guys soon," Max grinned with a salute and followed the man.

"Good luck!" The three called out before Max disappeared around the corner.

Max's opponent walked out first to a cheering crowd. The knight raised his hands in the air, clearly enjoying the praise. Once in the middle of the arena, he turned and waited for Max to enter. Moments later, Max walked in dressed in a knight's attire and with a broad, radiant smile. His joy, even from where Koen sat, was contagious. The crowd stood and roared with excitement.

"They sure know who Max is!" Koen yelled to the twins.

"No kidding!" David yelled back.

They watched as Max made his way to the middle, while the crowd continued to roar. Max waved at the crowd and then turned to his opponent with a goofy smile, making the other knight laugh. They shook hands and then stepped back from each other to get into their fighting positions. Both knights lowered their visors and unsheathed their swords. Once the signal was made, Max's opponent advanced. Max was ready for it, though, and parried the advancement. He continued to fight in defense, occasionally making a quick offensive move. The opponent made one strike to Max's leg, making the crowd gasp, including Koen, Alaina, and David.

Max retreated a few steps and repositioned himself. The two knights stopped to breathe, but they quickly resumed the fight. Max advanced with a volley of substantial cuts, making the opponent retreat. He left no room for the opponent to make another strike. He made his first hit, and the crowd cheered. Max didn't seem to tire for a second, as he continued to swing his sword around.

The opponent did his very best to defend himself, but Max was too advanced for the other man. Soon, Max found his chance and hit the opponent's breastplate hard. This made the man stumble back, trip on his feet, and drop his sword. Max was on him in a split second with the blade to the man's chest. The knight raised his hands in defeat, and the judges called it to an end.

The crowd stood and cheered for Max's victory. Max raised his visor, reached to help the man up, and gave him a pat on the back. Once he handed him his sword from the ground, he waved at the crowd again before walking out of the arena. Koen, Alaina, and David joined in with the cheering crowd.

Soon, Max was back in the stands with the others.

"You were great!" David told him.

"Thanks. It felt good to be out there again," Max smiled. "Your turn," he said as he turned to Koen as soon as the next match ended.

"How do you know?" Koen looked confused. "Did they call me?"

Max shook his head and then raised his hand with five fingers up. "Five, four, three, two . . . one."

"Koen?" The same large man who had called Max spoke.

"Yes, sir?" Koen turned around in his seat.

"You're up," the man said, motioning for him to follow.

Koen turned to look at his friends and silently hoped they were praying to their God for his safety. He rose and went after the man.

"This way," the man said. "Just enter through that gate and walk straight down the middle until you reach your opponent. You're new, right?" The man asked.

"Yes, it's my first time," Koen nodded and glanced at the man.

"Okay. Your opponent is new, too. You'll be fighting against the levels the judges have assigned to you, so you should be fine. Good luck," the man said. Koen nodded in response.

One by one, Koen took his steps out of the gate. Suddenly, the nervous feeling returned as soon as his eyes met the massive crowd. He swallowed down the nerves and plastered a smile on his face, hoping it would spark excitement instead.

He met the opponent in the middle of the ring and shook

his hand. The other man was kind and returned his handshake with a smile. The man's red hair seemed to match the color of his armor.

"My name is Mark," the man said, his deep blue eyes sizing up Koen.

"I'm Koen. It's good to meet you," Koen answered, sizing up the other man.

"Same to you. I'm rather new at this, but I hear this is your first time?" Mark asked before taking a step back to get into a ready position.

"It is," Koen nodded and assumed his stance.

"Well, just for a heads up, I'm afraid I won't be going easy on you," Mark smirked.

"Neither will I," Koen gave a challenging smile.

The signal went off, and Koen waited for Mark to advance. Mark slid into Koen's space and made a powerful slice through the air, which was stopped by Koen's strong block. The swords clashed and clanged while they cut at each other.

Koen kept his mind sharp and attentive, always waiting for a slight opening. Koen switched to offense to see how Mark would take it. The man wavered for a few moments but quickly regained his rhythm. That's when Koen saw the weakness he'd been searching for. After a few more thrusts and blocks, Koen advanced again with the same movements as before, hoping Mark would waver again.

He did, and that's when Koen went for it. The sword plunged toward Mark's shoulder; it knocked him off his feet and onto the ground. His sword dropped into the dirt, and the crowd was immediately on their feet, cheering for the newcomer. Koen had won.

He turned his head toward where his friends sat and saw them cheering. His smile widened, and he realized his nervousness had disappeared. He could do this. Sword fighting was one of the things he loved to do, and he had spent most of his life perfecting it. He knew he could make it to the end of the tournament. He would have to be at his best, though.

The fights continued, with Max remaining undefeated, and Koen improving with every fight. Max came out with an injured shoulder one fight, but he was determined to keep going. Koen was now at the master level. The sun made its way across the sky, and it was now evening. The air began to cool down as the crowd held its breath for the last few fights. If Max won this next fight, he would have to fight Nicholas. If he lost, Max's opponent would fight him. If Koen wins his next fight, he will fight the winner of that round. Even if he or Nicholas did not make it to the last round, Koen felt there would be a fight.

Max made his way to the center of the arena and exchanged a handshake with his rather large opponent.

"I hope he makes it out okay. His shoulder seemed to be giving him trouble," Alaina said.

"I'm sure he knows what he can take," David reassured her.

Koen nodded in agreement and watched as Max started the fight. This fight was the most intense one yet. Max would fall back in weakness only to come back suddenly with great force and determination. The other knight wasn't as quick, but his movements were more powerful.

Koen feared that with Max's injury, any one of the knight's thrusts would end it.

Just when the thought crossed his mind, what he had feared happened. Max hit the ground, and the sword clattered out of his hand. The three of them were on their feet instantly, stretching their necks to see if Max was okay.

The other knight made his way over to Max and bent down to raise his visor. Several breathless moments later, Max was on his feet, and the crowd sighed. One of their most favored knights had done well and made it to the master level after being out. The city was proud of Maximillionous; his friends were too. They met Max at the gate and helped him to a seat.

"That kinda hurt," Max winced.

"Kinda? You were out cold," Koen laughed.

"Oh no, don't make me laugh," Max said while suppressing a laugh.

"Sorry," Koen smiled.

"Koen, you're up, lad!" the announcer called.

"Good luck, kid," Max said.

"Thanks," Koen nodded and turned to the arena. The fight was hard, brutal, and exhausting. Koen and his opponent had to step back to catch their breath several times before advancing again.

Koen felt he had met his match. As he stepped back to breathe, sweat dripped down his nose, and his heart beat rapidly inside his chest. The fight seemed to continue forever. Then, the same sound at the starting signal went off, startling the two opponents.

"That was five hits. The fight is over," a judge announced. Koen and his opponent looked at each other and raised their visors.

"Who won?" his opponent asked the judge.

"The winner of this round is," the judge paused to read the paper before him. Sir Koen of Norwest!" The judge announced. The crowd went wild! Koen's eyes widened, and his mouth dropped. Here he was, fighting in a tournament for the first time, and he had made it to the final round. "Amazing," Koen shook his head in disbelief.

"Good job, mate. You're a real fighter," his opponent said before walking past him toward the gate.

"Congratulations, Sir Koen. You have made it into the final round. You will compete against the winner of the next round," the head judge told him and the crowd. Koen had no doubt Nicholas would win.

After being congratulated and receiving a million handshakes, Koen finally sat down with his friends.

"Took you long enough," Max laughed at Koen's exhausted expression.

"Please tell me they take a break before the final round." Koen leaned back so his head could lie on the seat above.

"They do," Max laughed.

"That looked like a close fight. How did it feel?" Alaina asked him.

"It was tiring. It seemed like it would never end. We just kept matching each other's rhythm," Koen answered as he sat up again.

"Yeah, you guys matched each other's fighting styles perfectly. Do you think you were holding anything back?" David asked curiously.

"You mean, do I have anything more to use against Nicholas? You're wondering if I'll be a match for Nicholas or if I've reached my limit. Right?" Koen asked David.

"Yeah. What do you think?" David asked.

"I think I can do better," Koen said.

"Well, good!" Max clapped his hands, but then he cringed when reminded of his shoulder's pain.

"Nicholas is coming out!" Alaina said, grabbing the attention of everyone around them.

They watched him stroll out of the arena gate with a strong stride and a chin held high. He was clearly confident in his abilities as a knight. He smiled and waved at the crowd like he was the King. Nicholas's eyes swept the cheering crowd until they landed on Koen. As their eyes locked, Nicholas smirked, and Koen's nervousness returned.

Once in the center, the opponent who beat Max approached Nicholas. By his stride, it was evident he was also confident, but looked less proud than Nicholas.

The head judge stood up from his chair and silenced the crowd. The two knights turned toward him and listened to the rules.

"Five hits to end the fight, or one strong enough to knock down the other knight," the head judge said aloud for everyone to hear. "Assume ready positions."

Koen watched Nicholas as he bent at his knees and unsheathed his sword. Soon, the signal went off, and the fight began. Koen studied Nicholas hard and observed how he countered his opponent's movements. Not only was he strong, but he could back that strength with speed. He had it all. His skill seemed almost flawless. Almost.

"Right there. Did you see it?" David spun in his seat to look at Koen.

"The crooked foot? I saw it, but what about it?" Koen asked, squinting at Nicholas in the arena.

"His crooked foot throws him off balance. Hit him in the

right spot and you got him," David pointed out.

"He hasn't always had that crooked foot," Max interrupted.

"He hasn't? Was it an injury?" David asked.

"Yes, he almost lost his leg in a battle. He was helped in time, though, and was able to save it. However, the medical supplies were limited, and it was the best they could do. Unfortunately, the best they could do was leave him with a crooked foot," Max explained.

"That can help Koen, though. You must time it right. Be sure he doesn't know you know about it; otherwise, he'll be careful not to put himself in a vulnerable position," David told Koen.

"Makes sense. Thank you," Koen replied.

"No problem," David nodded.

Nicholas's opponent went for a thrust that he was sure would end the fight, but Nicholas had planned for it and blocked it in time. Then, when his opponent was momentarily surprised, he offered a blow of his own that sent the other knight to the ground with a loud thump.

The crowd gasped only momentarily before they roared into applause yet again. Nicholas won. Koen would fight him in front of all of Linencrest. He swallowed a gulp of fear and watched Nicholas celebrate with the crowd.

Then, the head judge stood up, and the crowd momentarily silenced. "The championship fight will start after the two knights have had a chance to rest." The crowd sighed their disappointment, but soon forgot it as they went on to cheer with renewed excitement. A brand new knight would be fighting a well-trained, well-known knight of Azgalia. Koen had no desire to win the championship. He did, though, have the desire to live, and if that included winning, then he would do it.

"How are you, kid?" Max put his hand on Koen's shoulder.

"I'm hanging in there." Koen laughed anxiously as he tried to hide his nerves.

"You have to be confident, Koen. To beat a confident knight, you need to be confident as well," Max told him.

"I understand. I'm working on it." Koen nodded and took a deep breath.

"You do have a good chance. He's very, very good, but I've watched you. You have a good chance at beating him," David added in.

"Thanks, David," Koen said. He wouldn't admit it now, but he appreciated David's vote of confidence. "I think I'm going to grab some water." Koen stood up from his seat and walked down the steps.

"I'll come with you," Alaina said as she followed him. "I'm not an expert at sword fighting or knight tournaments, but I do know enough to agree with David," Alaina said as they walked.

"Thank you. I agree with him, too. Although, I'm still struggling with the life on the line part. It's not like I'll lose the championship if I lose to him. If I lose to him, I could lose my life. Then again, I shouldn't complain too much, because after all, this was my doing," Koen said while his eyes searched for a water bucket.

"True," Alaina said before she spotted a bucket of water and pointed to it. "I think Max would have told us to leave if he didn't think you would make it," Alaina suggested. "And besides, he'd have to go through all of us to get to you."

"Thanks," Koen said with a weary smile. He reached for the spoon and lifted it to his mouth to drink.

Before heading back to David and Max, Alaina stopped Koen and looked him in the eyes. "Koen, I don't believe for one second that God brought you to me and my brother only to lead us this far. I believe everything happens for a reason, and I don't think you have yet accomplished the task God has set for you. I don't know His plan, but I can only hope and pray He allows you to continue so you can do something great for him with your life." Koen watched as Alaina searched his eyes for his response.

Slowly, Koen smiled. "I truly respect you and your faith. I hope that one day I can have the same hope you do. Thank you, Alaina," he said with genuine thankfulness.

"You're welcome," Alaina smiled brightly.

They made their way back to Max and David to wait for the announcement that the fight would start. It didn't take long for the judge to call the crowd to their seats for the last fight of the day.

"Ladies and gentlemen. It is time for what you all have been waiting for, the last fight of the night," the announcer said for the crowd to hear. "Call out the knights!" he yelled. The crowd began to drum the steps with their feet.

"Sir Koen! You're up!" the man called him once again.

Koen stood and turned to his friends. "Hopefully, this won't be our last day together." He tried to keep the humor light, but inside, he was terrified.

"Sir Nicholas!" Koen heard the man call Nicholas, and his stomach dropped.

"Confidence, Koen. Confidence," Koen whispered to himself as he was handed his helmet.

"Go on now," the man nudged him into the arena.

"Right, sorry." Koen shook his head and, step by step, walked with the most confident stride he could muster. The crowd started cheering as soon as he entered the arena. Even through his nervousness, Koen couldn't help but smile at the sound of the cheering. Something about the sound made him excited. He glanced down at his Mizcriean sword that was sheathed at his hip. Max and David had helped him cover the Mizcriean design so he could still use the sword. Max suggested it since Koen was used to its weight and balance.

"You'll be more at ease and comfortable," Max reasoned. As he thought about his sword, images of his training in Mizcriea began to flash through his mind.

He remembered training with his brother and the rush of adrenaline it gave him. He remembered the smile his mother gave him every time he won a fight; the pride she displayed for her son. He remembered this was something he loved. He was good at it. He could do this. He believed that even though he was far away from his mother, she was still right there with him, cheering him on. "I can do this," Koen said as he lifted his chin. When he made it to the center, he turned in his place to watch as Nicholas strode out into the arena with unwavering confidence. But this time, it didn't bother Koen. Once he had reached the center, he stared Koen in the eyes and squinted.

"You're going to wish you had never made that bet, young man," Nicholas said, determined to scare Koen. It didn't work.

"Maybe," Koen smirked, which made Nicholas give a prideful snort. Both Nicholas and Koen listened to the head judge tell them the rules for the fight. Koen mouthed the last words along with the judge. "Five strikes to end the fight, or one strong enough to knock the other knight down."

"Or one fatal blow," Koen heard Nicholas whisper. Nicholas readied himself and flipped down the visor to cover his bloodthirsty eyes.

Koen followed suit and readied himself. With one last look at his friends in the crowd, he pulled down his visor and locked his gaze on Nicholas.

"Wait for the signal," the judge said.

Koen waited. He listened to his breath as it blew against the inside of his helmet. He concentrated on the beat of his heart to calm himself. He studied Nicholas's posture. Then the sound went off.

In one quick movement, Nicholas was on him. His advance was strong and fast, throwing Koen into momentary surprise. Koen recovered by blocking the hit and stepping back.

"Careful." Koen heard Nicholas taunt him.

Koen grunted in response and readied his sword for the knight's next blow. Nicholas cut through the air, not giving Koen any room to switch into offense. He was fighting with rage.

The crowd cheered and whistled as the fight progressed. It was only the beginning, and it was already looking bad for Koen. He managed to stay on his feet and remained balanced, though. He just couldn't find an opening. Koen was growing tired and knew he was done if he didn't act soon.

For the first time in his life, he found himself considering prayer. Inwardly, he prayed to the God of the Christians. He admitted his wrongs and asked for protection, hoping He would have mercy on someone who wasn't saved.

Koen saw a slight opening and took it. When Nicholas brought his sword toward himself, Koen brought his sword forward. Nicholas blocked it, just as Koen had hoped. It sent Nicholas back a few steps, giving Koen a few moments of rest. When he looked up, Nicholas looked frustrated that Koen had interrupted his rhythm.

"Whoops," Koen shrugged, glad Nicholas couldn't see his smirk. He remembered the crooked foot David had pointed out. With a renewed plan and wild idea, Koen readied himself and waited for Nicholas to advance. He had not observed this wild idea at this tournament, but he saw it done a few times in Mizcriea.

Nicholas swung his sword straight for him, but, just in time, Koen ducked under the blade and sprang up quickly to take the position of offense from Nicholas. Koen laughed at the surprise and confusion on Nicholas' face and advanced. One cut and slice at a time, Nicholas started to fall back.

The crowd was going wild with the unexpected turn of events. Koen knew they were all waiting for him to make a final move and end the fight. He could feel Nicholas growing anxious as he tried to anticipate Koen's last move. Koen was waiting, though; he was waiting for the right time. He watched Nicholas' feet while he continued to battle him.

The waiting paid off as Koen saw his opportunity. When Nicholas's crooked foot went backward, Koen used his sword to push him left by hitting his right shoulder. Stumbling, because his weight had shifted onto his crooked foot, Nicholas was thrown off balance and left open for Koen to make a move that would end the fight. If only the crowd could see Nicholas's face as soon as he realized his defeat.

Koen raised his sword and thrust it forward to end it all. Yet, Nicholas made a dramatic fall right before the sword made contact with his breastplate. Koen, confused, pulled up short and watched the man hit the ground.

Nicholas threw off his helmet to reveal a face filled with rage. His eyes met with Koen's, and that's when Koen's heart dropped to his stomach. Nicholas raised an accusing finger at him, "He's a Mizcriean!"

NINE

Suddenly, all eyes focused on Koen, and he could feel it. He felt smaller and more vulnerable than ever. Nicholas had exposed his identity, and now he was sure he was done for.

The crowd and the judges went silent as they awaited his response to Nicholas' accusation.

When Koen couldn't bring himself to respond, Nicholas stood up and shouted, "It's true! Look at his sword!" He snatched Koen's sword from the ground, knocked off the cover over the design, and held it forward for the judges to see. "See, the Mizcriean symbol? Not only is it made in Mizcriea, but it is also a Mizcriean knight's sword!" The crowd gasped, and the judges all stood up. "He's probably a spy as well!" Nicholas shouted, and the crowd gasped again.

"No!" was all Koen could muster.

"So, you're not a Mizcriean?" Nicholas turned on him with a deadly glare.

"No, I–I am–I just—" Koen sputtered, trying to find words that would help people understand, but all he could think was that there was absolutely no way out of this.

"Take him away!" Koen heard the head judge call. Koen's eyes went wide, realizing they were talking about him. Backing away from Nicholas, Koen wished he could back away from the entire situation.

"You can't leave. We haven't settled our deal yet," Nicholas said as he slowly started his way.

"No, I can't. Please—" Koen was cut off when a firm hand suddenly grasped his arm. He instinctively flinched in fear for his life.

"Koen," Max said, making Koen relax. But only a little. "Nicholas, what are you doing? You had a deal!"

"You really think I would let a Mizcriean beat me and go free?" Nicholas spat at Koen's feet in disgust.

"I had my doubts," Max said.

"Max—" Koen nodded toward a group of men coming to get Koen. "I need to get out of here."

"Yes, you do. The twins are waiting for us," Max said with a nod, and his eyes found their way to Koen's sword in Nicholas' hand.

"Waiting where? How are we going to get out?" Koen was starting to think Max didn't really have a plan.

"Don't worry. I'm good at improvising," Max grinned. Suddenly, Max pushed Koen off to the side, kicked out his foot, and knocked Koen's sword free from Nicholas' grasp. "Aha!" Max proudly said as he caught it in the air.

"You can't be serious, Maximillion!" Nicholas raged.

"Actually," he smirked, "It's Maximillionous." He tossed Koen his sword and blocked a cut Nicholas made at him with his own. "Not today," Max said as he put his right foot behind Nicholas' crooked foot and pushed back, making him fall onto the ground with a grunt.

"Until next time!" Max bowed to the judges and grabbed Koen's arm, propelling him toward the gate.

"I don't know how to thank you!" Koen shouted as they ran for their lives.

"Don't thank me yet!" Max yelled back and focused on what was up ahead.

Koen followed Max's gaze and saw that the gate was clear. Maybe the men hadn't heard what all the commotion was about yet.

But as they entered the gate area, men arrived armed and ready for their capture. Max and Koen slid to a stop and looked around for an exit.

"Max!" a familiar voice called out. It was Matthew, Max's friend. "Is it true, my friend?" Matthew's gaze shifted from Max to Koen.

"It is. You have to trust me, though. It is for a cause much greater than you know," Max told his friend.

Matthew searched Max's face and must have decided to trust him because he nodded and turned on the other men blocking their way. "Let them through!" Matthew shouted. The men hesitantly moved out of the way and let them pass. Max thanked his good friend as they continued through the gate.

"He must be highly respected," Koen mentioned when they were almost to wherever they were going.

"He is," Max nodded, and they continued running through the tournament arena hallways. "This way," Max told him as he cut around a corner.

"Where are we going?" Koen asked between breaths.

"Just follow me," Max said before cutting around another corner.

Max didn't explain exactly where they were headed, but Koen trusted his plan nonetheless.

"They're right out there. Go on ahead. I'll meet up with you guys. David knows what to do," Max told him. Koen hesitated to leave Max alone but decided to listen.

"Okay," Koen nodded and ran out of the hallway.

"Over here!" He heard Alaina call from a wagon. Koen ran to them and hopped up beside her.

"Where's Max?" Alaina asked, looking behind Koen.

"He said he'd meet up with us." Koen raised an eyebrow to see if David knew what he was discussing. When David nodded, Koen sighed in relief. David clucked for the horses to move forward, and soon, they were on their way.

"It all happened so fast," Alaina stated. Koen looked up to see her peering at his face.

"Yeah. I . . . it all seems surreal. I don't think in a good way either. What do we do now? The whole city practically knows I'm Mizcriean." Koen worried that news would reach his father; a Mizcriean knight had competed in an Azgalian tournament. Surely, he would know it was Koen.

"Well, we have to leave the city," Alaina said.

"We do? No, we have to talk to Max! We can't leave yet!" Koen shook his head.

"There's nowhere to hide. Plus, they'll no doubt question Max about us and search his place," David said.

"I didn't mean for this to happen. I'm so sorry." Koen looked from David to Alaina.

"It's okay. We needed to leave soon. We really need to be on our way to Mizcriea," David said while steering the wagon off the road and onto a faded path through the woods.

"This is where Max said to go?" Koen asked.

"Yeah. He said there's a small cabin we can stay in for the night," Alaina told him.

As they made their way through the woods, Koen considered what had happened. Not only had he made it out alive without winning, but he had come so close to being champion. He was better with the sword than he thought. He remembered his prayer to the Christian God asking for help, and wondered if he should tell them about it. Did the prayer protect and guide him? Or just luck? Koen decided to keep his thoughts to himself, at least for now.

They pulled up to the small cabin, and Koen immediately felt safe. The cabin was surrounded by greenery, and white flowers decorated the ground.

"It's beautiful." Alaina jumped out of the wagon after him.

"Indeed." Koen looked around.

"Let's tie up the horses," David said while unhitching Blade from the wagon.

"Where is Wayne?" Koen asked.

"I believe Max is bringing him when he meets us here," Alaina said and went to help David.

"I'll go check out the cabin," Koen said. He made his way through the tall grass to the front door. The cabin's roof was not much higher than his head, but just tall enough that he could walk through the door. At first, the door wouldn't move, so being careful not to break it, he pushed it with more force. It finally budged and grated across the wooden floor. Dust filled the air inside, making him cough. He squinted against the dust and looked inside. It was a one-room cabin with a small stove and fireplace. There was a small bed beside a window, but he could tell it hadn't been used for a while. There would be enough room for the three of them to sleep on the floor, and at least there was shelter. It was better than nothing.

"What do you think?" a voice asked from the door behind him. Koen turned and saw Max peering through the door frame.

"It's small but better than sleeping outside." Koen smiled.

"True," Max nodded and stepped inside, followed by the twins. "I used to come here when I first trained for tournament fighting. Being out in nature and alone in a small cabin helped me focus. It's been a while, though," Max explained as he looked around.

"A bit dusty," Alaina coughed and covered her mouth with the sleeve of her dress.

"It wasn't this bad when I was here, but like I said, it's been a while." Max shrugged. "It should do fine for the night, though."

"What about you?" Alaina asked him.

"I'll go back to my place, and if Linencrest doesn't give me too much trouble for helping a Mizcriean, I'll head back to serve in the King's army," Max said. "Where will you go?"

Koen and Alaina looked toward David to answer, which he found amusing because he snorted. "We head north. We'll travel until we feel the need to stop in a city," David told Max.

"Well, make sure to stop in the King's City. I know this is no vacation for you all, but it still is a must-see place," Max said.

"Then we should plan on stopping there," Alaina said, looking to David to see if he agreed. He did.

"Great!" Max clapped his hands together. "Koen." Max turned to him. "It was truly a pleasure to meet you. I never thought I'd meet the prince of Mizcriea, let alone imagine him being like you. It was an honor." Max pulled him into a brotherly embrace. "I pray God shows you His truth and opens your eyes."

"Pleasure was all mine, Max. Thank you for all that you've done for me. If you were the only Christian I ever met, you made a pretty convincing case," Koen laughed.

"Thank you . . . I think," Max chuckled along with him. "And you two, of course." Max let go of Koen and turned to face Alaina. "Alaina, I am so glad you stumbled into that tavern and we met. I believe it was God's divine intervention that I met you three." He looked into her eyes. "I do hope we cross paths again soon."

He turned to David, "David, I expect to hear from you as soon as your quest is over. I believe you would be a great addition to the royal army, if you're interested." Koen thought David might cry. "I pray you both find your father and your quest is safe. God be with you," Max said, embracing them and stepping back. "Farewell and safe travels."

Max waved and rode out on the extra horse he'd brought.

Once he was out of sight, they all stood in comfortable silence and listened to the sounds of the leaves rustling in the breeze and the animals in the bushes. The sounds of nature were calming and mesmerizing, especially after the day's events.

Koen gazed down the path Max had taken, considering the quest ahead. Crossing borders could be extremely dangerous. He wondered if they would even make it past or if they would perish before finding out if the twins' father was even alive. He had to help as much as he could. What about his father? What would come of his returning home?

As his eyes caught sight of a delicate flower falling from one of the trees to join the others on the ground, he let out a sigh. He hoped that the twins' God would see them through.

♕

"So, wait, where are we going?" Alaina asked David as they traveled down the dusty road that led out of Linencrest. They woke early that morning to get a head start and to limit the risk of Koen being found. Most of the morning, Alaina's mind had been so consumed with thoughts of the previous day, and she realized she had no idea where they were heading. She knew it was north, but that was about it.

"Not sure," David answered as he squinted against the dust. His black hair was beginning to take on a more ashen appearance, making it appear darker than dark brown. His filthy face made his skin look darker, and his eyes looked brighter.

"What do you mean, 'you're not sure'?" Koen asked, confused. He had been quiet most of the morning, and Alaina was sure it was because he, too, was deep in thought about the day before.

"Well, if you would let me finish . . . " David glanced sidelong at Koen." . . . you would know. I was saying that I wasn't sure yet because we have two options: Fortingburk, which is off to the west and closer to the coast, or we go to Malikai City, which is off to the east."

"I thought we had planned to go to the King's City?" Koen said.

"Well, I thought it was more of a suggestion when discussing it. Unless you want to see the ocean instead, we can go to Malikai?" David looked at them.

"Is there more to consider? Besides, just where do we want to visit?" Alaina asked, wondering if there was a reason better than just an incredible visit.

"Both are just about the same distance to where we want to go, and both provide for our needs." David shrugged, meaning he didn't care which way they went.

"Do you have any ideas, Koen?" Alaina looked at Koen. She didn't have to ask him, but it felt more polite.

"I have no preference. It's up to you," Koen motioned toward her.

"Hmm . . . well, we never really did get to see the ocean," Alaina began.

"We should be able to see the ocean at Dragon Coast, though. So, you'll see it whether you choose Fortingburk or not," David told her.

"Well, okay then. I say Malikai City. It may be our only chance, and it would be cool to see the city our father visited so often," Alaina reasoned.

"I agree. Malikai City, here we come!" David shouted out of nowhere, making Alaina laugh.

"New adventures, here we come!" Alaina shouted after him.

"New dangers, here we come!" Koen joined in on the fun.

The three traveled for hours until they decided to stop by a lake. They dismounted and let the horses graze on the grass. Alaina spotted a tree casting the perfect shadow in the grass by the lake. She made her way over to the tree and sat in the shade. She glanced toward her brother and Koen to see them looking under a rock with pure fascination on their boyish faces. This made her laugh and shake her head in disbelief. She found it amusing that they could go from being so serious and tough-looking to a little boy looking at a snake under a rock the next moment. She was so blessed to have a brother, let alone a twin brother, because life would be so dull without him. Alaina watched as David asked Koen to hold the rock so he could catch the snake. Koen nodded and obliged. Carefully and slowly, David readied his hands and, with a quick movement, grasped the snake between his two hands. The snake fought his hold and hissed at the strange human who dared disturb his evening. David's face lit up at his accomplishment, and he turned to see if Alaina had watched. She laughed at him.

"Boys never really grow up," her grandmother used to say. She would wait a few seconds before continuing, "Thank goodness for that."

"Nice," she nodded, and David turned toward Koen to show him the snake.

"Look at his pattern!" Koen looked over the snake with fascination.

"Such an incredible creature," David said, marveling. "Do you want to hold it?"

"Sure!" Koen smiled and carefully replaced David's hold on the snake with his own. Koen held it still and waited for the snake to quit moving. "It feels so strange."

"Have you never held a snake before?" David asked him.

"Never. I've seen them up close, but I've never held one before," Koen answered.

"Alright, well, when you put him down, you have to move quickly," David explained how to handle the snake.

Alaina watched as Koen released the snake back to its habitat and laughed as he jumped out of the way of the snake's angry fangs.

The sun began to set soon after they started back on the road. They were only two days from Malikai City, and Alaina was ready to see civilization again. Sometimes, the road would end, and they would have to rely on their tracking skills to find their way, but Alaina knew the Lord would guide them. Alaina noticed Koen was quieter ever since they left Linencrest. She knew what he was feeling; she saw it on his face, though she couldn't tell his exact thoughts. She figured she'd wait until he was ready to share his feelings.

It was a cold, quiet night in Malikai City, and the cloud that blanketed the sky blocked the moon and stars, making the darkness even more pronounced. King Malikai had not gone to bed until late that night because he was too worried about the kidnapping of his men. Sir Dierks, his good friend and most trusted knight, disappeared just days ago. They could not find him, which greatly affected the King's heart.

He cried out to the Lord more times than he could count, asking why this was happening to him. Still, he stayed faithful and firm.

That night, the King crawled into his bed and lay beside his Queen, Laura. She was fast asleep and looked peaceful as always. The King's eyes shut, and his body relaxed, allowing him to fall asleep.

Just outside the King and Queen's quarters, a faint shadow lurked in the night. It made its way up to their window and skillfully unlocked it from the outside. Slowly, he pushed it open, making sure not to make a sound. Silently, the shadow crept through the window and hid in the room's darkness. Without a noise, it scurried over to the King's bed. The shadowed figure gazed upon the King with hate and disgust.

Suddenly, another shadow appeared on the other side of the bed. The other shadow peered at the Queen and smiled with evil glee. The first shadow nodded for the second to make its move. In a quick and silent maneuver, the second shadow covered the Queen's mouth with fabric and pulled her off the bed. She was startled awake and tried to scream for help, but to no avail. She tried to break free, but the shadow was too strong.

A third shadow, large in build, appeared next to the first and nodded that it was ready. At once, they covered the King's mouth with fabric and slid him off the bed. Surprised, the King jolted, almost making the two men drop him. When it dawned on the King what was happening, his face turned to rage. He moved his body violently, trying to break free. Yet, the shadows held him.

They set him on the floor, and the third shadow held the King firmly while the first forced a potion down the King's throat. Malikai choked on the potion as it burned his throat.

Only a few moments after swallowing, the King began to feel dizzy and extremely tired. The Queen's face was panicked at the sight of her husband. Darkness overcame his vision, and his eyes closed. He was once again asleep.

The men who were as dark as shadows tied the frightened Queen up in the bed. They moved to the window and lowered the King out. The next moment, they were gone as if they'd never even appeared. Queen Laura sat alone and terrified in the darkroom. She could do nothing but cry and pray for morning to come soon.

♛

Princess Evelyn sat up in bed and rubbed her tired eyes. Outside her bedroom window, the sun began peering over the distant mountains. This was strange, though, since she usually didn't get up until the sun had fully risen above them. She shrugged and rolled her neck to release the knots she'd acquired at night. She jumped out of bed and, after combing her hair, opened her door to peer down the halls. None of the servants were up and running the chores yet. She could hear the chef in the kitchen, though, probably making those delicious bread rolls.

After ensuring no one was in the hall, she went to her older brother's room. She gave a few solid knocks until she heard him groan out of annoyance.

"Good morning, Gavin." She laughed and skipped like a little girl to her parents' quarters at the end of the hall.

As the only princess and the youngest child, most people expected her to grow up to be a spoiled princess, or at the very least, a fragile one. However, she was neither of those. Her mother saw it in her, and her father was growing to see it. Evelyn knew she had to give him grace because she was still his little princess.

Evelyn was a strong spirit, held within a soft-spoken girl. Her pretty yet straightforward appearance fooled many. One of her favorite things to do was to surprise people with her true personality. She was intelligent and tough, and she could wield a sword almost as well as her brother.

At her parents' bedroom door, she raised her hand to knock. Something stopped her. She heard a faint whimpering and quickly burst through the door, her worry growing. Her heart dropped, and her breath caught in her throat. There, her beautiful mother sat tied up and gagged in her bed. Her father was nowhere in sight, immediately bringing tears to Evelyn's eyes. She raced to her mother's side, quickly untied her, and took the fabric from her mouth. Her mother fell into Evelyn's embrace and cried the hardest Evelyn had ever seen someone cry. The cry scared her, though. It wasn't a typical sad cry; it was a terrified cry.

"What happened, Mother? Tell me! Where is Father?" Evelyn spoke between fighting her tears.

"He—he—he's just—they just took him! There was nothing I could do! They just took him!" Again, she cried in agony.

It took Evelyn a moment to realize what had happened. "No!" Fear took over, and her body shook in sadness and fear. They had taken her father, the king. The Kingdom of Azgalia was now without a King.

"What's wrong?" Gavin was at the door. His face held a look of great concern and distress.

It took everything in Evelyn to force the words out of her mouth, "Father–he–he's gone." Evelyn buried her face in her mother's shoulder and cried. Gavin stood in silence as he watched his mother and sister. After minutes of silence, his expression changed from shock to anger and frustration.

"We can't allow this! This is the King who was kidnapped! Our father! We won't stop searching until he is found!" With that, he was gone.

Evelyn's tears ceased, but her heart still ached. Her mother sat and stared at the wall, saying nothing. Her heart broke for her mother. She couldn't imagine how she felt after her experience. Evelyn found her own spot on the wall to stare at as she sorted through her thoughts. How many of them were there? Who? It was unthinkable that these kidnappings had been occurring for years, yet every time, they were unprepared for it. These thoughts made her understand her brother's anger and frustration. What would they do now? How would the kingdom go on? Would it?

"Search parties are out as we speak. I have the entire royal army on the search. Everyone in and outside the castle is looking for him," Gavin reappeared in the doorway.

"Gavin," their mother spoke, which captured the attention of both of them.

"Mother?" Gavin walked up to their mother's side and took hold of her hands.

"Son, if this is anything like the other kidnappings, which we are quite certain it is, you must prepare yourself." Their mother spoke in a tone that worried Evelyn. She was heartbroken and scared, yet her tone was calm. It sounded as though she was unaffected by it all, even though she clearly had been.

"Prepare for what, Mother?" Gavin shook his head in confusion.

"Prepare to take your father's place as King," she said, leaving her two children speechless.

"Mother, he has only been gone a few hours!" Evelyn stood up, confused at her mother's words.

"Mother, we have barely begun the searches!" Gavin shook his head.

"You know it's true, though, son. Have we ever found any other kidnapped man? Why would this be any different? If not harder? They have the King!" Their mother said unwaveringly.

Evelyn continued to shake her head. A moment ago, her mother was sobbing and crying into her shoulder, and now, she was planning for Gavin to take his place as King? After only a few hours of him being gone. *This was absurd!* "This is ridiculous! You can't possibly be serious, Mother!" Evelyn held back her tears.

"She's right, Evelyn," Gavin said without looking her in the eye.

"Oh, not you too!" Evelyn backed away, shaking her head. "How can you give up so easily?"

"We're not. It's the most reasonable . . . " Gavin started.

"Reasonable? He is King. Father is the King, and I don't believe for a second he is gone for good. He and all those other men were kidnapped for a reason we don't know. I would like to know why, wouldn't you? I mean, do you think now that Father is gone, they're done? What makes you think they won't take you as well? It's time we ended this. So, while you're busy trying to replace him, I'll be looking for Father," Evelyn finished by slamming the doors shut and running down to her room. She grabbed her bag, packed it with certain necessities, changed into her riding clothes, and headed out the castle doors.

They may have given up, but she hadn't. She was going to find her father.

TEN

Hooves knocked on the cobblestone streets of Malikai City. People laughed and smiled as they went about their day, enjoying the beautiful sunshine. It was warm but not too hot, and a slight breeze wasn't too chilly. The day seemed promising, but still, Alaina sensed tension in the air. She was sure it was due to her discernment and ability to see things in others. She sometimes got "feelings" about certain things, and she was rarely wrong. David must have noticed her weary look since he asked how she was doing.

"Okay, I think," she responded. She was doing fine, but she had a strange feeling about something. That's what always frustrated her when she was younger: she could sense things but couldn't pinpoint why she felt a certain way. As she grew, she became more patient.

"I've just got this feeling . . . " Alaina said to David.

"What kind of feeling?" David asked. He knew about the "feelings" she experienced and could usually help her figure out the reason faster than she could on her own.

"A weird one. There's, like, this tension in the air," Alaina tried to describe it.

David tilted his head curiously and looked around at the surrounding people. Alaina knew all he saw was a beautiful day and happy people, but she also knew he trusted her judgment.

"I'll keep my eyes open," David said. Alaina nodded in return.

Koen followed closely nearby, but he was utterly lost in the city's atmosphere that was so unlike his father's kingdom. She followed his gaze to see what had momentarily captured his attention. Sure enough, it was an elderly man playing a gittern while he sang an Azgalian song. Alaina smiled as she watched the joyful man sing, and for a moment, she missed her childhood. The song being sung was the same song she used to sing while doing her chores as a little girl. She couldn't exactly remember when she had stopped singing, but she wished she hadn't. She hummed occasionally, but Alaina couldn't remember when she'd sung last. She decided to save that thought for later and focus on the task at hand.

"Where to first?" Alaina nudged Ophelia up next to David.

"Well, we seem to be fine on our necessities, so we don't need to buy anything," David answered.

"Are we planning on sleeping at an inn tonight?" Alaina asked him.

"I suppose we could. It will be our last stay in an inn, though, since we are low on money and there aren't many good inns up the northwest," David explained.

"Well then, I will savor every second of it," Alaina laughed. As much as Alaina loved the outdoors, she did love a comfortable bed to sleep in.

"Did I hear we'll be staying at an inn tonight?" Koen suddenly appeared next to Alaina.

"That is correct," Alaina said.

"Yes!" Koen said maybe a little too loudly as he pumped his fist, making the twins laugh.

Soon, they found an inn with reasonable prices and told the innkeeper to hold two rooms for them. Afterward, they decided to explore the city more. While they made their way around, they saw many soldiers scouting the city. Some were searching buildings, and others were stopping travelers. Some stood post throughout the city with a searching and urgent gaze.

"They look like they must be part of the royal army," David pointed out. "See their swords and golden chainmail? That's what Max had."

"That is what it looks like," Koen nodded in agreement.

"Why would the royal army be patrolling the city?" Alaina asked them.

"Could be a training exercise," Koen tilted his head in thought.

"I don't think so." Alaina shook her head. "Are training exercises normal?" Alaina wondered.

"No, not really. At least not in Mizcriea." Koen shook his head.

The royal army wasn't the only group of soldiers observed out and about, as the trio made their way around the city. Alaina knew there was more going on than just a training exercise, but she could not read the faces of the soldiers due to their helmets.

Suddenly, bells all around the city began to ring. Every citizen of Malikai collectively dropped what they were doing and began to make their way toward the center of the town, where the largest bell tower stood.

"What's going on?" Koen asked. Worry was plastered on the faces of the people, and they were making great haste to reach their destination. The bells continued to ring loud and clear.

The trio followed the people towards the center of town.

"Excuse me, miss, do you have any idea what's going on?" Alaina asked a girl not much younger than herself.

"The bells are ringing because an important announcement is about to be made. Everyone in the city must gather around to hear it. It rang four times, which means it's extremely important and most likely not good news," the girl answered. When Alaina thanked her, she ran off toward the bell tower.

As they drew closer, they could see a man standing on the bell tower by the bell. He would wait about thirty seconds before ringing it again four times. He did this until everyone was as close as they could get. Alaina, David, and Koen, all on horses, were surrounded by people. There was no way they could get out of the crowd, even if they needed to. They would simply have to wait.

"I've never seen so many people in one area," David said.

"I'm just glad we're on horses." Koen eyed the people rubbing against his horse's side and tried calming Wayne. "Well, maybe not."

"Ladies and gentlemen, I have an urgent announcement!" The man on the bell tower shouted for all to hear. "For those that can hear me, share with those who cannot!"

Alaina read his face when he looked out onto the crowd.

Worry. Urgency. Sadness. Fear.

He was a good man with a good heart. But his heart showed great fear, which told Alaina something was terribly wrong.

"In the middle of the night, His Majesty, the King, was kidnapped! The kidnappers are unknown, and the King is missing! The knights will be searching day and night for him! Please! If you see him or know his whereabouts, please report it. Again, the King has been kidnapped, and we must find him!" The man told the crowd.

At this, the crowd panicked. Horses rolled their eyes and flared their nostrils, and people ran by them without a care that an uncontrollable animal might trample them. Alaina and David's horses remained calm despite being tense. Koen's horse, on the other hand, was growing anxious.

"We need to get out of here!" Koen shouted over the people's frantic crying.

Alaina pulled her attention away from the crowd and tried to find a way out.

"Follow me!" David yelled.

Alaina and Koen kicked their horses in David's direction. They made their way slowly through the crowd and tried not to run into anyone along the way. From what Alaina saw, the people were scared—no, they were terrified. Their King had been kidnapped, and there were so many dangers they would be exposed to now.

Her heart ached for them, and she knew they were up against something much bigger than finding their father.

Later, they were in the woods once again. They decided there was no reason to stop and shop in the city while it was in chaos, and they thought they would help it more by continuing their quest.

Alaina spoke up, "How strange is it that our father was kidnapped, and now their king has been kidnapped, too?"

"It is strange, but it doesn't exactly mean that there is a similar reason," David answered.

"True, but we shouldn't rule it out, right? You must admit there is a good chance they're connected, and we're up against something bigger than we thought, right?"

"I guess. However, we need to focus on the mission at hand. If the Lord chooses to bring different matters along our way, then so be His will, but we cannot go and start making problems ourselves," David said.

"Wow," Koen spoke up.

"What?" David turned to him.

"Nothing, it just seemed like a really wise way of putting that." Koen shrugged, and Alaina snorted in amusement.

"Honestly, I think God has already brought different matters along our way. The fact that we met Maximillionous and what happened in Linencrest, I'd say this journey has already turned out to be more than we had originally planned," Alaina stated.

"I think you're right," David nodded.

"I'm disappointed we couldn't spend more time in Malikai City, but I also think it was best to leave. The longer we take, the less time your father could have," Koen stated.

"I agree. It's best we be on the move anyway. We can sightsee another time," Alaina agreed.

"So, David, what is our heading?" Koen asked.

"I believe the next stop is Dragon Coast," David said after pulling out a map.

"Dragon Coast? You mean, like, the coast with dragons?" Alaina said with uncertainty in her voice. She had read how tough their scales were, and if they got into a fight with one, her arrows would barely leave a mark.

Koen kept his eyes on the horizon and said in a mysterious voice, "There's only one place called Dragon Coast, and it's the place with dragons."

Alaina and David rolled their eyes. "What are the chances of us running into a dragon?" Alaina asked.

"Well, being that we're going to be riding in the woods that run right along the coast, there's a good chance we'll see one. However, the chances of us encountering one are very slim," David told her.

"Well, I've always wanted to see a dragon." Alaina shrugged and laughed nervously.

"I've seen one before as a kid," Koen said.

Alaina watched his eyes as he stared through his horse's ears. He seemed to be completely lost in thought, his mind focused on his memories. His face showed curiosity as he recalled what it was like to see a dragon, a pinch of fear that only turned into determination, and then anger. Alaina wasn't exactly sure why the anger had suddenly taken over his face, but she could guess a few reasons why.

"It was captured by one of the royal Mizcriean knights. It was massive, and it was the color of smoke. I remember the eyes were yellow. The knight captured the dragon to win the respect of the King, my father. Of course, he received what he was promised: respect and treasures. Though everyone cheered for the knight's accomplishment, I had a different feeling about it. I felt sorry for the dragon. I couldn't imagine what it would be like to be so big, powerful, wild, and free, only to be thrown into a crammed cage. I explained my thoughts to my father, only to be shut down and told I was being weak and soft," Koen explained.

"If you don't mind me asking, how was your mother on things like that? I remember you saying she was the only good thing in your father's life. Did she agree with the Mizcriean ways?" Alaina asked.

"She was never involved in those things. She was usually in her room because she never cared to be involved. I remember my father and her getting into an argument about a situation very similar to that. My father yelled at her so loudly, she never spoke the same after the incident. It made her quiet and scared. She knew that if she gave my father a reason to get rid of her, my brother and I would be left alone with him. That was the last thing she wanted." Koen's face showed anger once again.

"I hope your brother is well when you find him, for your sake," Alaina said. She went on to ride beside him in silence.

♔

Dragon Coast was exactly as they imagined it to be. It was misty and dark, and caves along the cliffside proclaimed that dragons ruled the mountains.

They arrived in the evening, just two hours before sunset. They would need to find a safe place to camp before dark.

"We'll find a space to camp and set up a fire. It should take us a few days to navigate out of these woods. The trees are thick and should help protect us," David said just loud enough for the others to hear.

"I hope to see a dragon," Alaina whispered. When there was no response, she turned to see them both giving her an "are you insane?" look. "What?" She laughed. "Not up close, of course."

"Oh, well then yeah, I agree," Koen laughed.

"If you see one here in the woods, it will be up close. We're headed into the thick part of the woods for safety, so you won't be able to see the dragons flying around," David told her.

"Ok, I guess I'll have to wait," Alaina huffed in disappointment.

Once they had found a campsite, they set up a fire and tied the horses closer than usual. Around midnight, they could hear the screeches of dragons as they flew over their heads. Alaina couldn't fall asleep for a while, so she continued to listen to the beasts' noises. It was an eerie sound, but it was quieter than what she had imagined. Alaina had heard they made a terrifying noise when angry or upset. Tonight, it was just their way of communicating. The misty clouds had gone away to reveal a starry night sky and a bright moon. Alaina continued to try to fall asleep, but her body wouldn't allow her to rest. She couldn't understand why and soon gave up trying. She sat up and looked around the campfire. Both men were sleeping soundly.

Alaina rose quietly, taking care not to disturb the others, and slipped away to fetch more wood for the fire. Staying within sight of the campsite, she collected dry sticks, knowing chopping wood at this hour wasn't wise. After tossing the sticks into the fire, she sat close to the burning embers, allowing the warmth to wash over her. She watched the flames flicker and dance momentarily, mesmerized by their orange light. Still unable to find rest, she decided to take a short walk. She retrieved her sword and bow from the horse and fastened the sheath around her waist.

Although she didn't plan to venture far, she pulled out her knife and began to mark trees. "Just in case," she whispered as if to reassure herself. "Probably won't even use it."

With a last look at the fire, she headed towards the beach. As she drew closer, the dirt gave way to sand, and the trees began to thin out. The dragons' shrieks were louder, and the sound gave her chills. When she reached the end of the woods and looked at the ocean, she stopped and decided not to step out into the open.

Alaina gazed out at the ocean and marveled at the moon's reflection. "Amazing," she smiled. Then she turned right and walked the tree line up a hill. The hill grew steep, but she continued forward. Soon, she reached a cliff that looked far down into a small cove formed by the mountains. Alaina got down onto her stomach and crawled to the cliff's edge to look over. It was further down than she had thought. She couldn't imagine she had climbed so high. She crawled back and stood up. Alaina looked at the ocean again and let her mind wander wherever pleased. She steadied her breath as she let her eyes adjust to the dark.

A cold breeze picked up and took Alaina's breath away for a second. She stepped back, and suddenly, her leg filled with a striking pain. In panic, she lifted her pant leg to see if something had stung her. When she looked down at her calf, her eyes went wide. A monstrous orange flower had latched onto her calf, wrapping its way further up her leg. She could feel its venom burning through her leg, and it took everything in her not to pull away, afraid a struggle would only make her situation worse. In the moonlight, she could see her leg turning purple, and she began to cry out in pain.

She cried louder, hoping David and Koen could hear her, but she feared she had wandered too far. She had not been aware of dangers on the ground and in the sky.

Suddenly, the pain subsided, and her leg became completely numb. She couldn't feel anything.

Just as abruptly, the entire right side of her body went numb, and she collapsed into the dirt. "Lord, help me!" she cried out. The world around her wasn't in focus and began to spin. Alaina was afraid she might die. Was this her life? Had God brought her all this way just to die from a poisonous plant on a cliff? Not even by a dragon? Her mind soon didn't make sense, and she could no longer think. The moon was fading from her sight.

The last thing she heard was a dragon shriek nearby. It didn't worry her, though, because she would probably be dead before it found her. It shrieked again, but this time much closer.

That's when her world went black.

David woke and found the fire had gone out during the night. "Strange," he thought to himself. Despite the foggy morning, it was warm. He looked around and saw that Koen was also just waking up. But when he looked around, Alaina was nowhere in sight.

"I think she might have gone to get firewood. There," Koen pointed to the ground over where Alaina had slept. Sure enough, footprints were leading towards the surrounding trees.

"Can you tell how long ago?" David sat up in his place.

"Um, let me see," Koen said, standing up and walking over to the footprints. He knelt and stared at them for a few seconds.

David watched as Koen squinted for a closer look. After a few minutes, David asked, "What is it?"

"Well, I mean they're very recent obviously, and it's hard to tell exactly when, since it was so recent . . . "

"How long ago, Koen?" David pressed.

"It couldn't have been too long ago. They're not fresh, but deep enough that it must have been a couple hours ago."

"What?" David shot up onto his feet. "It doesn't take hours to get wood for a fire."

"No, it doesn't." Koen shook his head and stood.

David walked over to Ophelia and checked for Alaina's sword and bow. "She took her weapons."

"We both know that if a dragon got to her, her chances of winning the fight are incredibly slim." Koen looked at David, worried.

"I know. We need to look for her. Come on." David picked up his sword belt and followed her tracks with Koen close behind.

"Well, she definitely went to get firewood," Koen said when the footprints led back to the campsite.

"Yeah, but then she left again. Look over there," David pointed to another trail. They followed it to the water and then up the mountain to the cliff where Alaina had been. David looked around, confused and more worried than he had been in a long time. He couldn't lose another person he loved. He couldn't lose Alaina. She was all he had left. David wasn't sure he could go on with the quest without her. "God, please, do not let me lose my sister," David prayed silently.

"They end here," Koen pointed to the ground by his feet. "It looks like she had some trouble, but she barely moves from this spot. Plus, her feet never leave the ground. She must have fallen here." Koen observed the prints in the ground. "I don't understand. Either there would be another creature's prints, or her prints would be leaving this place."

"Another creature . . . like a dragon," David said while staring blankly at the ground.

"Yeah, it's possible it was a dragon, but like I said, there would be prints." Koen shook his head in confusion.

"Like these," David said as a statement rather than a question.

Koen quickly made his way over to David and followed his gaze. "Yeah," Koen gulped. "Like those." These giant prints could only belong to one creature: a dragon.

"Is . . ." David couldn't bear to say it. "Is–" He had to know what Koen was thinking, because he couldn't think clearly at this point. "Is she gone?"

"Hold on." Koen took one more look at the dragon prints and then ran back over to where Alaina's were. "It doesn't make sense."

"What?" David asked.

"If the dragon had . . . " Koen looked to the ground instead of into David's eyes, " . . . attacked her, there would've been, um, remains. However, there are no remains; the only sign of struggle is shown here where she fell to the ground. And here, the prints don't make sense. They sort of look like–" Koen thought for a moment. "But that doesn't make any sense. Why would it do that?" Koen knelt in frustration and buried his face in his hands. "I just don't know."

"Why did she leave the campsite?" David asked no one in particular, but clearly fighting worried tears.

"David."

David looked up. "What?"

"It doesn't make sense . . . " Koen stared at the ground. "Unless . . . "

"Unless what?" David's eyes filled with hope.

Koen shot to his feet. "Those aren't all Alaina's footprints. Those are someone else's."

"What does that mean?" David asked, growing anxious to follow Koen's train of thought.

"I once read about a tribe from Azgalia that lived near Dragon Coast. They learned more about dragons than any other people alive, and by knowing so much, they lived in peace with the dragons. Some even learned to train the dragons so they could ride them."

"Ride dragons?" David raised an eyebrow.

"That's what I read."

"And you believe that?"

"Well . . . I wouldn't rule it out," Koen shrugged. "It's possible."

"Okay, so say that's true. What does that have to do with Alaina?" David asked.

"These are someone else's footprints. That right there," he said while motioning to the ground, "means she was dragged across the ground. The dragon doesn't move except for those prints over there, which means he landed, balanced himself, and flew away. But he didn't come alone; he came with a person and left with two."

"A dragon rider took Alaina?" David was trying not to lose

it.

"From what I see and know, that seems like the best explanation," Koen stated.

"So, how do we get her back?" David asked, calming his composure.

"Are you ready to get up close and personal with some giant lizards?" Koen smirked.

"I was afraid you'd say that," David exhaled in a stressed manner. "Let's go get her back." After a nod of agreement, they followed their marks and soon found the campsite. David grew increasingly worried with each passing minute. Just because they had a theory of what happened to his sister did not mean she was alive. Just because someone dragged her away didn't mean she was okay. In fact, she could be in real danger. After all, the person who might have dragged her away rides a dragon. People who ride dragons must be crazy, right?

He needed to find Alaina.

"David?" Koen asked, breaking David out of his thoughts.

"Yeah?" David said.

"We'll find her. I won't stop looking until we do. I know I've only known you two for a little while, but we've already been through a lot together, and now you guys are like family. We'll find her," Koen tried to reassure David.

Even though she wasn't his sister, David could see he, too, was worried about her. "Thanks, Koen." David nodded and mounted his horse.

ELEVEN

It was midday when Koen and David reached the sand. It had taken them some time to find a safe descent down the cliffs. They looked northwest to see the dragon caves clearly. The waves crashed ashore, and their horses danced sideways when they felt their riders' tension.

"The point of sleeping in the woods was to stay away from the dragons. Now we're headed towards them," David said.

"Funny how life does that, huh?" Koen said.

After taking a moment to find the quickest route, they made their way towards the mountain. In the light of day, it felt like they'd entered another, more mysterious land. Dragon Coast was beautiful, yet unnerving, as the plant and animal life seemed wilder and alive in its unfamiliarity. A bright red lizard with eyes the color of lemon darted up the rock face as they rode past, and David was torn between feelings of awe and fear for their safety in this foreign land.

"This place must have drawn many explorers because of its beauty, but I think it ended up being more dangerous than they had first thought. I don't think anyone travels to these parts anymore," Koen said, looking at the expanse around them.

"Something as beautiful as this place must have a defense from outside invaders," David said thoughtfully. Afterward, they rode in silence.

David knew there was only so much they could do at this

point, so he asked that God would protect Alaina if she were still alive.

The closer they got to the dragon caves, the more anxious David became. The largest animal he ever had to kill was a wolf or a large buck. He was good with a sword, but wasn't sure how to hold his ground against a dragon.

"So, what exactly is the plan?" When they reached the border between the caves and trees, Koen reined his horse. "Do we just look in every cave until we find her? Or call out hoping the dragon rider hears us?"

David tried to muster a plan, but he could tell his worry was clouding his usually calm thought process. "I—I—I'm not sure." David closed his eyes. "Give me a second." He dismounted and ground-tied Blade. He walked to the edge of the trees and looked up. Caves covered the face of the mountain, and some went as high as the very top. They were giant black holes that made you shiver just looking at them.

David tried to recall whatever he could about what he knew of dragons. Thoughts about their size, their behavior, and how they survived swirled around in his head. "Wait, the dragon riders you talked about. You said they lived in a village, right? We need to find the village," David said.

Koen nodded and looked around. "Well, I don't know about you, but I'm not asking the dragons for directions."

Something hurt. It hurt a lot. Then, it was cold and wet.

Nothing made sense because all she could think about was

how badly her leg hurt. Her eyes refused to open, and her limbs were motionless. All she could do was lie there and think about the pain. Wait, did her voice work? She moaned aloud. Yes, that worked; although her lips couldn't form words for her moaning to make any sense. She moaned again but stopped when she thought she heard something. Her hearing worked; that was good.

The footsteps came closer. Her mind told her to move, but her body ignored the command. She listened for the footsteps until they stopped at least a foot away.

Alaina held her breath, or at least it felt like she did, hoping she looked dead, just in case it was a dangerous stranger. Suddenly, a cold hand touched her arm and then reached to push the hair out of her face.

"Oh, thank goodness you're alive," said the voice of a young woman. "I hope you're not too frightened. You are safe here and have nothing to fear. I rescued you when I saw you lying on the ground by the cliff. I saw you were bitten by one of the Precarious Poppies, one of the deadliest plants in Azgalia. Luckily, I have the cure for the poison. Family recipe."

The girl went on, "Your vision will come back soon, and everything should be back to normal. Also, I have to say you're the prettiest girl I have ever seen! I mean, I haven't been around other people since I was under ten, but even then, I'm sure they weren't as pretty as you. I was told my mother was a beautiful woman, though." The girl stopped as though she was thinking of another topic to cover. Her voice sounded young, and it was clear she wasn't fully grown yet. She sounded kind, and her voice had a higher pitch. "Oh, I can't wait to actually meet you. I hope you're as nice as you look. I'm sure you're very nice.

I haven't had a conversation with someone in years! Also, I must warn you, I tend to ramble on and talk about things . . ." She cut herself off. "Rigel! Put that down right now!" A loud clatter followed the girl's yelling.

Alaina had to wake up and see where she was. As lovely as the girl seemed, she had to get back to Koen and David; they were probably going crazy with worry.

"Oh! You know what I was just thinking? I wonder if you're not the only one! I guess I'll just have to wait to ask you that when you wake up. Shouldn't be long now, you'll have your voice back first, and then you'll be able to move, and then your vision will come back."

Suddenly, Alaina's throat was open, and it felt like someone had removed their tight grasp from it. It felt so good that she thought she should yell and never take it for granted again. She coughed a few times and then finally spoke. "What's your name?" It came out raspy. Maybe she wouldn't yell just yet.

"Oh, your voice is back! It sounds a little hoarse right now, but that will go away too. Oh my goodness, I can't believe how much I've told you without telling you my name! My name is Harleigh. What is yours?"

"My name is Alaina," Alaina said. Even though her throat was open, the words still came out rough.

"What a pretty name!" Harleigh quipped. "Oh, I can't wait for you to meet Rigel. Are there any others with you here?"

"Yes, my brother, David, and our friend, Koen. They're probably looking for me right now," Alaina said.

"Oh, how wonderful! That means I'll probably get to meet them!" Harleigh said excitedly. "Are you in any pain yet?"

"What do you mean, 'yet?'" And just as Alaina finished

asking, a sharp pain shot through her body, making her cry out in pain. It only lasted a few seconds, though, for when the pain was gone, she could move.

"I suppose you can move now?" Haleigh asked cheerfully.

Alaina sat up and nodded yes. "That hurt."

"Yeah, that's what I've heard," Harleigh said with sympathy.

It was hard to read Harleigh with her vision gone, but from what she sounded like, Alaina took her for a sweet girl who just hadn't had enough socialization, which would explain her ongoing childlike joy. Honestly, though, Alaina looked forward to seeing a genuine smile and a girl around her age.

"I've been traveling with men these last couple of weeks, so I have to say it's nice to be in the company of a girl. Even under such poor circumstances," Alaina laughed a bit.

"Oh, I'm so happy that my company makes you happy!" Harleigh jumped up and down on the wet ground, splashing it onto Alaina. "Oh, I'm sorry!"

"It's okay," Alaina said, moving her hand to wipe off the water. "Where are we anyway?" She moved her head around as if she were looking.

"We're in my cave," Harleigh said.

"Your cave?" Alaina asked questionably.

"Yep!" the girl said. "Why don't you look around?" She giggled.

For a second, Alaina thought the girl was making fun of her, only to realize her vision was returning. Alaina blinked several times and rubbed her eyes. Everything finally came into view.

She blinked once. And then again. She couldn't believe what her eyes were seeing.

Was her voice gone again? She felt as though she couldn't mutter a word. There, right before her eyes, was a dragon.

She gulped and blinked twice again. Alaina rubbed her eyes and continued to stare in awe. "That–that–that's a–a–" Alaina couldn't find the words.

"That's Rigel, my dragon." Harleigh wore the most enormous and proudest smile Alaina had ever seen. This girl had a dragon.

"Wow. Incredible." Alaina stood up and continued to marvel at the giant beast. He stood over eight feet tall, and his scales glimmered in the sunlight like the color of a sunset. His wings seemed enormous but were nicely tucked behind him on his back.

"Isn't it?" Harleigh said, putting her hands on her hips.

Alaina then peeled her gaze from the dragon to the girl. She took this moment to get a good read on the girl who saved her.

Joy. Honesty. Love. Compassion.

She was thin, pale, a bit lanky, but beautiful. She had bright red hair and emerald green eyes that could pierce the soul. Her lips were rosy, and faint freckles were speckled across her face. She wore an old, torn dress that hadn't been washed in a long time, except maybe in a stream.

"You're very pretty," Alaina said, giving a kind smile.

The compliment made Harleigh's face light up. "Why, thank you!"

"Harleigh, how did you come to own a dragon?" Alaina asked curiously.

"Well, my village helped care for the dragons here and learned to ride them. My father gave me Rigel, so I've raised Rigel since his birth," Harleigh explained.

"That's how you brought me here? On Rigel?" Alaina asked.

"Yep!"

Alaina's eyes widened. "Wow. I almost wish I had been awake when that happened."

"I can give you a ride if you want!" Harleigh said with great enthusiasm.

"That would be so amazing! For now, though, I think I'd better stay for my friend and brother." Alaina thought for a moment. "Harleigh, where is your village?"

Harleigh's expression quickly changed to a solemn one. "My village burned down when there was an accident with a dragon. One man in our village always hated dragons, so he beat one in anger one day. It turned on him with its fire breath. The village burned down."

"And your family? Where are they?" Alaina asked carefully.

"Gone with the village," Haleigh said sadly.

"I'm so sorry. So, do you live here alone with Rigel, then?" Alaina asked.

"I do. Rigel and the other dragons," Harleigh smiled.

"Harleigh, how old are you?" Alaina asked.

Harleigh squinted as she tried to remember her age. "I think I'm sixteen years old."

"And how long ago did your village burn down?" Alaina was almost afraid to ask.

"Eight years ago," she said.

Alaina stared at Harleigh. She has been here for eight years, living with dragons. Alone.

She clearly has been able to care for herself, but still, Alaina couldn't imagine.

"Alaina, there is no need to feel sorry for me. What has happened to me was God's will. I was devastated all those years ago, and of course, I still miss them all. However, I know God has a plan for my life, and whether it's a difficult one or not, I plan to always trust him." Harleigh smiled, and it seemed her eyes twinkled at that moment.

Alaina smiled back, "Harleigh, you can count me as your friend for life."

Harleigh laughed and embraced Alaina. "Oh, Alaina, you can count me as yours as well. I knew there was something special about you the moment I picked you up."

"I'm so glad you picked me up in the first place," Alaina laughed.

"Oh!" Harleigh let go of Alaina and jumped back. "I almost forgot!" She ran over to the wall of the cave where Rigel lay. "Rigel, you're probably lying on them, aren't you?" The tiny girl put her hands against the dragon and pushed against him as if she planned to move him out of the way. "Move, you lazy lizard!"

Alaina watched with wonder as Rigel snorted and slowly stood, moving toward the girl, though he only crawled a few feet away from the place he was before. "You know, Alaina, despite what some people think, dragons can be extremely lazy. At least, when they're spoiled like Rigel here," Harleigh laughed as she bent down to pick up Alaina's sword, bow, and arrows. "Here you are." She handed Alaina her things.

"Oh, I forgot about these! Thank you!" Alaina said.

"No problem," Harleigh smiled.

"Do you think you could show me the way out? I think I

should go out in the open so my company can find me," Alaina suggested.

"Why yes! Follow me!" Harleigh motioned with her hand and headed toward the exit, which Alaina assumed was nearby.

Alaina followed her through the cave. It was dark, cold, and wet. The idea that she was walking through a dragon cave made her shudder a bit. Never would she have guessed she would end up in a situation like this. Not only had she seen a dragon up close, but she had been in his cave. *Wait until I tell Koen and David,* she thought to herself. It helped a bit to think that a tiny girl like her new friend could survive her whole life living at Dragon Coast. Maybe Alaina could survive a couple of days without them.

"Almost there," Harleigh said as she turned to her left. Alaina was about to ask why she had faced the wall when Harleigh disappeared into it. It was a tunnel! When Alaina turned the corner, the tunnel was lit up by daylight. It was much brighter than the rest of the cave. That's when she realized the light at the end of the tunnel was actually the end of the tunnel. Alaina couldn't help but smile.

"Harleigh, I am so glad I met you, and I wouldn't change what happened to me for anything, but I gotta say . . . I am so excited to get out of this cave." Alaina and Harleigh laughed.

"No hard feelings," Harleigh laughed.

Once they reached the end of the cave, Alaina paused just before the shadow met the light. She took a deep breath and stepped into the sun.

"The fog from the other day must have lifted," Harleigh noticed.

Alaina nodded, "It's beautiful."

"Alaina!" There was a faint voice that called out her name.

"Did you say something?" Alaina turned to Harleigh.

"No. Did you hear something?" she asked.

"I think so," Alaina closed her eyes to concentrate.

"Alaina!"

"There it was, again! Did you hear it?" Alaina asked Harleigh.

"Yeah, I did! Could it be your friends?" she asked.

"I bet it is! David! Koen! I'm here!" Alaina called out. "Come on, let's go find them!" Alaina ran in the direction of the voice, with Harleigh following close behind. "David! Koen!"

"Alaina!" They called again, and this time, Alaina recognized the voice.

"I'm coming!" Alaina called out.

"Alaina! Alaina, follow my voice!" David called out.

Alaina followed his voice until she knew she was close and slowed to a fast walk. When she pushed through thick tree branches, she caught sight of her brother and her friend. "Oh, you guys!" She ran to David and embraced him.

"Gosh, I thought you were gone for good," David said as he hugged her back.

"Yeah, no running off like that again, please," Koen smiled.

"Oh, I won't," Alaina laughed and walked over to hug Koen. "Thanks for coming all this way to find me."

"Well, of course," David said.

"Now, who are you?" Koen asked.

Alaina looked at him and followed his gaze to Harleigh, standing smiling by the trees. Alaina could see she didn't know what to say or do around these new people. She didn't have a slow introduction, unlike the one she had experienced with

Alaina.

"Koen, David, this is Harleigh. She saved my life," Alaina said, walking over to Harleigh and grabbing her hand. She encouraged her to come closer.

"Thank you, Harleigh," David thanked the girl with a genuine smile.

Koen tilted his head and studied her for a second. "Yes, thank you for saving my friend. May I ask you a question?"

"Why, you're most certainly welcome! I am so glad I could make it to her on time. I'm afraid Alaina would never have recovered if I hadn't found her. Oh, and yes! Ask me anything!" Harleigh clasped her hands together, her excitement evident. Alaina saw that she was joyful to be amongst people, with a smile all over her face.

"Were you a member of the Dragon Coast tribe?" Koen asked.

Harleigh's excitement dimmed, but not by much. She looked into his eyes and nodded. "Yes, I was. My tribe burned to the ground. My tribe and village were lost to a fire about eight years ago."

"I'm so sorry to hear that. You see, I read stories of your people. I was told they were myths, but others told me they were true. Is it true that your people rode dragons?" Koen asked.

Alaina thought Harleigh's smile couldn't be bigger, but the girl proved her wrong. Harleigh's smile broadened just a bit more at the mention of dragons. Koen was in for a treat. This thought made Alaina laugh, which earned her an odd look from her brother and friend. She made eye contact with Harleigh and winked.

"Yes, they did. In fact, so do I," Harleigh said.

"Do?" Koen squinted.

Just then, Harleigh whistled with her fingers in her mouth, and a couple of seconds later, the trees began to shake and a slight breeze picked up. Only for a second, though, for when the group looked up, there was a dragon.

Koen's eyes widened, and David's jaw dropped open. Rigel landed a few yards from the group beside Harleigh. At that moment, Alaina was glad the boys didn't have the horses with them.

"Wow," was all Koen could muster up.

"That's exactly what I said," Alaina laughed.

"Incredible." David shook his head with wonder in his eyes.

"Isn't he?" Harleigh beamed. "His name is Rigel."

"Truly amazing," Koen said as he looked back at Harleigh. "Since your village burned down, where do you stay?"

"I usually either sleep with Rigel or in the woods in the tent I built. It's quite relaxing and comfortable, actually," she said.

"Would you be able to join us? You're most welcome!" Alaina suggested. "We're headed to Mizcriea and could use a helping hand."

"We'll be leaving in the morning," David nodded in agreement.

"Oh, how wonderful that sounds! I'm afraid I shouldn't leave Rigel, though. He has not known life without me. I'm sure Mizcriea is not a friendly home for dragons. Please come back to visit me, though?" Harleigh said kindly, although Alaina saw there was a part of her that wished she could go.

"Why, of course! If you ever need anything, and I mean it, I will do my best to help you in any way I can," Alaina said as she looked into her new friend's eyes.

"Thank you, Alaina. I will be here if you ever need me." Harleigh smiled.

"You said you'd take me on a ride, right? I intend to come back for that." Alaina laughed.

"Of course." Harleigh grinned. "Well, since you leave in the morning, why don't I show you around?"

"Sounds good to me." Koen nodded.

"Let's go get the horses first," David suggested.

"Do you have Ophelia?" Alaina asked, and when David nodded, she said, "Okay, I'll go with you."

"Wonderful. I'll meet you at the bottom, then. I know the most beautiful beach," Harleigh said.

"We'll meet you," Alaina nodded, and with that, Harleigh walked to Rigel and leaped onto his back. They took off into the sky together and dove down the mountain out of sight.

"Now that's something you don't see every day," Koen said.

"The girl or the dragon?" David asked.

Koen laughed, "Both."

TWELVE

"How close did you say we were to the border?" Alaina turned in her saddle to face Koen.

"That was like an hour ago," Koen laughed.

"Yeah, but what did you say?" Alaina ignored his laugh.

"I said we were about an hour away," Koen smiled.

"Wait, so . . . " Alaina's eyes widened. "We're here?"

"We're at the border. Or at least, that's it over there. Just beyond those intertwining trees." Koen pointed ahead of them. "Only problem is that there is a river we have to cross."

"A river? How are we getting across?" David asked.

"It's shallow enough that we can swim the horses across safely. However, once we're across, we'll have to tie you two up with the horses. You also may not be aware of this, but unfortunately, it's not a strange thing for a Mizcriean to cross borders and kidnap Azgalians for slavery. It's not common, but it's also not very rare. So as long as I say I captured you two as slaves, they will let you enter with me," Koen explained.

Alaina nodded. "Okay. Whatever it takes." Her heart broke over the thought that Azgalians could be taken like that.

They passed under the trees that Koen had pointed out and arrived at the riverbank. There was a current, but thankfully, it wasn't strong enough to cause trouble. Alaina dismounted along with Koen and David.

"We'll go across and tie you up on the other side, but we'll have to hide so they don't see us cross," Koen said.

"We can do that," David said. "Let's go."

Each grabbed their mount and piled their valuables on the saddles to avoid as much water as possible.

"Won't the water get to them anyway?" Alaina wondered out loud.

"It all depends on how deep it is. When I came over, it was shallow enough that the supplies didn't get wet. It could have risen, but we'll see." Koen shrugged. "I'll go first." He walked up to where the water met the land and lowered his foot into the flowing river. Stepping in, he touched his foot to the ground and continued to drop in the other.

"Wow, that is cold," Koen said, shivering. He ignored the urge to jump out and instead signaled Alaina to follow. "David should bring up the rear."

"Okay," Alaina said. Part of her was scared she wouldn't be strong enough to walk through the current or that a horse might act up, and it would all go wrong. Ophelia hadn't had much experience with water, at least not to this extent. She prayed the Lord would allow the horses to stay calm. After swallowing her worry, she took a step forward. There was no way she could turn back now.

Ophelia shook her head when she reached a hoof into the water. "It's alright, girl." Alaina stroked her neck. As soon as Ophelia was calm once more, they continued. Alaina could feel the adrenaline rush through her as the excitement and danger of what was happening hit her. The water was freezing, but she continued to move.

"You okay?" David called over the sound of the rushing river.

"Yeah! Come on in!" Alaina called back through chattering teeth.

David came in and followed closely behind. They moved through the current slowly but steadily. Every few seconds, they checked in with each other and their surroundings. Each was shivering and praying they'd make it to the other side.

As Alaina stepped through the water, she focused on her footing. The rocks beneath were slippery, making it hard to gain traction. She was thankful it was shallow enough to walk through, so they wouldn't have to swim, but the rocks were challenging to navigate.

Without realizing it, her bow slipped off Ophelia's saddle. Out of the corner of her eye, she saw the rushing water catch the tip of her bow and pull it towards itself. "No!" Alaina cried out.

"What's wrong? Alaina!" Koen yelled, trying to see what was happening while keeping his horse still.

"My bow! It fell off and it's floating away!" Alaina was just about to make a desperate swim for it when David stopped her.

"Alaina, I know that bow is special to you, but you can't possibly rescue it without being pushed too far away from us. You have to let it go," David tried to reason with her. He always seemed to remain so calm somehow.

She could see he felt terrible, but that bow meant so much to her. She had grown up using it. Her grandmother had helped her make it and taught her how to use it. It took everything in her not to swim after it. She considered it and squeezed her eyes shut. Then she let out a deep sigh. *Keep moving*, she said to herself.

Opening her eyes again, she looked ahead.

Koen was now a couple of feet away from the other side. So far, the area seemed clear and safe to climb onto land, but they'd have to do it quickly.

"Alright, this part can get tricky. You'll have to climb up before your horse, so ensure you have a way up before jumping into it. It has to be done quickly; otherwise, your horse will get restless," Koen called back over his shoulder, and with that, he placed his free hand on land, swung his right foot up, and all in one motion made it onto dry land. His horse came right behind him in one great leap.

"That easy, huh?" Alaina said, but the roar of the water drowned out her voice. "Alrighty then."

Alaina was next. She knew Ophelia would wait for her to climb up; Ophelia would probably even let Alaina climb on her back and ride up. However, she didn't have time to test out her theory. Mimicking Koen's movements was slightly more complicated since Alaina didn't have the height Koen had to swing her leg over. Alaina's move was more like a jump, push-up, wiggle, and a face plant.

"You okay?" Koen asked, clearly trying to hold back a laugh.

"Yeah, yeah." Alaina waved it off. Once Alaina got to her feet, Ophelia gracefully leaped from the river and landed easily on dry land. "Good girl." She stroked Ophelia's face.

Next was David. He'd taken Blade on daring adventures around Norwest, so it wasn't surprising when he easily completed the jump.

"You make it look so easy," Alaina told him.

"It is easy," David smirked.

Alaina rolled her eyes. "Whatever."

"Alright, let's get you two tied up," Koen interrupted, turning their banter into seriousness.

First, David tied Alaina, and then Koen tied David. Koen put a little more effort into tying David to make it look more realistic. David was a strong young man and would need more bonds than a young woman. He then moved up to tie the horses to one another. "You guys ready?" Koen exchanged eye contact with each of the twins.

Alaina gazed at Koen.

Honor. Bravery. Determination. Hope.

He was nervous, but he was overcoming it. She then turned and searched David's eyes.

Faith. Readiness. Bravery. Protectiveness.

He was scared, whether he'd admit it or not. But he was equally, if not more, determined to find answers.

"We're ready." Alaina looked back at Koen and nodded.

Silently, they proceeded toward the Mizcriean soldiers guarding the border. Alaina held her breath as they stepped through the trees and into the open. This was it. This was the moment that decided whether their trip had been worth it. Her heart picked up pace, and all she could do was pray.

As soon as they emerged from the trees, the soldiers turned toward them and rushed to surround them. They were covered in armor and held their swords at the ready. Koen put his hands up, which showed surrender.

"Who are you?" the soldiers demanded of him.

"You're kidding, right?" Koen responded sarcastically in Azgalian, knowing that's what they thought he was. He couldn't resist.

The soldiers, not satisfied with that answer, moved toward

him. Before they got too close, Koen unsheathed his sword and called out a command in Mizcriean. The soldiers abruptly stopped and stared at him until their eyes grew wide.

"My prince!" a soldier cried out. "My apologies!" They knelt in front of him.

"Stand up. I won't kill you. Where is my uncle?" Koen asked in an impatient and authoritative tone.

A soldier with dark hair and a pointy nose glanced suspiciously at Alaina and David.

"They're with me," Koen stated sharply.

"This way." The soldier stood.

Alaina and David easily understood Mizcriean since their grandmother repeatedly told them the importance of knowing it. She would tell them that one day they might need it, and that they would be thankful for having learned it. This would now give them a great advantage. This was the day it would serve them well. They followed closely behind Koen while surrounded by soldiers who watched their every step.

They followed them into a camp filled with men and small tents. There were horses tied to posts and soldiers with armor that reflected the sun into Alaina's eyes. The sun at that moment seemed hotter, making the ropes around her wrists more uncomfortable and itchy. That grass felt nice underneath the thin sandals Koen had insisted she wear for the plan's sake.

"Uncle!" Koen called out. Alaina followed his gaze to a man who was bald except for a tiny portion of hair pulled back into a ponytail.

An interesting choice of hairstyle if she'd ever seen one.

His tiny ponytail was comprised of black hair, and he had a long, narrow beard. He turned at the sound of his nephew's voice and searched with his dark eyes for Koen. When he saw him, he smiled and opened welcoming arms for his nephew.

"My boy! My nephew! You have returned, just as I told your father you would!" His uncle embraced him.

If Alaina couldn't read faces, she would have believed Koen had betrayed her and David and that he had actually missed his uncle.

"Uncle, I just needed a break from it all. I'm sure you understand." Koen stepped back from the hug but kept a hand on his uncle's shoulder.

"Well, of course I do. When I was a young prince, I, too, did something similar." His uncle smiled.

When his uncle turned to face Alaina and David, Alaina almost had to look away. She had never seen a heart as wicked as this man's.

His gaze was dark, but not just because of his eyes. Alaina kept her expression downcast and timid.

"These are two friends I picked up along my way back," Koen said, slurring the word "friends" with sarcasm.

David spat on the ground, and Alaina gave a fake whimper. A soldier tried to advance, but Koen cut him short.

"Leave them be. I brought them along as slaves and as gifts for my father. They're Azgalians."

Koen's uncle started to laugh. It sounded like one that boiled from the pit of his wicked stomach. "How wonderful."

"I would like to head home as soon as possible. I'm sure you can imagine my longing for a real bed." Koen gave a half-laugh.

"Yes, yes, of course. There is a minor issue, though," his uncle said.

"Which is?" Koen raised an eyebrow.

"There have been problems in the past with shipping female and male slaves in the same carts, and shipping the men in a cart makes for an easier escape than if he were on a boat instead . . . " his uncle started.

"So?" Koen wondered what his uncle was implying.

"So, we now ship men by boat to a coastal city that is closer and holds a large majority of soldiers who can transport. We still ship ladies by way of cart; it's just that your boy here won't be able to come with you. Though you will see him at the castle shortly after you arrive yourself," Koen's uncle said, smirking at David while saying so.

Koen tried to keep an indifferent expression. "That's perfectly diabolical." Koen laughed, and his uncle joined in. "I am curious, though. Would you be able to make an exception for me, uncle? I'm not sure I trust the slave boat captain. I know of his reputation, and I want to make sure my slave arrives in one piece," Koen said, trying to keep it light.

"Certainly I would if I could! You know I would, my boy!" Koen's uncle put a hand on his shoulder. "Unfortunately, it's a direct order from your father, and we both know what he does when he hears of exceptions being made. With all his soldiers around." His uncle gave Koen a knowing glance.

Koen let out a big sigh and glanced at Alaina to show her how sorry he felt. "I see, Uncle. It will have to do then. I need the captain to know that it is of utter importance that my slave arrives to me in a timely manner," Koen asserted.

"But of course, my prince!" His uncle grinned, but Alaina saw deceitfulness run down to his core.

Alaina looked at David and, without words, asked if it

would be okay or if *he* would be okay. David gave a slight nod and softened his eyes. Only Alaina was able to notice things like this, but she was extremely thankful for it at that exact moment. When Alaina looked back toward Koen, their eyes met, and without his uncle seeing, she gave a nod of assurance.

"Will I be able to transport the girl myself? I'd like to keep her as my personal servant," Koen told his uncle.

"Why, of course. If that is what you want." His uncle put his hands on his hips and scanned Alaina. "A rare one indeed." He nodded in approval.

"That is what I want. Soldiers, take them to that tree and await further orders. When I leave, you may transport the boy." Koen referred to David as "the boy" to make himself seem superior, even though David was only a year younger.

"Yes, sir." They saluted and tugged on the twins' ropes, so they followed them to a nearby tree. Alaina and David sat down at the tree's roots and watched Koen and his uncle disappear into a tent. Before going inside, Koen looked over his shoulder at the twins.

Even though David wouldn't travel with them, everything was still going according to plan.

"David? Are you going to be okay?" Even though Alaina already knew the answer, she still wanted to hear him say it.

"Of course. I'll be able to find my way. As soon as we land, I'll find a way to escape or go along with the rest of the men. Either way, I'll end up at the castle and find you and Koen," David said.

"Right, it's just . . . "

"It's just we've never been this far apart for as long as this before," David finished for her.

"Plus, I'll be with Koen. I trust him, but that still doesn't take away my nervousness," Alaina told him.

"I understand. You think I want to leave you alone with Koen? I trust him much less than you do; however, I trust the Lord ultimately. Grandmother taught us well, and she prepared us for situations like this. I have to believe we will be alright. Our father's life depends on it," David said, hoping to comfort his sister and himself.

"You're right, as usual." Alaina laughed. She then became serious. "David, I just realized something."

"What is it?" David leaned in.

"Koen's uncle. He knows our father."

David's eyes widened. "How do you know for sure?"

"He recognized us," Alaina said.

"That's impossible." David shook his head.

"Unless . . . " Alaina led on.

"Unless he knew our father," David finished nodding.

"Exactly. We hold so many of our father's features that if someone knew our father, they would know we belong to him. Max is proof of that," Alaina explained.

"So, you're saying he has met our father?" David said.

"He could be our connection to finding our father," Alaina said.

"Or the reason we don't," David glared at Koen's uncle from where they sat.

"Alright! Get them up!" Koen's uncle called from the front of the tent as he stepped out.

The soldiers walked toward the twins.

"May God go with you, David, and keep you safe!" Alaina called out to him as they dragged her brother away. Tears began to well up in her eyes. She was uncertain she would ever see him again; she could only hope and pray.

"God, keep him safe," Alaina prayed silently.

Koen then said a word to his uncle, and after a nod of approval, he made his way over to Alaina. "We should head out now," he said, speaking Azgalian.

"Koen, I think your uncle . . . " she began.

"I know. He was asking questions. I pretended not to know anything about you. I took care of it. For now, at least. So, we need to go." Koen grabbed her arm and helped her to her feet.

"Okay. What about the horses?" Alaina whispered.

"I'm afraid we can't bring Blade with us. It'll be safer and easier to travel with just the two of us. We'll take Wayne and Ophelia. My uncle will have Blade transported to my stables."

"Okay," Alaina nodded and followed Koen to their horses.

After Koen helped her into the saddle, he temporarily tied her horse to his. "Just until we ride out," he said. He mounted and continued through the camp while nodding to his soldiers. Once they reached the trees on the other side, Alaina breathed a sigh of relief.

"I feel the same way. I hate being a prince," Koen laughed.

"I can't imagine," she said. "You know where to go?"

"You're kidding, right?" Koen laughed. "You're in my kingdom now."

THIRTEEN

The smell was dreadful. David wanted to gag every time he inhaled it. It had to be the rotten fish. It seemed like the only purpose of the fish was to make the slaves' lives more miserable.

The slave transportation ship had already left the dock the day before. Yesterday, David said goodbye to his twin sister and was forced to trust a Mizcriean with her life. Ever since he stepped foot on the ship called "The Forgotten," it had given off a horrible stench.

"Don't worry, mate," said an older man. You get used to it eventually." David tried not to vomit as he introduced himself. "You can call me Mr. P. I was transported on this ship myself about ten years ago when I was taken, and they've kept me on permanently."

It was hard to believe you could get used to a smell as bad as rotten fish, but he hoped it would be soon. As he looked around, the name of the ship made more sense. Most of the men on the ship seemed as lonely as possible. Looking into the horizon, all that lay ahead was the sea. As far as the eye could see, there were blue waters. No land or people in sight. He could imagine most of the men had lost all hope, with nothing on the horizon.

David thought back to Mr. P and the day before. "By the way," David asked, "what does the P stand for?"

"Stands for permanent," he laughed. Still chuckling, he walked away with a smile that held as many teeth as this ship held nice people, which wasn't many.

Permanently a slave. What a life to live. David shook his head at the thought.

From what little he had observed, the captain didn't treat his crew members any better than he treated the slaves, but at least the crew was getting paid. Mr. P also told David that they still had a few days of travel ahead, which made David feel nauseous just thinking about it. He didn't believe he was seasick, but the very thought of being stuck on this boat sounded dreadful.

So far, he'd spent most of his day sitting in a wet corner below deck or scrubbing something somewhere on the ship. "There always seems to be somethin' to scrub," a man complained.

"So, lad, what be your story?" A large man plopped down beside him. His arms were as big as a blacksmith's arms, and his legs were like muscular tree trunks. The man was intimidating next to average-sized David.

"I uh–um–" David started, unsure if the man was curious about his story, or if he was looking for an easy kill.

"Don't worry, boy. My bark is worse than my bite," the man laughed, putting a hand on David's shoulder.

David laughed nervously. "Yes, sir. Well, um, it's a long story."

"I've got the time. What about you?" The man laughed again and motioned to the boat around them with his hand.

"Yes, I suppose I do. What's your name?" David asked.

"Jamie. And yours?" He asked.

"David," he said.

"Ah, a mighty name, David is. It's a pleasure to meet you. Am I right to assume you're a follower, yes?"

"By follower, you mean . . ." David raised his eyebrow.

"Follower of Christ, of course!" Jamie smiled.

"Oh yes. Yes, I am. How did you know?" David asked.

"Sometimes you can just tell, you know? There was something about you when I first saw you, lad." Jamie gave David a toothy grin.

David smiled back. "What about you, Jamie?" David asked, excited that he'd already made a possible ally.

"Yes, I am!" Jamie's smile somehow widened even more than before. "Now tell me, what's your story? We all seem to have one on this boat."

"I came to Mizcriea on a quest with my sister and . . . " David paused before saying it, "and a friend."

"And where are they now?" Jamie asked.

"We were separated at the borders. My sister and friend stayed together, and they took me on this ship," David said. He was unsure how much information he should or shouldn't tell this man.

"Are you Mizcriean?" Jamie asked.

"No, I am Azgalian," David told him.

"May I ask what quest a young Azgalian like you found yourself on?" Jamie's eyes danced with curiosity.

David so wished he had his sister's gift in situations like this. Should he trust this man with his information? David decided to befriend the man and pray he wasn't being deceived. "My sister and I have come to find our father. When we were very young, he was captured by Mizcrieans."

"Oh, really? What makes you think he could still be alive?" Jamie asked.

"We heard that our father had sent a letter, so we hope he is still alive. The risk is worth it to us, since we are the last left in our family," David said.

"I see. So, where is your sister now, and how are you planning on continuing your search if you are trapped as a slave?" Jamie asked.

"No, no. You see, the prince of Mizcriea requested that his uncle bring me to him as his personal slave. That is how I get to the castle," David told him.

"You sure about that, lad?" Jamie looked worried. "I'm pretty sure I overheard the border guard tell the captain to sell you at shore along with the rest of us here." Jamie motioned to the other man around them.

"Are you sure? That's not what Koen said . . . " But then David realized Koen's uncle had deceived them. "Why that . . . " David started to fume.

"Hey now, lad, we have to trust the Lord." Jamie put a hand on David's shoulder and offered a soft smile.

David sighed, "You're right." How was he supposed to escape? He'd only have one chance. Mizcrieans cared very little about Azgalian lives, and they would kill easily if one didn't follow orders.

"Well, my sister is safe with a friend who has helped us through our journey, and they are continuing without me for now. As for me, I'm not sure how I will escape, but I know I must," David said with determination.

"Well, I would like to aid in your escape. If possible, I will help, and we can both escape. What do you say?" Jamie held out his hand.

David usually worked better alone, but in this circumstance, David could see that having an ally would be of extreme help. "It's a deal." David grabbed Jamie's hand and shook it.

"All hands on deck!" the captain called from above.

Jamie and David scrambled to their feet and followed the rest of the slaves up the stairs.

"Usually, when the captain calls everyone to deck, it's for a head count, a new rule put forth, or it means we're under attack. As far as I can tell, we aren't under attack, so I think we're okay," Jamie told David.

David had no clue what to do, so he was thankful he could follow Jamie. Jamie knelt alongside a line of other slaves on their knees, so David followed suit. The crew stood behind them, their hands behind their backs.

"They seem awfully well-mannered for a crew. From books I've read, I would assume them to be a bit unruly," David whispered to Jamie.

Jamie nodded. "These men used to be knights. The king ordered them to take on new roles as crew members. The captain used to be a head knight himself. The king didn't trust just any sailors to ship slaves, only knights who had the same mindset as the king himself."

"Interesting." David nodded and watched as the captain made his way to the ship's center, along with his first mate.

"Finwick! Count the heads of the slaves!" The captain ordered.

A man jumped out of line from the rest of the crew and began counting the heads of the captured men. One man spat at Finwick's shoes when his head was counted, and his response was a kick in the back from a crew member behind him.

"We'll have respect on this ship!" the crew member yelled.

"And I'll be the one giving orders!" the captain yelled over the crew member. "Finwick, continue."

As Finwick got closer, David noticed something very interesting on Finwick's arm. "Thirty, thirty-one." Finwick stepped in front of David, and before he could say "thirty-two," David said loud enough for only him to hear, "How long have you had that marking?"

Finwick's eyes quickly made eye contact with David, but he chose not to respond. "Thirty-two." He turned around and reported to the captain that he counted thirty-two slaves on deck.

"Good, that is correct." The captain nodded, and Finwick stepped back in line with the crew.

David wasn't sure what the story was behind Finwick, and he didn't have his sister's gift, but from what he saw in his eyes, David had a feeling he'd just found a new ally.

"We arrive back on land in two days! Back to your stations, men!" And with that, the captain walked off to his quarters.

"We must be going on land this time," a crew member told another, and David wondered what that meant.

"Back below, come on," Jamie told David. They stood up, and as they made their way down the stairs, David again made eye contact with Finwick and then began to descend.

"Jamie, what do you know about Finwick?" David asked him as they knelt, leaning against a barrel.

"Not much. I've only been here a few more days than you. Although you learn a lot in a few days." Jamie paused to think. "What I've heard is that he was previously a knight like the rest of them. Although I was told that a conversation was overheard about how none of them know exactly where he comes from. None of them remember seeing him in the royal army, although there are reasonable explanations for that. I suppose they're suspicious of him, but the captain seems to favor him above the rest. He's a hard worker and always gets the job done right," Jamie explained.

"Interesting." David stared at the floor in deep thought.

"Why the sudden interest? You know it is impossible to kill on a boat and get away with it," Jamie chuckled.

"No, no, I'm not going to kill him! I saw something on his arm," David said.

"The three lines? I saw it too, but don't most seamen have strange markings anyway?" Jamie raised a brow.

"Well, sure, but not like the one he had. I saw the same thing, on the same spot, back home in Azgalia," David looked up at Jamie. "On a knight."

"What are you saying?" Jamie raised his eyebrow.

"I believe Finwick is from Azgalia. Those markings were given to the knights of the King's royal army." David was getting excited.

"How sure are you?" Jamie asked.

"If I confront him and am wrong, what do I have to lose? They already know I'm from Azgalia, and I'm already on a slave ship, so . . . " David said.

"Good point. I don't think he would kill you . . . " Jamie began.

"Wow, that's comforting," David said jokingly.

"Hey, just trying to help a friend," Jamie winked.

"Okay, I'll plan on confronting him tonight." David leaned back against the post and decided right then and there to take a nap.

♛

A few hours later, David awoke to Jamie shaking his shoulder violently. "What–what's going on?" David asked groggily as he struggled to open his eyes.

"The captain is headed our way," Jamie whispered. "We have to salute when he steps in the room."

David stood as fast as his tired body could and watched the stairs like every other man below deck. *Someone must have been on watch to warn us*, David thought. These men may not have been friends, but in some ways, they had each other's backs and shared a common enemy.

The captain came down the stairs loudly, almost as if he stomped his boots on them harder than needed, just to promote intimidation. He stopped in the middle of the room, and all at once, the men saluted. "Good." He nodded as he eyed the newcomers, including David. "I'll need a few men on deck during the night so some crew can rest." The captain looked around the room. "Mr. P!"

"Yes, sir, I am here." Mr. P came out from behind a group of men.

"Mr. P, I need you to pick out men you think will be best equipped for being on deck during the night," the captain told him.

"Yes, sir."

"Report back to me once you have the men," the captain ordered, turned on his heels, and stomped back up the stairs.

The room remained silent as the men waited to see who would be picked, and from what David could see, every man hoped it wouldn't be them. David backed up a step so that he was beside Jamie and quietly whispered, "Do I want to be picked?" Jamie looked at David and shook his head.

"Sorry boys, but ye heard the captain," Mr. P said. "Alrighty then, let's see." He scanned the room, picking out men. Some young, some old, but all looked strong and capable.

About seven men were picked out before Mr. P reached David's side of the room. Two men were picked, and then Mr. P locked eyes with David. David's heart sank in his chest as soon as he realized he'd been picked. "You, boy." Mr. P pointed at him.

David looked up at Jamie with questioning eyes. "You'll be fine," Jamie told him.

David nodded and walked to where the other chosen men were standing. Once the unlucky few were chosen, they followed Mr. P up the stairs and onto the deck. Mr. P placed them all where he wanted them to work. David was placed on the top deck with a mop and bucket. "It's just 'cause you're new, lad. Also, from here, you can keep an eye on the horizon for any dangers." Mr. P chuckled at David's unamused expression and walked off.

Although David didn't understand why they needed someone to mop the top deck during the night, he saw something that made him glad he had been chosen for the job. Just a few feet away, Finwick was steering the ship. This was the perfect opportunity to talk to him. He decided that he'd approach casually and then ask. So, he slowly made his way toward Finwick while mopping the deck. Once he was about three feet from him, David paused and stared in the direction Finwick faced.

"Do you need something, boy?" Finwick turned to face David, somewhat annoyed.

"Well, you see. I was just thinking . . . when the captain said two days until shore, did he mean today and tomorrow as two days, or tomorrow and the day after as two days?" David pretended to be dumbfounded.

"By golly, boy! E'rybody knows you never count the present day! It will be tomorrow and the day after." Finwick shook his head.

"Oh, I see." David nodded and then stared back at the ocean.

"Was there something else?" Finwick glared at him when David didn't go away.

"Oh, I just wanted to compliment you on such a great accomplishment," David said with an innocent-looking face.

"Which would be . . . " Finwick urged David to go on. Royal army or not, he was an impatient man.

"Earning that marking, of course," David said, then continued to mop.

"What are you talking about?" Finwick took a step toward him.

Without looking at him, David said, "The three lines on your forearm, right under your wrist."

"And what's it to you?" Fenwick raised an eyebrow.

David stood and walked up close to Finwick, this time with a more confident posture. "I know that it's from Azgalia. I know it is only given to those in the King's royal army. I also know a man with the same marking. His name is Maximillionous."

At this, Finwick stared speechlessly into David's eyes. "I—

you—" he stuttered, unable to decide how to respond.

"Listen, I am from Azgalia. If you're a friend of Max, then I'm a friend of yours. I only ask three things: Why are you on this ship? What exactly does the marking mean? And will you help me escape?"

Finwick crossed his arms, and seeing that David was un-moving, he relaxed and gave a slight smirk. "Max, eh? How's he doing?"

David smiled. He had been right. "He's well. We attended the knight tournament in Linencrest with him."

"Ah, yes. Max always did love those things. Now, he never told you what the marking meant?" Finwick asked.

"No, only that it's given to the knights of the royal army," David said.

"Look here, the top line is the longest because it stands as the most important; it represents God. The second, also the second longest, represents the people of Azgalia. The third, the smallest of the three, represents Azgalia's King. In this or-der, we are called to protect and serve—first our Lord, second the people, and third the King. Even though we are under the King's rule, the King holds the people higher than himself," Finwick explained with a spark of passion in his eyes.

"Amazing. Even better than I imagined," David marveled.

"As far as why I am here, the King ordered me to research the kidnappings. It led me to the border crossing, which led me to the Mizcriean army. They do not know I am from Azgalia, as I speak with a Mizcriean accent easily, and because of my attire. It so happened that the day I arrived, they were taking on knights and interviewing them for board positions on this ship. I used it as an explanation as to why I was at the border crossing. To make a long story short, I ended up here. I've stayed only because I have been able to help many and learn a lot about the Mizcrieans. Once I feel I have done enough here, I plan to return and use the information I have in Azgalia's aid," Finwick told David.

"Incredible!" David said, and then grew serious when a thought entered his mind, "Finwick? Did you hear about the King?"

"No, what happened?"

"He was kidnapped," David told him.

"No!" Finwick's eyes widened. Although clearly angry, he kept his voice lowered for secrecy. "I must return then!"

"No, you have to finish your work here. The Queen and the King's son are still there. There is nothing you can do at this point. I believe the kidnappings are only part of something bigger. We'll need all the information we can get," David calmed him.

"You're right." Finwick nodded. "How do you know so much? Why are you on this ship?"

"My sister and I were parted at the border crossing. We came to find our father, who was a helper to our King. We believe he was kidnapped like the others," David explained.

"How do you plan to find him and set him free?" Finwick questioned.

"Would you believe me if I told you the prince of Mizcriea is helping us?" David smirked.

Finwick remained silent for a moment before asking, "What's your name?"

"David, sir." He smiled.

Finwick looked up in determination, and a righteous fire

burned behind his eyes. "David, I am going to help you escape." He stood up straight. "As well as every other slave on this wicked ship."

FOURTEEN

It had only been two days since David was taken away, and Alaina struggled to sleep. She lay on her back by the fire that Koen started not long ago. They'd ridden late into the night because they wanted to cover as much ground as possible to escape the border crossing. She had to admit, it was weird traveling only with Koen. They found ways to pass the time joyfully by playing games and telling stories from their childhood. Koen was trying his hardest to keep Alaina's mood up. She enjoyed his company and the ability to get to know him more. She loved seeing someone become their best self. Since Alaina saw all sides of a person upon meeting them, she rarely got to know the growth someone experienced. Alaina wondered if there were other things to discover about her gift.

She stared at the stars, lost in deep thought, when Koen rolled over to face her. "Still can't sleep?"

Alaina rolled onto her side. "Yeah, sleep doesn't seem too welcoming tonight either."

"Have you been praying for him?" Koen asked.

Alaina smiled slightly, "Nonstop."

"Then I'm sure he'll be alright," Koen said, then looked up at the sky.

"As much as I wish it worked like that, it doesn't," Alaina said as she intertwined her hands atop her stomach.

"What do you mean?" Koen asked with genuine curiosity.

"Well, God doesn't always give you the answer you want; sometimes it's the opposite. Whatever it is, though, it must be his will," Alaina said.

"Then why pray for something if your request doesn't matter? I mean, if it has to be his will, then maybe he will go against your request? Isn't he going to do what he wants, whether you ask or not?" Koen asked, confused.

"Good questions, Koen. The best way I can explain it is that we pray as an act of faith. We can ask for what we hope, but God only does what he wills. If what we want aligns with what he wants, then that usually means your answer is what you asked for. When we bring our problems before God, we must recognize that we cannot change a situation without Him. Yet, we are also to pray, believing he hears us. We are given the gift of prayer to talk to God and go to Him whenever we need Him. We are given the gift to ask him and pray to him. Our hearts must always want his will, and if they do, then you will be glad no matter what answer he gives. He always knows better than we do."

Alaina watched Koen's expressions illuminated by the flicker of the fire to see if he was understanding. He was, so she went on, "In the Bible, it says in Romans 8:28, that 'we know that for those who love God all things work together for good, for those who are called according to his purpose.' The good he promises is good in his sight, though maybe not always in ours. But in the end, it is all for our good and his glory," Alaina said.

She hoped her words were clear for Koen. She, too, struggled with trusting in God's promises, because sometimes, it seemed like nothing was happening.

"Oh," was all he said in return. Alaina was sure what she

said would give him enough to ponder for the night; she did not complain about his short answer.

There was silence for the rest of the night, so Alaina drifted in and out of sleep. Once morning came, Alaina watched as the sun slowly brightened the sky. Just before she decided to lay her head down one last time, she heard something not far from their campsite.

She froze and listened. There it was again. Gradually, she could hear the sound a little better. It sounded like horses. Something, or someone, was moving their way. Then, she heard a faint voice. "Koen," Alaina crawled over to him and nudged him. "Koen, wake up."

Koen rolled over and rubbed his eyes. "What, what is it?"

"Someone is coming our way," she said, pointing in the direction of the sound.

Koen sat up and listened for himself. "Okay, they're too close to pack everything up and leave before they hear us. It doesn't sound like many of them, so we'll just have to prepare to defend ourselves if we need to. Just act like simple travelers," Koen said, crawling out from under his blanket.

"I'll get the breakfast things," Alaina said. She ran over to her saddlebags and pulled out a pan. Koen started a fire, and together, they cooked and waited for the strangers to reach them.

Koen stared into the woods and then looked at Alaina. "It almost sounds like . . . " Koen was interrupted by the sound of a child's scream.

"Oh, hon, you're fine. It won't kill you," a woman's voice replied, sounding somewhat annoyed.

"It's just a lizard," a man's voice said. "It wants to be friends."

"Get it off!" the child screamed.

"There, it's gone," the woman said as they walked through the trees.

"Oh, why, hello there!" the man said, smiling and waving. "Hope you don't mind if we pass through here." The man was short and slim, with a pointy nose and a chiseled jaw.

"Oh, not at all," Koen replied. They'd decided Alaina wouldn't speak unless necessary, since her accent would draw suspicion.

"Say, you look very familiar," the woman said while staring at Koen.

"I get that a lot," Koen laughed and glanced knowingly at Alaina. She had probably seen him before; he was the prince.

"Right," the woman smiled, but kept a suspicious eye on him.

"Where might you young travelers be off to?" The man looked from Alaina to Koen.

"We're headed north . . . to see family," Koen said.

"How wonderful! We are headed northwest. This is my family. My wife." He pointed to the rather plump woman beside him. "My daughter. " He motioned to the little girl, who no doubt was the child who had screamed. She had brown hair, like her father, and green eyes, like her mother. "And my son." He pointed toward a boy a few years older than the girl.

Alaina hadn't noticed the boy behind his father, mainly since he hadn't spoken. She subtly tilted her head to see him and was immediately stunned.

Nothing.

Alaina could not read anything about the boy. She couldn't see anything about him with her gift. Had it stopped working?

She looked at the wife and read her. No, it was still working. Why couldn't she read the boy? She asked the father, "What's your son's name?"

The father replied, "Lucas."

When Lucas heard his name, Alaina looked into his eyes. She smiled and held his gaze for a few seconds before he slowly returned her smile. He had hazel eyes and dark brown hair and looked surprisingly different from the rest of his family. His face was young and kind.

"Well, it was wonderful meeting you, but we must be going," the father said, motioning for them to move forward.

Alaina and Koen watched as they made their way out of the campsite. As Lucas passed by Alaina, he glanced at her, then at his family, and then back at her. He smiled, touched his forehead with his index and middle finger, then reached out and touched Alaina in the same way on the same spot on her forehead. When Alaina gave him a questioning glance, Lucas nodded and smiled. He turned forward and followed his family.

"That was weird," Koen said. He squinted and tilted his head. "Did you see anything in the boy?"

"I'm not sure," Alaina began to think. She couldn't figure out what the touch to the forehead meant.

"What was that forehead thing all about? It was almost as if he was trying to tell you something," Koen observed.

"I think he was, but I am not sure what." Alaina watched the group ride off before telling Koen, "Koen, I couldn't read Lucas."

"What do you mean?" Koen faced her.

"I couldn't read him! It was almost as if I didn't have the gift. I do, though. I could read the rest of his family and you without any problems, but Lucas was blank!" Alaina explained to him while trying not to lose it. "What does that mean?"

"Well, maybe there is an exception to your gift, and Lucas is that exception."

"I have never experienced that before. My grandmother never mentioned that my father had an exception. I don't get it," Alaina said, shaking her head in disbelief.

"Well, what do you want to do about it?" Koen asked.

"Nothing now," Alaina sighed.

"Well, we know where they're headed if we want to find them," Koen smiled.

"Then let's get going," Alaina said as she threw her saddle on Ophelia. "Oh, and Koen?"

"Yeah?" He looked back over his shoulder.

"Nice explanation earlier. 'Headed north to see *family*,'" Alaina laughed as she repeated his words.

"It's a good explanation, is it not?" Koen laughed with her.

"It is. We'll have to continue using that if we're asked again," Alaina said in amusement.

"Right. We should reach the next town before dark, which will allow us to stay in an inn for the night," Koen said as he ducked under a hanging branch. "As long as we don't run into trouble."

"Great, I could use a clean-up, and not to mention, I've been missing an actual bed," Alaina laughed.

"Me too," Koen said. Alaina prayed that today would be one of significant progress. She wanted to reach their destination as soon as possible to see if David had made it yet. Although the timing was in God's hands, it was still hard to wait.

The next few hours of silence gave her time to think about

Lucas, her brother, the quest, Koen, and how everything would play out. What exactly would she say if she found her father? Would he be happy to see her and David? Would he be the man their grandmother had always told them about? Alaina groaned in frustration, which earned her a weird look from Koen. She waved it off.

There were numerous things to worry about, and many things had to go right. This made her wish even more that her brother was here. He always seemed to have good advice on these things.

The rest of the ride was smooth, and as Alaina had prayed for, they had no trouble. The terrain slowly became sandier, which, according to Koen, meant they were nearing the desert. He said they may have to travel into the dunes if there is no other way out of the town. Either way, going through this town was the fastest option. This quest would definitely compensate for her lack of travel in her younger years.

As they rode, she tried to coax Koen into talking more about his past. She noticed that he did not readily share about his up-bringing. Because of her gift, Alaina could see things in him that were evidence of the past he had. She could tell he was hurting. He tried to deflect challenging situations with humor because it distracted him. He also had a desire to prove to people he was capable. These things and more she could see, but his past she couldn't. She wondered if she could see people's pasts and, if so, whether she would judge them more harshly.

Her grandmother told her, when she was young, that her father used to change himself to appeal to the different people he read. She warned Alaina against falling into the same trap of doing the same thing.

Alaina sometimes feared she was never her own person. Maybe she changed herself because of the people she read. What if she wasn't living to be the person God had created her to be?

Alaina thought deeper still. *Was she created with this gift for that reason? Was she supposed to only be the sum of those she came in contact with?* She used her ability on so many, but never on herself. *What would she see if she did use it?* Alaina wasn't sure she would ever find the answers to her questions, or if she was able, or if she would ever want to.

"Alaina?" Koen's voice made her jump.

"Huh?" Alaina blinked and refocused on the present world around her. She had been so immersed in her thoughts that she wasn't entirely sure where they were.

"You, okay?" Koen laughed. "You looked like you were worried."

"Oh, yeah, just deep in thought, I guess," Alaina said.

"Yeah, I've had a lot of time for deep thinking, too. You know what, Alaina?" Koen asked.

"What?" Alaina tilted her head.

"I hope we find your father and that he's everything you hoped he would be," Koen said with genuine care.

Alaina thanked him with a gentle smile. "Thank you, Koen. That really means a lot."

That night, they arrived in town later than they planned due to a wrong turn. Because they were exhausted from a long day of travel, they checked into the first inn they saw. Alaina told Koen goodnight and collapsed into bed.

The next morning, Alaina felt like she'd been run over by a cart from exhaustion. Her eyes struggled to open, and even though she couldn't see her hair, she was sure it was a complete mess. The room's darkness made her want to go back to sleep. "I've got to get out of here." She sat up, grabbed her things, and shut the door on her way out. She looked left and right down the hall, trying to remember which direction led to the front room.

"You go *right*, my dear," a short woman, who Alaina guessed was the maid, told her.

"Thank you," Alaina nodded and headed right. She followed the hall while she scanned the walls. The cracks in the wall, along with the peeling wallpaper and paint, showed her that the inn was aged. Despite its old age, it was inviting and comfortable. She silently thanked God it hadn't caved in on them in her sleep.

After following the unusually long hallway to the end, she took a left and found the front room. She saw Koen talking to another man, who seemed to be in deep conversation. Alaina decided not to interrupt and accepted a cup of tea from the innkeeper. She found a nearby chair that creaked as she sat on it. From its looks, the chair was just as old as the inn. The room was warm, and the front room held several chairs and tables to the left. To the right was the desk where Koen and Alaina had checked in the previous night. Behind the small desk was a door that led into what Alaina guessed was the kitchen. The people there seemed to keep to themselves for the most part.

Alaina was surprised Koen was so deep in conversation.

The man Koen was talking to was likely giving Koen directions.

Koen finished the conversation with a "thank you" and a handshake. His gaze then drifted around the room until he saw Alaina. When he did, he smiled and made his way across the room to her.

"Good morning," Koen said and took the seat beside her.

"Good morning. How early did you wake up?" Alaina asked.

"Before light. Even though I was exhausted, I couldn't seem to sleep towards the morning hours. It worked out, though. I met a man who was able to give me an idea of which direction we should be heading from here," Koen said while staring somewhere behind her. "It's frustrating not knowing where I am. I've never traveled this part of Mizcriea. I usually travel more through the East side."

"Interesting," Alaina nodded, amused. "What did he say?" Alaina took a sip of her tea.

"He said we should head toward the desert. That's the fastest way from this point," Koen said.

"How much faster is it going through the desert instead of around?" Alaina asked, not liking the idea of traveling through the dunes.

"Going around the desert can easily take a week, if not more. We could encounter all kinds of trouble in the towns and forests. Going through the desert usually takes three days." He thought for a moment. "Traveling through sand will be no easy task, but it will be undoubtedly safer than going through the towns of Mizcriea."

"Three days? I suppose even if we were to run into trouble

as far as our rations go, we could still make it out fine," Alaina thought aloud.

"Exactly," Koen agreed.

"So, when do we leave?" Alaina asked.

"Today. If you're up for it, that is. We'll need to fill our canteens with water and store more food, then we can be on our way," Koen said.

"Whatever gets us where we need to go faster," Alaina said.

After paying the innkeeper, Koen and Alaina went around the back to where their horses were kept. She noticed no one in the town smiled. Everyone seemed to be missing two crucial things: hope and true joy. Even their children followed their parents with dragging feet.

"Are all your people like this?" Alaina asked Koen.

"When an evil tyrant of a King rules you, then you tend to lose all hope. Those who hate my father, the King, live for the present, devoid of hope for the future. Those who love the King tend to be just like him."

Alaina's heart broke for the people there. She wished she could spend more time in each town, speaking the truth and showing them that there is a joy worth putting hope in. Since they were on a mission, she prayed over the town as they rode through the streets.

They both filled their cans with water until they felt there was enough. Then, they restocked their saddlebags with fresh food and treated the horses with grain from one of the stores.

Before heading out, they sat under the shade of a nearby tree to eat. The fresh fruit melted on their tongues; Alaina was thankful they could find some spare change. An apple never tasted so good, and Alaina was sure her horse couldn't agree more. Despite the people's overall mood in the town, Alaina still found joy in her heart and appreciated the warm air, the tree, the apple, and her companion. Their horses added to the moment's beauty, and she couldn't help but be thankful.

"Truly, the Lord is good."

"I admire that about you," Koen said suddenly.

"Admire what?" Alaina asked.

"How positive you can be about your faith despite what you've been through," Koen said.

Alaina smiled. "The bigger question is, how can my God be faithful in His goodness and promises despite what I've done?"

When Koen's expression showed bewilderment, Alaina went on, "God gave the first people He created on this earth a command, they disobeyed, and committed the first sin. Since then, sin has entered the world, corrupting many hearts and minds. We sin against God every single day, even though the laws He has given us are for our own good. We sin because it is in our nature, and without God, we are doomed to an eternity in Hell. However, since Christ died for our sins, we can be saved from our corruption and forgiven by God."

"So we sin, but how can you stay so faithful to your God when terrible things happen to you and others all the time?" Koen asked with curiosity.

"Koen, bad things happen because there are bad people in the world, not because our God is bad. And good things happen only because our God is good."

"Amazing." Koen blinked. "I'll definitely ponder that for the next few days in the desert," he said, and they both laughed.

"I'm not sure I want to leave the shade of this tree." Alaina rested her head against the bark.

“It’s almost better than the inn’s beds last night, huh?” Koen said.

“Oh, it’s *definitely* better.” Alaina laughed.

245

FIFTEEN

Dry. Evil. Boring.

If Alaina could read the desert, she was sure those would be the things she would see. They were a few hours into traveling through the desert, and Alaina already felt as if it had been days since her last sip of water. The sun beat down on them, and the sand blew in the wind, causing the air to feel rough and dry. Their horses licked their lips in thirst. *It's going to be a miserable three days*, Alaina thought. She had to remember that it would soon be over and she would be closer to finding her brother and father.

Koen seemed to be holding up okay. Before heading out, they had purchased head wraps to protect themselves from the sun and the sand. They hadn't talked much, if at all, since they'd decided it would keep them less thirsty. Even though Alaina had grown to dislike the desert, she couldn't help but marvel at how the dunes constantly changed shape.

The more the wind blew, the more one changed and another formed. They looked so soft from afar and had a beauty like no other. Alaina found out that the golden sand was indeed as soft as it looked, so smooth that her feet slipped beneath it as she walked beside her horse. They needed to give their horses a break from carrying them on their back through the silky sand.

She looked up at her saddle, and her eyes fell on the small tent they had purchased. In the desert, they couldn't depend on trees, branches, or wood to protect them from the sun. If they slept on the sand without covering, they may end up buried in it when they awoke. On this thought, Koen said they needed a tent, but unfortunately, between them, they couldn't afford more than one. So, they settled for one and hoped things would work out. Koen had offered to take shifts, but Alaina said it wasn't worth the risk, and it would be wiser to sleep with heads and feet on opposite sides. This situation made her wonder what would have happened if David had still been with them. They might've had to take that risk, which was just another unforeseen thing God had planned perfectly.

"Should we stop for a break?" Koen turned around to ask.

Alaina pulled her head wrap from her mouth. "Yes, please." So they stopped and unpacked their food and water. They first gave their horses water and vegetables and then proceeded to nourish themselves.

"Wow, I never realized how juicy fruit could be until now," Koen laughed as he chewed on his food.

"I couldn't agree more." Alaina closed her eyes and savored the flavor on her tongue. The sweetness seemed to give her body more energy almost instantly.

"Crazy, isn't it?" Koen said.

"What?" Alaina looked over at him.

"How did we end up in this moment? From how we met in the forest, and now, we're here in a desert, surviving on fruit?" Koen laughed a little.

"Yeah. God sure has a crazy plan," Alaina said.

"Yeah." Koen just smiled and took out his canteen of water. After taking a sip, he held it out for Alaina, and she took a long drink. With water being scarce, she didn't mind sharing.

"I know we just sat down, but we should keep going."

"Yes, we should," Koen agreed.

So, they began again. As the last few hours of the day came closer, the wind grew stronger and the night colder. Pretty soon, they would have to set up their tent and hope it would protect them as they slept. Without trees to tie up the horses, Alaina worried they might wander off during the night, but it seemed the horses were just as exhausted as they were. When Alaina took her saddle off, Ophelia lay down in the sand. "Looks like we won't have to worry about that problem," Alaina laughed. She and Koen managed to make the one tent livable, and before she fell asleep, she prayed for safety during the night.

The next morning, the sand made its way into the tent, and when Alaina sat up, she saw that the sand covered most of her blanket. Her mouth was dry, and Alaina felt as if she hadn't opened her eyes in days. She shook sand from her hair and wiped her face with her sleeve. "Koen?" Her words barely made it out of her throat before she coughed. She tried again. "Koen?"

Koen sat up on the opposite side of her and rubbed his eyes. He groaned when he realized he was rubbing sand into them. He tried his sleeve, which worked better. Once his eyes opened, he looked around. "Wow," he coughed. "Good thing we only slept for a few hours."

"We should get going," Alaina said, and the two of them crawled out of the tent. The horses were standing, but the sand reached up to their knees. "What a good girl, Ophelia." Alaina walked up and rubbed her horse's forehead. Wayne had also stayed by the tent during the night, and for that, Alaina was thankful. She looked out at the desert, which seemed to stretch on forever, and thought of her brother. When she saw him again, she had to tell him she'd crossed a desert for him. The thought made her laugh.

"What's so funny?" Koen peeked over the back of Wayne.

"Nothing." Alaina shook her head and continued to saddle her horse with a new sense of hope.

Pretty soon, they were headed toward their destination once again.

SIXTEEN

"All hands on deck!" the captain shouted from above the slaves' sleeping quarters.

"Time to get up, lad," Jamie nudged David.

"Yeah, I heard him," David groaned and rolled onto his other side.

"Well, I suppose you can just lie there. I'm sure the captain will be fine and dandy about yer stayin' down here," Jamie laughed.

David heard Jamie stand up. "You really think so?" David flipped onto his back and smiled up at the large man.

"Come on, kid." Jamie rolled his eyes and headed for the stairs.

With another groan from his aching muscles, David followed the rest of the slaves up the stairs. When they stepped onto the upper deck, the light momentarily blinded David. He squinted and walked in the direction he walked every morning since he'd become a slave. Every time he walked to the head-count line, he ended up in the same spot in the lineup. Jamie would end up beside him and would count silently along with Finwick as though it were a song to him. David admired how Jamie could bring light to a rather dark circumstance.

Although the morning routine was the same, the day would not be the same.

"One, two, three . . . " Jamie whispered, and David slightly shook his head, amused.

"You're going to get caught," David said loud enough for only Jamie to hear.

"For counting?" Jamie held back a laugh.

He seemed more joyful today, and David knew exactly why. Today was the day Finwick, David, and Jamie planned to escape. It was the day they would reach land, and during that moment, all the slaves would be off the boat and on land, and David would initiate the attack.

"So, the captain will order all the men in a line off the ship and onto land. You all will be led to the town square. You'll have to wait for my signal to begin the escape," Finwick had told them earlier below deck.

"I see," David nodded in thought. "Will the townspeople fight against us?"

"No. They will worry too much about their goods and run to protect them," Finwick answered.

"I think it'd be best to keep this plan between us three, in case of betrayal. That way, the men willing to fight will act immediately, and we won't run the risk of being found out," Jamie chimed in.

David could only pray that it would work out as planned— or better. He longed to get back to his sister and know that she was well. He believed Koen would take care of her, but there were many things Koen couldn't control, and that's what worried David.

"Thirty-two." Finwick counted David, made eye contact, and then reported to the captain.

"Very good, sir." The captain nodded at Finwick. "Now, listen up!" The captain spoke with an authority that captured all ears. "Today, we reach the docks, and I expect no trouble." He looked into the eyes of every slave. "You will go where you're commanded, in an orderly fashion. Is that understood?"

"Yes, sir," all the men said at once.

"Mr. P!" the captain called out.

"Sir?" Mr. P said.

"I want men below deck and men above deck. I want the ship spotless and without a trace that we used this ship," the captain ordered.

"Yes, sir," Mr. P responded and turned toward the men. "You heard the captain, up and at 'em! I want half of you on deck and half of you below deck mopping the floors!"

David had a sudden thought. "Jamie, what's the captain's story?"

"Aye, ol' Cap was a knight for the king of Mizcriea. He served in the army from a young age. I heard his mother died one day while he was out at sea, and after that, he requested his position be transferred to something that allowed him to stay at sea," Jamie whispered to David.

"Why did he ask to stay at sea after that?" David asked.

"I'm not sure, but they say he was too heartbroken to face the rest of his family, and so he used the sea as an escape," Jamie told him and glanced over at the captain.

David nodded, wondering if the captain's callousness and cruelty stemmed from his heavy heart. His story says he had a heart, one that was loyal to its kingdom and family, but his present character proved otherwise. He put his thoughts in the back of his mind and followed Jamie to where the captain had ordered them.

David and Jamie stuck together to clean the top deck. They

started with scrubbing the deck on their hands and knees. "I want to be able to see the land as soon as possible," David told Jamie.

"Same here, mate. The sooner we see land, the sooner I can leave this wicked ship," Jamie said.

David tilted his head. "Wicked? I think I can understand why, but what makes you use that word?"

Jamie sat up onto his knees, "First off, we're slaves. The way we were all captured and the way we're kept has got to be against the Lord's good design. Second, all the crew members' private lives are God-forsaken. All, that is, except Finwick. Not to mention, this is a Mizcriean ship! The kingdom this ship works for will no doubt one day fall under holy judgment, it will!" David could tell that if Jamie kept talking, he might punch the closest thing to him. Unfortunately, the closest thing to him was David.

"I see," David said in a calm tone, hoping Jamie would cool off. Jamie just grunted and scrubbed the floorboards harder.

Soon, they made their way over to a broom and a mop. "I'll get the broom and sweep the dust while you just follow me with the mop. That way it's a little faster," David suggested.

"I like your way of thinking." Jamie laughed and followed through with David's inventive idea.

Even though David's idea made the job faster, it still took quite a while to mop and sweep the whole top deck. He'd give anything to clean a couple of horse stalls right about now and would much prefer the horse smell over the fish smell that continued to linger. Even when they had finished, the land was still out of view, and they were assigned to scrub barnacles. While scrubbing a stubborn barnacle, David heard one of the crew members say they were less than an hour out from the first sight of land. That would mean they had about two hours until they reached land. David took a deep breath and kept scrubbing.

Every second seemed like a minute, and every minute seemed like an hour until finally, David's eyes witnessed the true meaning of love at first sight. He could see the outline of the town, which was surrounded by forest, with mountains on the horizon.

"All hands on deck!" The captain called out.

All the men scrambled to the top deck like chickens for their morning feed. The crew members shouted with joy, while the slaves maintained their composure, though David could see they were relieved to see land.

The captain ordered the slaves to stand to the side of the deck while the crew members took over the ship. They prepared for landing and readied the cargo for unloading. While David and the others stood by and waited, Jamie suggested that they pray. They did and even managed to have some other men join in. It was a relatively quick prayer, but meaningful. Pretty soon, they came upon the shore, or as Jamie had whispered to David, "the land of faith."

David turned to give Jamie a weird look. "Of faith?" His face told Jamie he didn't exactly agree.

"I'd like to call it 'land of faith.' Everything we plan on doing as soon as we're off this ship will be done out of pure faith. We can only trust that God will deliver us," Jamie told him.

"Oh," David nodded. "Right, and we must also have faith enough to trust him even if it doesn't look good," David said as he watched the land grow before his eyes.

"Amen, mate," Jamie said.

Soon, they had made it into the docking area. While the crew members aboard readied the ship for takeoff, men on the docks below tied the ship down.

"Finwick!" The captain called the man who, ironically, had been instructed to ensure that none of the slaves escaped the boat.

"Aye, sir?" Finwick called back.

"Drop the anchor!" the captain ordered.

"Aye aye, Captain!" Finwick rushed over to the anchor and, with ease, lowered it into the water below.

"I sure don't mind resting, but I've never felt more useless in my life," Jamie said, slightly joking.

"I was about to say the same thing," David agreed as he and Jamie stood with the other slaves. They watched and waited while the crew did all the labor for once.

Then the order came, as if they had waited a century to hear it. "Alright, everyone off the ship! Mr. P, lead them down!"

"Aye, sir!" Mr. P answered. "You heard the captain, move along. First, you'll eat, then unload the ship. The captain wants all the ship's belongings in there." He pointed to a large wagon on the docks below them.

Jamie and David made their way to the middle of the group and followed Mr. P down the ramp onto the docks. The sun beat down on them from above, making them drip with sweat in their thick clothing. They were brought to the edge of the docks, and each given a bowl with rice and fish inside.

Suddenly, a man shot to his feet and took off in desperation. Before he reached land, though, a crewmate caught up and shoved him into the water. David's eyes went wide, and he looked at Jamie.

"Take this as a warning, men!" the captain called out. "There will be no escape!"

"Aye, I applaud him for courage," Jamie said.

If David were a crew member, he'd find the idea of shoving him into the water quite clever. However, in his situation, it was cruel.

The fish and rice not only tasted bad but also gave off a rotten stench. He prayed that they were safe to eat. David and the others were quickly growing tired of the taste and smell of fish.

As he sat and ate his meal, David watched the crew members laugh and joke with one another. He looked at the men sitting beside him. Each one had torn clothes that were barely hanging on, and each of them looked exhausted. Not only were their clothes worn, but they were as well. Their skin was burned from hours in the sun, and they were all malnourished. Their eyes were sunken in, at least the ones he knew had been there the longest. David hadn't been aboard long enough to experience all that they had experienced. *How did it ever come to this?* he thought to himself. *Since when did we start holding one person's life more important than another's? When did we decide that some men would be slaves to other men and treated as animals?*

David couldn't fathom how these men standing before him treated human beings this way. After all, wasn't each of them created in God's image? The fall of man had never been more evident to David than it was those few days aboard the ship.

Once all the men had finished their meals and placed their bowls in a large bucket that was passed, they were led onto the ship once more. There was a strange feeling in the air as they boarded again. By the weary look of the slaves, David was sure the rest of the men felt the tension. It was as though the men were afraid they would be stuck on board the ship. None of the men had any desire to step back on the ship. Yet, they had no choice. They boarded and unloaded everything the crew had left for them.

Thankfully, it did not take long. A sigh of relief escaped the lips of every man when they were officially going into town.

"I want two lines formed behind the wagon! I want Wilmar and Eric armed, and on both sides of the slaves!" the captain ordered his crew members.

David, Jamie, Mr. P, and the others formed two lines behind the wagon. Two crewmen then came along and tied each of the slaves' wrists together.

When it was David's turn, he looked around for Finwick but was unable to spot him. David thought of how the shackles would make their plan more difficult, but he knew it wouldn't stop them from getting free. They started towards town one step at a time.

David looked around at the men beside him. Each, including himself, was covered with dust and dirt. David quickly found that wiping his hands on his trousers only made things worse. Their clothes matched the dirt below their feet, and David was sure he was unrecognizable even to a family member's eye. Walking behind the wagon had quickly become a problem and an annoyance for the slaves, but of course, the crew members didn't care at all.

As they grew nearer to the coastal town, David observed people as they walked and talked. They were completely oblivious to the men headed their way. David observed the towns-people and was surprised to find that most of them seemed to be wealthy, as the town seemed to be of a higher social class. Their clothing was made with fine linen, and their architecture was more advanced than anything David had seen in Azgalia.

"Make way! Make way!" a crew member shouted. The people then realized the large group of men was heading their way. Mothers hurried their children away from the slaves, while others stayed to watch with curiosity.

As they walked through the town, David had never felt so low in his life. He was no more valuable to the people around him than an animal. They looked at them with either greed or disgust. The very thought of that made David's heart break, yet at the same time, filled it with righteous anger.

"Alright, men, get these slaves on their knees. I want them on the platform behind me," the captain ordered.

The platform looked as though they had taken a large chunk out of a ship's deck and raised it with stilts beneath. The wood was dark, and it creaked beneath the men's feet. It had wheels on the sides, which David assumed they used for moving the platform.

David grunted as he fell to his knees on the platform beside the other slaves. Those who followed orders fell to their knees. Those who were more reluctant were shoved or kicked down by a crew member. Pretty soon, they were in line and on their knees. It was back to the headcount like on the ship.

He watched the captain adjust his hat, force a smile on his face, and walk to the front of the platform. "Hello, good people! Today, I present you with a strong and well-equipped group. You will have no problem finding a good worker among these men. Now, shall we start?" the captain said. He then turned and motioned for someone.

David looked over to where the captain was looking and saw Finwick. Where had he been? The captain whispered in Finwick's ear and walked off the platform.

Finwick turned to the townspeople. "Each man is up for bidding, so call your offer as you wish." He turned and signaled for a slave to be brought forth. A man named Adam was brought to the front beside Finwick.

"David," Jamie leaned over and whispered, "What is he doing? I thought we were all escaping?"

"I'm not exactly sure, but he said to be ready," David assured him, although Jamie still looked a bit doubtful.

"Bids start at a pound!" Finwick said to the crowd. The crowd began to murmur amongst themselves.

"Two!" a man shouted amongst the noise.

"I'll bid four!" another countered.

"Six!" someone called out. The rest of the people didn't seem to want to go any higher until one man emerged from the crowd to stand in front of the people.

"I'll bid one hundred; actually, I'll bid seven thousand pounds. Wait, no, I want to go higher than that!" the man said proudly with a grin.

The people looked at him, astonished and bewildered. They were all whispering to each other in confusion. What kind of man in his right mind would bid that high on a slave?

David looked at Jamie with a confused look and shrugged.

"Who are you? What do you want?" The captain stepped forward.

"My name is Christopher, and I am here for some hard-working men," Christopher said with an unwavering stance. He had deep brown eyes and sandy blonde hair. His facial structure was defined, and his presence radiated courage. "You see, most of you may be surprised that I would bid so high for what you call a 'slave.'" He turned toward the crowd. "I, however, believe you can never go high enough to pay what a life is worth."

"What is your point?" the captain growled. He was growing impatient.

Right before Christopher answered, David stole a glance at Finwick and saw something; he was smiling.

"My point is, you shouldn't be trading men like cattle. Humankind belongs only to God, and I am here to set them free." Christopher looked over at the line of men, including David.

"By yourself?" The captain gave a hearty laugh.

"He's not alone." Finwick unsheathed his sword and, in a swift swing, cut the ropes that held the tied-up slave. He helped him up and stepped in front of the man as if to protect him. "Sir, you imprison men who do no wrong. You take men from their families so they can slave away here for other families. You mistreat them; their food is less than the least generous, yet you expect perfection in their work and behavior. They are not pigs; they are people. Same as you and I. So, if it is all the same to you, I would very much like to resign."

"I have to say, Finwick, I am a bit surprised," the captain said with disappointment. "But as good as you may be, you will not be able to set the slaves free."

The crowd had grown deathly silent as they watched the scene unfold before them.

"Don't be so quick to assume you know all, sir," Finwick smirked. Suddenly, men started pouring out of the crowd towards the deck where the captain stood. They ran with swords, their minds set on one mission: to set the captives free.

Swords began to bang and clang against the men from the crowd and the crewmates of the ship.

"God bless you, Finwick!" Jamie shouted in joy, but fortunately, their guard was too busy in combat to beat Jamie for his words.

Finwick was able to overtake the captain and tie him up, just as he had done to the slaves. David and Jamie were untied somewhere in the chaos, so they set to helping untie the other enslaved men. Some ran off, while most stayed to help fight the crew members.

David's heart was beating so hard he thought he might be able to hear it. The adrenaline rush was unlike anything he had ever felt before. He was good with the sword but couldn't recall that he'd ever been in a fight where his life was on the line. For a split second, he took in the entire scene and sent a prayer to God for protection. He thought of the Apostle Paul and how much he had endured for the sake of Christ. David hoped the Lord would use him and these circumstances to advance His kingdom.

At this point, some angry men from the village jumped into the fight against the enslaved men. Soon, the majority overtook the crew members, and the last couple escaped back toward the boat docks.

There was an erupting cheer of victory among the men. David and Jamie embraced each other with brotherly love. "You did good, lad." Jamie patted him on the back.

"Not so bad yourself," David laughed. He then looked around for Finwick and saw him standing by Christopher.

"Come on," David motioned for Jamie to follow.

"David!" Finwick said when he noticed him walking his way.

"Finwick, you had me worried for a second. I couldn't find you, and then you showed up on the deck to sell us off! I knew you hadn't changed your mind, but your plan was up for question. That is, until Christopher showed up!" David said and smiled at Christopher.

"I already had a plan that night you and I talked on the boat," Finwick smiled. "Now, David, please meet my friend Christopher. He and I met one day when the ship docked for more supplies. I came into town, and Christopher noticed my tattoo when my sleeve slipped down. He approached me about it, and we quickly became allies. He used to live in Azgalia, but now works here in secret," Finwick explained.

"Very nice to meet you, David," Christopher said, shaking David's hand. He was a kind man, and David already liked him. He didn't need Alaina to know he was a Godly man.

"Thank you, sir." Jamie thanked him by placing a hand on Christopher's shoulder.

"I live alone most of the time to avoid being discovered. I do a lot of underground work, sneaking around and doing quiet tasks. So, when Finwick here asked me to speak up about something, I was thrilled! It was about time I spoke aloud. So, thank you!" Christopher smiled

"No, Christopher, you must understand . . . " It looked as if tears were welling in Jamie's eyes. "You've undoubtedly changed the course of my life." Jamie shook Christopher's hand, but Christopher pulled him in for an embrace. When they let go, everyone exchanged knowing glances.

"So now what?" David looked at the three men beside him. "Where do we go now?"

"Well, some men who wish to go home to Azgalia will take the ship with me. With the Mizcriean flag, we should be safe to sail. For those who wish to go home in Mizcriea, or those who have a mission," Finwick winked at David, "they can continue with Christopher."

"And where are you headed?" Jamie asked Christopher.

"There is a camp in the forest. It is placed toward the center of Mizcriea so that all those who go have an equal way home. The best part is, it's Christian-based. They welcome all those who aren't enemies, hoping you'll either leave a Christian or leave having heard the truth," Christopher said.

"Sounds like I'll be going with you then," David told Christopher. "From there, I can go to the King's city and find my sister—Lord willing."

"Great! This will be quite an adventure. I assume you're up to it, though?" Christopher asked David.

"Absolutely," David nodded.

"Well, I'll be going with my mate David here. I need to be a part of this quest of his and make sure he has some fun along the way." Jamie wrapped an arm around David's neck.

Finwick announced the plans to the rest of the men. Most of the men headed back to the ship because many longed to go home.

"Sorry to have to part after just connecting, but I'm sure the Lord will have us cross paths again." Finwick shook hands with Jamie, David, and Christopher before leaving.

"I understand. It was an honor to meet you. I hope to connect again one day soon." David smiled and shook his hand firmly.

"I will continue to pray for your quest and that you find your father," Finwick said. He then turned to Christopher and said, "And you, thank you for your friendship. See you soon." Finwick and Christopher embraced before he said goodbye to Jamie and walked off.

"The Lord is truly good," Christopher said.

"Indeed," David and Jamie said together.

SEVENTEEN

The townspeople weren't too fond of the now-free men who escaped the slave trade. Families retreated inside, locked their doors, and hid their children behind their backs.

David couldn't blame them, though. He and the rest of them all looked the way they felt—enslaved, exhausted, hungry, and in desperate need of a bath. He imagined they appeared quite scary to the people. Not to mention, the men among them who were Azgalian were not welcomed into Mizcriea and would be arrested once someone found out. Christopher reminded them to keep their gaze fixed forward so they could reach the outskirts of town quicker.

"How are you holding up, my friend?" Christopher came up beside David.

"As well as can be expected, I suppose." David managed a smile.

"That's how the rest of the men seem to be. I've seen how the slave ships run, so I can understand your weariness," Christopher said. "Don't worry, though. I know where each of you can get rest for the night."

David looked up in surprise. It was almost as if he had read his mind! "Who will have us?"

"Well, you know, of course, I'd let you all stay at my home; however, there is just not enough room. I do know an elderly merchant who lives on the very corner of this town. His house lies right along the tree line that leads into the forest. We became friends one day when he found me sneaking around a young girl who had escaped slavery. I hid her under the baskets while I went to retrieve her food. When he found us, he immediately told me not to run and that he knew of my 'rescue missions' long before that day. From then on, he'd help protect me from guards and hide people for me when needed. He works closely with the faithful camp we plan to attend. So, in the morning, we'll slide through his back door and escape into the woods," Christopher said, then smiled widely. "Isn't God good?"

"Yes, He is." David nodded and smiled back.

After walking another mile or so through the town and avoiding eye contact with most people, they finally arrived at the elderly merchant's house. It was a two-story house that David could tell had once been a beautiful home. It seemed the man had let it go. David knew that if Alaina were here, she'd disagree. She'd say it looked even more beautiful this way, with the vines growing around the house, and the bushes so overgrown they couldn't stand upright. Because the plants were so lush, they provided many flowers to marvel at. The paint on the house's walls was old and chipped. Alaina would have said it gave it character. Still, with all the things that could be called wrong, there was at least a walkway to the door. David guessed that this was the only part of the greenery the man had chosen to trim.

"What's the owner's name?" David heard Jamie ask Christopher.

"His name is John," Christopher said.

As they walked to the front door, the bushes rubbed their

legs. "Why doesn't he trim the plants?" David asked Christopher.

"Because I don't see why we should cut back life. It should be able to grow, but with direction, of course! Which is why, as you see, the plants have not grown into the street, but rather back to my house or into the forest!" a man said, whom David assumed was John.

"That sounds like a good enough reason to me," David smiled and held out his hand for John to shake.

"Indeed, young man." John grasped David's hand firmly in his old and withered one. "What is your name, boy?" he asked in a Mizcriean accent.

"David, sir," he replied.

"What a mighty name!" John exclaimed.

"I could say the same for you," David said.

"Christopher," John peered around David to see his friend. "I like him already! Now, please come in, all of you!" He motioned for them to follow, and they did.

The inside of the house was nothing like the outside. It was clean and orderly. The shelves were filled with handmade pots, vases, and kitchen tools. It also seemed smaller than it appeared on the outside. Off to the left of the main room was a slightly open door through which David could see another room, most likely John's sleeping quarters. To his right was the desk where people would pay for their merchandise. There didn't seem to be much else, yet David was sure there was more. Where was the back door that Christopher had mentioned? Where did John hide people?

"Is it just me, or does it seem rather on the small side here?" Jamie said as he moved next to David.

"That's what I was thinking," David said as he looked around.

"Do you really think I'd have my hiding rooms out in the open and easy to find? That's ridiculous! No, no, no! Come, look at this." John hobbled as best he could, on what seemed to be a bad leg, behind the desk. He reached down and pulled out a key. He then hobbled over to the door of his room.

David looked up at Jamie and raised his eyebrows with a shrug.

Instead of going to his door, as everyone in the room anticipated, he stopped near the wall beside it. There was a picture frame holding a picture of a door decorated with brightly colored flowers and plants.

"Hidden in plain sight is what I like to call it," John said smugly, reaching under the picture frame for a very small notch. It was just big enough to slip a fingernail in. With his finger, he pulled out a handle. Everyone in the room was excited about what the hidden handle would reveal. John unlocked the handle with the key he held, and a door appeared in the wall almost as if by magic. They could make out a very faint outline upon looking closer.

Before he pulled the door open, he looked at the group of men with a humorous grin. David could tell this was one of his favorite things to do. He wouldn't be surprised if John let people hide here just to show them the hidden door. David didn't blame him; it was quite fascinating.

"Right this way, boys," John said as he opened the door without a creak.

Behind the door, David saw a large room with light, yellow walls. In the far-right corner, beds were stacked on top of each other. A large round table was near the center of the room, a few desks with flowers, and rugs were spread out in various places across the floor. It seemed more like an expensive inn than a hiding room. The colors were calming and made a person feel safe, so David could see why these things were chosen.

"Now, you see," John started as the men around him marveled at the room, "I've had many people stay in this room for days because it was unsafe to leave. Sometimes I have people coming in and out of the shop all day, making it impossible for those in hiding to come out. So, I made these rooms comfortable enough to stay in for days." John said this proudly but with a humble spirit.

"Wait, you said rooms?" Jamie asked.

"Indeed! Right over here." John walked back over to where the door was, but stopped a few feet from it and to the left. He used his foot to move aside a rug before bending down to pull up a hidden shaft. "This was hidden as well, so if soldiers found this room, people could go down here to hide." After pulling up the shaft, John walked down the steps inside. The other men followed with much curiosity. At the bottom of the stairs lay another room. This one was not as large but just as, if not more, important.

"I decided to add a kitchen for those who stayed. Most of those who had to hide for more than a couple of days would not have eaten were it not for the kitchen here," John explained.

As David looked around the room, he saw that John had spared no expense here either. He had wanted the best for people, and a question popped up in David's mind for the first time. The thought suddenly worried him, and he felt he needed to talk to Christopher about it as soon as the tour was over.

After they finished admiring the kitchen, they returned to the hidden room. The men helped unstack the beds from the corner, so they were ready for the night. Some would have to share beds because there wasn't enough for all.

"Now, is there anything else I can get you men?" John asked before leaving the hidden room.

"Is there food down in the kitchen right now?" one man asked.

"Why, of course! Help yourselves! Clean me out! The food will go bad soon anyway, so I must get rid of it somehow." John laughed and disappeared into his shop.

As David helped prepare the room for their night's stay, he couldn't find peace until he had an answer to his question. So, as soon as the last bed was ready, he found Christopher and asked him to talk to him alone.

"Of course. Shall we talk outside?" Christopher suggested.

"That would be good," David nodded, and they headed out to the plant-filled yard. They found a bench among the plants that gave them enough room to sit comfortably.

"What's on your mind, my friend?" Christopher asked.

"Well, seeing you, meeting Jamie and John, you all show strong faith in Christ. Also, hearing about the faithful camp, I just couldn't help but wonder, what's there in my country? Do we have people going and sharing the truth? Caring for those in need? Protecting the faithful?"

"I understand your worry and admire your caring for your country." Christopher smiled. "David, do you know how Jamie, John, and I found the truth? Besides God's mercy, of course."

"I . . . I don't," David said.

"Azgalians! Your country may not be faithful, but your people come from faithful origins. Your King made it known that the country's beliefs and rules are based on God's Word. Of course, there are still missionaries in your own country to reach those who still have not received eternal life, but there is no need for a protection camp. This country persecutes Christians; your country welcomes them." Christopher put a hand on David's shoulder. "Having a country like Azgalia at your back is a blessing."

"It's strange, though," David said in deep thought.

"What do you mean?" Christopher asked.

"If Azgalia is full of the faithful, and we supposedly have a faithful country at our backs, then why isn't more of Mizcriea saved? Why aren't there more over here?" David asked.

"That is a good question. As sad as it is, many faithful individuals choose to remain comfortable in their homes, rather than face the truth. Those around them also know the truth, so they stay together and remain naive to the wickedness that crosses borders. Many do come. That's why I have been able to do the work I do. That's why there is hope for the faithful here. Though, I agree with you, when you say there should be so much more," Christopher said.

"With a nod of agreement and disappointment, David said, "Comfortable is exactly how I'd describe the townspeople where I grew up." David looked at Christopher.

"What's even more heartbreaking is that some claim to know the truth only because it is the social norm. However, we must also consider the positive aspects. We must have faith that the Lord will work things out for the good of His kingdom because He will," Christopher said.

"I know it." David nodded. "Thank you for talking with me. It helped, and I think I've found a new mission."

"I will be praying for you, David," Christopher said.

♕

The next morning, David awoke to a strange ceiling and a soft bed. It felt like forever since he'd slept in a bed, and since the few days on the ship had felt like weeks, he was thankful to have had a good night's rest. As David sat up slowly, he looked around to see some men still asleep and some men missing. No doubt they were already eating breakfast. He continued to observe the room from the viewpoint of his bed and noticed a Bible lying on a desk. He got up out of bed and walked over to the Bible. He picked it up and brought it back to the bed to read. He'd left his Bible in his horse's saddlebag. Unsure of what he should read, he flipped it open to a chapter in Psalms to start reading.

After a few moments, a man from the kitchen below peeked his head up from the stairs. "David," he whispered.

"Yes?" David looked up.

"You want some food?" the man, whose name David had forgotten, asked.

"Very much!" David whispered as loudly as he could. So, from the other side of the room, the man tossed a loaf of bread to David. Even though it surprised him, David managed to catch the loaf.

"There's more down here," the man said and returned to the kitchen.

David eyed the loaf of bread in his hand, and after deciding it looked fine, he took a bite.

After finishing the bread and reading another few chapters of Psalms, the rest of the men started to awaken. Some men groaned as they sat up, while others quietly stood and headed straight for the kitchen. It was quite entertaining.

"When are we heading out?" a man asked Christopher as he walked through the hidden door. David hadn't even realized he hadn't been in the room.

"We'll head out at noon," Christopher said, and all the men nodded a silent response. "Mind you, most of you have slept until the eleventh hour." And immediately, all the men stood up and rushed to the kitchen. Christopher chuckled and turned toward David. "Have you eaten?"

"I've already had two kinds of daily bread, but I suppose I'll have a little more," David said, following the rest of the men down.

Later, after they had eaten and packed their things, all the men met back in the hidden room. John showed them yet another secret door that led outside. This was the "back door" that refugees used to escape, and it would also be the door that the men would use.

"This door leads straight to the forest. The guards know nothing about it, and my outside plants give enough cover that they will never see you," John explained.

"It is the perfect escape, John," Christopher told him. "We couldn't be more grateful for your hospitality."

"Only by God's grace." John smiled. "Now, you boys be safe! And be sure to tell my brother hello for me when you get there," John said.

David looked at Jamie with a questioning glance. "I heard he has a brother at the camp we're headed for," Jamie whispered.

"Oh," David nodded. After the men thanked John, they watched him return to the shop.

On his way, he turned and patted David on the shoulder, "May the Lord be with you, son," and continued.

"Alright, men! Let's move out!" Christopher said.

EIGHTEEN

"My name is Evelyn, and I am looking for my father. My name is Evelyn, and I am looking for my father. My name is Evelyn, and I am looking for my father." She hoped she wouldn't lose her sanity if she repeated it enough.

It had been a day or so now since Evelyn crossed over the border into Mizcriea. She'd safely made it over by taking the "secret crossing" way. Her father had his knights watch over the border for months in different areas to pick the perfect spot to cross secretly at the right time. Evelyn used the knowledge she had gained to do so herself. It worked. Thankfully, her horse remained calm while crossing the river, and no one saw or heard them.

As Evelyn looked around, she thought it would be wise to keep her mind focused on positive thoughts. She had heard stories of travelers who would lose their minds while traveling alone for long periods. Since Evelyn didn't know how long she would be alone, she thought it would be safe to take precautions.

"My name is Evelyn, and I am looking for my father."

She looked around and named the types of trees around her in her head. She loved nature and science when she was young, and could name the type of almost any tree. It helped in this situation as well. Everything around her was unfamiliar, but knowing the trees made it more familiar. Was she scared? Absolutely. Was she about to let that stop her? Absolutely not.

A tree branch brushed up against her and made her jump, which made her horse sidestep a little.

"Yep, definitely scared," she laughed nervously. As if someone might make fun of her, she looked around slightly. The forest seemed to go on forever in every direction. The sun shone through occasionally when it found a break in the leaves. The hooves of her horse quietly crunched the leaves and branches beneath. It was a calm yet terrifying feeling altogether.

The farther she got from home, the more she realized she may never get back. As doubt crept its way into her thoughts, she started to pray.

"Lord, protect me on this journey. Lord, if you're willing, help me find my father." She paused and thought for a moment, "And I don't know if I need it, but I would really like some help finding my way through the forest." And as if someone had heard her, she looked around at her surroundings. Nothing. She breathed a sigh of relief.

As the next hours passed, she decided to put more thought into the disappearances. The first one happened about a year before she was born. The most recent was her father. It seemed like her father was the last piece of a puzzle they had been assembling. The way Mizcriea was, though—it seemed like something they'd be behind. If all else failed and she never found her father, she promised herself she wouldn't leave Mizcriean ground without answers. "I promise," she said.

"This way!" A voice shouted from far off to the side, which made Evelyn jump and her horse spook.

"Oh no." She started to panic slightly. "No, no. Stop, Evelyn." She needed to calm herself down, especially if she wanted to stay alive.

"Aye, what do ya make of the Azgalian news?" a man's voice asked, this time closer.

"About their King? I say we celebrate tonight. No doubt King Cleatus already is," the other man said in a jolly tone.

That made Evelyn sick. The news had spread. Azgalia would quickly become an unprotected land in the eyes of Mizcrieans citizens. Evelyn could only pray that her brother Gavin was prepared.

As the men approached closer, Evelyn couldn't decide what to do. She could fight, but Evelyn knew two men against one woman weren't the best odds. She could just gallop away. "They'd hear us, though," Evelyn said under her breath. Plus, her horse might be too tired to outrun the men's horses. She thought of hiding, but there was no hiding a horse behind trees.

"But I can hide." Evelyn looked at her horse. "Please don't leave me," she said as she dismounted and let the reins fall to the ground. She ran to a nearby tree surrounded in brush and hid.

Slowly, the men came into sight. "Aye, I bet it was King Cleatus himself who kidnapped the Azgalian King," one said.

"I wouldn't be surprised," the other said with a chuckle.

"Eh, you do see that horse, too?"

Evelyn could see them better now. One was short and slender, and the other was tall and broad. Both were aged and looked experienced. She was glad she hadn't chosen to stay and fight.

"Yeah, I see it," the tall one said and looked around.

"I bet he left his owner somewhere all alone," the short one laughed.

"If that's true, the horse left his owner to die," the tall one said, and Evelyn's eyes widened in fear.

They made their way closer to Evelyn's horse. When her horse finally noticed the strange men, she lifted her head, and her ears perked forward.

"I'll go," the short one said. He slowly inched toward the horse while hiding behind his own. While the two horses exchanged greetings, he snatched the reins.

Evelyn watched as he looked over her horse and wished she could do something. Oh, how she loved that horse.

"Aye, now that's interesting," the man said.

"What?" the tall one asked.

"This be an Azgalian horse." The short one looked over at the tall one. "Should we be scared or joyous?"

"Check the saddlebags," the tall one said. So, the short man looked in the saddlebags and pulled out one of Evelyn's skirts.

"It's a lady's horse." The short one smirked.

"Then we have nothing to worry about. Take the horse, and let's keep moving."

Evelyn almost shouted out to stop them, but there was no doubt it would only end badly for her. So, she watched the short man tie her horse to his, then ride out of sight.

A tear ran down her cheek as it suddenly hit her. She was alone. She looked around the forest, and everything seemed bigger and louder than before. Before doubts started to creep in deeper, she looked up to see a ray of sunshine peeking through a tree. She decided she wouldn't give up. She would walk and pray that the Lord would protect her. "Now would be a great time for help," she said. Then she looked forward in the direction the men had gone. She took a deep breath and walked on.

About an hour passed before she heard another voice in the distance. She caught her breath and listened closely. Had the men come back to look for her? Maybe she could find a way to get her horse back. She listened.

Yelling. A whip. A cry.

"What on earth?" Evelyn turned in the direction of the sounds. Slowly, she made her way near a larger tree and watched until she could make something out.

Two horses pulling a caged wagon came into sight. She could see the coachman urging the horses on, but he wasn't the one holding the whip. She could see a man standing up, and he was the one with the whip. What was he doing?

Another cry.

"No." Evelyn's heart sank. "No." Her nose began to burn, and a tear fell down her face. "God, please help me." She shook her head as though it would stop the wagon from coming closer. The man standing was whipping people. Slaves. It was a Mizcriean slave wagon. Evelyn knew she was the perfect capture for them. She quickly looked around and bolted without giving it a second thought. Her feet hit the ground as fast as she could get them to go. The trees around her blurred, and the breeze on her face whisked away her tears. Her breathing quickened, and her heart raced to keep up with the sudden burst of movement. All this she ignored, hoping to escape the slave wagon.

When she believed she had gone far enough, she sank behind yet another tree and tried to still her breath. In and out, she breathed, trying to be as quiet and still as possible.

She told herself she would have to wait until the following day, where she was, just to have peace of mind that the slave wagon wouldn't find her.

"Ha, gotcha!" A deep voice rang loudly in her ear, and she was yanked from her hiding spot before she could fight back.

"No! Please, No!" Evelyn cried. "Help me! Help, please!" she cried louder, hoping someone would hear her.

"Thought you could get away, didn't ya?" the man snarled. He had tanned skin and had dark features. He wore a pointy hat with a black mustache hanging off the corners of his mouth. He wrapped his arms around her as she kicked and tried to break free, but to no avail. He grunted as he dragged her to the wagon, where other captured women looked through the cage at her.

"Please no!" Evelyn continued to try to fight.

"A feisty one, aren't ya?" the man said with a disturbing chuckle. Once they arrived at the back of the wagon, he threw her to the ground.

Evelyn hit the ground hard, and pain jolted through her body. She groaned, and her body folded as she tried to escape the pain in her abdomen.

"Now then, you have two options, Azgalian." Evelyn wondered how he'd known. "You can run off from here, but keep in mind, I have a bow and arrow. Or, you can climb into the wagon." The man looked down his nose at Evelyn.

How sick, Evelyn thought. He either lets people commit suicide or, out of their own will, chooses to climb into the wagon, thereby making them a slave. She had heard of the treatment of Azgalian slaves in Mizcriea. She sat up just an inch more to peer into the woods.

"Yes, yes, take your time." Evelyn could basically hear the man smirk.

She couldn't run. She would be hit and surely die in the forest. She would have to climb in. She wasn't sure how she would escape. "God, please help me," she whispered, crying for help, and then looked up at the man. She glared at him as she rose to her feet. The man only chuckled all the more, knowing he'd won. Slowly, Evelyn crawled into the wagon and found a place beside another woman.

"Come on, Alaric!" the coachman called out to the man, and Alaric went to join the coachman at the front of the wagon.

As the slave wagon started on its way again, Evelyn looked around at the women in the wagon.

"Does anyone know where we are going?" Evelyn asked the people. All but one person stayed silent.

"We are to be auctioned off in the next city," a younger girl said.

"Do you know how far away that is from here?" Evelyn asked her, and the girl just shook her head. Evelyn thought for a moment. Her knife! She still had her knife in her boot! She looked over at the cage gate and saw that it was fastened with a rope. It was not tied, but instead had a lock on the end. This is why no one could untie the rope and escape. Evelyn thought they would likely be afraid of being pierced with an arrow even if they did. The rope could be cut, though. She would just need to handle the bow and arrow problem.

She looked out at the man named Alaric and saw that he had a bow and arrow on him. While keeping her eyes on Alaric, Evelyn leaned closer to the young girl and asked, "Does he ever put the bow and arrow down?"

"Only when they have to relieve themselves," the young girl said, and Evelyn nodded.

"What's your name?" Evelyn asked her.

"Lily, Miss. You?" Lily looked up at Evelyn.

"My name is Evelyn." Evelyn smiled. "Lily, I have an idea." Evleyn leaned in closer so she could whisper in her ear. "I have a knife in my boot. I will move closer to the cage gate and start cutting the rope. So, the next time they stop to relieve themselves, we will escape."

Lily looked at her wide-eyed, "What if they don't stop to relieve themselves before the city?"

"We just have to pray they do," Evelyn said while eyeing Alaric.

Lily looked shocked. "Are you Azgalian?"

Evelyn looked at her. "I am actually the princess of Azgalia," Evelyn told her.

Lily's eyes widened. "Princess?" she whispered rather loudly, drawing the attention of the other women in the wagon.

"Princess of Azgalia?" a woman next to her sneered.

Evelyn was surprised at their response. "What do you have against princesses?"

"Not princesses," another woman chimed in. "Azgalians." The woman gave Evelyn an awful look.

"Oh, I see." Evelyn nodded in disbelief. These women had been captured by their very own people, and yet, they still choose to hate Azgalian people who have done away with slavery.

"Whether you like me or not, I know you all want to escape. Well, I have a plan to do so. Are you with me or not?" Evelyn kept her voice down, but loud enough for the women to hear her. The rest of the women, including Lily, looked around at each other, as if to contemplate whether they would choose slavery over making a deal with an Azgalian.

"Fine, we're in. But as soon as we escape, you're on your own," the woman beside her told her.

"Agreed," Evelyn nodded.

As the plan made its way to each woman, they discreetly made room for Evelyn to move closer to the cage gate. Once she was up against the rope, she worked the knife out of her boot while another woman blocked the view from the coachman and Alaric. Thankfully, they hadn't noticed a thing. She managed to get the boot out and put it behind her back. She felt for the rope as she faced forward, and when she found it, she started to cut. Now, all he could do was pray and cut as fast as she could.

The bumpy forest floor didn't help at all. With each bump, it threw her hand off course of their cutting. She tried to continue to focus and not give up. Then, suddenly, a sharp pain shot through her finger, and it took everything in her not to gasp aloud in pain. She removed her hands from behind her back, and sure enough, she had cut herself. The woman beside her saw that she had been cut and took the knife from her. Evelyn looked over at the woman, surprised.

"Let me do it," she whispered, and Evelyn thanked her with a nod. Slowly, she scooted over so she could reach the rope.

"Please, Lord," she whispered a prayer.

Finally, after what felt like an eternity, the rope was cut. It was now time to wait. Evelyn looked over at Lily and nodded to let her know the rope had been cut. Lily nodded and spread the word.

"Hey!" Alaric yelled, and everyone froze. "Don't any of you move!" he told them, and Evelyn could feel her heartbeat speed up. "Stop the wagon," he told the coachman.

"What for, Alaric?" the coachman asked him with annoyance.

"You'll see." Alaric turned his head toward the slaves with an evil smirk. Would he search them? Had he overheard a whisper? Evelyn felt as though her heart would jump out of her chest now.

The coachman slowed the wagon to a halt, and Alaric jumped out. "Don't any of you move now." Alaric scanned the wagon with his eyes. "I'll be right back."

"Alaric, again? Really?" The coachman was clearly annoyed.

"When nature calls!" Alaric laughed. "Man, you should see your faces! Scared for your lives!" Alaric laughed at the slaves, which only infuriated Evelyn. Thankfully, though, Alaric set the bow and arrow on the wagon and walked off to relieve himself.

This was it. Lily made eye contact with Evelyn, and they both nodded together.

Evelyn quickly, but carefully, removed the rope from the gate and pushed it out while the coachman was distracted fixing his boot strap. Evelyn let the woman beside her get out first, for hers and another woman's job was to grab the coachman, along with the bow and arrow. As the first woman climbed out, the gate had to be opened just a tad more so she could fit through. That's when the gate squeaked. The coachman's head whirled around, and his eyes grew wide. "No!" He yelled out.

They would need to move fast now. "Go, go!" Evelyn urged the women out. The women reached him first, while the coachman struggled to grip the bow and arrow. Evelyn jumped out of the wagon cage and held the gate wide open for everyone to escape. Some ran off, and some stayed.

Evelyn looked around, worried, until she finally saw Lily pulling at a lady's arm at the gate.

"It's okay, mama, it's safe. Come out, mama," Lily said.

"Lily, is that your mother?" Evelyn asked, and Lily nodded.

"What's her name?" Evelyn asked.

"Rose," Lily told her.

"Rose," Evelyn said the name with a smile. "Rose, please come out. It's safe, and you and your daughter are free now." Evelyn tried to encourage her, too. Rose looked up at Evelyn with fearful eyes, but Evelyn met them with a look she hoped told Rose she could trust her. Rose slowly stood up, following her daughter out of the wagon's cage. Once she was out, she turned to Evelyn and gave her a small smile.

"Hey! What's going on?" Alaric had made his way back to the wagon.

When the women heard him, they gathered together to create a wall. Unmoved, they stood their ground and taunted him to overtake them. One of the women had the bow and arrow in hand.

"Whoa, whoa, whoa, come on now, ladies! I'll let you all go, it's all good! We're good, right?" Alaric said, laughing nervously while raising his hands.

None of the women took Alaric's word for it, because the next thing Evelyn knew, they had Alaric in the back of the wagon with the gate shut.

Evelyn made eye contact with Rose, Lily's mother, and made her way over to her. "Rose, I know I am considered your enemy, but for today, can we be allies? Do you know which way the King's Castle is?"

Rose stared at Evelyn for about a full minute before she slightly nodded. She raised her hand and pointed in a direction Evelyn guessed was North. "It is that way," Rose told her.

"Thank you so much!" Evelyn smiled at her.

"Give her a horse, please!" Lily begged one of the women, and to Evelyn's surprise, a woman reluctantly untied a horse from pulling the wagon and gave it to Evelyn.

"Alright, now go. We had an agreement," said the woman who had sneered at her.

"I'm leaving now," Evelyn said while she turned her horse to leave.

"Thank you!" Rose suddenly called out.

Evelyn turned to look at her and smiled, "You're welcome."

♔

She'd lost her horse, been captured as a slave, and escaped, all in the same day.

Evelyn was determined to complete the mission she'd set for herself. She'd considered returning home a few times but was too stubborn to let herself quit. So, she continued through the woods in the way she hoped was a town. She needed rest, food, and new clothes. Evelyn was sure that her own mother wouldn't recognize her in her current condition.

Keep moving.

Repeatedly, she'd say that to herself so she wouldn't slip off the back of the horse. She could only pray that Rose told her the truth. With her weakness and only a small knife to protect her, Evelyn wasn't sure she could survive another "bump in the road."

By now, she would've been so close to the castle, but she had no idea where they'd gone after being captured.

"God, please give me the strength to walk until I find help. Please let me get through this so I can find my father," she said in a cracking voice. Her nose stung, and her eyes threatened to let tears loose, but she wouldn't let them. "Keep going."

She looked ahead at what seemed to be miles of forest. In the back of her mind, she knew she could not make it. Her face was scratched, and blood was coming from somewhere on her forehead. She had too many bug bites to count, and her legs were bruised and bleeding. She hadn't bathed since the river crossing, so she was covered in dust and dirt. She couldn't imagine what her hair must look like.

"What does it matter, though? There's no one around to see." She looked around, "No one."

Suddenly, her stomach cramped, and her head felt light. She slipped off the back of her horse and stumbled over to a tree to stable herself. "No. No. No." She shook her head and squeezed her eyes shut. "I have to keep going." She tried to push away from the tree but collapsed onto the ground instead. The world was spinning, and her limbs wouldn't budge. *This is it*, she thought. She had tried.

"Lord, protect my family." She squeezed her eyes again, and the world went dark.

David hadn't traveled on foot in a long time. He was fit and determined, but it was undoubtedly hard. He'd always preferred horseback—he and his horse taking things on together. Although now that David thought about it, he didn't travel much at all before this quest he and his sister had set out on.

"How are you holding up?" Jamie came up beside him. From what Jamie told him, he had traveled quite a bit before being captured. It was his job to transport goods.

"Doing alright," David said. "The fact that we're going to a secret Christian camp in the middle of Mizcriea makes this all the more exciting." David smiled.

"I was thinking the same thing," Jamie laughed. "Hey, Chris!"

"Yes?" Christopher called back.

"They have somewhere to bathe there, right?" Jamie asked, and all the men laughed.

"They sure do," Christopher laughed.

"Praise the Lord!" one of the men, who was named George, said.

David smiled and turned to Jamie, "What's his story?"

"His story is pretty amazing," Jamie said. "George had been a pastor of a small church in Azgalia until a few years ago. After retiring, his family died in a fire, so he became angry at God and ran away. Mizcrieans then captured him, and he became a prisoner. George repented to God and started preaching to the Mizcrieans that held him hostage, and in return, they cut off part of his tongue."

"His tongue?" David's eyes widened.

"Yeah. They were tired of losing their guards to him," Jamie said. "Although, he eventually learned how to say and form certain words. Plus, they didn't realize he could write, too."

"Really? Wow," David shook his head in astonishment.

"On board the ship, he remained reserved and obviously didn't speak. So, I never approached him, which I regret now," Jamie said. "While you were outside with Christopher, John asked George his story too, and George wrote it all out for us."

"Amazing," David marveled.

"Sure is," Jamie said. "So, tell me, did you and your crew have a plan once you reached the castle?"

David hesitated. "Well, we had part of a plan, I suppose. We were still working on it. I wanted it to be planned, but Koen wanted to leave room for last-minute changes."

"Koen? Is that the other guy traveling with your sister?" Jamie asked.

"Yes. I still can't believe I let us get separated. There was nothing I could do, though." David shook his head at the thought.

"Why'd you let him come along again?"

"He's originally from Mizcriea," David said.

"Oh, that's right." Jamie nodded.

"And more specifically, he is the younger prince of Mizcriea." David glanced at Jamie's face to see his expression.

"Wow. You don't say." Jamie lifted his eyebrows. "I understand your worry." Jamie laughed, "But I don't understand how you ever trusted him in the first place."

"I didn't. It was my sister. She has a way of reading people. She can tell everything one would need to know about a person at a single glance. So, when she met Koen, she saw something that I clearly didn't. She's never been wrong, so I had to trust her. Although for the sake of being her protective brother, I was still cautious," David explained. It felt good for him to share his perspective. He never had a close friend besides his sister with whom he could share his thoughts and life experiences.

"And how does he feel about you both being believers? Assuming he isn't one?" Jamie asked.

"He was very tolerant. All he knew about us was what his father had taught him, and his father wasn't exactly someone he admired. He began asking many more questions as we progressed further in our quest. He is more than willing to help us get our father out using his own power in the castle," David said.

"How fascinating." He paused to think. "From what you told me about your sister, she can take care of herself, I'm sure?" Jamie said.

"Definitely. She's better than I with a bow and almost as good with the sword," David said with pride, but inwardly, he hoped Alaina wouldn't need to use her skills.

A few more miles in, the sun was an hour or two away from setting. "Just a bit more, men, and then we'll set up camp for the night!" Christopher told everyone.

David spent most of his time planning their rescue and escape. Repeatedly. He looked up into the trees and studied them. He thought it was convenient that most trees were thick enough to hide behind. A whole army could hide behind these trees; they wouldn't know it until it was too late. That thought gave him a brilliant idea.

"Hey, Jamie . . . " David began to say.

"Wait, what's that?" Jamie investigated the distance.

"What?" David followed his eyes.

"Christopher! I see a horse in the distance," Jamie told him.

Christopher looked in Jamie's direction. "Indeed." He raised his eyebrows. "I don't see a rider. Let's move closer, but ready your weapons."

David and the men nodded in response to the sudden urge to remain silent. He unsheathed his sword and moved forward with the group.

As they moved closer, it became clear that it was a horse. They stopped a few yards away, and Christopher called David to the front. "I hear you're pretty good with your sword?"

"Yes, sir," David said.

"Great. Move with me. Everyone else, stay back and stay alert," Christopher said, motioning for David to follow. "We must be prepared for anything. An ambush is very possible in these parts."

They moved slowly, just in case there were others in the area, and so they wouldn't spook the horse. The closer they got, the more they realized the horse truly was alone and the rider was gone.

"Wolves," Christopher said after observing the horse's wounds. "The horses got away faster, and that's why we couldn't see that they were hurt from a distance. Not too bad, though," he said as he looked it over.

"Odd, isn't it?" David raised his eyebrow.

"What is?" Christopher asked.

"A knife is attached here, but this isn't a regular riding tack. This horse was pulling a wagon," David observed.

"You're right." Christopher walked around to the horse's

other side to observe the knife. "Well, now, that is an interesting find."

"What is it?" David stepped forward.

"This knife is Azgalian," Christopher said.

David's eyes widened, and he moved closer to Christopher. "You're right! That symbol is the same one I saw on the Malikai city flags. What is it doing here?"

"It could have been stolen," Christopher wondered.

"I don't know. I would be more inclined to think this horse was stolen. This is Mizcriean tack, but it is tack for a wagon horse. The rider must have stolen this horse from a wagon. I'm betting they were Azgalian."

"Whether you're right or not, whoever it was must be gone by now." Christopher motioned toward the wound on the horse.

David suddenly felt his stomach turn at the thought of leaving without answers. "Christopher, if there is an Azgalian close by, and dying, I can not do nothing. Can you give me an hour at most to search? If I see nothing, I will return."

"I'll do you one better, David. I say we camp here for the night," Christopher said, and after they returned to the men. "You can head out as soon as someone is taking first watch."

So, they set up camp and tied the injured horse to trees. While David helped set up the fire, he couldn't shake the thought of the horse and its missing rider. *Why? How? What had happened?*

"I don't know why this is bugging me so much."

"What, the bug? I know, it keeps flying in my ear," Jamie said annoyedly.

"No," David said before a bug tried to fly in his own ear. "Well, yes, but that's not what I was talking about. I mean the horse. What if—I don't know—what if the rider is still out there?"

"I don't know, mate. It's a pretty big guess to assume. What about there being wolves and all?" Jamie said.

"Yeah. I was thinking earlier, before we found the horse, how all these trees are thick enough to hide behind," David said.

"And?" Jamie prodded him on.

"And what if they had seen them coming before they reached him or her?" David looked into the trees. "I mean, the horse shows they were traveling. Unless they were moving fast, which they probably weren't, the rider would've seen the wolves before they reached them. Maybe the rider dismounted."

"And hid," Jamie added.

"Exactly," David said.

"It's possible," Jamie nodded. "What do you want to do about it?"

"I'm going to go look around. Not very far, but I at least need to try," David said.

"Sounds good, but be careful, mate," Jamie told him.

"I will." David nodded, got up, and grabbed a horse. He picked up a lantern, mounted, saluted Jamie, and rode off behind the camp. He wasn't exactly sure why he was so set on figuring this mystery out. He had to find his sister and follow their plan, yet he felt he needed to help whoever this rider was. Surely God had His own reasons.

"Probably both," David said aloud.

He rode through the trees looking for any signs that would give him a hint. After a few minutes, he spotted a piece of fabric that had ripped on a branch. He slowed his horse to a stop and dismounted. He picked up the fabric and examined it. It was an expensive fabric, but it had been through a lot. And by the look of the pattern, it looked like Azgalian colors. His eyes focused next on the ground, where he spotted a footprint. Then another, and then they continued. They showed signs of slow movement and heavy steps. Wherever this rider was, David could tell they were in weak condition.

"I must've passed the rider!" David ran back to his horse, and in one fluid movement, he mounted and kicked his horse forward. He moved as fast as he could while watching the ground for hints. He was sad to think of it, but he couldn't imagine the rider's state if wolves had attacked them. They couldn't have gone much further from where he had just been.

"Lord, please," he said under his breath.

And then, he saw her.

NINETEEN

It took everything in Koen not to quit. He hated nothing more than the desert and endless seas of sand. The heat on his back was enough to irritate anyone, but just add sand in the eyes, and you may lose your mind. However, Koen knew how important it was for Alaina to cross this desert, so he kept moving. He tried to tell himself to toughen up like his father would, but how tough can you possibly be? He was already pushing through, hadn't said one complaint, and only grunted when something made him mad. Koen thought he was being pretty tough.

Alaina, though, showed a whole different kind of strength. It was almost as if she were happy to be here. Even when she wasn't smiling and Koen thought she'd given in to frustrations, she'd look up at him and say, "We got this."

Koen wouldn't say it, but it actually helped. Having someone with optimism in a situation that was far from positive helped.

"Is it just me, or does it feel like we've gotten nowhere?" Koen gave a half-laugh.

"It does, but that's just because what's in front looks just like what's behind. You said three days, right? Tomorrow we'll see the end of it," Alaina said, being optimistic as usual.

"Yeah, true," Koen said. He took a deep breath and watched his feet. They'd slide through the sand with every step, then he'd have to pull them back out with a forward motion of his body. After a while, he could feel his legs tiring, his back aching, and his hands cramping from holding his horse. The key was just to watch your feet and keep pretending that the more you paid attention, the easier you could make the stepping process. Then again, you also had to pay attention because one wrong step could send you sliding down a mountain of golden sand. Which, Koen thought, sounded rather fun; he just had no desire to climb back up.

"So, your gift, does it work on animals too?" Koen asked Alaina.

She laughed, "No, but I wish it did! What I would give to know what's on Ophelia's mind!"

"Yes, I was going to say that would be extremely useful," Koen laughed.

"Are there any animals in the desert?" Alaina asked.

"There are, but not many. And they're hard to spot," Koen said.

"Any dangerous ones we should be on the lookout for?" She asked.

"Well, sure, but I don't imagine we'll come across any since we haven't yet. There's a sand-spiked lizard. Those are venomous but mild. There's the white raven; they need to bite anything in sight just to see if they can eat it."

"A white raven?" Alaina raised her eyebrow.

"It's not really a raven; they just call it that. It is white, though," Koen said.

"Wouldn't a white bird be easy to spot?" Alaina asked.

"Well, sure, if you were looking up. How many times have you stared at the sky today?" Koen laughed.

"True," Alaina smiled.

"There are other lizards, but none that are worth worrying about. There are snakes, though. Only two are venomous. One is a tiny snake that preys on insects and smaller lizards. It's no worse than a bee sting if it bites a human. The other is extremely venomous. It's called the serpent of paradise," Koen said.

"Wait, serpent of paradise? That seems rather contradictory," Alaina said.

"Exactly. It's called that because the venom causes you to have hallucinations. Those who've been bitten always claim they've seen some sort of oasis, or, like the name, a paradise. They feel free and overly happy, until they're not. The venom takes only a few hours to consume the body and kill the victim fully."

"That's horrible. What does it look like? Have you ever seen someone who was bitten?" Alaina asked with curiosity.

"It's pretty dull looking and blends in with the sand. I have seen two people who were bitten. One died, and the other barely made it. It was pretty crazy. He went from being super delirious and making those around him laugh to being completely unresponsive. Because it took so long to get the treatment, he ended up with brain damage," Koen explained.

"Wow. Who knew the desert had such a dangerous animal?" Alaina said.

"Well, no one did until someone thought it was a great idea to use the desert as a shortcut," Koen said.

"Well, it seemed pretty smart until now," Alaina shrugged.

"That's what the first guy said, too," Koen laughed and looked back at Alaina, rolling her eyes. This was good. He was laughing. He looked forward at the horizon to see if his eyes would play with him, but just as he did, he realized he needed to keep an eye on his feet.

"How's our water?" Alaina asked.

"We'll need to refill tomorrow when we get out of the desert, but we're good for now. Do you need some?" Koen asked.

"If I could," Alaina said from behind.

"Whoa, boy." Koen halted his horse and reached into the saddle pack to pull out their water sac. "Here ya go."

Alaina took a few sips and wiped her mouth. "Do you want some?"

"Yeah." Koen nodded and took the sack from her to quench his own thirst. "Water never tasted so good." Koen closed his eyes to savor the taste. Alaina shook her head and smiled. "What?"

"I'm just glad I'm not doing this alone," Alaina said.

"Well, of course, you wouldn't have made it out of your hometown without me," Koen said jokingly.

"Are you kidding?" Alaina laughed. "We almost didn't make it out of Norwest city because of you!"

"True." Koen shrugged. "But we did."

Alaina punched his arm. "No thanks to you."

"Ouch," Koen said. They stood for a few seconds, letting their laughter end while they looked around them. Koen was thankful for the compass he brought along. Otherwise, they probably would have become lost.

"We should keep moving," Alaina finally said.

"Right," Koen nodded and shifted his feet carefully toward the direction they were headed. After walking through the sand for several hours, they came to a flatter terrain. Koen was relieved that they were no longer walking on top of sand dunes.

He continued to watch his feet, but the flatter surface allowed him to look up once in a while.

"No white raven," Alaina said from behind.

"No, but the flatter surface is more common for the other animals," Koen told her.

"Wonderful," Alaina said nervously and began watching her feet again. Koen did the same. He looked for any movement and, once in a while, was tricked by sand sliding on its own. In such a barren land, Koen wondered how animals could survive. Life was a strange thing, he thought. He began thinking about Alaina and David's God again, what Max said in Norwest, and what he heard growing up. Koen never had this much time to think before. He had always filled his thoughts with the next step for the moment in time. He never really gave much thought to the future.

"Did you see that?" Alaina said suddenly.

"Huh?" Koen stopped in his step and turned in question.

"I think I saw something." Alaina looked at the ground. Koen followed her gaze to the ground. He searched the sand for any movement or odd pattern.

"You sure it wasn't just the sand? It's been messing with me all day." Koen looked at her.

"Maybe. I thought I did, though," Alaina said, unsure. "I guess we should keep going. Just watch your . . ."

"Ah!" Koen let out a scream in terror. Pain shot up his leg as he crumpled to the ground. It felt as if his leg were on fire, so he reached for it. He saw something move past him out of the corner of his eye. Fast.

"Koen!" Alaina threw the reins of her horse and fell to her knees beside him. "I saw a snake! What should I do?" Koen could barely hear her voice over the pain that he could feel spreading.

"Look at the bite," Koen said through gritted teeth.

"Okay." Alaina nodded and searched for the bite on his leg. "What am I looking for?"

"Is it big?" Koen forced the words out and groaned.

He saw Alaina examine the bite, and as if she had just remembered their recent talk about the big and the little snake, her eyes widened in horror. "Yes, it's big."

Koen squeezed his eyes shut. The pain now covered his entire leg. The serpent of paradise had bitten him. He didn't have long, and they were in a desert. His chances were extremely low. He forced thoughts to form in his head to tell Alaina something.

"Of course this happens to me!" Koen cried out.

"Koen, what do I do?" she said, kneeling beside him, desperate to help.

"In about thirty minutes, I'm going to start hallucinating and become delirious. It will seem like the pain is gone, but it'll actually be worse. My body will be affected by the venom by telling itself I'm fine while ignoring the pain. If I move, the venom will spread faster." Koen took a deep breath and groaned again. His mind was beginning to fog up already. "You need to find help. Anyone you find will be able to point you to a cure. You'll have to leave me here."

"How will I find you again?" Alaina was on the verge of tears.

"Tell whoever you find I'm in the flat terrain. They'll know what to do," Koen said, all this with little hope she'd actually find someone, but they had to try. "Go, Alaina."

Alaina stood up and mounted Ophelia. "Koen, hang in there. Please." She kicked her horse forward, and they were off. Koen let out the loud groan he'd been holding in and let the tears start coming. It stung more and more as it climbed past his leg. Once he felt it in his chest, the hallucinations would start.

He decided to examine the bite for anything odd before he lost himself to the hallucinations. Slowly, he sat up, freezing a few times to gasp in pain. Leaning over a little more, he reached for the end of his pant leg and lifted it. He winced. His leg was swollen, red, and bleeding. For a moment, he thought he saw bubbles, as if his blood was boiling in the heat.

He looked closer. Besides being a nasty bite, a doctor would probably call it clean. The snake must have made the strike and pulled off right away. There were no tears. However, that didn't make it feel any better, and his chances of living were not altered. It was still an impossible situation.

Then it hit him. He could die. He could die right here, all alone, in the desert.

His stomach started to sting, which caused him to yell in pain.

"God, why?" he cried out. He didn't know if he believed in God, yet he was asking why he'd allow him to die like this. Did he believe then?

From what they said, it was a yes or no question. No maybes. Death or life. David told him that one night. In death, you can live in Christ. In life without Christ, you're dead already.

"So what do you think, Koen?" David's voice played in his head. "Death or life?"

Koen squeezed his eyes as a sharp pain struck his chest.

Alaina couldn't hear her horse's breath over the sound of her own. She was slightly panicking, and she knew her horse could feel it. Thankfully, they were in the flatlands now; otherwise, there was no way her horse could keep up with the speed at which she was going.

Alaina could only pray. Over and over again, she prayed. They weren't supposed to reach the end of the desert until tomorrow, which meant the closest town was miles away. By the time she arrived, explained her situation, and hopefully avoided capture for being Azgalian, it would be too late.

"I can't let him die there, God. I can't." Alaina let the first tear fall from her eye, and it caught the wind. Her face was deprived of the feeling of wet tears, so she took that as a sign not to give up yet. She sniffed and fixed determination on her brows. "Come on, girl." She urged her horse towards the horizon.

She squinted against the sun and rubbed her eyes. "What is that?" she said while looking at a black dot on the horizon. "Hopefully something." So, she kept Ophelia galloping toward the black dot. Soon enough, it started to take shape. "Please, Lord, please." She prayed that whatever it was could help her in some way. Time was ticking for Koen. "It's a horse!" she exclaimed as it came into view. Soon, she saw the rider. She kicked Ophelia, hoping there was another boost of speed left in her. "We're so close." Then, they suddenly moved more slowly. "No, no, no." Alaina looked around, confused. They had hit the sand again! "No!"

Alaina looked up to see where the horse and rider were. They weren't facing them, and they were headed away. Alaina tried calling out, but the rider didn't hear. She looked at her horse and knew Ophelia wouldn't make another sprint through the sand without collapsing on the way back.

Alaina dropped the reins. "Stay here," she told her horse. She looked ahead and took a deep breath. "Lord help me, " she said, and she ran.

The sand swallowed her feet with every step, and her heart began pounding not far in. The sun felt hotter than she'd ever felt before, and her lungs, she thought, might just explode. The image of Koen lying on the ground played in her mind to keep her going. She was almost there but lacked the strength to call out. She used her arms for momentum through the slick sand.

Finally, the rider must have heard her breathing because he turned and looked at her. He stopped his horse and pulled down his face covering. His skin was familiar to the sun, his hair was wavy and long, and his eyes were a light, piercing blue.

Alaina stopped where she was and took several heavy breaths before she was able to speak.

"Miss? Are you in need of help?" the rider asked in Mizcriean.

Kindness.

Peace.

Wisdom.

Generosity.

Alaina praised God inwardly. "Azgalian?" Alaina hoped he knew her language.

His eyes showed surprise. "My apologies. Are you in need of help?" he said in her language.

"Yes," she took a breath. "My friend. A serpent of paradise bit him. He doesn't have long," she said in desperation.

"Where is he?" the man asked with worry.

"He's back in the flat lands. I followed a straight path north," Alaina told him. "Can you help me?"

"I do have the cure on me. I can only try," he nodded. "Let us go. He must not have long now." The man reached down for her to take his hand, and without hesitation, she took it and mounted up behind him. They rode as fast as his horse would move through the sand and ended where Ophelia stood faithfully.

Alaina dismounted from the man's horse and mounted onto her own. "Straight ahead." She pointed forward, and the man took off with Ophelia close at his heels. They continued for what seemed like forever, when Koen finally came into view. "There!" she yelled over the sound of the horses. The man nodded and urged his horse faster. Pulling up beside Koen, the two riders dismounted and quickly were by his side.

"Well, hello there, friends," Koen said in a goofy tone. He was in the delirious stage, Alaina thought.

"I hope this helps your friend," the man said with hope. "What is his name?"

"Koen," Alaina said.

"Yup, that's my name. Probably a better name than yours." Koen started laughing. He lay on the ground just as Alaina had left him, but his demeanor was completely different.

"Koen, I need you to drink this," the man held out a cup of what Alaina guessed was the cure.

"Only if Alaina says," he giggled. "I trust her." He gave a not-so-subtle wink, which almost made Alaina laugh.

The man raised his eyebrows. "Alaina?"

"Yes?" Alaina looked up.

"Will you give this to your friend?" He slowly handed the cup to her, and she took it.

Alaina nodded, "Koen, please drink this."

"I'd do anything you ask," Koen laughed while he slurred his words. Alaina carefully lifted his head and held the cup up to his mouth. He took a sip but immediately spit it out. "Whew, that stuff is disgusting!" Koen shook his head and made a sour face.

"Koen, please, you're very sick," Alaina pleaded with him.

Koen rolled his eyes jokingly, "I guess." He shrugged. "Give me some more of that potential poison." He laughed before taking another drink. This time, he finished it. "There, I did it. You proud?" He grinned up at Alaina.

"Yes." Alaina managed a smile. The cure wasn't guaranteed to work, but she prayed it would. "Now what?" She looked up at the man across from her.

"We wait. And we pray," he said.

Alaina looked up at him and smiled, "Will you?" The man nodded, although Alaina saw that he was slightly surprised that she wasn't surprised.

"Of course." He bowed his head and prayed aloud. "Lord, we come before you in this desert land. We have no hope and no control. You are our only hope, and you are in control. Lord, we come before you as your humble servants in desperate need of your intervention for Alaina's friend, Koen. Lord, I pray for healing and restored health. May your will be done. Amen."

"Amen," Koen said in a loud shout. "Whoa."

"What is it?" Alaina saw the change in his expression.

"You know, I'm not feeling too well." He nervously laughed. "Probably that nasty drink you gave me," he joked.

"We don't know until after the slumber," said the man.

"Slumber?" Alaina asked.

"There is a moment when the body either gives up or shuts off function to completely fight off the poison with the help of the cure," the man explained as he looked into her eyes.

"How do you know if he's fighting, or if he's given up?" Alaina asked with worry.

"It takes a full day for the fighting to be complete. Or to find out if he's given up." He lowered his gaze in sympathy.

"A full day? Will we wait here until then?" Alaina asked, confused about what they would do.

"Alaina, dear, I have not introduced myself. My name is Peter. I lead a camp north of here, home to many like you and your friend here—those who seek shelter and safety. We welcome all who God brings our way, but our camp is built and run by the faithful." As Peter explained this, Alaina gave thanks to God. The odds of finding Peter in the desert on this day were only what could be described as divine intervention by God.

"You have no idea what a blessing it is to hear you say that," Alaina said with tears in her eyes.

"I will bring you and your friend back with me. You may stay as long as you need," Peter said.

"Thank you so much." Alaina smiled.

"You knew, didn't you? That I was of the faith?" Peter smiled.

"I did. I—," Alaina hesitated. She sighed and then smiled. "I have what my grandmother called the gift—."

"Say no more, my daughter." His smile widened. "I know

of your gift. Come, let me show you the way." He rose and helped her up.

Koen spoke up."Hey, that's nice to hear you guys are great friends now, but I'm going to nap." His eyes began to flutter closed. "I'm just gonna—," and his eyes closed. His words went silent, and his breathing slowed. Alaina covered her mouth and held back tears.

"He has reached slumber." Peter laid a hand on her shoulder. "Let us go." He reached down, and together, they lifted him onto Koen's horse, who still stood by. Peter led Koen's horse, and Alaina rode beside him on Ophelia.

"Won't it take all day to reach the grasslands?" Alaina questioned.

"That is the beauty of our camp. It is unknown because we are closer than people think. They follow the maps to what they believe are the closest grasslands, when really, our camp lies only an hour west of where you found me." Peter smiled at Alaina's expression.

"Wow!" was all that Alaina could say. She couldn't express the overwhelming feeling of God's goodness. Her friend lay on his horse, yes, but God had provided everything they needed to get through it. She could only give thanks and continue to pray.

The camp finally came into view, and Alaina could only smile. She hadn't seen greenery or color in days and would never take them for granted again.

"This is my home. We've been here for the past eighteen years," Peter told her.

"Eighteen? Have you ever had intruders?" Alaina was surprised to hear they'd been around for so long. Eighteen years ago, her father had been kidnapped.

"We've had our fair share of dangers and intruders; however, God has always kept our place hidden. Most, and it's a very small number, that come to us by accident are people who have run away from something. They look for somewhere to go, and we take them in. They either leave a new man in faith, or they simply promise never to tell a soul," Peter said.

"How can you trust their word?" Alaina asked.

Peter looked at her with wise eyes and smiled, "Just wait and see, my child."

Alaina looked forward to the camp and wondered what God had in store for them there. She then looked back at Koen, and her heart sank. He lay there on his horse, motionless and pale. If she didn't believe Peter, she'd think he was dead. He looked helpless and weak. It definitely wasn't a good sign for Koen to be that way. "Oh, Lord," she prayed.

Soon, they were at the tree line, and she could see people.

"Welcome home, Peter!" the people said with joy.

"Thank you," he smiled. "These are our guests. A serpent of paradise bit the man and needs a room to recover," Peter told them, and so, two of the men stepped forward to lead Koen away into the camp.

Alaina followed close behind, and as she entered further into the camp, she saw more colors and people. It was like a small village! The people were walking, working, playing, talking, but most of all, they were joyful.

"Beautiful, isn't it?" Peter asked.

"It is." She smiled. Their homes were either small huts or tents. It was simple, but they didn't seem to mind.

Alaina watched as Koen was led to a tent, and the two men helped lift him off the horse and into the tent. For some reason, she had a sense of peace and knew he was in good hands.

"This way," Peter motioned for her to follow, so Alaina followed him to another tent that wasn't much further. "This will be yours." She nodded, then thanked the people who held her horse while she dismounted. "Before you settle for the night, I hope to show you something."

"Of course," she said and followed him to the most enormous tent in the village. Before they entered, Peter looked back at her and smiled widely. Alaina smiled back but wondered what could be more exciting than the village itself. As they entered, Alaina was surprised by the size of the tent. There were two large tables in the tent's center and chairs stacked everywhere. A pulpit was at the back of the tent, and a cross hung above it. It was simple, yet beautiful.

"We have our church, studies, and meetings here," Peter said, then turned to someone in the tent. "Charles, will you go get the William family for me?"

"Yes, sir," the man said and walked out. Not long after, he appeared, and the family Peter had called for entered behind him.

Alaina gasped, "Lucas?"

TWENTY

Alaina stared at the child who walked into the tent. It was the same boy from the forest she and Koen had seen! Along with his family!

"Alaina, you know these people?" Peter looked at her.

"Yes, I . . . we . . . " Alaina started, but was finished by the family father.

"Why, yes! We briefly met her and her companion in the forest a few days ago! Nice people. What brings you here?" the man asked Alaina.

"The serpent of paradise bit my friend. Peter helped me bring him here," Alaina said, still shocked.

"Yes, her friend is in critical condition," Peter said, and the room was silent for a few moments. "Alaina, I wanted to introduce you to the Williams family for a special reason." He smiled and looked down at Lucas.

Alaina looked at Lucas, who smiled at her. He waved, and Alaina was reminded she could not read his face. She looked at William's father, "Are you all Azgalian?"

"We aren't, but Lucas is. His biological family was good friends of ours and lived in Azgalia. When they died in a fire, we received word about Lucas. His parents were also friends with Peter and were of the faith. They left instructions that they would want Lucas and any other kids to be sent here if something were to happen. Even though we are not of faith, we consider him family and wish to do as his parents had hoped," the mother explained to Alaina.

"That's incredibly kind of you. May I ask, why though?" Alaina hesitated. "Is there a reason the parents would risk the journey for their son to come here? I mean," she looked at Peter, "there has to be a reason." Alaina hoped she didn't sound rude.

"There certainly is." Peter smiled again. "Lucas here is a lot like you, Alaina." Alaina wondered what he meant. "Lucas has the gift."

Alaina's eyes widened, and she locked eyes with Lucas. That must be it! "That's amazing! I have so many questions!" Alaina couldn't contain her excitement. Lucas smiled widely and stepped forward toward her. Like in the forest, he touched his forehead with his index and middle fingers and reached up to touch Alaina's forehead the same way.

"That's his way of telling you there is a connection," Peter said. "Is Lucas the first you've met?"

"The first? You're saying there's more? I had always thought it was just my father and me." Alaina looked back at Peter.

"You are not the only ones, Alaina, but there are indeed very few of you. And your father, where is he?" Peter tilted his head.

Alaina sighed, "That's a long story."

"I have the time." He turned towards the William family. "Thank you for coming to meet me. You may go now. Lucas, you can stay or join your family for dinner."

The Williams family turned to go, and Lucas followed them after nodding politely to Alaina. Peter then turned to Alaina, "Shall we?" He motioned towards the table and chairs that had been set there. Alaina nodded and sat.

After she finished telling the story of their journey, all the way from when her mother passed when they were children, to now, where they were, she took a deep breath and let out a nervous laugh.

"Yes, that's quite a story." Peter smiled. "Your father has your gift, you said?"

"Yes, that's what my grandmother said," Alaina said.

"Fascinating. Well, my dear, if you ever need anything from me or my camp, I know many of us will help you in a heartbeat—anything to make this terrible thing right. I have been in the presence of the King of Mizcriea before, and he is not a kind man. It's truly amazing that the prince is here now. The Lord sure does work in mysterious ways," Peter said.

"He sure does." Alaina smiled. "And thank you for the offer to help. I hope it doesn't come to that, but he's not a kind and easy man like you said."

"I will be praying for what the Lord will do through you. I have a feeling the Lord has more in store for you and your brother than just rescuing your father," Peter said with wisdom shining in his eyes.

"Thank you. Now, if you don't mind, I think I may need some rest," Alaina said, trying not to sound rude.

"Of course! You know where your tent is?" Alaina nodded. "Wonderful. I will see you in the morning then. May the Lord give you rest."

Alaina made her way out of the main tent and towards her own. On her way, she saw the tent where they had brought Koen. She looked at her tent, then back, and then decided to check on him. She held up the opening to walk through and saw him lying there on a bed. It was more of a cot really, but it made do. She quietly walked to his side, as if she might wake him. Looking down at him, her heart sank. He lay there helpless and pale. His breath was so weak, she had to stare at his chest to see if it'd move. She hadn't known she was holding her breath until she saw her chest rise and fall. "Thank goodness."

"We won't know until tomorrow," a woman said behind her.

Alaina turned around to face her. "I know. I just . . . " she said, looking at Koen again.

"You're worried." The woman nodded and showed sympathy.

"Yes," Alaina said.

"You need to rest. There's nothing you can do right now." And when Alaina still hesitated to leave, the woman said, "I promise to come get you if anything changes."

Alaina looked up. "Thank you." She ducked out of the tent and slowly walked to her own. She watched her feet the whole way, afraid that if she met the eyes of anyone in the camp, the floodgates would open. She sniffed and went into her tent. It wasn't any different than the one Koen was in, except there were flowers on her pillow. They had been picked from the forest, and a note was next to them. Alaina picked it up and read.

Alaina, it was a pleasure to make your acquaintance. It is truly amazing that we cannot read each other! I have only experienced it once before with my sister. She passed away, along with the rest of my family, in my homeland. Alaina, I wanted you to know that even though I cannot read you, I know I would read wonderful things. I pray that we can become friends and that you will be willing to ask for my help whenever you need it. Alaina, whatever brings you to Mizcriea, trust the Lord for your journey. Without Him, we can do nothing. I pray the Lord will help you and supply your needs. Your brother in Christ, Lucas

Alaina blinked tears away from her eyes and sat on her cot to think. He was incredibly wise for his age. She thought about the fact that they couldn't read each other. She wondered if she would be able to read her father. Being too tired to think further about it, she decided to give in and finally fall asleep.

♔

The following day, Alaina awoke to the sound of children playing outside her tent. She could tell the sun was shining because a ray of sunlight shone through her tent opening and right into her eyes. She sat up and brushed her dark hair out of her face. After rubbing her eyes, she stood. "Oh!" She collapsed back onto her bed when her legs went weak. She groaned, "I guess running through sand is a really good exercise." Her legs were sore from the day before, but she had to get up to see Koen. When she finally managed to exit her tent, she stopped to watch the people walking by.

The kids she heard earlier ran by with laughter and squeals. "You can't get me!" one little girl laughed as her friend chased her.

"Kelly, come here and finish your breakfast!" a woman who Alaina assumed was the mother called out after the girl.

"Good morning, miss," a man greeted Alaina as he passed. Alaina nodded back.

"Did you sleep well?" a woman came up to her.

"I did, thank you," Alaina said.

"Wonderful! And are you hungry?" the woman asked.

"Not at the moment, but thank you." Alaina smiled and watched the woman walk away. Alaina marveled at everyone smiling.

"It's the joy of the Lord," a kind voice off to her right said. Alaina turned her head to see Peter.

"It's beautiful. Even many Christians in Azgalia don't show this kind of joy." Alaina looked back at the people as she thought about her hometown.

"These people are taught daily in the Word. They are constantly growing in their faith and learning about God. Sadly, as you have seen, many Christians in Azgalia are simply Christian because their parents were. It's the Kingdom's religion, and so many adopt it, without ever making it their own. Or in most cases, the parents assume that it is good enough if they live by example. This is not the case, as you know. The children must be disciplined and discipled in the truth. Thankfully, though," Peter looked at the people and smiled, "there are still many like this."

"Do you think that Azgalia is getting worse? Do you believe that we are headed toward being more like Mizcriea?" Alaina asked Peter with concern.

"What do you think?" Peter asked.

"My grandmother would talk of a light future. Full of goodness and faith. I'm not sure anymore, though. Maybe she was talking about when we go to Heaven." Alaina thought for a moment, "And after all the things I saw on my journey here, there's so much—," Alaina paused to think of a word.

"Sin?" Peter asked. When Alaina nodded, he smiled, "My dear, there is much sin because we are sinful people. So yes, you will still see it. Yes, maybe the many Christians you have seen aren't filled with the Lord's joy and truth, but the Lord's name is still proclaimed freely in your streets. The very fact that this camp has survived so long shows hope. Alaina, do you believe God is great enough to redeem your sin?"

"Of course," she said.

"And do you believe He is great enough to redeem a whole kingdom and have them follow His word?" Peter continued.

"Yes, of course," Alaina said, but wondered where he was going.

"Alaina, it's all about how you look at it. If you see nothing but death, destruction, sin, and the wrath of God in the Bible, then that is what you will see. However, if you truly look at what the Word says, He is a just God. He is a God of love. He is a God who sent His son to redeem the lost. He is a God who has already defeated the enemy. Do you believe He has?" Peter asked her again.

"I do," Alaina nodded.

"Then you know. He said that He shall make all enemies His footstool. My dear, the Lord always wins in the end. His kingdom is always ruling. We are His soldiers who are called to fight for Him. What kind of soldiers are we if we only see sin and not hope? Remember, we hope in the Lord, for He never changes." Peter smiled.

"Incredible." Alaina smiled and shook her head. "Your words perfectly align with my grandmother's stories. I have so much to learn." Alaina shook her head in amazement.

"And yet you know so much more than I did at your age.

The Lord knows exactly what you know and when you will know more. Be patient with it. Now," Peter gestured towards Koen's tent, "go see your friend."

Alaina's face dropped as she was reminded. She had been so encompassed in the joy of the camp that she had forgotten Koen! How could she? She nodded at Peter and spun on her heels to race to Koens' tent. Someone probably thought she was crazy for running from one tent straight into another, but she didn't care. She needed to be beside her friend and was ashamed she hadn't been there sooner.

Alaina stopped at the tent's opening before going in. She took a deep breath, "Lord, prepare me if I must be prepared." She squeezed her eyes, and once she opened them again, she took a step forward.

"Oof." She ran into something. Or, someone?

"Sorry, there," a deep voice responded.

Alaina's eyes widened, and she brushed the tent out of her face so she could see. "Koen!" She grinned, "You're . . . you're . . ."

"I'm not dead!" Koen finished for her with his hands in the air and smiled as he stepped out of the tent. "Come here," he laughed and hugged her.

Alaina pulled away. "I was sure we were going to lose you." She shook her head. "You were so pale and helpless." Alaina looked at him with sympathy.

"Oh, wow. Yeah, that's usually not a good look for me. Probably best to forget the whole thing," he waved his hand in dismissal.

"Yeah, you're probably right. It was pretty bad," Alaina joked back, then smiled. "I'm so glad you're okay."

"Me too." He smiled. "So, uh, where are we?" He looked around at the people, confused.

"Right! Well, while you were unconscious, Peter took us to this camp. The closest green land was closer than we thought," Alaina explained.

"Strange. I've never heard of a camp here before. It must be close to the castle, though," Koen scratched his head.

"Just a couple of hours away. It's a faithful camp." She watched his expression to see how he reacted.

"Really?" Koen looked back up at the camp as if looking at it for the first time. "How long has it been here?"

"For eighteen years," Alaina said

"Eighteen?" Koen's eyes widened. "That's incredible! And my father never found it?"

"I don't think so," Alaina laughed.

"Wow." Koen shook his head. "Wait, who's Peter?" Koen furrowed his eyebrows.

Alaina laughed, "You missed a lot. Follow me." Alaina led him to the main tent in the camp, stopping just outside. "Wait here. I'll be right back."

She returned, but not alone.

"Lucas?" Koen said in a surprised voice. Lucas smiled and nodded. "What? How? What is he doing here?"

"You'll see. Lucas is Azgalian, and he has the same gift as I do! He was brought here by family friends when his family died. He's come to stay in the camp," Alaina smiled widely.

Koen looked at Lucas. "Incredible! Did you know that was possible?"

"My father had the gift, but I never really thought of any-one else having it." Alaina smiled at Lucas. "I wish you could speak to me to tell me more about it."

Lucas smiled and nodded in agreement.

"Well, hello there, Koen. It's good to see you sitting up-right." Peter came into the tent.

"It's good to be sitting up." Koen smiled. "Are you Peter?"

"I am. Last time you saw me, you were lying on the desert floor," Peter said. "The Lord is merciful, though, and it is good to see you here with us."

"Indeed." Koen nodded. "Thank you."

"Of course! I see you've met Lucas. Shall we eat now?" Peter looked at the three young people.

"Oh, yes, please," Koen groaned and stood up. "I feel like I haven't eaten in days."

"That's because your body spent all its energy fighting off the poison," Peter explained.

"That would explain how I feel right about now," Koen laughed.

They followed Peter to an outdoor table. Once they sat down, the camp women put food before them. It smelled amazing, and they enjoyed it slowly. It felt good not to be in a rush for the first time in days.

"We should be on the move soon," Koen turned to her, and Alaina laughed on the inside.

"Should we really be rushing? You just healed," Alaina asked, concerned it would be pushing it too soon.

"It's fine. After I eat, I'll feel like myself again. Besides, I'll have all the care I could need at the castle," Koen said. "I'm a prince, remember?" Koen smirked.

"That is, if your father welcomes you with open arms," Alaina said, raising her eyebrow and folding her napkin on the table.

"True. I have a good feeling he will. Especially after the run-in with my uncle at the border. From what Peter told us, Azgalia is the weakest it's ever been. It's only a matter of time before my father uses the advantage. He'll be in a good mood." Koen wiped food off his chin. Alaina could only stare at him. He met her eyes. "What?" he asked, dumbfounded.

"It's just that I hadn't really thought about that. My kingdom, people, and home are all in grave danger. I— I guess it's just hitting me." Alaina's gaze slowly sank to stare at the table.

"I'm sorry, I didn't mean to worry you," Koen said, feeling sorry.

"No, it's okay. I just wish there was something we could do about it."

"Who knows, maybe there is." Koen shrugged. "We'll have to pray about it."

Alaina looked at him and smiled. "Pray?"

"Yeah, pray." Koen smiled back at her.

She gave him a knowing glance and shook her head. "Well, as long as you think it's a smart move to head off already," Alaina said, looking at him with a questioning glance.

"I hate that you can see everything, but you hide everything so well yourself." Koen shook his head, and Alaina smirked. "Yes. I think it's the best idea to head off already," he said firmly.

"Alright. Then we will. I'll go pack my things." And so she got up to do just that. Koen followed her back to the tents and went to clean up and get ready to leave.

As Alaina packed, she thought about how much unknown was ahead of her. So much could happen in the next few days, and just the thought gave her butterflies. She knew what was expected of her. She was afraid, but she knew she had to do it. The questions hung in the back of her mind: *How would she find her father? Would this all be worth it?* She could only pray that the Lord would lead her to him and that when the time came, she would read correctly which man was her father.

After packing her things, she took a deep breath and stepped out into the world. It wasn't a big step, yet it felt like the most important one she'd taken.

TWENTY-ONE

"Whoa, boy." David pulled up on the reins to stop his horse. He could hear his own heavy breathing and his heart pounding in his chest. He had found a young woman lying on the forest ground a few feet away from him. She was unconscious and looked like she'd been through so much. Her face was pale, and her lips were chapped due to dehydration. He dismounted and knelt to examine the situation. Her dress was torn at the bottom, with rips throughout. She was bleeding on her forehead and looked as though she'd been there for a while. He looked around to see if someone might be nearby to help, but when there was no one to be found, he placed the lantern by his feet. Kneeling once more, he tried to see if she'd wake up. He wasn't sure if she could hear him, but it was worth a shot.

"My lady?" David shook her shoulder softly. When nothing happened, he spoke louder and shook harder, "My lady? My name is David, and I am Azgalian. I am here to help you."

He slipped his arms behind her knees and shoulders for support. With a breath in, he lifted her and carried her to where the gray horse stood. He placed her across the horse's back as gently as he could. This was the only time David wished for a shorter horse.

"There you go." David sighed and watched her face to see if there were any sign she would wake. When nothing moved except her chest, he nodded and took the reins. He'd have to walk back on foot, so he prayed there wouldn't be any wolves to worry about.

On the way back to camp, he wondered how she had ended up here. He had been here to find her entirely by God's providence. He wasn't exactly sure what shape she was in, but she wouldn't have lasted much longer if no one had found her.

As he headed back, he looked at the girl. She remained unconscious, and David worried that he'd found her too late.

When the camp finally came into view, the fire was still going, and a prominent, dark figure was moving toward him.

"David! You're back!" David heard Jamie say. He came towards him and slowed down just in time to not run him over.

"Jamie, is anyone awake?" David asked, remaining calm.

"No, they'll sleep through anything. I tried making howling noises because I was bored, and no one made a sound." Jamie shot the camp a joking glare. "Wolves could've taken me, and they wouldn't have known. But anyway, did you find the rider?"

David nodded and held up the lantern to show the woman lying on horseback. "She needs help right away." David tied the horse to a tree and slowly removed the woman from his back. He laid her down on his blankets. "Her breathing looks as though it's slowing." David examined her chest and looked at Jamie in concern.

Jamie nodded. "I'll get Chris." Jamie walked over to where Christopher slept and shook him awake. "Chris. David found a woman, and she needs help."

"He what? A woman?" Christopher sat up and rubbed his eyes, trying to get a grasp on his surroundings. When things clicked, he got up right away and made his way over to David and the woman. "You found her," he said.

"Yes. She wasn't very far from here when I found her, lying on the forest floor unconscious," David said.

Christopher knelt and checked her pulse. "She's breathing, but slowly. From the looks of it, she's extremely dehydrated." Christopher looked at her scrapes and torn dress. "She's been through a lot. Jamie, would you get me a wet cloth?"

"Of course." Jamie handed the wet cloth to Christopher, who used it to clean the young woman's head wound. He also cleaned her scraped legs, which had dried blood in various places.

"This wound doesn't look deep, but how it happened concerns me most. We need to try to wake her so she can drink water and hopefully tell us what happened," Christopher told them.

"I tried shaking her and talking to her. Even moving her didn't make her respond at all." David shook his head in confusion.

"Jamie, raise her legs for me. David, I'll need you to talk a little louder to her. I'll ensure her chest is positioned correctly to get as much airflow as possible," Christopher ordered them.

"What happens if she doesn't wake up, Chris?" Jamie asked.

"There would be something much more serious wrong with her—probably a head injury. We'll try this before worrying, though," Christopher said. "Okay, ready?" Both Jamie and David nodded in return.

David looked down at the young woman and spoke, "My lady, my name is David. Can you wake up?" David looked at Christopher.

"Keep going. Louder." Christopher watched for signs and

prodded David on.

David nodded. "Miss, can you hear me? We're here to help you. Can you wake up to drink water? My name is David, and I am from Azgalia. I have come to find my father."

"There, see!" Christopher sat up straighter. "Her finger twitched."

David looked back at the young woman, and when nothing else happened, he repeated what he said. "I've come to Azgalia to find my father, who was taken." Then suddenly, the woman moved, her breath deepened, and her eyes opened.

"My lady, can you hear me?" David said. The woman looked scared and confused. Her brown eyes searched David's blue ones until she seemed to feel safe.

"Can you hear us, miss?" Christopher asked, and without looking at him, the woman nodded yes. "Wonderful. Do you think you can sit up? You need to drink some water."

The young woman nodded again, and with David supporting her back, she sat up and drank from a cup Christopher offered. "Miss, my name is Christopher; this is Jamie," Jamie nodded with a smile, "and this is David, who found you in the forest." David nodded.

"Thank you." The woman spoke, which surprised the three men.

"If you don't mind me asking, what happened to you?" David asked her.

She looked down at her dress and flinched when she touched her head wound. "Too much." She took another sip of water. "I left to find my father as well." She looked at David. "The King was kidnapped, and we have reason to believe he was taken here. They tied my mother up and took him in the night."

"King?" all three men said in unison.

"Yes," she spoke directly to David. "You are Azgalian, are you not?"

David hesitated. "I am," he nodded.

"Your accent gave it away," the girl shrugged. "Well, I am your princess. King Malikai is my father, " she said.

"If you're the princess of Azgalia, what are you doing here in Mizcriea?" Jamie asked.

"As I told you, I have come to find my father. He was kidnapped. Surely you have heard?"

"I did hear of the King's kidnapping. I am terribly sorry," David answered.

"You seem suspicious." The princess raised an eyebrow at him.

David laughed. "I'm sorry. It's just hard to believe I just rescued a princess in the forest of Mizcriea."

"Fair enough." The princess smiled. "But believe it. I am very grateful and am most definitely in your debt." Before David could decline, she continued, " I left to find my father against my brother's and mother's wishes, of course. I was making my way when I crossed paths with two Mizcriean men. I hid from them, but unfortunately, they took my horse and belongings. I was left alone, and that's when my problems began," she explained to them.

"I believe we found your horse. Just over there." Jamie smiled and pointed out the gray horse David had ridden.

"Well, that is not my original horse, but thank you," the princess said. Then suddenly, her strong demeanor fell, and her eyes began to tear up. "I'm sorry. I just—I'm just in a bit of a tender state, it seems." She tried to laugh through the tears.

"May I ask your name, Princess?" Christopher asked her with kindness.

"My name is Evelyn," she told them. "I prefer you don't call me princess."

"It's a pleasure." Christopher lifted her hand and kissed the back of it. "Tomorrow we will reach a town, and you will be able to clean up."

"That would be heavenly. Thank you," Evelyn said.

"For now, it's late. We can all rest for the night now. David, get to sleep. I'll take watch for a little while," Christopher said.

The next morning, the camp awoke, and they were undoubtedly surprised by the presence of a woman in their midst. David stood by his things as he packed away his belongings and watched Christopher gather the group of men. Christopher explained to the group who she was, and Evelyn introduced herself.

"My name is Evelyn. The King of Azgalia is my father, and I have come here to find him," Evelyn told the men.

David watched as they began to nod and whisper among themselves. It was strange that she traveled alone, but it was very bold of her to make such a journey. It was something David admired about her. He hadn't given much thought to royalty; he isn't easily impressed by titles. Even though in desperate need of new clothes and a wash, Evelyn seemed to have something about her that caught David's interest. He wouldn't admit it to anyone else, but he was secretly interested in discovering more about her.

"Pack up, gentlemen! We head to town," Christopher announced.

Jamie walked by David and gave him a good morning nod, and David nodded back. "Here's your horse, my lady." Jamie politely handed Evelyn the reins to her horse.

"Thank you, Jamie. You can call me Evelyn, you know," Evelyn said as she mounted in one swift motion.

"Of course. However, until we are more acquainted, I'd prefer to use my manners." Jamie grinned and bowed before walking away, which made her roll her eyes.

David hid a grin as he cleaned his sword.

"Now that I am more awake, I wanted to thank you again for helping me." Evelyn's voice came from behind him.

He turned around to look up at her on her horse. The sun shone perfectly behind her, giving the illusion of a halo. She was beautiful, he had to admit. "I'm just glad I was able to find you," David nodded.

"If I may ask, what made you ride out to find me? I heard some men saying you were told to wait until this morning to look?" Evelyn tilted her head in curiosity.

David looked down at his feet. *Why did he feel nervous*? He noticed his sword was off balance. While adjusting it, he answered, "I couldn't sleep knowing that there may be someone in need of help, especially if they were thought to be close." David looked up. "Just how I was raised, miss." David smiled.

"Well, thank you." Evelyn smiled back. As she turned her horse to walk away, she said, "I look forward to hearing about your quest for your father."

Her sentence made his mind jump back to reality. Alaina

and Koen were still somewhere, and he still wasn't with them. His sudden change in attitude must have also shown in his body language.

"You okay, mate?" Jamie came up beside him.

"Yeah. Just thinking about Alaina," David said.

"We'll find them soon enough. The sooner we get to town, the sooner we get to the camp and get answers." Jamie patted him on the back. "By the way, Christopher wanted to talk to you."

David nodded and made his way over to where Christopher was helping clean up the fire. "Chris? You needed me?"

"Yes, I want to put you in charge of caring for the princess. You found her, so I think she will be more inclined to trust you and feel safe with you. Is that okay?" Christopher asked.

"Yes, I can do that," David nodded and turned to find a horse he could ride alongside Evelyn.

Choosing one that resembled Blade, he mounted and rode over to Evelyn, where she pensively looked towards the mountains in the distance. The fresh, open air and the clear blue skies were breathtaking. "Looks a lot like Azgalia, doesn't it?"

Evelyn turned her head and softly smiled. "It does." She looked down at his horse and said, "So, I see you'll be riding?"

"Yes, Christopher told me to keep an eye on you," David said with a smile.

"Oh, he did? Well, thank you. Once I wash and change, I'll be sure to feel more confident about taking care of myself again," Evelyn said.

David nodded. "You ready?"

"Yes," she said, following him to where the group was already approaching departure.

After some riding silence, David blurted out, "Are you a believer?" He wasn't sure what made him ask that so suddenly, but he wouldn't let that show.

"I am, yes. I assume you are, too, David?" Evelyn asked him.

My grandmother raised my twin sister and me to know the Lord," David told her. *Why do I feel like I could tell her my whole life story?*

"That's wonderful! My parents raised my brother and me the same. You have a twin sister?" Evelyn looked at him with her bright brown eyes.

"I do," David nodded shyly.

"Where is she? In fact, where are all you men headed?" Evelyn looked around at the group. "And why is it just men?"

"Well, my sister and I got separated at the border. She was allowed to pass through with our guide; actually, he's a prince of Mizcriea," David explained.

"How are you holding up, Miss?" Jamie asked, moving his horse's pace to catch them.

"Very well, thank you. How about you?" Evelyn said, eyeing David to let him know she wanted to hear more.

"My pleasure! Ever since we got off that boat, I've been great!" Jamie smiled.

"Boat? What boat?" Evelyn asked curiously.

"David here hasn't told you our story?" Jamie raised an eyebrow at David. David shook his head with an embarrassed smile.

"No, he hasn't," Evelyn laughed and brushed a piece of her golden brown hair away from her face.

"Well then, let me start. Feel free to jump in whenever,

mate." Jamie winked at David and began telling Evelyn their story.

David listened as Jamie told the story and laughed to himself as he realized how good a storyteller Jamie was. His facial expressions and hand movements kept the listener engaged. David had lived it, yet he was as interested in listening as Evelyn.

"And now, that story, I'll save for later, but you should hear how my mate, David, ended up here," Jamie winked again at David before walking away.

"May I ask how?" she prodded.

David smiled and began to explain his story, starting with the quest to find his father.

"Wait, you traveled with the prince of Mizcriea?" Evelyn's eyes widened.

"I'll get to that later," David laughed and continued to talk about their adventures at the knight tournament, the dragons, the people they met, the border crossing, and the split. He told her about how he met Jamie and Christopher, and all about the escape. He then explained how Alaina was still with Koen, and he wasn't sure where.

"I'm not sure what to say. Your story is something I've never heard before, not even in legends. As for your sister, I do hope to meet her. I have a feeling our paths crossed for a reason," she said. "Your father's kidnapping seems like it may be linked to the kidnapping of my father. They haven't been the only kidnappings either." Evelyn looked forward and sighed, "David, I do believe we can find our fathers, and I would definitely like to help you find yours."

"I would be honored to help in your search as well. Are you

good with any weapons?"

"You think it will come to that?" Evelyn looked at him.

"I think it's what we must expect," David said confidently.

"I know that. I guess I was hoping you had a hidden plan," Evelyn said. "But yes. I can handle a sword quite well."

"Now that is music to my ears," David smiled. "The sword is my specialty. When we arrive at the hidden camp, I'd like to see what you can do."

"I look forward to the challenge," Evelyn said.

"Great," David smiled.

"The faithful camp; is it like a haven for people of the faithful?"

"It seems like it. I only know what Christopher has told us," David said.

"Well, that's quite exciting then!" Evelyn smiled, and David couldn't help but return it.

They became lost in their thoughts and rode in silence, and David used the quiet to pray. He prayed for the group's journey, his sister, Koen, and his father. Even more so, he prayed that even if they didn't find their father, God would still use their quest for His glory.

They couldn't get to the faithful camp soon enough.

"Not long until we reach town!" Christopher called out. David watched Christopher slow his horse so he could ride beside Evelyn and David. "Evelyn, I don't want to risk anything, so when we reach the town, do you think you could wear this around your head? I'd hate for someone to recognize you." Christopher handed her a strip of fabric that would work as a head scarf.

"I'll wear it," she nodded. "But I doubt I'm recognizable in my current condition."

"Good. Be ready," Christopher nodded and rode back up to the front of the group.

TWENTY-TWO

Bustling and charming, Beckett was full of busy people. The markets were filled with buying and trading; market merchants shouted their prices to shoppers passing. Children played in front yards, while parents gardened or swept porches. It seemed as if everyone was doing something. No one was at rest enough to notice the newcomers.

Jamie made eye contact with David and shrugged his shoulders. They were thinking the same thing. David stayed alert as citizens crossed the road without looking and children played in the street. He steered his horse cautiously. Christopher told them the cottage was just at the end of the road. It was small and didn't stand out, but that was just what they needed. When they finally reached it, the riders dismounted and made their way through a crowd of people toward the stalls on the side of the cottage.

The familiar smell reminded David of his home in Azgalia. Their stalls were a place of solace for him. Sometimes, going out to the stalls was just to be there and think. Sometimes, even using the excuse of cleaning stalls for some alone time was welcome instead of doing house chores. His heart ached at the reminder of his grandmother; what he would give to hear her call him back to the cottage to help her with house chores one more time.

He gazed around and was surprised to find them smaller

than his stalls in Azgalia. "How many horses fit in here?" he asked one of the stable boys assisting the group in resting their horses.

"Ten horses, sir," the young boy answered, and David nodded in return.

"Will you hold him?" Christopher held out his horse's reins to David. "I'll go check in with the innkeeper to see if we're good to stay," he said, then disappeared inside.

"Oh, it's perfect," Evelyn said, walking up beside him.

"Perfectly *small*," Jamie said with a laugh as he came up to stand by them.

"The cottage or the stalls?" David asked.

"Both," Jamie snorted.

"Exactly. It's been a long time since I've stayed in such a quaint little place," Evelyn smiled. "Quite charming."

"Careful, miss, your princess is showing," Jamie joked.

Evelyn's eyes widened, and she covered her mouth. "Oh, my. I may blow my cover." Evelyn laughed when Jamie paused to decide if she was joking back or not.

"Ha! I like a friend who can joke back," Jamie laughed. "Not bad, Princess."

"Thank you," Evelyn smiled proudly.

Jamie did not need someone to encourage his humor, yet Evelyn seemed more than happy to do so. David's grandmother and Alaina would have loved their humor, which made him more willing to do more than put up with it, but enjoy it.

Christopher returned. "Alright, men. Split into groups of five and pick a room. The inn is ours, but let's keep that to ourselves, okay?" The men began to pair up, including Jamie and David. They decided to bunk with Christopher and two other men in the group.

"Are you okay, then?" David asked Evelyn before she headed inside to her own room.

"Yes, thank you, David," she said with a nod.

He nodded and followed Jamie inside the inn. The foyer was filled with warm lighting and dark wood. Upon entering, there were seating rooms on either side, and ahead of them was a long hallway that opened into a large room at the end. David looked around at the sitting rooms and noticed there wasn't much light coming from the outside. Most of the lighting was from the candles around the room.

Continuing through the hall, doors opened to rooms on both sides. Men from their group were already filling them.

"Honestly, I don't think it matters which room we pick," David said as he watched Jamie look from side to side at the rooms when he walked by.

"Sure, it does, mate. It's gotta be the one closest to the kitchen," Jamie said in a serious tone.

David laughed, "Then why are you looking in each room?"

"I'm nosy," Jamie shrugged with a smile. David shook his head and laughed. They continued a little longer down towards the room at the end of the hallway. When Jamie spotted someone he didn't recognize, he asked, "Excuse me, miss, where might the kitchen be?"

The woman looked up from dusting a desk. "Oh, are you looking for the innkeeper?"

"No, just the kitchen." Jamie smiled.

"Oh. Well, you're not exactly allowed in the kitchen." The woman looked down at her feet nervously.

"We don't plan on going in there. My friend here just wanted to make sure we had a room closest to the food," David said in a light-hearted tone.

The woman slowly looked up with a willing smile. "In that case," she hid a giggle, "the kitchen is through those doors and in the room to the right." She turned to continue dusting.

"Thank you, miss," Jamie said politely and scanned around to choose a room.

"She was clearly nervous. Why didn't you just tell her why?" David asked as they entered a room with two cots and two small beds.

"I don't exactly like to tell everyone my secret to choosing a room," Jamie laughed.

"Ah, I see," David pretended to be enlightened.

"What's so funny in here?" Christopher appeared in the doorway with a grin. He always seemed to be in a good mood. His friendly face and warm smile brought peace to those he helped.

"Jamie here has a secret to choosing a room." David motioned toward Jamie, who shrugged.

"Let me guess, the one closest to the kitchen?" Christopher entered the room.

"How'd you know?" Jamie asked, bewildered.

"Jamie, you seem like the kind of man who loves food." Christopher shrugged. "And because your room is the closest to the kitchen. The only thing good about being the closest to the back of a stuffy, cramped inn is that you're close to the food."

"I'm impressed." Jamie put his hands on his hips. "Are you always this observant but never say so?"

"Maybe," Christopher smirked and fell onto one of the

beds. "*Finally*," he sighed.

David did the same on the other bed and was surprised at how good it felt to lie on a usually less-than-comfortable bed. He closed his eyes and thanked God for bringing them safely here.

"Okay, not fair. There's no way you can do that on these cots," Jamie interrupted the peaceful moment.

"Here, take mine," David said and got up. "I'll go check on the horses." David left the room and walked back down the hallway toward the entrance. When he reached the front two rooms, he saw Evelyn and the person he assumed was the innkeeper in a deep conversation. He exited the inn silently and took in Beckett's scenery. The inn sat at the end of a cobblestone road. The end of the road was surrounded by bright green bushes that reached to David's hips. Behind the bushes, it looked out into open land. He looked to his right and saw where the stables were, so he stepped off the entry stairway. Making his way around the front of the inn, he could see back to the town's main street, where horses and people were.

Rounding the corner, he walked into the horse stables and approached his horse. "Hey, boy," David said as he stroked the face of the horse. He couldn't help but wonder where Blade was. He hated not knowing where his faithful horse had gone and hoped he could ride him again.

"You okay?" Evelyn's voice came from behind him.

David, slightly startled, turned around and nodded. He realized he was clenching his fists. "I was just thinking."

Evelyn nodded, unconvinced. "Isn't it a perfect space for the horses?" Evelyn smiled as she took in the area.

"It is nice," David said as he followed her gaze to look

around again. "We have a barn back in Azgalia where we live. My sister and grandmother spent a lot of time around the horses, so they wanted a proper place for them."

"That's wonderful." Evelyn unlatched the lock to her horse's stall. "Maybe after this ends, I can invite you and your sister to Malikai City. I'd love to thank you for your help properly, and I know your sister would love our stables."

"That would be nice," David agreed. "Thank you."

"Of course," Evelyn said.

"Excuse me, miss?" It was the woman from the inn.

Evelyn peered out of the stall. "Yes?"

"We're ready for you now," the woman said shyly.

'Oh," Evelyn nodded and exited the stall. "Excuse me," Evelyn said kindly to David as she walked by to meet the woman.

David nodded and watched as she disappeared around the inn's corner. Where was she going?

After stroking his horse's neck one last time, he went to see if Jamie and Christopher would want to walk around the city for a bit.

David, Jamie, and Christopher entered Beckett's busy street and went to the farmer's market. David observed the people's mannerisms as they passed by. Most didn't look up to make eye contact, and those who did were trying to sell something.

"Sir, you will *love* my cabbage!" The man followed David for a few steps before he finally listened to David's decline.

A few other merchants tried to sell the three men produce,

but they weren't exactly looking to carry produce back to the inn. As they kept walking, David observed the carpenter's shop and saw the wife weaving baskets on the floor while he carved into a table.

"That's talent," Jamie pointed out a cabinet with detailed carvings.

"True," David nodded. "The baskets as well," he said, marveling at the designs on the baskets. "Alaina would love this." David picked up a small basket that looked perfect for putting fruit in.

"I'm afraid it may be ruined on our ride, mate," Jamie said while observing it.

"I was thinking the same thing," David nodded. Reluctantly, he returned it and made a mental note to tell Alaina about the baskets if they survived this quest.

"Now that's something I want to see." Jamie suddenly picked up his pace, making David look up.

David's eyes locked on a blacksmith with arms like tree trunks hammering away at a brand new sword. The blade seemed to glow, though David was sure it was just him. The blacksmith continued to hammer as he shaped the blade. David not only loved swords, but he also loved the process that goes into making them. He had never made a sword, but he hoped to try it one day. Prying his gaze away from the blacksmith, he observed the rest of the shop. The different metals on the walls were so beautiful that David couldn't help but smile.

"Goodness boy, you might as well have seen the lady of your dreams!" Jamie shoved him in laughter.

"Blacksmiths in this area are said to be some of the best," Christopher said.

The blacksmith had massive arms, and his forearms were covered in markings. It looked like Mizcriean language. "He used to be a knight in the Mizcriean army," Christopher whispered to David. "That's what those markings are for. They represent victories."

David looked back at the wall of finished swords. He immediately made his way over to get a closer look. Taking one from the wall, he scanned the craftsmanship and marveled at its design.

"Now *that's* a sword." Christopher came up beside him.

"Let me see," Jamie said, holding the blade. The design was perfectly crafted and glimmered when it caught the sun's light. Indeed," he nodded and handed it back to David. "Although I prefer a bigger blade," Jamie shrugged.

David smirked, "Because you're not agile enough to fight with a smaller blade."

"I have my reasons," Jamie laughed.

"Right," Christopher laughed and continued to walk toward the knives.

"Do you wish to buy one?" the blacksmith's voice rumbled in Mizcriean. His voice was just as David would have expected it to be.

Better with the language, Christopher answered, "We are only looking for now. My friend is interested in your sword. How much?"

"Two pounds," the man said.

"Two pounds?" Christopher's eyebrows raised.

"What'd he say?" David leaned into Jamie's ear.

"Two pounds," Jamie whispered back, and David's eyes widened. He looked down at the sword he held and quickly put it back on the wall.

"Will he take seventeen shillings?" Jamie asked Christopher silently.

"Will you take seventeen shillings?" Christopher asked the man.

The blacksmith laughed deeply. "No, no, no. Two pounds," he said again.

David watched Christopher's expressions because he had no idea what was being said. The Blacksmith's accent was thick.

"We can do a pound," Christopher said to the blacksmith.

The man stopped his hammering and looked Christopher straight in the eye. It was as if he were waiting for Christopher to apologize for whatever he said and run away. Yet, Christopher stood his ground.

David walked over to Jamie. "What is going on?"

"Christopher asked if he'd take a pound for the sword," Jamie told him.

"What? I don't have a pound to spare," David said, shaking his head at Christopher, trying to get his attention.

Jamie looked at David and then at Christopher. "I have no idea what he's thinking."

"No less than a pound and a half," the blacksmith said firmly.

"It's a deal," Christopher smiled. David and Jamie stood and watched him shake the blacksmith's large hand, pay the blacksmith, and then go to take the sword off the wall. He walked straight over to David, placed the sword in his hands, and turned to walk out. "Come on, men," Christopher nodded for them to follow. David was pretty sure his jaw was stuck open.

"Christopher!" David ran up beside him once the shock wore off. "What were you thinking? I cannot pay you for this. There's no way I have enough to pay for it."

"Don't worry about it. I have more than enough for myself. Plus, I've always liked a good negotiation. That sword is worth a whole lot more than the blacksmith knew." Christopher stopped and looked at him. "There's only one thing I ask in return."

"Of course." David shook his head vigorously.

"I only ask that you follow the opportunities the Lord brings. When it comes to finding your father, you and I both know that there is something bigger here, especially after meeting Evelyn. This is bigger than your story," Christopher spoke with wisdom.

"You're right. Part of me is afraid to go there and find something bigger. Yet, at the same time, I pray that I can be used for something bigger. I won't let you down, Chris."

"I believe you," Chris slapped his shoulder, and they continued to where Jamie stood waiting. He raised his eyebrow and put a hand on his hip.

"Everything okay?" Jamie asked.

"Sure is," David smiled and looked down to sheath his new sword. They made their way back down the street toward the inn, and as they drew closer to the carpenter and basket shop, David spotted a young woman observing the basket he had wanted for Alaina. The girl's back faced them so that they couldn't see her face. She wore a tan and white gown that draped elegantly on her. Jamie followed David's gaze and saw the girl as well.

"Aye, mate, she's going to get that basket before you do," Jamie said half-jokingly.

David looked from Jamie to where the girl stood. "Fine, " he said and started towards the basket shop.

"Mate, where are you going?" Jamie tried to pull him back, but David was already walking that way.

Being the gentleman he was, instead of taking it from her hands, he asked, "Excuse me, miss? Do you plan on purchasing that basket?"

The girl turned around, and much to David's surprise, Evelyn looked up at him. She smiled, and David's heart lurched in his chest. He'd never seen a girl quite so beautiful. She must have washed up at the inn, because her skin glowed and her face was no longer tainted with dirt. "I'm not sure yet," she smiled. "Hi David."

Stop staring, he thought to himself. He tried not to look surprised at how different Evelyn looked. "Uh, hi. I didn't realize it was you."

Evelyn laughed, "Oh, I don't blame you. One look in the mirror at the inn, and I didn't recognize myself until I washed. I apologize to anyone who saw me in the state I was in." Evelyn's cheeks flushed in embarrassment.

Her brown hair seemed to shine even more, and David realized it had an auburn tint. She looked like a princess. "It wasn't too bad," David smiled.

"Oh, don't be silly; it was terrible," she said, and they both laughed.

"Princess!" Jamie walked up with Christopher. "You are looking well!" he grinned.

"Why, thank you. Hello, Chris." She nodded kindly to the

men.

"Evelyn, glad to see you feeling better," Christopher nodded.

"Thank you," Evelyn said, looking back at David. "Why were you asking if I would buy the basket?"

"Well," David cleared his throat. "I had my eye on it earlier because I wanted to get it for my sister, but decided it would be too hard to travel with," David explained.

"Oh, nonsense! You could tie it to the horses and leave it at the camp we're going to. I'm sure it will be fine." Evelyn picked up the basket and placed it in David's hands. "She'll love it," she said with a glowing smile.

David bought the basket for just a couple of shillings and was glad he did. The group returned to the inn for dinner and retired to their room early to rest for the day ahead. Tomorrow, they would reach the camp.

TWENTY-THREE

Alaina and Koen continued their quest after Koen started feeling better. Since it was not long until they reached the castle, Alaina prepared herself for one of the craziest things she might ever do. The fact that her grandmother or brother wasn't with her made her that much more nervous.

"Not long now," Koen said from in front of her. Alaina wondered what was going through his mind. He had memories here and reasons not to want to return, whereas Alaina only went off imagination.

"How do you think your father will respond to your arrival?" Alaina asked.

"I'm not sure. He likes to make a scene, so I imagine it won't be without something dramatic. I don't think it will be anything violent, though," Koen swallowed. "At least at first."

"You really think he'd do anything to you?" Alaina rode up beside him.

"I wish I could say no. However, certain things make you question. I would never have imagined he would go after my mother. He's too unpredictable." Koen shook his head. Alaina could see his anger rising.

"You're not alone this time," Alaina tried to be reassuring.

"Thank you," Koen nodded and faced the castle as it came into view. Alaina watched his face as a storm of emotions rolled over him. "Alaina?"

"Yes?" she tilted her head.

"Do you think we could pray first?" Koen looked at her, and she could see his fear and worry.

"Definitely." Together, they looked up at the castle, and without closing their eyes, Alaina prayed for their safety and God's guidance through the days ahead.

"Thank you," Koen said. "Here we go." They urged their horses forward toward the front gate.

Alaina spotted the guards by the gate and tried to read their faces, but they were hidden behind their helmet guards. The castle was huge and frightening. The entrance gate was made of black iron, and the curtain wall surrounding the castle was massive. She took it all in and marveled at how overwhelming it looked. It seemed impenetrable. She'd say it was impossible if it weren't for her faith.

Once they appeared through the trees, the guards at the gate saw them and immediately raised their swords. "State your business, " the guard on the right said. As soon as it was spoken, though, both guards' faces turned to ones of embarrassment as they recognized Koen.

"I am Koen, Prince of Mizcriea. I order you to let us in and bring me to my father," Koen said in an authoritative tone that Alaina had never heard him use before.

The guards knelt, and the one who had spoken said, "My apologies, your highness. We'd heard of your disappearance, but the King told us not to expect a return," the guard said.

The other guard said, "We are surprised to see you." He cleared his throat, obviously nervous, "But welcome home, Prince Koen."

"Thank you. Now take me to my father," Koen ordered

again.

"Yes, Your Highness." The guard looked from Koen to Alaina, but chose not to ask even though he was curious about her presence. "This way," the guards signaled the gatehouse guards to raise the gate. It rose slowly so they could pass through.

The grounds of the Mizcriean castle were shocking. Alaina's eyes widened, but she did her best to hide her surprise. What once must have been beautiful grounds and lush grass was now brown, and any greenery that wasn't dead was overgrown.

Stealing a glance at Koen's reaction, he too was hiding his shock, but she could see he was just as surprised as she was to see the grounds in such poor condition.

"It's changed so much," Koen said aloud.

"How long has it been?" Alaina asked.

"A couple of weeks? A month? I'm not sure, but I never expected everything to have changed so much. My father must have let everything go." Koen shook his head in bitterness. Alaina saw that the gardens had been a special place for his mother.

"Yes, the King wanted to prioritize the royal army, and there has been a decrease in ground maintenance. All the gardeners were ordered to join the army," the guard explained. Koen and Alaina looked at each other.

Once they reached the castle's front entrance, Koen gave instructions for the horses to be taken care of and brought to the royal stalls. "And please ensure they're taken better care of than the grounds."

"Yes, sir," the guard answered and directed the stable boy. While the boy walked away with the horses, Alaina saw him staring at Koen over his shoulder.

Fear.

Worry.

Hatred.

Anger.

Sadness.

Strange, Alaina thought. His emotions and characteristics of loyalty, kindness, and justice didn't make sense. How did those relate to Koen?

"This way, please," the guard led them in through the doors, which two other guards opened.

Inside the castle doors was the largest room Alaina had ever seen. Massive pillars lined each side of the scarlet carpet that ran straight ahead to the King's throne. Each side of the throne held two knights, who stood unmoved. Without acknowledging their entrance, King Cleatus sat listening to the latest report on the kingdom. His almost black eyes, tan and wrinkled skin, and dark-haired beard made him look even more intimidating than she had imagined. Alaina saw impatience as the messenger rambled on about the countless problems in Mizcriea. One by one, the King's fingers tapped on the armrest of his throne.

"Sire?" the messenger asked.

King Cleatus blinked and looked at the messenger, "Yes?"

"Sire, how would you like to respond?" the messenger asked hesitantly.

"Is it unclear that I wasn't listening?" the King growled.

The guard guiding them asked them to wait by the doors until the King was finished.

"Ah, my apologies, sire," the messenger cleared his throat. "I had asked how you would like to respond to the escape of the slaves by the ports along the coast?"

"There was an escape? That hasn't happened in years!" The King stood up. "Whose ship was it?"

Alaina and Koen looked at each other. David had been placed on a slave ship; could he have escaped? She could only pray that it was the case and that he was now safe.

"It was The Forgotten. Captain Bennett, sir," the messenger said.

"Captain Bennett? Captain Bennett! He had the strongest crew in all my slave ships! How on earth did this happen?" King Cleatus demanded while turning red in the face.

"The slaves were taken off the boat as usual to be sold at the docks. The First Mate betrayed him to help the slaves," he answered while cowering in fear of the King, fuming in anger.

"This is outrageous. Where are the slaves now?" The King sat back in his chair, full of anger.

"Their location is unknown," the messenger said, covering his face with his paper.

"Unknown!" Cleatus bellowed, and the messenger all but sank to the ground in fear. The King stared at him until finally Cleatus let out a low groan as he sat back into his throne. "Let them be for now. I have more important matters now." The King waved his hand, and the messenger quickly departed from the throne room.

The guard nodded to Alaina and Koen before speaking to the King. "Sire, if I may?" the guard bowed.

"What is it?" the King asked. "It had better be better news than the messenger before you."

"Indeed, my King, it is." The guard nodded. "Your son has returned."

The King's eyes widened, and for a moment, Alaina saw fear behind his mask of confidence and brute strength.

"My son? Koen?" The King looked behind the guard to where Koen and Alaina stood. "Koen, my son!" The King stood and forced a smile. "You've returned," he said with arms stretched open. Alaina wanted to laugh.

Koen looked at Alaina before walking forward. "Stay behind me," he whispered before he walked up, passed the guard, and stopped just short of the steps that led to the throne. "Yes, I'm back."

"Where on earth did you go, my son?" The King's voice shook slightly as he tried to hide his nervousness.

"I just needed to be alone for a while," Koen answered blankly.

"I see you were not so alone." The King's gaze fell onto Alaina.

"Yes, I ran across an Azgalian girl on my travels. I want to keep her as my personal maid," Koen said firmly.

"Azgalian, you say?" The King raised his eyebrow, and Alaina avoided eye contact, just as Koen had instructed.

"Is that a problem?" Koen asked, averting his father's gaze back to him.

"No. So long as she works for us. It can be done." The King then smiled. "Why don't you go visit your brother and get settled? In the meantime, there will be preparation for a celebration of your return!" The King stood again. "Guards, take his maid to the servants' quarters so she may change into appropriate attire." Then, he turned back to the guard who had brought Koen and Alaina into the throne room. "And you! Immediately begin preparations for a celebration tonight by spreading the word through the castle!" The guard ran out to execute the orders, and other guards came to escort Alaina out.

"Koen," Alaina said before the guards began taking her away. She knew this was the plan, and yet, the force with which they took hold of her frightened her.

Koen whipped around to face the guard standing by her. "Treat her as one of the head maids. She is my personal servant, and I would prefer her to be in the best conditions."

"Of course, my prince." The guard nodded and loosened his death grip on her. He led her away.

Before walking away, Koen looked one last time at his father before going to find his brother. His father met his gaze and ordered the rest of the guards to leave momentarily. He didn't break eye contact until everyone left the room. His father's face quickly lost its smile, and his eyes darkened. He returned to what Koen truly knew of his father: dark and evil. "You'd think if you really cared, you would've stayed and fought."

"What does that mean? How could you ask your son to murder his mother?" Koen exploded in anger

"It means you should have stayed and fought for her life if you truly didn't want her to die. Some son you proved to be." His father's face slowly formed an evil smirk.

"You killed her," Koen said without question in his voice. His heart broke all over again. His throat and nose burned.

"Did you believe I would change my mind? Or that I wouldn't take matters into my own hands?" The King sat back comfortably on his throne.

"Why?" Koen's voice rose, and he felt like he had been punched in the gut. *He's right. I left her with him. How could I do that to her?*

"Why? She was an inconvenience!" Cleatus sat forward. "She was ruining all my plans to make this kingdom great! I believe she was involved with the people we call *the faithful!*" he said, sneering at the name. "She needed to be stopped before brainwashing our kingdom."

"You never even loved her!" Koen mistakenly let a tear run down his cheek.

"Of course not. Marriage isn't about love but convenience for the families involved. Sadly, those who marry for love are mistaken. It is all a misguided emotion. When I realized she was no longer a convenience for this family, it was time for her to go." He folded his arms and spoke as though it were a casual, unfortunate event, which infuriated Koen.

"You will regret this," Koen said through gritted teeth.

"Careful, son." The King's eyes seemed to darken even more. "Didn't your mother ever tell you that history repeats itself? Now, why don't you go to your room and think things over? If you come to the celebration tonight, I will forget this ever happened, and we will move on."

Koen didn't say a thing, and instead of unsheathing his sword and lunging toward his father like he wanted to, he turned to find his brother Cronin. It took every ounce of him not to slam his feet down with every step. He curled his fists and clenched his jaw. He had never felt as much anger and hatred as he did then. "God, why?" Koen said under his breath and surprised himself. *Just like I said in the desert.* He thought back to when he was in the desert and cried out to God. He had asked God why, then, too. Did he believe in Alaina and David's God? Or was he just used to them talking to their God all the time, and he just picked up on their habits? *Don't kid yourself. You know He must be real.* Koen shook his head. He couldn't believe his thoughts. *Wait, mother was scheming with the faithful? Had she been one of them, too?* He thought about David and Alaina's openness with their faith and wondered if his mother had been faithful and why she had never shared it with him.

Pressing through the doors that led out of the throne room, he ignored the guard's welcome greetings and asked them where Cronin was.

"He was last seen in his chambers, my prince," the knight bowed.

"Thanks." Koen turned again and made his way through various halls and turns until he ended up at his brother's chambers. Upon reaching the door, he stared at the wood before knocking on it. He hadn't spoken to his brother since the day his father had asked him to murder his mother. How did Koen know that Cronin wasn't a part of this? Did Cleatus and Cronin work together on it all? Or did Cronin now despise Koen because his father may have blamed their mother's death on him? All Koen knew was that Cronin had always been a faithful brother to him. He had always stood up for Koen, despite never being the best influence. For that, Koen had to give him the benefit of the doubt. So, with that, he knocked on the door.

"What is it?" Cronin's deep voice came from inside.

"Cronin, it's Koen," Koen answered from behind the doors. There was silence, and then Koen heard the door unlock.

Cronin opened the door, and when the brothers' eyes met, his face lifted, and they both smiled. "Brother." He embraced Koen and squeezed. "You've returned."

"I have," Koen said, feeling like a burden had dropped off his shoulders. He stepped back to get a better look at his brother. His features were so much like their fathers. His brother's hair had grown longer, and his beard was thicker. Usually, his dark and sharp features made him quite intimidating, but for some reason, Koen noticed something softer in his presence. Koen tilted his head. "You do look a bit softer." Koen smiled at his brother and laughed while Cronin playfully punched his arm.

"Maybe that's because I am." Cronin raised his eyebrows and pursed his lips. "You, Koen, you have definitely changed."

"How's that?" Koen put his hands on his hips and raised a brow.

Cronin paused to think. "You look wiser."

Koen was a bit surprised at the observation his brother had pointed out. "Really? I'll take that as a compliment."

Cronin smiled. "Please, come in. I believe we have much to talk about. It looks like you've been on quite a journey."

"I like to call it a quest," Koen said as he sat beside his brother.

"A quest, you say?" Cronin brushed a piece of his black hair away from his face. "Have you reached the end of your quest? Is that why you've returned?"

Koen smiled. "No. I returned to finish the quest. I need to ask you about something." Koen looked into his brother's eyes. "Do you know why I left?"

Cronin's eyes dropped to the floor. "I believe I do. When I

first noticed you were gone, I went to ask Father, and he told me you killed our mother and left. He tried to tell me you betrayed us." Cronin took a deep breath. "I couldn't believe it. You loved our mother. So, I slowly searched for answers and put things together. Plus, I went through mother's diaries and discovered so much I didn't know about our mother." He looked up at Koen again. "I only leave my room to go to the kitchen or out into the gardens. I haven't seen Father since that day. I know what was done, and trying to deal with it has been the hardest thing I've ever experienced."

"Cronin, I am so sorry I left you. I was so upset and dismayed; I needed to leave." Koen let his tears fall this time.

There was a moment of silence between them, as they felt there wasn't much either could say. They had already faced the fact, but it seemed more real being with each other again. Cronin reached out and, to Koen's surprise, drew him in for an embrace.

"I needed that." Koen brushed away a tear as he stepped back.

"As did I." Cronin smiled wearily.

"Remember when you and I would get into a fight, and one of us always ran to mother to cry and complain?" Cronin asked.

"And she would always embrace us before she said anything so that we could calm down." Koen nodded.

"It always worked." Cronin smiled.

"Still does." Koen gave a soft laugh.

Koen broke the silence, "I spoke to Father." Cronin looked up at him. "He's never looked so dark, Cronin."

Cronin nodded. "I always ignored that about him. I always thought it was necessary to run a kingdom. Be tough and unmoved; command what you want because you're the King. How Mother put up with him, I'll never know." Cronin shook his head. Koen could tell there was something more he wanted to say. "Koen, there's so much to tell you. Will you hear me out?"

"Of course. That's why I came to you. I needed to talk to you. Tell me what you know," Koen encouraged his brother.

"Koen, I need to tell you honestly." Cronin looked nervous. "Koen, I've decided to join the faithful. Though I didn't have much contact with the outside world when you were gone, I did converse with the servants and go through my mother's diaries. Well, I am convinced." He breathed out and waited for Koen's reaction.

Koen could do nothing but smile at that moment. "Cronin, that's amazing." Koen shook his head and laughed. "Congratulations, brother." Even though he was thrilled to see his brother doing well, a part of him felt awkward. He believed it to be so since he himself wasn't of the faithful.

"Really? I thought you would be against it! Or at least seriously question it?" Cronin looked confused but grateful for his brother's support.

"Cronin, I have much to tell you. I have met several people who have changed my life. All of them have been part of the faithful." Despite his twinge of awkwardness, he was truly happy for his brother.

"So, you are faithful as well?" Cronin asked eagerly.

Koen paused, and his smile fell. "I guess not." Koen looked out the window. "I'm not sure why. I've seen all the evidence. The faithful have been nothing but kind to me. I believe their God is real, but for some reason . . . " Koen shrugged and looked back at his brother.

"You're not sold out for it," Cronin said, and Koen nodded.

"I'm not dismissing it. I've been thinking about it a lot. And I promise I will continue to do so," Koen said. "I need to discuss the reason I've returned, though."

"Please." Cronin motioned for his brother to continue.

Koen explained to his brother what had happened while he was away and why he had returned. He talked about the kidnapping theory, and that they had reason to believe that Alaina and David's father had been kidnapped and brought to Mizcriea. "They believe he is still alive."

"Wait, just a minute. You said you heard of King Malikai's disappearance?" Cronin interrupted.

"Yes?" Koen asked, wondering what Cronin was saying.

"I believe they are connected." Cronin looked at Koen seriously. "Koen, I believe there is something big Father is planning. That's the reason he kept saying mother was in the way. The King and your friend's father are not the first to be kidnapped. Plus, isn't it odd that Father always seems to be acting strange around the time Azgalia is in a rough spot?" Cronin pointed out.

Koen thought about what Cronin was saying. He was right; these weren't the only kidnappings he knew of; these were just more important people. Once Mother was gone, he decided to kidnap King Malikai. Surely, it all had to be connected, but how?

"You're right. Cronin, I'm not sure what Father is planning, but I feel we can figure it out. Do you know where I can find out if their father is still alive, and if he is, where he may be kept?" Koen asked.

"It would be with the rest of the parchments. Only Uncle and Father have access," Cronin told him. "You ran into Uncle on the way?"

"Yeah, at the border," Koen answered.

"He should have been back before you then," Cronin said skeptically. "He may know nothing about what Father is planning. He's always gone when something like this happens."

"I don't know. I'm not sure I can trust anyone outside the faithful right now," Koen shook his head.

"Even yourself?" Cronin raised his eyebrow with a smile, and Koen waved him off.

"You know what I mean," Koen said, standing up. "I need to find out where Uncle is. If we can trust him, I can get the key into the parchment room without Father growing suspicious."

"Sounds like a good plan to me," Cronin nodded in agreement.

Koen looked at his brother, who had longer hair and a beard. He was otherwise a handsome man, but in the last couple of weeks, he had let go of maintaining his appearance. "Will you come to the celebration with me tonight?"

"I should have guessed." Cronin rolled his eyes. "I will," he said, giving in and nodding.

"Great." Koen turned to leave, but before he stepped out, he said, "Please don't come unless you clean yourself up." Before walking down the hall, he heard Cronin laugh.

He had been afraid to return to the castle, but now, no matter what happened, he was glad he spoke to his brother.

"Now I need to find Uncle," Koen said, walking down the hall.

"Looking for me?"

TWENTY-FOUR

Walking through the dark halls with tall ceilings and no outside light made Alaina nervous. The fact that she was in King Cleatus's castle didn't make it any better. While two guards escorted her on each side and a hand on each of her arms, Alaina remained silent.

"Pretty strange that the prince wants an Azgalian girl as his personal maid," the guard on her right said. His breath was hot against her ear, making her shudder.

"He probably views her as a prize," the other guard on her left said with a disgusting smirk.

"True. I mean, look at her eyes," the guard on the right said, pulling her to a stop and leaning in towards her. He had snake-like green eyes, blonde hair, and a scar across his cheek. Alaina shrank back from him, which made him laugh.

Lust.

Deceitfulness.

Recklessness.

Arrogance.

Alaina's heart sank at the thought that he may not take her to the maids right away. *Please, Lord, let them just take me to the other maids so I can be with Koen again. Protect me!*

"What's your name?" the guard with the snake eyes prodded.

"Alaina," she answered, averting her eyes from him.

"Alaina," the guard slurred in a playful tone that made Alaina feel sick. "No doubt you're an Azgalian." When Alaina didn't reply, the guard on her left spoke up.

"You're pretty lucky to be kept alive. Usually, the royals would have you beheaded just for entertainment. Why, you're actually the first Azgalian to be working in the castle. Must be something special to the prince, huh?" the guard said. When Alaina didn't reply again, they both laughed.

"Sure isn't because of her voice," the snake-eyed guard said. "But I bet I could get something out of her." He ran his eyes over and pulled her closer to him.

"Tristan, we have orders, " the guard on her left said, and Alaina almost let out a sigh of relief.

Tristan, the one with the snake eyes, glared at the other guard, but only for a moment. "Why do you have to ruin all my fun, Cyrus?"

"Because I would like to keep my head," Cyrus responded, and Tristan snorted. Cyrus stepped forward, and Tristan followed suit.

Thank you, Lord, Alaina thought to herself as tears threatened behind her eyes. She really thought Tristan was going to take advantage of her, and she prayed never to see him again.

They finally reached the end of a long hallway with a door on the right and a door on the left. The guards led her to the one on the left and knocked on it. "It's the King's guards; let us in!" Immediately, the door opened to reveal an elderly woman dressed in servant attire. "We have a recruit for you, ladies. She is to be Prince Koen's personal maid."

The elderly woman looked at Alaina with kind and gentle eyes. She nodded at the guards, and they released their grips on her. "Have her ready for the celebration," Cyrus told her.

"And make sure she gets cleaned up," Tristan added in. With that, they were gone, and Alaina let out a breath when the door shut.

"Don't worry, my dear. We will take good care of you here. We're all in this together." She put a comforting hand on Alaina's shoulder.

Kindness.

Gentleness.

Empathy.

But among those good things, Alaina could tell she was not of the faithful. She still possessed questionable characteristics.

"Thank you," Alaina smiled. "May I ask your name?"

"My name is Laura." The woman tilted her head. "Are you new?"

Alaina saw she meant new as a maid. "Yes, I am new," Alaina nodded.

"Bless you," Laura said before turning and motioning for Alaina to follow her.

Alaina followed her into a larger room. Walking through drapes, they entered the larger room that held many other girls. There were all ages, from younger than Alaina to older than Laura. Alaina's heart broke for the girls who were slaving away. Many were clearly exhausted.

"This half is the workroom." Laura pointed to the right side of the room. "This side is the resting room," she said, pointing to the left side of the room. "The right side is for those who must sew, fix, clean, or anything else you can do sitting in place. There are girls around the castle as we speak, doing other work. The left side is for those waiting for their turn. Since there is so much to do, we work in shifts and rotate out." Laura then led her through another doorway and pushed through another set of drapes. "Each room has one window, but they are stuck half open. It helps with the breeze on hot days but leads to bug problems and chilly nights." Laura pointed to the window in the room.

"What is this room for?" Alaina asked as she looked around the room they stood in. It had been filled with tables and chairs, but was empty now.

"This is where we have our meals," Laura answered. "Now, the next room." She walked toward another doorway with drapes and stepped into another large, dull room. "This is where we sleep and stay. There's a closet off to the left where you can pick a maid's outfit," Laura said, and pointed to the closet.

"Thank you," Alaina nodded and walked over to the closet. As she looked through the clothes that hung, her heart saddened. These were the lives these women lived—this is what most of them knew as life. And for them, there was no escape or hope for a better future. At that moment, she asked that God would provide an opportunity for her to help the women in some way one day.

She finally found a dress that fit and looked down at the simple, worn dress. It looked like the rest of the servants' dresses. The fabric was old and had tears in various places. The white had faded to ivory, and the blue on the sleeves had gone dull. Her apron had stains on it, but it was the least of her worries. After she changed, she went back to Laura.

"Perfect," Laura winked. "Now, tell me everything." She sat down on a bed and patted the spot beside her.

Alaina joined her on the bed and sighed. "Everything?" Alaina searched Laura's eyes and knew she could trust her. Perhaps Laura could even provide some helpful information.

"Everything, my dear," Laura smiled.

Alaina put her hands in her lap, and while staring at nothing in particular, she told the story of her quest. She watched Laura's face turn from shock, confusion, wonder, admiration, and worry, and Alaina didn't blame her a bit. As she recounted all the events to Laura, she realized how much she had been through in such a short time. Through it all, God surely delivered them.

"My brother is somewhere in Mizcriea. I believe he may have escaped his slave ship, but I'm not sure. Koen is helping me find my father, and I am here until he gives me news." Alaina finished but refrained from telling Laura about her gift.

"My dear. I don't know what to say," Laura shook her head. "We have many of the faithful here. I am not, but I have great empathy for those who are." Laura smiled sweetly. "Alaina, dear, your story is extraordinary. I would love to help you finish your quest if you would be willing?"

"Yes, of course. I need all the information you can provide," Alaina nodded.

"Okay. Listen closely," Laura leaned in closer and her voice faded to a whisper, "I've heard there is an underground level to the castle that few know about. I'm not sure how true that rumor is or how that would tie in with your quest, but it may be worth looking into." Laura looked around. "I also know there are many secrets the King is keeping. He tells his people less than half of what they really should know. The Queen is said to have passed unexpectedly in her sleep a few weeks ago; however, I don't believe that for one second. She was in perfect health. I was her personal maid."

Alaina's eyes widened when she realized she knew the truth, but Laura did not. "You said the King of Azgalia was kidnapped in the middle of the night with no trace. Well, I heard some whispers about the King sending two of his best men out one night without explanation. That is not common, my dear." Laura looked seriously into Alaina's eyes. "And one more thing."

Alaina nodded for her to continue, but a woman suddenly came into the doorway and said, "Stand at once. A knight has come to give an announcement."

Women rushed to standing positions, and those changing hid or hurried. The knight appeared in the doorway with his face hidden by his helmet.

He spoke, "There is to be a royal celebration tonight for Prince Koen's return home. All of you are ordered to serve guests. That is all." Before he turned to leave, he spotted Alaina and spoke to her, "You. Prince Koen asks that you be sent to his room promptly. He wishes for help in preparing for the celebration." And with that, he left.

The girls resumed their tasks, but this time, they whispered about Koen's return and the new maid he requested. Alaina noticed many of the girls looking her way.

"Many of them are jealous of your position. You're new, and you've already been assigned to be a personal maid for the royal family. Let alone Prince Koen." Laura winked at Alaina. "From what you say, he's a changed man now?"

"He hasn't decided upon his faith; however, he truly wants to follow the truth. He has been a good companion through it all. He promised my brother as much and has done his absolute best to keep it," Alaina smiled.

"That is wonderful. I believe you have somewhere to be?" Laura quickly adjusted Alaina's messy hair and motioned for her to leave the room.

"Yes, I believe I do." Alaina nodded and headed toward the doorway. "What was that one more thing?" Alaina turned around to look for Laura, but she was already gone. "Well, I guess I'll have to ask her later." Alaina turned back around and found her way out of the girls' servant quarters. On the outside of the door was a knight standing guard. Alaina was thankful it wasn't Cyrus or Tristan. "Sir, where might I find Prince Koen's chambers? I am assigned as his personal maid."

"Follow me." Alaina hurried to keep up with his long strides down the dark and long halls. Along the way, she could feel many of the King's staff eyeing her and whispering to each other. It only took one look to know they were talking about her. It appeared the castle already knew of the Azgalian serving the returned Prince.

Alaina could hear voices around the corner when they finally reached the great hall. The knight stopped abruptly and turned to face her. "Wait here." Alaina nodded and watched him walk around the corner. She inched a bit closer so she could hear what was being said. She recognized a voice and realized it was Koen.

"Pardon me, Lord Dolion and Prince Koen." Alaina peered around the corner to get a better look. The knight looked at Koen. "Prince Koen, do you still wish for the presence of your maid?"

"Yes. Have her wait in my chambers," Koen nodded and

looked back at his uncle.

Deceit.

Secretive.

Pride.

Arrogance.

Conceit.

Koen's uncle was not a man to be trusted.

The knight slightly bowed and turned back toward Alaina. Alaina quickly resumed her proper posture and awaited the knight.

"This way. You will wait for the prince in his chambers," the knight said, and Alaina nodded in response. She followed the knight into Koen's chambers and was told to wait in a seat until the prince returned. She nodded again and waited for the knight to shut the door.

Immediately, she stood up and pressed her ear against the large wooden door. The voices coming from the hall were muffled and hard to make out.

" . . . have you back," his uncle said. " . . . border crossing."

Koen's voice came next, "Good . . . in the castle." Alaina closed her eyes in hopes she could hear better. "Slave ship . . . escape." The words that followed were too quiet to understand. She backed away from the door and stared at it until she heard footsteps coming toward the door. She quickly returned to where she was seated before, just in case it wasn't Koen. The door creaked open, and Koen stepped in. He looked out and then proceeded to shut the door.

He turned around and looked at her before laughing. "Why are you just sitting there?"

His smile made her heart skip, and Alaina told herself it was because she was glad to be safe and with her friend again. "The knight said to wait here," Alaina shyly smiled.

"And you listened?" Koen laughed in disbelief.

"No, of course not," Alaina smirked.

"I thought so." Koen shook his head and walked over to sit on his bed. "Did you hear any of the conversations with my uncle?"

"Very little. The doors were too thick to make out what you were saying," Alaina said. She glanced around the room and took in the decor. *Everything is so dark here*. She noticed the tall ceilings and the wallpaper showing battles.

Koen laughed again. "Yeah, they're pretty thick." He cleared his throat. "I talked to him about the slave ship that escaped."

"And?" Alaina leaned forward.

"He, of course, remembered your brother, so I asked him if he knew anything. He said it was the same ship your brother was on. There was an escape, and from what my uncle knows, all the slaves escaped," Koen told her.

Alaina jumped up, "Is that good news? Did he say if they knew of their whereabouts?" Alaina felt unsure of what that meant for David. Did David know where he was? Was he okay? Did he partake in the plan to escape?

"I'm not sure. It depends on how the escape happened. My uncle said they escaped at the docks, but that is the last known whereabouts," Koen told her, looking disappointed he couldn't tell her more.

"That's ridiculous!" Alaina stared out the window in the room overlooking the gardens. "So, do you think it is good news then?"

"As far as I'm thinking, yes. Hopefully, he can make his way here. But if my uncle learns about his whereabouts, I can have him bring David here," Koen suggested.

"No," Alaina shook her head.

"No? Why not?" Koen furrowed his eyebrows.

"I don't trust your uncle, Koen, and I don't think you should either." Alaina looked at him. "I read him. He's hiding something, Koen."

"Really?" Koen took a deep breath. "I thought maybe I could trust him. At least, in the small things. And what could he be hiding?"

"I don't know." Alaina placed a hand on his shoulder to show sympathy. She knew Koen felt like his family was falling apart, and that's because it really was. After a moment of silence, she removed her hand and thought she'd change the subject. "Did you see your brother?"

"I did." Koen looked up with a smile. "He is doing well. He told me that he has joined the faithful."

"That's wonderful, Koen!" Alaina smiled at him.

"It is," he nodded and stood up. "Cronin told me there may be information about your father in the parchment room. The problem is, the only people with access to that room are my uncle and father," Koen said.

"How are you going to get it, then?" Alaina crossed her arms.

"I was going to ask my uncle," Koen said with a hesitant smile.

"I don't think you should," Alaina shook her head. "Is there a key?"

"Yes. I'm not sure where it's kept, though." Koen thought

for a moment. "What if I got my uncle to trust me? If he believed I was trustworthy, he might be willing to let me in."

"At what cost would you convince him, though?" Alaina sat back in the chair and watched Koen's face mull over the idea.

"I guess I'll find out tonight," Koen said. He stood to change, and when he walked by Alaina, she saw him hide a laugh.

"What's so funny?" Alaina smiled.

"Nice clothes!" Koen grinned.

"Psh, it's your fault." Alaina rolled her eyes jokingly.

Things were finally coming together. King Cleatus sat on his throne, watching the lips move on another messenger, and he explained what was happening on the east side of his kingdom. He didn't hear a word, but then again, it didn't matter. Nothing ever happened in the east, and his current plans were much more critical. His fingers continued to tap one at a time on the armrest as he waited for the man to be done.

With Koen's return, things could finally fall into place. His brother was back at the castle now as well. Cleatus held back a smirk as he thought everything was perfectly playing out together. Since he killed his wife, he was finally able to focus on his plans solely. She was always hovering over his shoulder, trying to speak "wisdom" to him.

"Wisdom?" He scoffed at her once. "Wisdom clouds instinct if you ask me. A man uses instinct and strength to get through life. I'll leave the wisdom for you."

He still stood by his words. After all, who was the one who

had perished? She never saw it coming; so much for wisdom. Another thought stirred in his mind about the servant girl Koen had brought with him. She had looked strangely familiar, but he assumed it was because she was Azgalian. They all looked strange to him.

"Sire?" the messenger interrupted his thoughts.

"Sounds good." Cleatus nodded at him and waved him away.

"That's all for the day, my King. Would you like the maids to prepare you for the celebration tonight?" the knight to his right spoke.

"That would be fine." Cleatus nodded and stood up from his royal throne. "I will walk there myself." He walked down the steps toward the great hall where his chambers were. On his way, he passed his brother, to whom both gave a slight nod of acknowledgment.

"Things are being set in place," Dolion told him as he passed.

"Good." Cleatus looked forward and smiled with pleasure.

The celebration started, and many people from the surrounding cities and towns attended. Fiddles and gitterns could be heard everywhere. People clapped and stamped as they danced. *Dramatic as always.* Koen shook his head. The kingdom's dark blue and green colors, along with a golden yellow, decorated the castle grounds, making up slightly for the dead landscape. The finest and most expensive linens covered all the tables, and gourmet food was laid out for the people to enjoy. It was a celebration, but Koen didn't see it that way. With so many secrets and hidden motives, he couldn't trust his father in such a dark time. He couldn't help but wonder if the celebration was a cover-up for something else. Not only that, but now he also had to worry about his uncle.

"Ah, Prince Koen, it is good to have you back. We were all a bit confused about why you ran off." Lord Darius slapped Koen on the shoulder. "Why *did* you run off?"

Lord Darius's grin made Koen want to cringe. His teeth were yellowed as if he hadn't cleaned them in years. *Did the man have any hygiene? Probably not, he's too busy carrying out my father's evil orders.*

"Oh, you know," Koen managed a fake laugh. "Just wanted to see more of the world before I get old."

"I get it." Lord Darius raised his eyebrows and laughed. "Wasn't that long ago I was young and had that freedom like you. Gotta take the chance while it's there; that's what I always say."

"Exactly," Koen laughed and watched him walk away. He'd known Darius since he was very young, and the man had definitely never used that saying. Koen shook his head. He looked around for Alaina and avoided getting into lengthy conversations. He spotted his brother and made his way over to him. He was wearing a dark blue tunic that had gold trimming. His trousers matched perfectly, and his hair and beard had been nicely trimmed. "You look good," he smirked as he stood beside him.

"I miss my long beard," Cronin said, stroking his stubble.

"No, you don't," Koen laughed.

"You're right," Cronin smiled. "I don't. Thanks."

"What are brothers for?" Koen wrapped his arm around Cronin's shoulder.

"Although it really should be me helping you. I'm the older brother after all." Cronin gave Koen a side glance.

"Oh, believe me, you owe me," Koen said jokingly.

"Have you seen Uncle? He's back," Cronin said.

"Yes. I spoke to him earlier. Alaina said we shouldn't trust him," Koen said in a low voice.

"I wouldn't put it past him to be involved with Father's plans," Cronin shrugged.

"Agreed," Koen nodded. "I'm going to convince him I think otherwise. I need the key to the parchment room."

"That's dangerous. Uncle can pick up on motives quickly. He can recognize his own game." Cronin looked out at the crowd.

"Yes, but when has the fact that something was dangerous ever stopped me? Plus, I just have to play his game long enough to get the key," Koen said.

"True, I guess. Just be careful." Cronin's "older brother" tone was coming out. "I feel so useless, though. I want to help."

"We'll need your help soon, I'm sure. If you start poking your nose in things now that I'm back, Father may grow suspicious," Koen said as he continued to look for Alaina.

"You're right," Cronin snorted. "You looking for Alaina?" He nodded toward the left corner of the room. "I'm guessing that's her. She's pretty." Cronin smirked, and Koen rolled his eyes.

"She's too young for you," Koen said, dodging Cronin's shove with a laugh.

"Go on, get." Cronin shook his head, laughing.

Making his way toward Alaina, Koen kept his gaze on the ground to maneuver through people without making eye contact. Suddenly, he ran into a tall, hard figure. He looked up, and his eyes widened slightly.

"I'm sorry. I really should stop surprising you." His uncle gave a smirk that made Koen feel uneasy.

Koen tried to show relief, as though he was glad to see his uncle. "I'm sorry. I thought you were another eager mother trying to set me up with your daughter," Koen said, hoping his uncle believed him.

"Understandable," his uncle said, clearly not persuaded. "This is quite a celebration." His uncle looked around at the party.

"It is. Glad to see I was missed," Koen said. *Why am I so nervous?* He needed to shake the nerves before they ruined his and Alaina's plans.

"Well, it's good to see you haven't lost your sense of humor. Say, how was your trip after I saw you at the border?" his uncle asked.

"It was difficult. We went through the desert, and a snake bit me." Koen was careful not to share too much information.

"Really?" His uncle raised his eyebrows, "Well, you seem alive and well." His uncle laughed and patted him on the shoulder.

"It seems so." Koen laughed, growing more relaxed. His uncle didn't seem so suspicious. *Maybe I'm paranoid.* "Uncle, I've had a lot of time to think recently," Koen paused to make sure his uncle was paying attention. "There's something I've been meaning to ask you."

"Go ahead. Ask anything," His uncle nodded.

"All this time being away has made me realize how much I want to do more for the kingdom. I'd like to train to become part of the royal army. I'd like to be your right-hand man in battles and training," Koen said, ensuring his face and voice didn't waver.

His uncle looked surprised for a moment, then grinned. "My nephew, there's nothing I'd love more. I think you would be a perfect fit. From what I've seen, you already wield a sword well. We'll just need to focus on your hand-to-hand combat. When would you like to start?"

"Tomorrow," Koen said confidently.

"Good answer. Well, then." His uncle straightened his shoulders. "See you bright and early." As he walked off, Koen let out a sigh of relief.

"Koen," Alaina came up beside him. "How was that?" She looked around where his uncle had gone.

"I'm in," Koen said and looked at her. She looked worried. "What's wrong?"

"Koen, I was watching your uncle. For some reason, things seemed worse. He's hiding something big." Alaina looked into his eyes. "And whatever it is, it's about you."

TWENTY-FIVE

"It's kind of amazing, isn't it?" Evelyn asked David as they sat in the grass watching everyone. They had finally arrived at the camp that morning and were waiting for Christopher to find the "man in charge," as Jamie had said. The group stayed in the grass and watched the bustling camp. The people set up tents in an open field and made their own village. The people walking by were friendly, and the kids went about their day as if strangers were a picture of normalcy.

"Yeah," David nodded. "I can't believe this is so close to the castle, yet the King has never disturbed it." He shook his head in wonder.

"Truly God's providence," Evelyn nodded and smiled.

"Alright," Christopher came up and clapped his hands, being his usual upbeat self. "Peter would like to meet everyone, and he says there's enough room for groups of four to five to have their own tent. Those who plan on staying here until further notice, you will have your own tent made as soon as possible," he said, and the group clapped and hollered.

"Okay then," Christopher grinned. "Follow me."

Together, the group followed. He led them to what looked to be the main tent. It was larger than the others, and David guessed it might be large enough to fit the whole camp if needed. "If any of you need to meet, if there is ever a meeting called, or anything of the sort, this is where that all happens."

They made their way through the opening, and Christopher approached a man with tanned skin, long hair, and bright blue-green eyes. His smile was warm, and his eyes seemed filled with wisdom and kindness. "Everyone, this is Peter."

"The man in charge?" Jamie spoke up.

"That's right," Peter laughed along with everyone else. "Welcome, everyone. We're a welcoming camp serving the true King, the Lord Jesus Christ. We only ask that you keep our location to yourself," he smiled. "Now, I'd love to talk to each one of you individually, but seeing that there are so many, please come to me on your own time. Tell me your names for now, and I'll have some of our people show you to your tents."

David waited patiently with Jamie and Evelyn as the rest of the men introduced themselves to Peter. Once Peter reached them, Jamie reached out and shook his hand. "My name is Jamie; it's an honor to meet you, sir. Christopher has told me a lot about you."

"It's a pleasure, Jamie," Peter kindly smiled. "I feel this camp will love you and your sense of humor."

"That's a high compliment, sir." Jamie laughed and nodded when a woman approached and asked him to follow her to his tent.

Evelyn was next. "It's a pleasure to meet you, Peter. My name is Evelyn."

"Evelyn, I hope it's alright, but your friend Christopher said he had the princess of Azgalia in his group." Peter smiled knowingly at Evelyn.

"Yes, that would be me," Evelyn laughed, knowing she was the only girl in the group.

Peter smiled. "Princess Evelyn, it's a pleasure to have you

here. I am deeply sorry for what has happened with your father. I do hope you find him," Peter told her.

"Thank you, Peter. Maybe we could talk about that," Evelyn said with a longing look.

"Yes, of course. I look forward to hearing more and seeing if there's anything I can do to help." Peter shook her hand and placed his other hand on top of hers.

Peter directed his gaze to where David stood; he blinked twice and tilted his head.

"Sir," David nodded respectfully. "My name is . . . "

"David," Peter said, which surprised him.

Peter smiled at David's confused look.

"How did you know?" David looked over at Christopher. *Christopher must have told him about me, too.*

"David, your sister told me so much about you. I have to say, I am so glad you found your way here," Peter smiled and embraced him.

"You know my sister?" David's heart leapt. *His sister was here!*

"Indeed. I ran into Alaina while she was seeking help for Prince Koen. Praise the Lord, I was there to help. Koen wouldn't have made it," Peter shook his head.

"What happened? Is she okay? Where did they go?" David realized he was getting ahead of himself. "I'm sorry; I just have so many questions."

"Why don't we sit down?" Peter motioned to the tables, and David nodded.

"Christopher and Evelyn, feel free to join us until you are shown to your tents." Peter invited them, so they did. "My son, your sister was in perfect health when she was here. She left here about a day ago with Koen. A serpent of paradise bit him, but he pulled through it well.”

Christopher’s eyes widened when he recognized the deadly animal. “Serpent of paradise?” He shook his head. “Wow.”

“Indeed,” Peter nodded. “She told me of your quest. As we speak, your sister is in the middle of it right now. They headed to the castle as soon as Koen was well.”

David stared at the table. “I need to be there.”

Peter shook his head. “I think that would make it more difficult, David. I agree you should leave as soon as possible, but it seems the Lord has you separated for a reason,” Peter said.

David was surprised to find that he was struggling to compose himself. *Didn’t Peter understand the urgency of their quest? Maybe Alaina didn’t tell him everything.* “Why do you think it would make it more difficult?”

“I know Koen is the Prince, and Alaina is posing as his maid. They both have a place in the castle where they won’t be questioned. You, however, don’t have any cover.” It was a reasonable point.

David was silent as he mulled over his thoughts. What was he supposed to do then? If he didn’t go now, then when? When would it be safe to go? *Never*, he thought. “You make a valid argument. Still, I’d like to leave tomorrow.”

Peter looked at David and slowly nodded. “I understand.”

“I’m going with you. I came here for the same reason, and I plan to see it through,” Evelyn said firmly.

David admired her for a moment. “Are you sure?”

“Yes.” She looked at Peter. “I know I am.”

Peter looked at Christopher and then at Evelyn and David. “Well, please let me know what you both need.” David nodded. "Please meet me before you leave. I would like to pray for your quest before you head out."

"We will," David said before heading to his tent for the night.

There was a sudden banging in Koen's head. His eyes squeezed shut in hopes of drowning it out.

More banging. It was a knock at the door, "Ugh." He groaned as he rolled over.

"Koen, training starts in half an hour. Meet me at the gate in fifteen minutes," Dolion's voice pierced through Koen's groggy brain.

"Oh!" Koen's eyes shot open. "Uh . . . " He shook his head to get some bearings. "Yes, Uncle. I'll be right down," Koen called. For some reason, while he slept, he'd felt like it was all a dream. None of this could truly be honest, right? He knew it was real, but it seemed so lovely to think it wasn't, just for a moment. "Okay, I need to get going." He hopped out of bed and dressed in his tunic and trousers. He would put on armor at the training grounds. He didn't bother looking in the mirror; he hadn't used one the past couple of weeks.

Since his mother's death, he knew it would never be the same if he returned home. Yet, it was worse than he imagined. Every corner he turned, every window he peered out, reminded him of his mother and the memories with her. The guilt gnawed away at his heart with every memory that passed through his mind. *It's my fault she's dead. I need to make things right.* Opening his bedroom door, he took a deep breath and let it out. His eyes glanced towards the corner of the hall when he sensed movement.

"Alaina," his tense body eased when he saw her.

"Prince Koen." Alaina formally nodded and motioned toward the other servant behind him.

Koen nodded knowingly and spoke in what he called his prince voice. "I will be at my uncle's training all day today. It should give you plenty of time to finish the tasks I asked of you," Koen said. When the other servant turned around to resume a chore, Koen raised an eyebrow and smirked. He loved playing pretend.

"Yes, of course, my Prince," Alaina bowed her head and answered perfectly in sync.

Koen nodded and went on his way down the hall. When the other servant disappeared into a room to clean, Koen turned around, pointed at the door the servant entered, and gave a pretend, mocking laugh. He earned a giggle from Alaina, which made his heart happy. *Cronin was right. She is pretty.*

"Be safe," she mouthed before slipping into his chambers. With that, he turned to head to the training grounds.

Koen went through a series of halls until he finally reached the arena. A stone wall with a curved doorway led out into another narrow hall. Koen stepped through the doorway and looked left, then right. Straight ahead was another stone wall, but each direction led to different entrances into the stands or the arena. When he was younger, Koen read plenty about combat. He and his brother would also play-fight for hours on end. They dreamed about the wars they would fight in, and all the kingdoms they'd conquer together. Koen was a skilled swordsman; he'd go so far as to say he was better than his uncle. There was only one way to find out.

"Koen. This way." His uncle appeared from the left. Koen nodded and followed him through to the spectator stands. "I want you to watch my men fight first. I know you have watched before, but a refresher is always important," Dolion said with a focused gaze on the men below.

"Of course," Koen agreed. If only his uncle knew about the knight tournament. He averted his eyes to watch the men below meet each other in the middle of the arena.

When Dolion called out for them to begin, they immediately started to combat.

Thrusting and slicing, but pulling back to avoid real injuries, the knights moved around the arena. The slightly taller man ducked when the shorter one went to attack his helmet. The taller one then delivered a cut at the shoulder of the shorter one and made a dent in his armor. The knight stumbled back and quickly regained balance to attack forward again.

Finally, the shorter one took advantage of his speed. The taller one, not realizing how to use his height, fell and was defeated by the shorter one.

"Very good," Dolion clapped slowly as the men finished and helped each other stand. Dolion turned to his nephew, "You know the basics. Just as the knight down there did." Dolion motioned toward the tall knight. "However, you will have to learn to use your advantage. Like this boy." Dolion then motioned toward the shorter knight. "Sure, he is a smaller opponent, but he can be quicker than you," Dolion explained, and Koen nodded. "Do you understand?" Dolion asked Koen.

Koen met his eyes, "Yes." His uncle led him out of the

stands and down the stone hallway. They walked down a steep staircase until they came to the training ground. He followed him out into the arena. Dolion took the sword from one of the knights and handed it to Koen. With the sword in hand, Koen turned to face the smaller knight.

"No armor," Dolion said, and the knight looked at him in surprise, but when Dolion didn't budge, he complied. The shorter knight took off his armor and faced Koen.

Sword in hand, Koen readied his stance and crossed blades with the shorter man.

"Good," Dolion said and backed away. "Begin."

The shorter man quickly rotated his blade to thrust toward Koen's torso. Koen jumped back and swung his sword to knock the knight's sword off course. With the momentum, the knight spun his body, and Koen anticipated it before he could initiate his intended move. Koen wasn't short and speedy or tall and heavy. He was, however, strong, quick-thinking, and agile. Koen dropped to his hands and twisted his body to remove his opponent's feet. The shorter man tumbled forward, and Koen jumped back to his feet. Now on opposite sides of where they started, the shorter man had to regain his bearings. He had speed, but he didn't think very fast.

Koen smirked and released a series of combinations David had shown him. He even added a few steps from the Azgalian culture dance that he had done with David. The knight was taken aback and struggled to keep up with Koen's unpredictable movements. He gave the knight no room for anticipation or ability to memorize his movements and patterns. Koen slipped up once by allowing a pause, and that's when the knight surprised Koen with a quick slice at his shoulder. Koen groaned at the sting but quickly recovered, driving the knight back with even more strength and force. The knight finally fell back and threw his hands up in surrender.

"Alright!" he shouted.

Koen pulled up just short of his chest and looked into the knight's frightened eyes. "Good job," Koen smiled and sheathed his sword. He reached out a hand and helped the knight up.

"You are better than your uncle said," the knight declared.

"Thank you," Koen said and looked over at his uncle. He stood there, emotionless.

"Very good," he nodded. Koen still couldn't tell if he was proud, angry, impressed, or surprised. "You have improved much since I last saw you in combat."

"I've practiced since then," Koen stated.

"Good," Dolion said with a nod of approval.

"Uncle, would you say I've surpassed even you?" Koen smirked, knowing his uncle couldn't pass up a good challenge.

"Of course not," his uncle waved him off.

"Really? I think I have," Koen said, shrugging.

"Please, my boy. I have many more years of experience," his uncle said. "Don't let the first win go to your head."

"Right, but isn't it about using one's advantage?" Koen raised an eyebrow.

Dolion stared at Koen and squinted. "What are you getting at, Koen?"

"I'd like to propose a challenge. You against me." Koen crossed his arms.

"Why would I do that?" Dolion raised his chin and eyebrow at the same time.

"Because if you win, I will tell you how to penetrate Azgalian border protection and overrun the castle." The knight Koen beat stood by, his mouth wide open in shock. Koen stared deep into his uncle's eyes. He had thought long and hard about what he could give his uncle, and even though it was risky to promise such a thing, he knew it was irresistible to his uncle's curiosity.

His uncle's eyebrows raised. It was probably the most emotion he had shown all day. "And how can I be certain you aren't bluffing?"

"Because if I am, you have the power to end my life," Koen stated, which again, surprised his uncle.

"And if you win?" his uncle crossed his arms.

"I get the key around your neck," Koen said bluntly.

His uncle's eyes squinted. "Whatever for?"

Koen was doing his best to compose his nerves. He couldn't let his uncle be suspicious. He needed to be convincing. He needed to be like his uncle at that moment. To beat his uncle at his own game was the only way to make this work.

"I have always wanted more power in this kingdom. I can help my father immensely if I expand my knowledge and understanding of Mizcriea. I know that's the key to the parchment room." Koen pointed to the key.

Dolion stared deep into Koen's eyes, searching for any deceit. Finally, to Koen's relief, he smirked, "You got me." Dolion approached his nephew with an amused expression and shook his hand. "Challenge accepted."

He couldn't tell if he was breathing harder or if his breathing sounded louder in his helmet. Koen adjusted his breastplate and put his boots on. He looked to where his uncle was putting on his armor. He was really going to do this. He would never have imagined he'd be sparring with his uncle. His uncle was an excellent swordsman, and growing up, Koen watched him defeat every knight he trained in the arena. Koen wasn't about to back down now, though. Koen rolled his shoulders back and walked out into the middle of the arena.

Dolion stood up straight and walked over to meet Koen in the middle. Swords sheathed, nephew and uncle sized each other.

"Last chance, Koen." Dolion raised his eyebrow.

"You want to forfeit?" Koen gave a mischievous grin.

Laughing, Dolion shook his head and reached up to flip down his visor. "Not a chance."

Koen's humor quickly diminished, and his expression became serious. He backed up and unsheathed his sword. Staring at his uncle, he flipped down his visor and readied his stance. Feet placed firmly in the dirt below him and holding a steady breath, he crossed blades with his uncle. He hoped Alaina had prayed for him that morning.

The smaller knight, Oswald, stood off to the side to make the call. He crossed his arms and whispered something to the tall knight. They looked smug. They believed Koen was going to lose. "Ready?" the knight asked. When Dolion nodded, the short one took a breath. "Begin."

Koen's eyes widened when Dolion exploded with a decisive advance. His mind was momentarily stunned; Koen was surprised he held his ground. But he couldn't afford to be surprised.

Releasing a series of deflections, both men knew Koen was on the defensive. Dolion had the advantage of experience, but Koen was smart enough to know that didn't always guarantee a win.

Dolion's sword flew faster, but Koen caught every thrust and refused to give up his ground. Their swords danced, arced, cut, and sliced in a volley of mastery. Koen found an opportunity to reverse the roles and took the lead. As he gained control and increased his speed with quick thinking and unwavering strength, Koen felt the tension in the arena as more knights came to witness this duel.

Once Koen held the offense, he could sense Dolion's anger. Koen only grew more determined. The short knight stepped forward as if he wanted to interfere.

"No!" Dolion yelled between hard breaths. "Back off!"

Koen saw an opening. A cut from Dolion had put his sword too far outside his torso, which left him unbalanced. He countered with a diagonal cut, then began a quick thrust that he was sure Dolion wouldn't be able to parry.

Halfway through his thrust, Koen realized it had been a trick. Dolion had shifted his left foot slightly to recover from his "mistake."

Koen pulled his thrust up just in time to block what his uncle intended to be the victory move.

Surprised, Dolion was now out of position. Koen smirked behind his visor and attacked. Sword flying, muscles burning, and breath heating his helmet, Koen put his uncle in a desperate retreat. While his uncle was exasperated and clearly trying to recover, Koen saw his chance. With one final powerful blow, Koen's sword met his uncle's and sent it flying.

Victory.

With a thud, Dolion's sword pierced the dirt, and the knights stood stunned. Koen had bested Sir Dolion in a sword match. Dolion's hands went up when Koen put the tip of his sword to his chest. "I found my advantage."

"Clearly," Dolion said bitterly.

With the edge of his sword, Koen tipped off his uncle's helmet and used it to hook the necklace his uncle wore. Raising it over his head, Koen grabbed the key and held it in his hand. "I assume training is over?"

"It is," Dolion waved off Koen's offer to help him and stood alone. He picked up his helmet and turned to Koen with a suspiciously wide grin. "You've made me proud today, Koen. You bested me before my knights, which is truly an accomplishment. You surely have great talent."

"Thank you," Koen said. *Why is he so kind? What does he want?*

"I'm sure my knights would greatly develop under your training and mine combined. What do you say?" Dolion asked.

"I'll . . . " Koen looked around at the knights and wished Alaina were there to tell him his uncle's motives. "I'll think about it."

"Of course. Sleep on it. Let me know by tomorrow, will you?" Dolion continued to be uneasily generous.

"Yes, sir." Koen faked a smile and a respectful nod. He needed to get out of there. He walked out of the arena with a nod to the knights who were obviously still stunned.

TWENTY-SIX

Twirling the key around his finger, Koen paced through the halls. When he came to the hall where his quarters were, he peeked inside his room to see if Alaina was still around. "Alaina?"

"Over here." Alaina's voice came from around a corner. Koen walked around to find her reading a book in a chair. She looked up from her book, and when she saw it was Koen, she snapped back to reality. She folded her book, stood up, and looked at him.

Koen waved the key in the air with a smirk and raised eyebrows. "You got it!" Alaina grinned.

"You bet I did." Koen gave the key another twirl and stuffed it in his pocket. "I'm going to the room now. I'll return for you here as soon as I find what we need."

"Koen . . . " Alaina couldn't finish her sentence, but her expression showed she was thankful.

"We both want answers," Koen said, walking toward the hallway again. "Lock the doors. Only open the door if you hear my voice." He slipped out his door and walked down the hall while steadying his breath. He was trying to calm the nerves that churned in his stomach. Hurrying through the halls, he tried not to draw any attention from the servants. Soon, he reached the parchment room. Koen took a deep breath and pulled out the key from his pocket. *Why am I so nervous? I won the key fair and square,* he thought. Yet, he couldn't shake the feeling that chilled his spine after he won the fight with his uncle. After looking left and right, with a trembling hand, he inserted the key. The door squeaked open, and he slipped inside.

The room was smaller than he imagined, but every inch of the wall held parchments on shelves. In the left corner was a desk and chair with parchment paper and a quill pen. He looked around for any direction that would make the search for what he needed easier. He took a step closer to examine the shelves and saw some dates indicating the times the parchments were relevant.

"Eighteen years ago," he whispered, tracing the shelves with his finger. His eyes flickered back and forth to find the parchment. Finally, his finger stopped, and so did his breathing. "There," he said and reached to pull it out.

Dust swirled around his head as he pulled out the old parchment. He blinked away the dust and stared at the parchment in his hands. Slowly, he unrolled it. His sea-green eyes scanned the parchment, and his heart began to race.

Mizcriean soldiers had abducted Alaina's father under King Cleatus, his own father.

Shivers ran down Koens' body, and he blinked hard as anger boiled inside him. He read on.

It read that her father was taken to the "dungeon below." Koen furrowed his eyebrows. *Dungeon below? We don't have a dungeon below.* He shook his head and kept reading. A capture order was put in place.

Koen blinked. "He's alive." Chills ran over his body as he realized it. "He's alive," he said again. He read more. His heart sank when he read that her father was beaten to comply with their plans. Cleatus used him for his gift to build Mizcriean armies. At the end, the parchment read "capture order two." *If this is two . . .* Koen's eyes widened. "That would mean . . ."

He looked back at where he had taken the parchment from. Tracing his fingers down the shelves for a similar parchment. He pulled it out and scanned it. *Another abduction from Azgalia? But who?* He retraced the shelves. Another capture. He did it again and again and again. His heart was beating fast, and he started to sweat. His father had been behind all of this. *Why, though? What was he planning?* He picked up what seemed to be a recent parchment, and his heart sank when he read what it held. It was King Malikai's capture.

Then, he froze.

Suddenly, he realized something was missing. Where was capture number one? He looked back to where Alaina's father's parchment was and scanned for "capture one."

The door squeaked. Koen's head whipped around just in time to see his uncle behind him before everything went black.

The wind blew through the forest, rustling the leaves as the clouds covered any sight of the sun. David's horse side-stepped nervously.

"Looks like he's not too fond of the wind," David stated as he tried to relax his horse.

"I don't blame him," Evelyn said, trying to keep her hair out of her face. They could see the castle entrance gate from where they were. Peter provided them with Mizcriean clothes so they could pass as common folk. The Mizcriean clothing contained warmer colors, primarily brown, tan, and ivory. The men wore ivory or tan-colored trousers and a brown tunic, which was tucked in. Evelyn wore a lighter brown dress with an ivory apron tied around her waist.

Peter told them that commoners visit the castle often to plead for extra time to pay their taxes since prices were so high in Mizcriea.

"It's there," David pointed to the gate. "Ready?"

When Evelyn nodded, David urged his horse forward despite its hesitance to move in the wind.

Coming upon the gate, the guards unsheathed their swords. "What business do you have here?"

"We've come to plead with the King," David said, ducking his eyes, which Peter said showed respect.

"Very well," the guard nodded and signaled for the gate to be raised.

David and Evelyn thanked the guards and entered. The fields behind the wall were not at all what David imagined. The fields surrounding the castle were just as dull as their clothing. The colors were almost completely gone, and the flowers looked dead. The view only added to David's uneasiness. He couldn't explain it, but it just felt evil.

"It's hideous," Evelyn said aloud, breaking David's thoughts.

"Shh, keep your voice down," David laughed. "Someone may hear you."

"Well, maybe they should; the gardeners have done a terrible job maintaining the gardens." Evelyn nodded as she gazed at a sorry excuse for a castle garden. Azgalia's castle grounds were lush and bright. The colors glimmered when the sun shone down on the morning dew.

David nodded in response. He couldn't agree more and thought it was strange that almost no one was outside. Finally, he saw a man in the garden, staring at a large dead tree. David thought it was strange and wanted to investigate. "Follow me." David nodded toward the man.

"Shouldn't we enter the castle?" Evelyn asked.

"We have nothing to plead for. We just need to find Alaina and Koen," David said. He turned his horse in the man's direction.

As they drew closer to the man, David could now see that he wasn't much older than he was. He had a trimmed beard and a short haircut, but it was done without any skill. His clothes were of fine linen, yet they were in poor condition. With deep brown eyes and dark features, the man looked up at the tree with hands raised above his waist and palms up.

"Is he . . . is he praying?" Evelyn whispered to David. David shrugged.

David spoke quietly, not wanting to startle the man, "Excuse me, sir?"

Obviously surprised by the interruption, the man spun around with wide eyes. When he saw David and Evelyn, he eased slightly. "Can I help you?" he asked.

"Possibly," David looked at Evelyn, then back at the man. "Ah," he hesitated, hoping his following few words wouldn't give them away. "We're here for business with Prince Koen. Do you know where we might find him?" David asked.

The man furrowed his eyebrows. "Prince Koen?"

David swallowed, and his horse side-stepped, feeling David's nervousness. "Uh, yes. Prince Koen."

The man stared at David for a few seconds and then looked at Evelyn. "What are your names?"

"My name is David, and this is Evelyn," David answered, praying the man wouldn't know Evelyn.

"David?" The man squinted. "Let me ask you, David. Do you know who I am?"

"I, uh," David stuttered, "I can't say I do." David shook his head, hoping for the best.

There was a long pause before the strange man suddenly burst into a wide grin. "David." He began to laugh. "This is truly wonderful." He shook his head in wonder.

David, who was extremely confused, smiled, "I beg your pardon, sir. Who are you?"

"Why, I am Prince Cronin, Koen's elder brother," Cronin smiled.

David's eyes widened. "I had no idea; my apologies . . ."

"Please, please." Cronin held up his hands. "Koen told me about you and your sister, Alaina. I was pleased to hear he was in faithful company during the time my brother was away." When David gave him a questioning look, Cronin said, "You'll be pleased to hear I am of the faithful."

David looked at Evelyn to see if she was thinking the same. How did they know this wasn't a trap? *I wish Alaina were here. She would see if he was being honest or not.* "I'm sorry if we are hesitant to believe you."

"No, I get it," Cronin nodded. "Now, I know Alaina is with my brother, so who is this?" Cronin motioned toward Evelyn.

"I am Evelyn, a new friend of David," Evelyn said, knowing not to reveal her true identity.

"It's a pleasure, Evelyn," Cronin bowed. "Now, would you like to see Koen?"

"Yes, and if it is at all possible, and my sister as well," David said with eagerness.

"Of course." Cronin nodded. "Please follow me." Cronin led them to the royal stables and helped them bring their horses in. After telling them to wait in the stables, he left to find Koen and Alaina.

♕

Alaina stared out the window in Koen's room, biting her lip. She was growing anxious, waiting for him. Surely he should be back by now. Of course, he could still be searching for the parchment, or he could have been called to another matter, or . . . something worse. But she was praying that wasn't the case.

Laura would start searching for her soon. Alaina could get in trouble if anyone found her waiting in here. "Ugh, Koen. Where are you?" She continued glancing at the door, hoping he'd suddenly enter. She brushed the hair out of her face and paced back and forth, thinking about what to do. Alaina looked at the time and decided that if he weren't back in the next twenty minutes, she'd leave the room and write a note to let Koen know she'd gone to look for him. She sighed and sat down on his bed. Suddenly, she jumped at the sound of a knock on her door.

"Koen? Are you in there?" A familiar voice came through the door. Alaina stared, wondering who it was and what she should do next. "Koen?" This time, the voice called louder.

Alaina looked around frantically and, without thinking, knocked over the chair to let the person know someone was in here. She didn't want to give away her identity yet, though.

There was a pause, and then, "Is Koen in there? It's Cronin."

Alaina sighed in relief. She slowly unlocked and opened the door to find Koen's brother standing there. "Cronin," she spoke.

He looked at her, surprised. "Alaina? What's going on? Where is Koen?" Cronin looked in the room.

"He's not here. He went to face Dolion this morning and won the key to the parchment room. Last I saw him, he told me to wait in his room until he returned. That was hours ago." Alaina shook her head in worry.

"I didn't see him on my way here." Cronin's features twisted while he thought. Alaina now became aware of how tall and intimidating he was. However, his dark features were softened by his mellow presence. "We need to find him. Oh, and Alaina, your brother and his friend are here to see you."

"David?" Alaina asked, confused. "Friend? When?"

"He's outside by the stables. He's come asking for you and Koen. We need to find Koen, because they cannot wait there for too long," Cronin reasoned.

Alaina nodded, her heart skipping in excitement and gladness. *David was alive! David was here!* She silently praised God and thanked him for protecting her brother. She prayed they would find Koen soon. Alaina followed Cronin as they walked back down the halls searching for Koen. On the way, Cronin stopped and asked the maids and servants if they had seen where his brother had gone. So far, Alaina could see that they all told the truth.

"I can see how your gift is extremely useful," Cronin said as they walked.

Koen must have told him of her gift, she thought. "It can be," she said.

"Alaina!" Laura spotted Alaina passing by.

Alaina spun around at the sound of her authoritative tone. "Laura, I . . . " She tripped over her words.

"Prince Cronin, I apologize. Miss Alaina was supposed to report back to me long ago." Laura gave Alaina a furious glare, although Alaina knew Laura meant no harm to her.

"Laura, it's fine. Alaina is helping me." Cronin looked down the hall and then back at Laura. "Say, would you happen to know where my brother is?"

Laura's eyes widened just quickly enough for Cronin not to notice. "I . . . I'm afraid I do not," she said blankly.

Cronin looked at Alaina, and when Alaina didn't meet his gaze, he pressed Laura again, "Laura, I must find my brother. I will personally reward you for any truthful information you can provide."

Suddenly willing to cooperate, Laura said, "Prince Cronin, you understand I was told to keep this to myself by Sir Dolion himself. You can understand why I had to lie to you just now." Laura looked around nervously and fidgeted with the cloth in her hands. "However, I do love you and your brother dearly. Keep your reward." She paused. "I believe your brother is in danger." Alaina's heart sank.

"Laura, please," Cronin urged her to go on.

"Well, you see, I was cleaning when I saw Koen go into the parchment room. He looked as though he wasn't supposed to be going in there. So, of course, I waited to see what was going on. Not long after, I saw Sir Dolion walk inside. The next thing I knew, Sir Dolion walked out, dragging Koen behind him. He was unconscious." Laura shook her head. "My goodness, I blew my own cover when I gasped at the sight. Sir Dolion saw me and threatened to have me killed if I told a soul. He then dragged him off," Laura said, and looked down the hall as though she was afraid Dolion was listening.

"Laura, what else?" Alaina saw there was more.

"I followed him." Laura shook her head, ashamed of her behavior. "He ordered a knight to bring around a carriage. He threw Koen in the back, then stepped inside himself. The knight got in the front to drive." Laura breathed in. "And then, would you believe it, the King himself walks out of the castle and steps inside too!" Laura shook her head. "I have no idea where they were going or why they did such a thing with Prince Koen, but I'm afraid neither of them was in good spirits," Laura said.

"We need to go now. Thank you, Laura," he said, and he and Alaina sprinted down the hall.

When they finally reached the main entrance, Cronin turned to Alaina. "Alaina, someone needs to tell your brother. I can go with you, but I must warn you: I fight poorly."

"Okay. Cronin, tell my brother. I will go get Koen."

"How? Both my father and uncle are the masterminds behind this!" Cronin said.

"I just need a bow. Cronin, please," Alaina stared into his deep brown eyes.

Cronin sighed, "I wish I could offer more." He shook his head and turned to speak to a knight. "Get me a bow, arrows, and a horse." The knight ran off to do as he was told. Cronin turned to Alaina again. "Perks of being a prince," he said with a smirk.

The knight didn't take long to return with what Cronin had requested. "Thank you. Now leave your post for an hour," Cronin ordered him, and the knight nodded, although his eyes told Alaina he was confused as to why.

"Here, let me help you up."

Alaina nodded and accepted his hand so he could help her into the saddle. "Thank you." She could feel her heart pounding as Cronin handed her the bow and arrows.

"Alaina, be careful." Cronin put his hands on her knee and looked up at her. I will be praying for both you and Koen." His eyes welled with tears, and he fought to blink away. "I cannot lose another."

Alaina steadied her breath as she looked into Cronin's face. She understood him completely.

Her grandmother and David had taught her how to use a bow and sword well. She was prepared—she had to be. Alaina prayed for her own safety and kicked her mount forward.

Four words entered Koen's mind.

Cold. Wet. Dark. Pain.

He could barely breathe. Something was covering his head, preventing his vision. He was on his side and lay on something hard, wet, and bumpy.

I'm in a prisoner's cart.

How did he get here? The last thing he remembered was . . . falling asleep. *Had he been abducted?* He couldn't remember.

The cart continued to bump up and down. His shoulder was sore from repeatedly hitting the floor of the cart. He then remembered Alaina. *She was still back at the castle! If he were kidnapped, what would happen to her? I have to get out!*

He tried to focus his mind on moving his hands. They were tied up.

He wriggled and twisted, but no success. He kicked his feet, but they were too tightly bound. So, he did the only thing he could think of.

He yelled.

Suddenly, the cart stopped. He stopped yelling and listened. He heard footsteps and a lock move. Then, the cart doors swung open, letting in cold air.

Koen shivered and rolled over so that he could face the open doors.

"Ah, so he finally awakens," his uncle said.

What?

"Is he awake?" another voice sounded, followed by an evil laugh that could only belong to one person—his father.

Koen moaned when he felt a sharp pain in his chest.

"Oh, shut up," his uncle said. "Yes, he's awake!"

"Let me see him." Footsteps met his uncle.

"Koen, my boy, this is nothing personal. You'll understand soon," his father's wicked voice said.

"Let me out!" Koen's voice rose with frustration, which brought back the pain in his chest. He winced.

"I'm afraid I cannot do that," his father's voice returned.

"Why are you doing this?" Koen asked with a painful tone.

"Like I said, you'll soon understand." He laughed and pushed the doors shut.

Koen had to get out, because if he didn't, he might never come back.

TWENTY-SEVEN

The cart came to an abrupt halt, jolting Koen awake. His head swirled in confusion and pounded in pain. The cart doors swung open, and he felt the sun on his face.

"Get him out." A jerk at his feet followed his uncle's command. He was thrown on the ground with a thud. Pain shot through his body. "Father!" he cried out in anger.

His father ignored him. "Get him up, will you?" Koen was pulled to his feet and felt the rope around his ankles released, allowing him to walk.

"What is the meaning of this?" Koen called out, desperate for an answer. He was only assuming the worst.

"Where do you want him, sire?" the extra man asked. Probably a knight.

"That tree," his father said. Koen was pulled, stumbling to gain his balance, toward "that tree." As Koen realized what might be happening, he decided to fight. He threw himself against the knight holding him and felt his grip loosen. Koen used that moment to break free of the knight. The only problem left was that he was still blindfolded and his hands were tied. This caused Koen to hesitate long enough to be seized again by the knight. The knight was bigger and stronger than he was, so Koen could not break free again.

The knight grabbed his hands tighter, and Koen grunted as he was pushed further along. "Nice try." The knight's whisper in his ear only made his anger burn more. He was pressed against the tree, roughly, and his hands twisted back around the tree. They were tied so tight Koen was sure he'd lose circulation.

"Now the sack." Suddenly, the sack was ripped off his head, and the sun momentarily blinded him. He squinted to focus and saw his father standing a few yards from him, with a sword in his hand. His uncle stood a bit further away with his arms crossed. He showed no emotion.

The cart was nowhere in sight.

"Father, why?" Koen's raspy voice asked.

His father's hateful expression slowly changed into a twisted laugh. "I've been waiting years for this."

Koen felt his anger slowly start turning into sadness. His eyes threatened to release tears. He couldn't, though. Not now. "Father, what are you doing? Why?" He knew he had his mother killed. He wasn't surprised to find such hatred in his father, but being the target left Koen crippled with fear.

"I suppose you at least deserve an explanation," Cleatus said and turned to look at Dolion, who still had a neutral expression. "Well, my son, it all started before you were born. The war between Azgalia and Mizcriea had gone on for ages, you know. For generations, Mizcriea has been looking for a way to conquer Azgalian land with no success until it was my turn to try." Cleatus formed an evil grin and twirled the sword in his hands. "I had the brilliant idea of faking revenge. If Mizcriea had a reason to break the peace treaty, there would finally be a cause for war. But that was when we found out you would be born."

"What does this have to do with me?" Koen asked, feeling

the heat rise in his body.

"My wife was also pregnant when we discovered your mother was to have you. We lost our son, but you were born." Cleatus paused in amusement to watch Koen's reaction.

Confused and uncertain what to think, Koen could only yell out in frustration. "Father!"

"I don't think you understand, Koen," he smirked. "You are not my son. You are the missing prince of Azgalia."

All at once, Koen's world crumbled. His life was a lie. The tears broke through, and his mind raced to understand, but it felt too clouded by despair, hurt, anger, and sadness to make sense of anything. Somehow, he knew what his father said was true. He believed him. His gut wrenched, and his heart felt as though it had been shattered. He wished he could fold into a ball right there. He wished his mother were here to tell him everything was alright, but even his mother wasn't his mother. As he peered into the eyes he had known as his father's all his life, they quickly changed to a stranger's gaze. Any amount of respect he had tried to hold onto for him vanished. All he could think of was the next thing. He might give up altogether if he allowed himself to think further than this moment. He looked down through blurred vision and tried blinking away the tears.

Cleatus continued, "Because of the peace treaty, an Azgalian healer came to try and save my son. When he couldn't, I realized Azgalians were all liars. That's why my ancestors hated them so much. They all proclaim to have the answers and be the best, but they're liars. So," King Cleatus paused to adjust his stance, "of course, I jumped at the chance. I had you kidnapped. No one knew of our son's death; I had the healer killed afterward. So, pretending you were ours was easy. I threatened my wife to keep it a secret, otherwise, I'd kill you. The plan was that when you grew, I would kill you myself on Azgalian soil. I would then blame Azgalia for the murder of my son and have a cause for war." His face twisted again into a smirk. "The beauty of it all, though, is, of course, the irony. I would be killing the Azgalian prince. The son of their own King."

"You sicken me." Koen spat at the ground. His heart and soul had not yet recovered. Koen wasn't sure how much more "truth" he could take. "My moth . . . " Koen stopped himself short, "Your wife, why did you kill her?"

"Ah, you're smarter than you look," Cleatus said. "She turned to the faithful. She told me she could no longer lie about your true family. She would tell you the truth, but that would ruin everything!" Cleatus recalled in disgust.

"So you would have me kill her!" Koen burned with fury.

"Exactly." Cleatus stared him down. "But, that's in the past now. Your time was served, and the end has come to start the beginning of my rule, finally." Cleatus adjusted his sword so he could clean it on the hem of his garment. "Oh yes, and as for your maid friend, I was suspicious of her when she walked in. I knew something was familiar about her, but I couldn't put my finger on it. Then, later, I knew. I had her father kidnapped years ago! He had what I was told was called the gift." Koen's eyes widened in fear. "I had no idea he had children! If I had known, I would have had them killed a long time ago; however, I am obviously now aware. She poses an even greater threat of being here. In case you were wondering, she will be killed as soon as we return to the castle." King Cleatus spoke with no remorse.

Koen began to shake. It was all his fault. He should never

have led David and Alaina to Mizcriea. Now, she would die without any answers of her father, and David would hate him even in death. He refused to sob, even though his heart was broken. His chest ached, his nose stung, and his throat felt like it might never allow him to speak again.

"And now that your heart is broken, your death shouldn't hurt as bad." Cleatus looked at Koen with a look of pure evil. He began to advance, slowly, toward Koen. Koen knew he would make death slow and painful. Koen's eyes shut instinctively as he prepared for the sword to impale him. Cleatus raised his sword and swung.

There was a CLANG followed by a THUD. Koen's eyes shot open, and he watched King Cleatus jump back, startled. The sword had been knocked out of his hand by . . . an arrow? Koen looked around, confused. Then, he saw it. Or . . . her.

Alaina's heart was racing, and sweat was dripping from her brow. She kicked her horse faster as she flew by the surrounding trees. "I can't believe . . . " She was too frustrated to finish her sentence. She should have said something, she knew. She didn't know this would happen, but maybe she should have known. She should've warned Koen more about the evil of his father and uncle. "Fast, come on!" she urged the horse beneath her.

She could see tracks on the ground where the cart carrying Koen had been. They seemed to go on forever. *Where could they be taking him?* Soon, she slowed when she thought she noticed a change in the tracks. They had stopped. There were some footsteps, but none led away from the cart. They had moved on. She kicked the horse beneath her, and it sprang into a gallop immediately. The horse could feel Alaina's sense of urgency.

Lord, please allow me to reach Koen in time. Protect him. Give him whatever strength he may need in this moment, Alaina prayed.

Soon, she saw the wagon in the distance. She slowed her horse to a stop and dismounted, never taking her eyes off the wagon. The back doors were open. Alaina's heart dropped. *Was she too late?* Without hesitation, she threw the rope around the tree. It was faster than tying and a fine temporary hold for a horse.

Alaina slowly made her way toward the wagon while being aware of her surroundings. She had a bow in hand and an arrow in place, ready to fire at any moment. She breathed quietly as if she were hunting. They may have horses with them, and if they sense her, they would blow her cover. *Not that you have any,* Alaina shook her head. She was in a very vulnerable position; she knew that. Focusing her thoughts again, she reached close enough to the wagon to see no one around. There were horses that pulled the wagon, but she wondered if they had taken an extra. She walked up beside the horses and quietly, but quickly, unhitched them from their harness. She would let the horses figure out on their own time when they were free. She didn't want to risk them ruining her plan to launch a surprise attack. Walking away from the horses, she followed the footprints to where she believed they would be. As she drew closer, she could hear voices. It was King Cleatus!

"My wife was also pregnant when we discovered your mother was to have you. We lost our son, but you were born," Cleatus said. *He's talking to Koen!*

Alaina, closer now, saw Cleatus facing away from her. She jumped behind a tree in fear he might turn and see her. Slowly, she peeked out and scanned her immediate view. She saw Koen's uncle waiting with his arms crossed. The knights who had come along with them stood with sword in hand, ready to obey a command. She turned her gaze back to where Cleatus stood. She reached her neck out a bit farther and finally saw Koen. Her heart sank. He was tied up to a tree and completely vulnerable.

"Father!" Koen cried out, and his desperation gripped her heart. She listened as Cleatus explained his master plan to Koen. Alaina's throat hurt as she held back tears, watching Koen as Cleatus told him he was the lost prince of Azgalia. She felt as if she might puke. It was so awful. The pain she saw in Koen's face was unbearable. *The lost prince of Azgalia?* She looked away from them and leaned against the tree to process the news momentarily. *Oh Lord, be with us now*; she could only pray.

Alaina turned back to listen when she heard mention of her. And her father! Her heart began racing again, and the next few things Cleatus said were blurred by the emotion that welled up inside her.

" . . . she will be killed as soon as we return to the castle," she heard Cleatus say. Alaina watched Koen, and a tear slipped down her cheek. Cleatus went on, "And now that your heart is broken, your death shouldn't hurt as bad." Cleatus stepped forward, and that's when Alaina knew it was time.

Alaina jumped out from behind the trees with bow and arrow in hand. She shot an arrow to knock the King's sword out of his hand. The knights on duty advanced toward her, but luckily, Alainas' arrows flew faster than their feet moved. She released the arrow, and it pierced the first knight's shoulder, sending him to the dirt with a thud. She quickly shot the other knight in the thigh. Koen's uncle looked at her wide-eyed and stunned. Her long, dark hair flailed around wildly as she moved. With another arrow drawn, she pinned Sir Dolion to where he stood and kept an eye on Cleatus, who looked extremely disappointed that his plans had been interrupted. Slowly, King Cleatus and Sir Dolion raised their hands in surrender. The knight whom she had shot was rolling back and forth on the ground in pain.

"Koen, are you alright?" Alaina called over her shoulder, breathing hard from the adrenaline.

"I am now," Koens' voice croaked. As he watched, he noticed that the dark-violet cloak she wore blended with her black-blue hair. Her face, determined, showed a strength and beauty Koen had never witnessed before.

"Drop the sword, Dolion." Alaina didn't bother with giving him the respect of calling him "sir."

Sir Dolion slowly bent down to place the sword on the ground. "Now move." Alaina motioned with her head where he needed to move. When he was a good distance from the sword, she ordered him to stop. "Now, King Cleatus, make your way over to Dolion unless you want the next arrow a little lower than my last." Reluctantly, King Cleatus made his way over to his brother. Sending another look at the knight whom she had shot, she noticed he was no longer moving.

Alaina cautiously stepped over to Koen and momentarily

took her eyes off the two rulers to untie him.

"Thank you," he whispered.

"Don't thank me yet; we need to get out of here," Alaina whispered.

Suddenly, Koen noticed Cleatus advancing toward Alaina with a sword in hand. "No!"

The knot around his hands loosened enough. He broke free and threw himself before Alaina. With eyes closed, he braced for impact. He heard a thud, and his breath caught. Opening his eyes, he met the eyes of the man he had believed to be his father for so long. For the first time, Koen saw his father afraid. Shocked, Koen stepped back, his eyes wide as Alaina grabbed his arm from behind. King Cleatus fell to the ground, lifeless.

Reluctantly, Koen raised his eyes to meet Dolion. Towering over the King, Sir Dolion had killed the King of Mizcriea, his own brother.

"Koen, let's go." Alaina tugged at his arm, but he could only stare into Dolion's eyes. Alaina pulled harder this time, forcing his feet to move.

"This is only the beginning!" Dolion yelled after them.

His life had crumbled in moments. Even though King Cleatus proved to be the worst father figure any boy could have, Koen had been raised his whole life believing that man was his father. To have Cleatus die that way, in front of him, no matter how he viewed him, broke his heart. And he hated it.

"He deserves no pity from me," Koen said under his breath. Alaina knew he was still processing, so she kept quiet while waiting for him to speak. He appreciated that.

Alaina mounted her horse and Koen took one from the wagon. They then raced through the trees, back toward the castle.

What did Dolion mean? What was he planning? Whatever it was, something told Koen it could be even worse than Cleatus' plans.

Alaina glanced over her shoulder at Koen as they rode back toward the castle through the trees.

Confusion.

Brokenness.

Hurt.

Fear.

Worry.

"Alaina, slow down for a second," Koen yelled. Alaina pulled on her reins and slowed the horse to a trot and then a walk, pacing with Koen's horse. "I can't thank you enough for coming. How you knew, I don't know, but thank you," Koen said, and Alaina saw the genuine gratefulness in his eyes.

"I'm just glad I was there in time, Koen," Alaina replied in sympathy.

"Alaina, this is bigger than we thought." Koen began to explain his father's plan. "We need to get back to the faithful camp as soon as possible and warn them. There needs to be preparation for a war. As for your father, I know where he is. He's alive, but we will need more help to rescue him."

Alaina's eyes began to well with tears at the news of her father. "Praise God," she said and silently processed it all. Their quest had become so much more than they had expected—so many more highs and lows than they thought possible. Yet,

Alaina could see God's hand in it all. She prayed her father was in good health when they found him. She could only imagine what they may have put him through. "Koen." She shook her head to focus. "David is actually at the castle with Cronin right now." When Koen looked at her, surprised, she nodded. "That was my response, too!" Alaina said. "But wow, Koen, I'm not sure what to say . . . you're the missing prince of Azgalia?" Alaina was still trying to wrap her head around it.

"So it seems," Koen nodded, looking ahead at the trees. "I missed one of the kidnapping parchments, and that's when Dolion knocked me unconscious. I believe that parchment holds the information regarding my kidnapping," he said in sorrow. "All this time." He shook his head.

"Koen, I'm not sure why God allowed this to happen, and I'm not going to pretend I do, but I do know God's will is perfectly ordered." Alaina tried to help him deal with the shocking news. Though she could see his internal struggle and feelings, she found it challenging to find the words to say to him that might help.

"I think I'm beginning to understand." Koen nodded.

"Really?" Alaina looked at him as he smiled at her.

"None of this makes sense, and things seem the worst they have ever been." Koen paused. "Somehow, the only thing that makes sense is the God you believe in."

Alaina felt her heart swell. A smile pulled at her lips as she watched Koen process.

"I believe we have God on our side. I don't know why, Alaina, and I can't explain it," he shook his head as if he couldn't believe what he was saying, "but I have faith."

Alaina believed him through and through. She felt as

though her heart might burst with joy. God had chosen one of the darkest moments of Koen's life to break through to him. Why? Sometimes God works in ways that bring Him the most glory. She thought of how her grandmother used to say God liked to be dramatic sometimes, but in a really amazing way. Like how he designed the butterflies and the fish in the sea. Or how he chose to swoop in at the last minute to save his people. It always left her in awe. She prayed at that moment for God to continue working on Koen's heart. "Amen to that." She flashed a smile at him before they urged their horses onward again.

♛

When they made it to the castle, they pulled up just short of the royal stables and swung off their horses. "They were in here when I left," Alaina said.

"They probably went somewhere safer," Koen suggested.

"Where would Cronin have taken them?"

Koen smiled. "I have a pretty good idea where they're at." Alaina saw a childish spark light up his eyes. "Follow me, " he said, and they mounted.

Alaina and Koen rode toward the back of the castle and straight for the treeline inside the castle grounds. Once they reached the treeline, Koen dismounted and tied the horse. They walked into the trees, and Alaina watched Koen look at the ground as if he expected it to tell him something. She decided not to question him but waited instead.

Koen squatted down and scratched his head as he searched the ground. "Usually it's much easier to . . . " Suddenly, he stood up and grinned back at her. I found it."

"Found what exactly?" Alaina asked, amused by his childish excitement all of a sudden. He didn't answer, but instead just continued forward. Then Alaina asked, "Oh, is it a treehouse?"

"Nope," Koen said with a mischievous smile. Alaina furrowed her eyebrows. *Where in the world would his brother have hidden here?* She looked around through the trees. No building on the ground, and as far as she could see, there was no treehouse.

Then he stopped. "Here."

Alaina raised her eyebrow and looked around. "Okay, you got me. I have no clue what you're trying to find." Alaina huffed, and Koen smirked. He then proceeded to stomp his foot three times, pausing, and then stomping two more times. He winked, stepped back, and then kicked a woven piece of grass, leaves, and sticks off what looked like a knight's shield.

"What . . . ?" Alaina looked down at it in wonder. Then, there was a strange noise. "Is that what I think it is?"

"Maybe." Koen remained amused. He looked down at the shield. "I can't believe he brought them here," he said, "but it makes sense."

Alaina watched as the shield opened up toward them. A hand pushed it up from underneath. "Cronin, I had completely forgotten about this place," Koen said happily.

Alaina, still amazed, shyly waved at Cronin as he popped his head out of the ground.

"I'm surprised you even thought to look here, but a part of me knew you would remember." Cronin smiled. "Please, come in," Cronin said and backed down the ladder out of the way.

Koen looked at Alaina. "After you."

Alaina gave the hole in the ground a weary look. "If you say so." And with that, she got down on her hands and knees. Dipping one foot at a time into the hole, she slowly lowered herself. Koen followed her. Together, they climbed down through a narrow shaft that allowed just enough room for Koen to fit; his sword rubbed against the walls and dropped dirt on Alaina's head. She coughed.

"Sorry. Last time we were in here, we were kids," Koen said.

"Makes sense," Alaina laughed.

"At the end, just drop. It's not a far drop, so you'll be fine," Koen told her, and she nodded.

Sure enough, just like he had said, she reached the end of the ladder to find she would have to drop the rest of the way down. Hesitating, she tried to determine the height of the drop. But then, she heard David's voice.

"Alaina?" David's voice carried up into the shaft. It was enough encouragement for Alaina not to think twice about letting go of the ladder and plunging to the floor beneath. She bent her knees to embrace the impact. Standing up to regain balance, she looked up and took in the room. It was small, and the walls were insulated with wooden beams. The furniture inside it was small and looked to be made by an unskilled craftsman. The decor was humorous. Straight ahead was a table with two chairs. Beside that was a large carpet, which took the prize as the nicest thing in the room. Surely it was stolen from the castle. No doubt, this had been Cronin and Koen's bunker as kids.

Koen dropped behind her, and Cronin went to greet his

brother. "You're okay, " he said simply, but Alaina had seen their brotherly love for each other.

"Alaina." David's voice grabbed her attention, and she looked over to meet eyes similar to hers.

"David!" she cried and ran to embrace her brother.

He squeezed her tight. "You can't just run off like that."

Alaina pulled back to look at his face. Though he was clearly kidding, she playfully hit his arm. "And you just can't leave me like that."

He smiled, but then looked serious. "Never again."

"Never." She held back tears and backed up to get a better look at him. He looked well but tired. His clothes were worn, his hair was a little longer, and he looked wiser, but there was more. Alaina noticed something else about him.

"What are you thinking?" David asked knowingly.

Before Alaina could answer, a young woman walked out from around a corner. She looked to be their age, with sandy brown hair, deep brown eyes, and a fair-skinned face. "Who is this?" Alaina asked, interested.

"This is Evelyn," David introduced the girl.

Evelyn smiled and politely bowed her head. "It's an absolute pleasure to meet you. David has told me much about you, Alaina, " she said.

"Ah, David," Koen interjected and embraced him with a pat on the back. It's good to have you back with us. I'll admit it was much harder without you," Koen said with a wry smile.

"Likewise," David smiled. "I met Evelyn while I was traveling with my group. We found her lost and injured in the forest. I brought her back to our camp in dire condition, but she recovered well." David paused as if preparing his next words.

"She is with me because she is looking for her father as well."

Alaina looked at Evelyn. "Who is your father?"

"King Malikai," Evelyn said.

The news momentarily shocked both Alaina and Koen. Princess of Azgalia? Alaina's eyes widened slightly as she realized. Quickly, she curtsied with a bow of her head.

"That's not necessary," Evelyn said sweetly. "Thank you, though."

Alaina smiled back and looked over at Koen. They shared a knowing glance. Not only was she Azgalian royalty, but she was also Koen's sister! "Princess," Alaina started.

"You can call me Evelyn, Alaina," Evelyn said.

Alaina nodded, " Thanks. Evelyn, have you come alone to find your father?" When she nodded, Alaina looked again at Koen.

"Why don't we take a moment to sit down?" Koen suggested. When the group agreed and sat down, Koen took a deep breath and said, "Alaina, you first."

Alaina nodded. "David," she smiled, "Our father is alive and we know where he is. We just need to plan a rescue mission." Alaina watched as thankfulness and hope swirled around in David's mind.

"That's wonderful," David said as grateful tears filled his eyes. He sniffed and reached over to squeeze her shoulder.

Alaina then turned to Koen and nodded for him to tell his news. His news was the most shocking and would alter the group's plans.

"Cronin, as you know, father kidnapped me," Koen said, and when Cronin nodded, he continued, "He tried to kill me twice. Thankfully, Alaina came to save me before he ended my life. However, before trying to take my life, he explained why." Koen told them of the King's plans, and when he began to explain his biological family, Alaina saw the shocked expressions of both Cronin and Evelyn.

"Wait, brother." Cronin shook his head in confusion. "How is that possible? Surely, I would have known."

"They hid it from us, Cronin. I mean, it explains why I look so different, doesn't it?" Koen asked, and Alaina's heart broke for the brothers. "Nonetheless, you're still my brother," Koen reassured him.

"So, Azgalia's lost prince? My lost brother?" Evelyn asked in disbelief. Alaina could see she was still processing. She trusted David, so she trusted them, but she was hesitant. Alaina didn't blame her.

"There was a kidnapping parchment I missed. It would've occurred at the time of my birth, before Alaina and David's father. I didn't read it, but it would hold the truth; although, I'm positive it is true," Koen said sadly. "My heart breaks for your father. I read his abduction parchment as well."

"You did? What did it say?" Evelyn asked.

Alaina watched Koen's gaze drop. Koen hadn't told her anything about the King of Azgalia until now, yet Alaina knew what he would say before anyone else in that room.

"There was a time of death," Koen said, and deep breaths from Evelyn followed silence.

Evelyn refused to cry at the moment, although Alaina knew she needed to grieve. Alaina saw strength in Evelyn. "We need a plan, then. A good one." Evelyn arose with newfound determination. "We need help and resources, which we cannot find underground. We need to go back to the camp and form a rescue plan for your father," she said, looking at Alaina and David. "And then with his help, we will decide what to do about King Cleatus's plans."

"I have reason to believe my uncle will most likely continue with my father . . ." he cut himself short, "with Cleatus's plans," Koen said.

"I can second that," Alaina nodded in agreement. "I saw it in him."

"I'll go with you. My uncle will find out soon enough that I've helped you all," Cronin said.

The group nodded in agreement and decided to do precisely what Evelyn said. They gathered their belongings and climbed the ladder back out of the underground room.

Standing below while the others climbed out, David and Alaina stood beside each other. "A lot has changed since we crossed the border," David stated.

"A lot has changed since we left home," Alaina corrected him. "David, what are you thinking?"

David winked. "You already know." He looked at the ladder before jumping to grab it. He said, "You and me." He paused. "We can do this."

TWENTY-EIGHT

Together, they arrived at the faithful camp after escaping the castle grounds for the forest. Upon their arrival, Jamie and Christopher ran to greet them.

"David, we're surprised to see you back here so soon," said Christopher.

"As am I, my friend," said David as he dismounted his horse. "We need to speak with Peter immediately."

"Of course. I'll have someone send for him."

"I see you picked up a few new friends," said Jamie.

David laughed and introduced them to Koen, Cronin, and Alaina.

"It's like meeting fictional heroes," Jamie said.

"My children," said Peter as he approached them. "It is so good to see you all together and well." He welcomed them inside the meeting tent to continue their conversation.

"Peter, we have something urgent to discuss with you," Alaina said as they sat down.

"Of course," Peter nodded for her to go on.

David observed Peter's reaction after explaining the last couple of days. As far as David could tell, he remained calm and understanding. David looked over at Alaina to see if she was reading him.

"I know you're concerned," Alaina started.

"But I will not worry." Peter put his finger up as if to put her words on hold.

"We believe the next step is to rescue my father. There is much he could help us with," Alaina finished.

"I see." Peter nodded, taking it all in. "That makes sense. You say your father possesses the same gift as you?" Alaina nodded. "Then, they kept him alive for a different purpose than you may think. I believe he was targeted first for a reason. I assume they are using his gift for their gain. It's correct to put your father's rescue as the top priority," Peter said confidently.

David and Alaina nodded with satisfaction. They had thought the same, but wanted to make sure they weren't being selfish.

"I was thinking," Koen said. "There are still some things we can prepare before we rescue your father. Assuming the rescue mission is successful, it will undoubtedly make my uncle angry. He'll waste no time in attacking. We should have things set in place," Koen reasoned.

"I agree," David said. "We need to warn Evelyn's mother and brother about the possibility of a coming war. They will need to prepare the Azgalian armies."

"Yes, although we may need more than that. While Cleatus was ruling, my uncle was in charge of training the armies. I know for a fact he has grown them. He's taken all the extra men and trained them," Koen said.

"What will we do then? We can't exactly ask all Azgalian men to fight. We have armies to protect those who can't protect themselves," Evelyn said. David saw she was worried for Azgalia. He couldn't imagine the weight on her at the moment. Her father was dead, and she was now the only royal member of Azgalia who knew of the war, possibly only a few days away. Well, David thought, there was Koen now. He still couldn't get over that Koen and Evelyn were fully brother and sister, yet they were raised in opposing kingdoms.

"We can ask, but they will not be ordered. From what I've heard and experienced, Azgalian people are very protective of their land and people. They seem like they will be more than willing to fight for that," Koen assumed.

"I agree," Alaina nodded.

"Great, we'll ask. I was also thinking of the people we've met." Koen looked from David to Alaina. "Like Max and Harleigh," he said.

"Harleigh? The girl with the dragon?" Evelyn asked.

"Yeah, I mean, I know it sounds crazy, but having a dragon on our side could be a real asset," Koen shrugged.

"He's not wrong," Peter laughed.

"How would we get word to her? How do we know she's in the same place?" David asked. Alaina smiled; she missed his practical and wise thinking.

"We'll just have to assume she hasn't moved. Regarding getting word to her, I'm sure we can spare a soldier or two to find her. Or maybe a carrying pigeon." Koen looked to Evelyn for confirmation.

Evelyn nodded. "I'm sure that can be arranged."

"And Max," Alaina said. "He would want to help and may also know some people who would join."

"That's true," Koen nodded in agreement.

"You also have us," Christopher said, walking into the tent. "The men here would be more than willing to help in any way they can."

"I believe they would as well," David said.

"Since we do not have much time, we should attack two things at once," Peter suggested. He looked around at the rest of the group, "Evelyn, along with a few men, should ride down to Malikai city to warn her family and Azgalia of the coming war. There, she can also give orders to find . . . " He paused to think. "The girl with the Dragon and this Max, you speak of. While she accomplishes that task, David and Alaina will rescue their father here," he said.

"I think that would work," Alaina said as she thought it through. "David? Evelyn? Do you agree?"

"Yes," they said in unison.

"Unless you think otherwise, I should stay and help with the rescue of their father." Koen looked around the table.

"I think you should, too." David nodded. "You know the castle well, and Cronin?" Cronin looked up at the sound of his name. "You could create a diversion if need be." When Cronin nodded, David asked, "How are you with a sword?"

"Not as good as my brother here, but I've defeated him a few times in practice," Cronin smirked at Koen.

"He's right," Koen laughed.

"Good," David said. "I say we all start . . . well, today? If you are all up for it?" David asked, looking around. When everyone at the table nodded, David stood up. "Good. Christopher, would you see if some men could escort Evelyn to Azgalia starting in the morning?"

"Of course," Christopher nodded.

"I'll go with you," Evelyn said, following him out of the tent.

"Peter, do you think you'd know some men in the camp willing to help in case we need backup going into the castle?"

David asked.

"Most certainly. There are many men here who are willing and able," Peter responded. Alaina could see that he wanted to help in any way he could. "I will find them now."

"Thank you." David smiled and then turned to Alaina and Koen with the determination Alaina always admired. "We need a plan to get our father back."

"I assume you already have one?" Koen said from behind Alaina's shoulder. Koen was already picking up on David's way of thinking.

David smirked, "Of course."

Having already completed most of the plan, David led the conversation while Koen jumped in with a strategy and helpful facts about the Mizcriean castle. Cronin watched and listened along with Alaina. She enjoyed watching them form a plan. She noticed that despite their many differences, they made a great team. She loved to see how David's heart had softened toward Koen and how Koen's respect for David had grown. A part of her was overjoyed at this, having grown to admire Koen.

"Koen and I will go first to ensure there aren't more men than we assume. We'll need to take the bell tower guards out first, then the watchtower men. Once we take out the watchtower men and the gate guards, you'll have to be ready to climb the wall. Cronin, you'll have to climb from another point. It's easier to spot two people climbing a wall together than it is to spot only one. We don't want to cause suspicion," David explained.

"We'll have to replace the gate guards with two of our men. That way, people won't notice that they're gone, and they can raise the gate if needed," Koen suggested.

"That makes sense," David nodded.

"Climb the wall?" Alaina interrupted, and all eyes fell on her. She tried to hide how crazy she thought the idea was. She knew it was possible, but had difficulty picturing herself scaling that enormous wall.

"I know it seems a bit far-fetched of an idea, but I do think it's possible," Koen said, looking around for other opinions.

"It'd be the best way in. It's worth a shot, if you think it's possible," David said, and Cronin nodded. "Okay, so we'll attach a grappling hook and a cord to some arrows. We can use it to climb the wall," David told her.

After noticing her hesitation, Cronin said, "We can practice on some of the boulders outside. I saw a steep one not too far from here that would be perfect."

"Okay, that makes me feel much better," Alaina laughed nervously.

"Good," David nodded and continued with his plan.

"Once the guards are in place and Alaina is inside with us, we'll need to find the underground dungeon where you said our father is still located." He looked at Koen.

"I can get you there," Cronin suddenly said. The three young people looked at him expectantly. "I had a lot of time to wander the castle while you were gone, Koen." He paused as if to pity himself. "There was always this one door that was never unlocked. It was in a far-off end of the castle, and quite ugly."

"An ugly door?" David raised his eyebrow in question.

"I know it sounds odd, but you won't understand until you see it. Anyway, I don't know for certain that's the door, but it's worth a shot," Cronin shrugged.

"I agree with Cronin," Koen stated.

"And if it's not that door?" David questioned.

Koen took a deep breath, "Then we try every other door and hallway until we find him. In the order that Cronin assumes, it could be so. And if that fails, I will find Dolion and drag him by the ear until he tells me."

David stared at him briefly, then smiled. "Boy, am I glad God brought you into our lives."

"I think that's the nicest thing you've ever said to me." Koen smiled, holding his face and pretending to cry.

David rolled his eyes, and Koen laughed. Alaina appreciated their willingness to stay light-hearted despite the circumstances. There was a lot at risk in this plan. So much could go wrong that one would think they would be stressed and serious. However, she felt it was important to remain thankful and joyful, as Paul called the church to in Philippians. "Okay, so, once we find the door . . . ?" Alaina encouraged David to continue.

"Right," David regained focus, "Once we find THE door, Koen and Cronin will stand guard of the entrance while you and I go in. I'll be there if any guards are inside and, of course, to help find our father."

"Okay." Alaina nodded slowly, and her heart beat faster at the thought of all this happening tomorrow. *What would it be like when she finally found her father? Would he recognize them? Would he even remember that he had kids? What if he wasn't anything like she had pictured all these years? What if being imprisoned all this time had changed him?*

"I say it's best to keep our plan loose. That way, we can easily adapt if things go wrong, and we're not so tied to a plan,"

Koen reasoned.

"Only this time will I agree to that," David said with a finger raised. "I'll go tell Christopher and Peter."

"I'll go with you," Koen nodded.

"I'll show Cronin to his tent," Alaina said. "We'll meet you at dinner then?" David and Koen agreed, and they all parted ways.

♛

Later that night, at dinner, Peter arranged to celebrate God's faithfulness in past events and future events.

"Whatever happens in the days to come, we will be the people of God. Our Lord will always remain faithful and unchanging, so it is our duty as His children to remain faithful even through this." All the people nodded, and there was an echo of "amens. "Now, let us praise Him," Peter said, cueing for the music to begin, and the people sang in praise.

The sweet melody of the music brought Alaina to the verge of tears. "Creator of the Starry Height" was one of her favorite hymns. God was truly good. No matter what happens tomorrow, even if they fail to protect Azgalia, God is good and always will be.

Alaina felt her twin put his arm around her shoulder. Together, they sang along, and the evening ended with a prayer for the safety of God's people and the fulfillment of the Lord's will.

They said farewell to Evelyn and the men who were to travel with her early the following day.

Alaina knew from that moment that David cared much for Evelyn, so she prayed silently for Evelyn's safe return.

"Tomorrow," Koen said when David, Alaina, and Cronin stood in a circle before heading off to sleep.

"Tomorrow," they said back in unison.

They will return to the Mizcriean castle tomorrow, scale its walls, and rescue her father.

♕

Tapping his fingers one by one, he stared blankly at the wall before him. The room was dusty as no maids or servants were allowed to enter, even to clean it. A parchment lay before him, much like the ones he had found Koen looking at. He took a deep breath and pulled out his quill pen and ink.

A smirk pulled at Sir Dolion's lips as he signed the bottom of the page. It was the last capture to have taken place, and it wasn't the King of Azgalia.

His brother Cleatus had been so naive. He made all of Dolion's ideas his own without considering how he felt. He willingly shared his ideas with Cleatus, but there was always a hidden agenda. His brother thought Koen's death was only about getting revenge on Azgalia. However, that wasn't the case. Yes, Dolion was frustrated that Koen was alive, but that wasn't the primary focus.

Cleatus was dead, and Dolion was now in charge of Mizcriea. *That's* what mattered.

All he needed to do now was blame his brother's death on

Azgalia and wage war to conquer the Azgalian kingdom and make it his own.

The thought of Koen and his little friends crossed his mind, but they couldn't possibly disrupt his plans. They may have "the gift," but Dolion had both "a gift" and now the entire Mizcriean army.

"Sir, you called?" Dolion's head soldier arrived at the door to the parchment room.

"Yes." Dolion grew serious and looked up. "Bring me head maid Laura. I have reason to believe she has committed treason."

TWENTY-NINE

A chill made its way through the dungeon like it always did, making the man in the cellar shiver like he always did. Sitting on the cold, hard floor, he forced another bite of what the soldiers called food down his throat. It was better than nothing— at least that's what he always thought.

"I don't know why he never eats on his cot." He heard one guard whisper to the other. They stood some distance from his cell, but he could still hear what they said. They were young guards. He'd seen many come and go all the years he'd been there. Those who left were either sent to join the King's army, died, were killed, or all three.

He chose not to answer; they weren't speaking to him anyway.

He swallowed another bite and looked around the dungeon at the others in the cells. Some were actual criminals, some were innocent men taken prisoner for multiple reasons, and some, like himself, were kidnapped. It had been a while since they brought anyone new in, which was unusual. Seeing a new prisoner once or twice a week was normal, but he hadn't seen one in a month. He couldn't get a read on the guards either, as to why, but he suspected they didn't know anything either.

It was as dull as could be in the dungeon. He wondered when he last saw a bright color. Even the guards were required to wear a dull white tunic and dull armor. He wondered if their swords were also dull. A light came in during the day from a far wall. It lit the dungeon just enough to see the food in front of him and the guards, but mostly, his world was darkness.

He shifted his sitting position when his foot started to feel numb. Looking up, he saw a guard approaching his cell with something in hand. The young guard stopped at the cell door and reached through the bars of his cell.

"Would you like your water now?" the young guard asked politely.

"Yes, thank you," he answered and took it. They nodded at each other, and he went to sit back down to watch the guard walk away. This young guard, in particular, had taken an interest in him since the beginning. Titus, the young guard, had questioned why he had been imprisoned. When no one could answer, Titus asked him himself. They soon became friends, and Titus proved to be an ally.

Looking down at the water Titus handed him, he pulled a piece of paper from the bottom of the cup. This was how Titus kept him updated on the castle's happenings. Recently, Titus hadn't provided much news because he simply had nothing to give. So, opening it, he expected the same.

He unwrapped the folded paper and scanned the writing. His eyes froze on the first sentence.

Prince Koen murdered King Cleatus.

No one else knew Koen wasn't a Mizcriean prince. He was Azgalian. So, how did that happen? Did Koen find out and seek revenge?

The prisoner wiped the corner of his mouth with the back of his hand.

He continued further down the page. Suddenly, he felt as

though someone had just set him free. His heart lurched in his chest. He read the next sentence over and over again just to make sure it was true. Goosebumps covered his body.

How was it possible? Why? What had happened? Is this tied to the King's death? Looking back down at the page, he reread it.

"Your daughter and son are in Mizcriea."

THIRTY

Alaina took a deep breath as her hair was caught up in the wind. Any minute, an arrow would fly into the soldier at the bell tower, and he would drop. Alaina will climb the wall to meet with Cronin, Koen, and David as soon as that happens. Together, they would find the hidden dungeon. She would then need to read the faces of every prisoner to find her father. He should be easy to find because of his eye color, and she could see the gift in him.

The woods were quiet, just as they were before she left on this journey with her brother and Koen. In this moment of silence and anticipation, thoughts flooded her mind.

Her first thought was Koen. She wondered where he was with his belief in God. She'd watched his faith grow so much over their journey. *Lord, please draw him to you.* Aside from the fact that she hoped he would believe because it would save his soul, she also had growing feelings for him, but knew she wouldn't make them known unless he shared her faith. She thought about the continually growing admiration Koen had for her. After all they had been through together, it had only been a matter of time.

She thought about herself and the growth she'd experienced since leaving on this quest. Although her faith had been challenged at every turn, she was thankful for all the ways the Lord had provided her with growth opportunities. But even after all these challenges, she still felt weak in the face of the daunting task of entering the castle. She knew she had to trust God with what they were about to do.

Alaina sighed. So much had happened, and she just hoped it wouldn't be for nothing. She looked up when she heard a thud. The arrow had found its mark, and the soldier was down; it was time to move. "Lord, help us," she prayed as she sprinted towards the wall.

Her eyes locked on the wall that was growing closer, and her heart raced to pump blood throughout her body. Spotting where she was to begin the climb, her eyes followed a straight line to the top of the wall.

She was moving quickly so no one would spot her. Finding her mark, she skillfully slowed her pace to raise her bow and release a grappling hook with a rope trailing behind it. She slung her bow over her shoulder and kept hold of the rope, which she tied around her waist as Koen had shown her. Once she reached the wall, taking a leap of faith, she jumped and landed her feet on the vertical wall. Using all her strength, she began the climb. The wall had more grip than Alaina had anticipated, but she wasn't complaining. She refused to look down or around her, fearing she would want to stop. She prayed Cronin was doing well with the climb. It hadn't taken long for David and Koen to get over the wall.

"Right hand," she took a deep breath. "Left hand," she repeated over and over again out loud.

Her legs were burning, her back and neck ached, and her arms felt like noodles. She was also pretty sure the rope around her waist might end up separating her body into two halves. Yet, she went on.

Trying to distract her mind from the strain, she picked out details to focus on. The wall was rough, allowing for a firm grip and sound footing. The sky was blue, and the sun peeked through a few clouds. Her breathing was heavy, and she was about halfway at this point.

"So . . . close," she said, struggling to make sense of even her own words.

Finally reaching the top of the wall, she gripped the edge with her right hand and left. She pulled herself up and over using any strength she had left at that moment. She rolled over and looked around for danger before collapsing on her back. She heard footsteps and raised her head to look. It was Cronin.

"Are you okay?" he asked out of breath. At least she wasn't alone in her suffering.

"Yeah, just needed a second," she said between breaths.

He laughed, "I'm winded." Reaching down, he helped her up to her feet. "Good?"

"Am now. How about you?" she asked him, but already knew the answer.

"Never better," he joked. "Let's go."

Alaina nodded and followed him along the top of the wall. He led her to a staircase that zig-zagged down within the wall.

"They should be at the stables by now," Cronin said as they ran down the stairs.

Making it to the bottom of the dark staircase, they came to a door that Cronin slowly pushed open. He put his finger to his lips to let Alaina know to remain quiet. Opening the door, the light shone in and momentarily blinded her. "We're good," he said, slipping out the door with Alaina behind. They ran along the wall until they saw where the stables were and stopped.

"I assume we're safe because the guards and watchmen are down, but just in case, don't stop running. If someone tries to fire at you, run in random zigzags to throw them off," Cronin told her, and Alaina nodded in understanding. "Ready?"

"Ready," Alaina nodded. Together, they made another sprint toward the stables. This sprint was longer than the one to the wall, and Alaina could feel the exhaustion from her challenge earlier again. However, seeing David and Koen waiting for them gave her the extra push she needed to make it across.

"How was it?" Koen asked them at the stables. Alaina looked at David, who was scanning the area for any signs of danger.

"Didn't run into any problems. Good job," Cronin told Koen and patted him on the shoulder.

"Good," David said. "Let's go then," he motioned for Cronin to lead.

"Of course," Cronin nodded. "This way." He led them away from the front entrance to the castle and more toward the side.

"The front entrance?" Koen questioned.

"No, there is a hidden entrance," Cronin answered.

"How?"

"Shh." Cronin stopped him and squeezed up against the corner of the wall. The group silently watched two knights ride by on horseback. There was a silence before Cronin looked at Koen with concern. "That's strange."

"Dolion must be readying his army," Koen said in disgust.

"Of course." Cronin nodded and moved on around the corner. They remained crouched down as they scurried along the wall of the castle. Due to low lawn maintenance, the grass provided great coverage to hide in. Stopping suddenly, Cronin turned around and pointed at the ground before him. Two wooden doors looked like they led to a cellar. *Much like at their cottage in Azgalia,* Alaina thought.

"How did you find this?" Koen laughed as he dropped down into it.

"Just wandering around," Cronin shrugged.

"It looks like a hidden hallway, not a cellar," David observed.

"Exactly. It leads straight to the kitchen, believe it or not. I think back before my father, this was used to smuggle certain items in the castle without the people knowing," Cronin said.

"Interesting," David said.

"Truly," Cronin nodded. "It gets quite dark, so just follow me," he said, and the group nodded. Cronin proceeded down the hallway at a quick but not loud pace. Alaina knew any loud sound would echo and be easily heard from either end of the hall. The last thing they wanted was to be found out.

Continuing down the hall, Alaina observed the perfectly carved stone hallway. It was rounded at the top, and the dark, wet atmosphere made it cool. It felt good to have a break from the heat outside. A few minutes later, they reached the tunnel's end and spotted a ladder.

"It leads up into the kitchen," Cronin explained. "I'll go first. The chef was in there when I came up the first time, so it won't be so odd seeing me do it again. I'll distract him," Cronin said, and climbed the ladder. He pushed up on the door above their heads and climbed into the kitchen overhead. The doors shut behind him, and the group waited in silence.

They waited for an eternity until the doors finally opened again. Cronin peeked his head through. "He was in here, but as

I said, he wasn't surprised to see me doing this again. He's off to pick up an order of vegetables, which he always insists on seeing himself. The coast is clear." He then opened the doors, and one by one, they climbed up.

Alaina pushed herself out of the tunnel into the largest kitchen she could imagine. It had the finest kitchen accessories, and the fruit in the baskets looked so ripe and juicy that it made her mouth water. Pots and pans hung from the wall, and the fireplace had beautiful details carved into the stone. "Grandmother would have loved to see this," Alaina whispered to David.

"Indeed," he said as he also admired the kitchen.

"One of my mother's many talents was design and decor. She designed every piece of this kitchen herself," Cronin pointed out. Alaina could see his pride in his mother and the sadness that clouded the memories.

Koen put a loving hand on Cronin's shoulder, and they nodded in understanding.

Making their way out of the kitchen, they carefully looked for any knights or maids they might pass. Pacing quickly down one hallway after another, Cronin halted in his tracks. He turned and put a finger to his lips. "Someone is coming," he said, looking around the corner again. "Back, back, back." He motioned for them in urgency. They hid behind whatever they could find and prayed that no one would notice their presence.

Alaina stared at the corner where they had just been. She listened to the footsteps as they drew closer, and her heart began to quicken its pace again. Suddenly, Alaina's eyes widened at Sir Dolion walking down the hallway. A knight was beside him, holding onto the head maid, Laura.

Alaina's heart dropped as she remembered that Laura had helped them find out what happened to Koen. She squeezed her eyes shut, hoping Dolion wouldn't sense anyone was looking. "Lord, please," she mouthed. She listened as the footsteps continued down the hall and breathed a sigh of relief when they faded out of hearing distance.

"We're in the clear." Koen tapped her on the shoulder. She nodded and followed him over to the corner.

"It's just down this way," Cronin said. They hurried down the hallway to two large doors that Koen and Cronin opened together. The door opened slowly, and thankfully, no one was behind them.

They walked through the doors to a short hallway with one door at the end. Alaina paused in her strides once she caught sight of it. The large doors behind her closed, and the boys joined her where she stood. Alaina could only think of one word to describe it.

"Ugly," Alaina said.

"Told you," Cronin laughed.

"I never thought there was such a thing as an ugly door." David shook his head in disbelief. "But there is no other word to describe it."

"Don't let it hear you say that; remember, we want it to open for us." Cronin winked and led them over to the door.

The coloring faded between an ugly brown-green and gray. She wasn't sure how it was possible, but there seemed to be things growing on it. It looked as though it was as old as the earth itself. How or why they let the door stay in this condition was beyond Alaina. *So strange,* she thought.

Cronin stood looking at the door and rubbed the black stubble on his chin in thought.

"Let me see your sword, David," Cronin said, and took the sword from David. Using its tip, he wedged it into the door and wiggled it. The wood on the door creaked and groaned. The sword chipped the timber and severed a crack by the doorknob.

"Well, you might as well just knock it down now." Koen held back a laugh.

"I would." Cronin looked at them. "But watch." He pushed the sword in even more until it hit something.

"Was that . . . metal?" Koen asked, confused.

"I've managed to see them open this before, and when they did, I saw the back of the door. It's made of metal. Which makes it heavier than the normal door," Cronin explained.

David tilted his head. "How do you plan on opening it with my sword then?"

"Making the door metal is where their genius stopped," Cronin laughed. With one hard shove, the sword plunged into the wedge between the wall and the door. It squeaked and popped open. Looking back at the group, he said, "I honestly didn't realize it would be this easy."

"Let's not speak too soon," David said and returned his sword. He turned toward Alaina, "Ready?"

"Ready." Alaina smiled at her brother, and they entered through the "ugly" door together.

Alaina's heart picked up again as her mind raced between emotions and different thoughts. They were about to find the truth about their father.

Entering the door led them to a dark staircase.

"What's with your people and dark passageways?" David shook his head as he started down with his sword ready. Following the stairs, there seemed to be a faint light at the bottom. The closer they came to it, the more they realized it opened into another room. Peering down, David checked to ensure no guards were in the way. He nodded when he saw that they were in the clear. Alaina followed him down, and they stood in the doorway of the entrance to the dungeon. It was massive.

It was dark, and a faint light came from somewhere in the room. Alaina felt a chill. A breeze was probably coming from a vent. Looking around, she saw so many cells and prisoners. No one had spotted them yet, so they took this time to take in their surroundings.

David looked down at Alaina. "Okay, I'll have your back. We'll go down one aisle at a time if we must."

"Okay." Alaina nodded and took a deep breath. "Follow me," she said and took a step out.

Walking down the first aisle, the prisoners seemed to stare at them as if seeing beings from another world. Looking from one face to the next was genuinely heartbreaking. Alaina saw each person as they were. Her heart broke in knowing that many of them were not only prisoners of Mizcriea but prisoners of their sins. As she passed cells, some reached out and tried to pull the hem of her skirt. She stumbled backward, but David kicked them away.

"Stay back," David hissed with a glare at a man behind bars. He glared at David with a hateful expression that sent chills up Alaina's spine. *There was evil in here, no doubt,* Alaina thought. Reaching the end of the first aisle, Alaina's eyes widened, and her heart sank.

"There are so many, David." Alaina shook her head. Fear started to cloud her mind, and she couldn't help but worry that they wouldn't find their father in time. "I don't know how I will read so many." She buried her face in her hands. It was too much. The faces, the people, their stories, she could see it all.

"Alaina, remember what grandmother taught you. Use it as a gift, for that is what it truly is. I know you feel burdened to know so much about so many, but you can't control everything. We must do what we can and trust that God will care for the rest. I'm here with you and know you're strong enough to do this, Alaina." David raised her chin, and Alaina's hands fell from her face. "God gave you the gift for a reason."

Feeling weak and vulnerable, Alaina managed a smile through her tears. She sniffed and wiped the tears from her eyes. "Thank you," she said, swallowing the frog in her throat. "One by one."

"One by one," David nodded. Alaina turned to walk down the next aisle. More prisoners were begging, pulling at her hems, and some just stared blankly, all while she read faces. Alaina prayed for strength.

"You shouldn't be in here." A voice came from a cell they had passed.

David looked at Alaina and urged her forward. "Guards!" the voice suddenly called out.

Alaina spun around to look at David, wide-eyed and worried. Guard footsteps were now making their way toward them. "David?" She searched him for what they should do.

"Stand behind me." He turned toward where the guards were coming and held his sword ready.

The guards turned the corner and locked eyes with David and Alaina. "Hey!" Their faces turned from confusion to anger. Alaina could see they hadn't seen intruders in their dungeon .

. . ever. "What are you doing here?" They started advancing with swords drawn. Alaina counted four guards. David backed up, slowly pushing Alaina behind him.

Refusing to stand back and wait for her brother to get severely injured, Alaina quickly loaded her bow and held the arrow pointing down. She didn't want to threaten them just yet.

"We're here looking for a prisoner. We don't want to cause anything, just coming peacefully." David held up a hand to show he wasn't planning on advancing.

"On whose command do you search the dungeon? This dungeon is strictly for special prisoners who have committed the worst of crimes," the one who seemed to be in charge said.

David hesitated. "We're here under the King's order."

"Sir Dolion?" the guard asked, clearly unconvinced.

"No," David said blankly. Alaina found it strange how quickly they switched their allegiance from Cleatus to Dolion.

The guard raised his sword impatiently. "If not Sir Dolion, then you serve an enemy King, and are therefore unwelcome."

"I assumed you'd say as much." David shrugged, and with that, the guards advanced.

Alaina raised her bow and released the first arrow. One guard went down, and the others advanced. One came after Alaina, and the other two attacked David. Alaina ducked under the first thrust her opponent delivered. She quickly recovered and immediately felt her combat instincts kick in. Her grandmother and David had taught her well. Throwing the bow over her shoulder, she backed up and unsheathed her long knife. The guard paused at the sight of her knife and laughed before advancing again. He delivered a volley of slices and cuts, but to his surprise, they didn't penetrate Alaina's defense one bit. She deflected each movement perfectly. Her wrist bent smoothly to deliver what she needed the long knife to do. She managed to strike his arm, which sent him into retreat. He held his arm instinctively, allowing Alaina to finish the fight. Swinging her body around, she raised her foot to knock the sword out of his hand. Her leg swung back around to balance her upright. The guard fell to the ground, and his sword clanged on the floor. Reaching down to pick it up, she sheathed her long knife and went to help David.

From what she saw, David held his own just as she imagined he would. Already, one of the guards was on the ground clutching his leg in pain. The other guard, who had been the leader, was holding up well against David. Knowing she would only get in the way, Alaina backed up but kept her sword and eyes ready for surprises.

Each cut and slice echoed in the aisle, and the prisoners watched, some in terror, and some she could tell were enjoying the most exciting thing they'd seen since being imprisoned. David blocked two thrusts the guard had tried, and finally decided he had to finish it. Just like he always did, which always made Alaina wonder. This is what made him such a good sword fighter. He could go on forever, while his opponent would eventually start to tire. Then, David would almost feed off the lack of energy and use it to empower himself. It seemed like he could outlast anyone.

With the last series, David released the now helpless guard. His sword fell to the ground, and the guard raised his hands when David's sword stopped just short of the man's heart.

"Leave," David said sternly. With that, the guard turned and sprinted toward the stairs with all the energy he had left.

"He may go tell Dolion, though," Alaina said.

"Not if Koen and Cronin stop him first." David sheathed his sword and looked at the two guards on the ground. "Let's go."

Alaina nodded and dropped the sword she had been holding. Leading again and reading faces, Alaina could still feel the adrenaline rush from the fight. She took a deep breath to calm her mind and focus. They turned about three more aisles when Alaina could feel herself growing hopeless. She wouldn't give up, but it wasn't helping seeing so many in such terrible conditions after only being imprisoned for a few months. Turning the next aisle, Alaina looked side to side, searching the different faces. Her hopes were low. Her adrenaline was now gone. She felt as though she was moving, but not feeling, growing numb to what she saw now.

Then, she stopped. Her feet wouldn't move. Her heart felt as though it had stopped. Her breath caught in her throat, and her limbs grew weak.

"David," her shaky voice whispered.

"What?" he leaned over to look at her. He followed her gaze and assumed almost the same position she held.

"David." A smile grew on her face. "It's him."

The man in the cell before them sat on the floor eating something Alaina couldn't identify. His hair was long, dark, and unruly. His beard was just as dark as his hair, but both had grey woven in between. He was thin, but not weak-looking, and his face held striking features. Alaina longed to see his eyes.

"Father," Alaina said aloud to capture the man's attention. He looked up, and Alaina's eyes immediately filled with tear.

Wisdom.

Faith.

Strength.

Fatherly.

The Gift.

Lightening blue eyes stared right back at hers. Their eyes locked, and his food hit the floor.

"Alaina," his eyes watered, "my daughter."

THIRTY-ONE

"Father." Alaina stared into her own eyes.

He looked at David, who stood beside her, and Alaina saw his pride in his son. "David, my boy," he said as a tear fell from his eye. "My children, how is this possible?" he asked as he slowly stood up.

"We'll have to explain later, we don't have much time," David said as he walked forward to unlock the cell. He had taken the key from one of the guards. Good thing he was with her, because Alaina might not have thought of that.

"Yes, yes, of course." Their father nodded and came to the cell door. Once David opened it, father and son embraced. The cool and collected David suddenly dropped, and Alaina saw the vulnerable side of her brother. Tears streamed down his cheeks—the side of him that longed for a father. Alaina watched her father's face sink into his son's shoulder, and her heart broke for him. He had been locked up for so long. They stepped back, and her father said again, "David, my son. You've grown up so much." He shook his head in disbelief.

Then he looked up at Alaina, and seeing her empathy, stepped away from David to embrace her. His arms covered her, and that's when she couldn't hold it in any longer. Like David, she let her tears flow freely down her flushed cheeks. Her father was with them now. They were no longer orphans. *What a gift!* Her heart sang in thankfulness.

His arms seemed to comfort her suddenly. "My Alaina, you are so beautiful. You are so much like your mother."

She backed away, and they stared at each other. Smiling through her tears, she said, "You're finally rescued."

"Oh my dear, I was rescued long ago by the Lord our God." He smiled. "But I couldn't be more thankful to be with my children finally."

David and Alaina shared a glance. The moment was surreal. "We found him, David," Alaina said as she sniffed and wiped her tears.

He nodded, "We found him."

Together, they walked out of the aisles and toward the stairs. "David, is it not strange that those were the only guards we've come in contact with?"

"It is, but then again," David looked back at her, "Dolion is gathering his troops. I suppose he didn't think the secret dungeon needed much protection."

"Did you happen to see a young guard? His name is Titus, and he is a friend," their father said.

David and Alaina looked at each other. "What did he look like?" David asked.

"Tall and thin. Brown hair, kind face, blue eyes," he offered a description.

"No, he doesn't sound like any of the guards we saw." David shook his head.

"I suppose that's good," their father said. "Titus has told me something about how this place works. So, how did you two manage to penetrate the door and have no one notice?"

"We have friends guarding the door for us." Alaina smiled.

"And they also happen to be the princes of Mizcriea," David said.

"Koen is helping you two?" their father asked. Alaina could see his mind piecing something together. He knew.

"Yes. You know his secret, don't you?" Alaina asked him.

"Yes. I was kidnapped before he was. Is it true he murdered the king?" he asked.

"No, sir. Dolion did. I was there when he did it," Alaina said. When her father looked at her in surprise, she told him, "I'll explain the details later."

"My question is," David chimed in from behind them, "How do you have the same name as Koen?"

Their father laughed, "Actually, he has the same name as me. His parents, the King and Queen of Azgalia, were close friends of mine when I served them at the castle. When the queen was pregnant with Koen, they told me they planned to name their son after me. Although I always wondered why King Cleatus didn't bother to change it. Rather arrogant and wicked."

David nodded while thinking it over. "Ever since we met him, I thought it strange that he shared your name. At first, that's why I thought Alaina trusted him, but I knew she had more reason than that," he said and winked at Alaina.

"It caught me off guard, too," she said.

"Well, so as not to add any more confusion, but I suppose I should tell you that I go by my second name more often, which is Aldrich," their father told them. "But of course, I would love it if the two of you would call me father." They all shared a moment of silence and wonder before continuing.

They were silent as they climbed the stairs to the door. Unsure of what was awaiting them at the top, they thought it best to be prepared for the worst.

After they had made it through the dark portion of the stairway, they could see the light up ahead from where Cronin and Koen should be awaiting them. Stepping lightly, they crept up the last few stairs and peered out the door. Alaina didn't realize she had been holding her breath until David nodded, saying they were good. Koen hurried into the doorway to help Alaina get her father up the last stair. Once they left the stairway, Koen shut the door behind them. Cronin and Alaina helped support her father, while Koen and David led them with swords drawn for defense. Alaina took a deep breath. They were almost out. They hurried through the large doors and down the hallway.

"It's so empty," Koen whispered.

"Dolion is making a lot of changes, it seems," Cronin said.

"They seem to be working in our favor," Alaina said.

"For now," Koen shrugged.

"Come on. We have to get back to the kitchen," David said.

Her father was awfully quiet, so Alaina glanced over at him to ensure he was okay. She looked at his face and realized his age for the first time. His face was wrinkled, and his hair had some silver in it. Surely the dungeon had taken a toll on his body, especially without proper nutrition. She watched her father's eyes as they bounced between people and thought this was the most excitement he'd seen in eighteen years.

Her father offered a smile when Alaina glanced at him once again. "I'm fine, Alaina."

Alaina smiled shyly. "I just want to make sure."

"Thank you. I am more than okay. I just don't want to be a burden by talking your ear off. I have so many questions," her father told her, and Alaina smiled.

"I can't wait to answer them all," she said.

They reached the kitchen and entered after Koen told them the chef was gone. "Okay, one at a time now," David said as he raised the floorboard. So one by one, they lowered back into the hidden passageway. Koen helped lower Alaina and David's father down to David. Alaina followed, then Cronin, and Koen was last. Cronin led the way to keep a quick but quiet pace.

"Isn't this something?" Alaina's father whispered.

"It's an old passageway for smuggling goods," Alaina told him.

He nodded and stared forward in silence. "I'm assuming we will be avoiding the gathering of the soldiers, correct?"

The group stopped in their tracks and looked back at him. "What do you mean?" Koen asked.

"My soldier friend told me that Sir Dolion was gathering his army on the castle grounds," his deep voice echoed in the silent tunnel.

"We didn't know," David said blankly. It was silent as they stopped to think.

"Well, for all we know, it could be on the opposite side of our exit," Cronin said. "And if it's right in the middle, we'll figure it out."

"I like this man," Alaina's father said.

"That's a compliment I'll hold on to," Cronin said with a smile.

"Okay, let's keep moving," David commanded, so they continued.

Alaina listened to their breaths echoing down the tunnel and could tell they were near the end when the echoes got quieter. "There it is," she said when she saw a ray of light breaking through. The group reached the end, and Cronin climbed the short ladder to reach the doors above. He pushed them up and climbed out. The group waited in silence, praying the army wasn't above them. The doors opened again, and Cronin stuck his head through.

"They're not here. But I can hear them. It seems as though they are the opposite way. We should go now," he said, reaching down to help each member.

Once above ground, they retraced their steps along the wall and through the tall grass. "To the stables," Cronin called from in front. When they reached the stables, all time seemed to speed up, and Alaina's heart pulsed.

Koen and David mounted horses and raced toward the main gate through the fields. Upon arrival, they ordered their men who were in place of the Mizcriea guards to raise the gate. As soon as the gate moved, Alaina mounted up with her father, and Cronin mounted another horse. Together, they raced for the gate.

Suddenly, an arrow passed Alaina's head, and she instinctively kicked her mount to go faster. They had been discovered!

"Swerve," her father said from behind her.

Of course, she thought. Nodding in response, she swerved her horse to try to throw off the archer. Arrows flew, but none struck. She sent up a prayer of thanks as her horse flew through the gate and into the forest. It wasn't until she reached the trees that she slowed down. David and Koen met her and Cronin when they were at a safe distance.

"Our men will meet us at the camp. They know what to do. Let's get Father to the camp," David told Alaina.

"Thank you, Lord," Alaina whispered and brushed away tears of thankfulness. Her father squeezed her hand, and they went toward the camp.

♕

Back at camp, they dismounted and placed their horses with the others. David helped their father down, and the group went to the main meeting tent. Alaina explained the camp to her father as they walked through it. Once they were seated inside the tent and awaiting Peter's arrival, David and Alaina went over the details of their trip.

Watching her father's face while they talked made Alaina's heart feel more at peace. Yes, he was surprised to hear about all the dangers they had lived through, but she saw how proud he was of them.

"My daughter was in the cave with a dragon and crossed the Mizcriean desert?" He grinned. "And my son," he looked at David and laughed, with tears starting to well in his eyes, "you escaped a Mizcriean slave ship and rescued a princess?" He shook his head in wonder. "My children are truly bold as lions. I couldn't be more proud." He laid a hand on each of theirs. Then he looked at Koen, who sat there smiling, "And you, Koen, it's an honor to meet you."

"The honor is all mine, sir. I believe I am named after you," Koen said with a wide smile.

"True," he laughed. "Thank you for traveling with my children and protecting Alaina towards the end."

"It was my pleasure," Koen shot Alaina a smile, making her

heart flutter.

"I'm sure it was," their father laughed. Alaina couldn't stop smiling from all the joy and gratitude she felt. The man she longed to meet, to know, to laugh with, was here in front of her, only by God's grace. He reached up to remove a loose strand of blue-black hair from his eyes. As he laughed, Alaina noticed the wrinkles around his eyes and mouth. There were signs of a long life, yet he was still considered young for a father. She saw the wisdom he had gained in the years he'd been a prisoner, but also that they weren't easy. Despite his ability to trust God in the hard times, Alaina knew that being in a cell that long wasn't an easy endeavor. She admired how he made it through and held onto his faith and gratitude, laughing with them and not in a pit of despair, only by God's grace.

"As I told them, though, since it may be hard to keep track of both our names, you can call me by my second name, Aldrich," he said, looking at Koen and Cronin.

"That works. However, I feel like I should be the one changing my name. After all, it was yours first," Koen joked.

"Nonsense. Only you can pull that name off," Aldrich joked back, and the group laughed.

"Ah, welcome to the faithful camp, Koen. After everything I've heard from your children, it's an honor to meet you," Peter said, coming in to shake Alaina and David's father's hand.

"It's an honor to be here. My children told me about you as well." He smiled. "And due to recent changes, you can call me Aldrich."

"Of course," Peter smiled back. "Please, let us sit down. I'm sure you know there is much to discuss."

"There is," Aldrich nodded.

Alaina listened as the men began talking about battle strategies and numbers. Chiming in her thoughts here and there, Alaina was glad to help. She knew most girls weren't up to such a challenge, but she and David read the same books growing up. Koen, Cronin, her father, and Peter all had experience in battle, which meant they could give better insight into specific details.

"You said you have friends from Azgalia that may prove to be valued allies?" Aldrich asked the young people.

"Yes," Koen said.

"The girl with the dragon and our friend Maxamillion from Linencrest. We think he may have connections," David said.

"Maxamillion? I believe I knew him way back when he was a boy," Aldrich said, recalling his memories.

"You did. He recognized me because I looked like you," Alaina told him.

"Remarkable," her father said, shaking his head. "It truly is a small world," he laughed. "That kid was a firebrand, but he was one of my best students."

"I also met another royal army knight on the slave ship. He helped us escape. I know he would be honored to be in the fight to defend Azgalia," David said.

"That's just what we need," Aldrich nodded.

"I know the knights at Linencrest weren't all the best team players, but I'm sure many of them would defend their own kingdom," Koen suggested.

"I agree," Alaina nodded in agreement.

"What about the princess? Evelyn, was it?" Aldrich asked, and they nodded. "Where is she?"

"She's getting word to her mother and brother in Malikai

city. She's hoping to get word to all the people we just mentioned about defending Azgalia. As soon as we get word from her, we will better understand our numbers," David explained.

"Are you all ready for battle here? The numbers we have here are what we have for sure," Aldrich said, and it was answered with silence. "I know it's a harsh word. Especially when there seemed to be peace for so long, but I'm afraid that's what this is all leading to. War isn't pretty, but it's Biblical. Defeating the enemy is Biblical. We must be ready with a defense, but we are also equipped enough to attack the enemy when the time is right." He paused to think. "And the reality is, there hasn't been peace. There is always a silent war happening between our two kingdoms. Cleatus was always finding ways to break the peace. The kidnappings are proof of that. Now is the time. I believe each of us has been brought together for a time like this, my friends." Aldrich spoke with such wisdom and truth. The young people nodded and let the words sink in.

"I couldn't agree more, my brother," Peter said. "The Lord has already defeated the ultimate enemy. Whatever comes of this war will only be what God has ordained," he said.

"Amen," Aldrich nodded with a smile.

"We're ready," Koen broke the silence.

"Are you, Koen?" Aldrich asked. Alaina could see her father's piercing gaze read Koen. He wasn't afraid to make Koen uncomfortable if it meant getting the truth. That must have been why the Kings found him such a strong asset.

Koen didn't seem to waver. But it was no surprise to Alaina. Koen was changing. He believed. "Yes, sir, I am. I believe God is the Author and Creator of my life. I have decided to commit my life to him fully and to fight for His kingdom. From what

David and Alaina say, I believe He has been adamant about drawing me to Him, no matter how much I don't deserve it," Koen said without breaking eye contact with Alaina's father.

Aldrich slowly formed a broad smile and stood up. "Koen, my boy, let me shake your hand." Koen's face broke out into a smile, and he stood up. "I can see you've come a long way, Koen. I am beyond glad that you've come to recognize the truth. Welcome to the family, Koen." Aldrich grinned back at the young man with pride.

Alaina was moved by what she saw in her father's eyes. She could almost feel his exact feelings because they were so strong. Even though he had been gone for years, he left a legacy of truth that trickled down into his children, leading to the salvation of Koen, who was named after him. Alaina knew her father wasn't proud of himself, but rather proud to be a Christian, to be a man chosen by God for such a legacy.

After more discussion about the war, Christopher entered the tent and became acquainted with Aldrich. Soon after, they received a letter from Evelyn, who had relayed the news to her family and sent word to Harleigh and Maxamillion. The letter also said that her brother had ordered the news of the war to be sent out throughout the kingdom. People were directed to seek shelter or to join in to defend their beloved kingdom. She encouraged them to prepare as quickly as possible, as her brother was already assembling the royal armies of Azgalia. She told them she had informed her mother and brother about Koen. They had reacted in surprise, doubtful at first, but after hearing the news, they were thrilled. She said she'd never seen her mother smile so big, and for once, she said, Gavin may have become teary-eyed. They couldn't wait to meet him.

After hearing about King Malikai, they were extremely thankful for some good news. Besides being broken-hearted for the king, they were well and trusting in the Lord. The letter ended with the exact words,

"We're ready for war."

THIRTY-TWO

David stepped out of his tent and stared at the sky. The clouds were thick, but they would burn off around noon. The birds were silent. It was almost as if they were holding their breath for the day ahead. They had received word that Sir Dolion was releasing the troops and would cross the border today and attack.

They also received word Evelyn was on her way back with help. David expected their arrival within the hour. He'd been praying faithfully for her safety every night and had been surprised at how much he missed her while she was gone. Gavin would come, along with their friends Max and Harleigh. She mentioned nothing about dragons, but David knew Harleigh wouldn't leave her dragon behind.

He looked around the camp and shook his head in wonder at how they had managed to bring all these people across the desert and over the border into Azgalia. He was amazed and overwhelmed at all God had done and continued to do. He truly believed it wouldn't have been possible without God on their side.

Across from him, his father, Aldrich, exited his tent looking well-rested and even better than when they found him in the cell. His eyes caught sight of David. He nodded and smiled before walking over to meet Peter. It had been a few days since they rescued their father. Now, he was here, strong and willing to fight. He had somehow found his way easily into leadership alongside Peter, who thoroughly enjoyed his company. His wisdom and character were Godly and kind, evident in how he treated people with graciousness, but also righteous and just, in how he handled tasks.

Just then, Jamie came running toward him with a grin the size of the sun. David laughed, "What is it?"

"Dragons! I've never seen them before!" Jamie said, wide-eyed and full of wonder, like a child.

David smiled and then paused. *They're here already?* As soon as his eyes caught a glimpse of the dragons, meaning there was more than just Rigel, his eyes widened. He followed Jamie to the cliffside in the distance, and his mouth dropped. It was so much more than they could have hoped for. Not only was Max there with royal army soldiers, but Finwick walked alongside them with many familiar faces from the slave ship. David recognized some tournament knights from their time in Linencrest. Harleigh rode on Rigel beside Evelyn, who rode alongside her elder brother, Gavin. Behind them were thousands of Azgalian knights ready for war.

"Almost brings me to tears," Jamie said as he stared straight ahead.

David swallowed the lump in his throat. The beauty and the awe of what God was providing were just too much for him to fathom. "I'd have to agree."

Alaina ran up behind them, with Koen trailing close behind. "They're here?" she asked, and then she followed his gaze to see what they were staring at. Pretty soon, the whole camp stood watching. When they finally arrived at the base of the camp, everyone cheered.

Evelyn dismounted and ran to hug Alaina, Koen, and David. "It's so good to see you all!" She grinned. "Gavin?" She looked back at her brother, who was making his way over. "Gavin, meet my friends." Koen cleared his throat and winked at Evelyn, which made her laugh, "And of course, our brother."

Gavin looked at Koen, and David could tell they were brothers. How Evelyn hadn't seen it before, David could only wonder. Koen, obviously unsure what to do, held out his hand to shake Gavin's. Gavin smiled and reached out for it, instead pulling him into an embrace.

"I can't begin to tell you how amazing this is," Gavin said with watery eyes. Being the man he was, though, he quickly pulled back and gave Koen a loving slap on the shoulder. "Looks like you take after your older brother with your good looks," he winked at Koen. Soon, they were all acquainted again with their old friends and now new ones. David showed the leaders towards their established meeting tent to discuss their battle plans.

As he looked around the table, David was reminded of the stories his grandmother would tell him about the legends of Azgalia and the lands before Azgalia was founded. The round table held everyone perfectly. Max sat beside Finwick and Aldrich. Harleigh and Alaina were talking. Koen, Evelyn, Gavin, and Cronin were all getting acquainted. Jamie and Christopher sat beside David, discussing Jamie's fascination with dragons.

David looked up when he noticed Peter had walked into the tent. He stood and waited for everyone to settle down before welcoming everyone to the camp.

"I cannot begin to say how great our God is." Peter smiled. "Amen?"

And all of God's children said, "Amen."

Alaina stood looking in the mirror that was sitting on her cot. She stared down at the reflection that looked back at her. They would line up and get into position for the attack in just a few moments. She was dressed in women's warrior clothing that Evelyn had brought for the women who had chosen to join. She had to admit she loved them. They were heavier than her daily clothes, making her feel more secure and strong. The dress featured dark blue and black colors, adorned around the neckline with small red flowers. These flowers represented the Kingdom of Azgalia. Her favorite part of the dress was the cross centered in the middle of the neckline. She raised her gaze to peer back at herself in the mirror. As she stared at her appearance, she realized she looked older, not from wrinkles or anything worn down physically, but more in a mature way. She took a deep breath and let her mind drift to the day before. She had been standing in the meeting tent, deep in thought about the war and extremely worried about the times ahead. Concerned about the safety of her loved ones: her twin brother, who will be in hand-to-hand combat, her father, whom she had just found, could be easily retaken from her; Koen, whom she had grown very fond of, could also very well fall into the hands of Mizcriea.

"Reflection of oneself is important." The words played through her mind. "You must understand yourself, your strengths and weaknesses, before you can do anything your best," her father told her.

She could see his face and his voice in her mind. The sun shone down and made his aged skin glow. His old, wrinkled face showed his wise old age, and his voice was raspy but comforting. He had a jawline and a chin that showed determination, yet eyes that showed kindness.

Throughout this journey, she told everyone she'd do her best. Yesterday, when he asked about her quest and the war, she answered with the same thing she had told so many, but she had not expected his response.

He asked, "Do you know your best? In fact, do you even know yourself?"

She had been confused by his response, unable to answer his quick comeback. "I'm not sure what you mean," she replied.

"What I mean is this: people have expected so much of you for so long. They expect a strong and fearless girl, so you've adopted that as your own thinking. You've taken their expectations and made them your reality. You don't even know who you truly are. When was the last time you examined yourself? When have you done your best *YOU* and not *them*? You go on reading everyone else's personalities and thoughts; you become so consumed by others around you that you forget yourself. You may have just met me a few days ago, but a father knows his daughter. And I have the same gift you do. I know the struggles. And you've never had someone read you, but I can. Do you understand what I'm saying?" He folded his arms and searched her eyes, much like his own.

"I . . . I think I do." The wheels in her mind began to spin. He was right. *Who was she really? What was her best? Does she have a best? What were her thoughts?* The sad thing was that she couldn't tell.

"You're right." Her eyes dropped to the floor, and she squeezed them shut. She would not cry.

"How do I find out who I am?" She opened her eyes but continued to look at the cobbled stone floor.

"By finding who you are in Christ. By letting go of everyone else's thoughts. By finding the truth." He placed a comforting hand on her shoulder.

She looked into his eyes and let them fill with tears—tears of joy, tears of happiness. She knew what she had to do.

"Thank you! Thank you!" She smiled and used the sleeve of her tunic to wipe the tears from her eyes.

"Anytime, my dear," he said with a kind smile.

She stood in the middle of the room with a new mind, new determination, new understanding, and new strength. She would be able to finish this now.

"Are you ready to go?" David interrupted her thoughts of the day before.

"Yes. I'm ready." She nodded and turned to face him. Their blue eyes locked, and after a few moments of silence, they walked out of her tent together.

Today was the day that they fulfilled their quest—the quest for the kingdom.

The troops were now lined up. Alaina stared ahead at the river, which separated the two kingdoms. She steadied her breathing so she wouldn't be nervous.

They had gone over the plan of attack several times; her father was thorough on the details. Everyone knew what to do; she was confident in that. She only struggled with the fact that today's war could go one of two ways: either Mizcriea overruns Azgalia, and many die, or Azgalia claims victory, and the kingdom's peace is restored. The Lord already knew the outcome of today.

As she continued to stare, she thought of her conversation with Max the day before. She had mentioned her worry, but the reminder he gave her encouraged her.

"Alaina, whether Azgalia conquers today or not, Christ has already won the ultimate war. Christ's kingdom has already won. There's hope no matter the outcome," Max said.

It was true. They can always have hope, even in the most uncertain things. Taking another deep breath, she glanced around her. She spotted several of her close friends and many Azgalians who had chosen to fight for their home. She spotted her father, and he was focused on the war ahead. They were to wait for his signal once he spotted a Mizcriean soldier. Once they crossed the border, they would carry out a surprise attack.

Suddenly, Aldrich raised his hand and pointed. Everyone followed his point and spotted the first few Mizcriean soldiers.

Now, they waited.

Her breathing was steady, but her heart was beating wildly. She heard a slight sound next to her and looked over. Koen knelt beside her and shot her a grin.

"I realize I probably shouldn't be smiling so big, but I've got a good feeling. I can't explain it, though," Koen said quietly.

"I'm still nervous."

"Me too. It's normal," Koen nodded.

They looked forward again and saw the soldiers crossing the river. Once they crossed the invisible line that Aldrich had made, they would make the advance. Some of the soldiers would still be crossing, but couldn't move fast enough through the water.

They were just a few feet away from the line.

"I've got your back if you get mine," Koen whispered, making her heart skip a beat.

Focus, Alaina. She nodded in response and pulled her first arrow of the day. Pulling up her bow, she placed the back of her hand against her cheek. Squinting one eye, she stared her target down. Once his feet crossed the line, she released.

The knight fell to the ground, and the others pulled out their swords in confusion. The Azgalians were on them in seconds. Koen and Alaina ran alongside them. Alaina had never felt adrenaline and power like this before. The amount of energy running through her body as she advanced alongside thousands of Azgalinas was such that she couldn't help but call out their battle cry along with them.

Koen swung at the first knight he encountered. A knight in his blind spot swung at him, but Alaina released an arrow before he could complete his swing. She felt her senses were heightened, and she was on high alert, ready for a strike at any moment. Koen turned and nodded in her direction. She nodded back and pulled another arrow to save David in the same way. Her sword was at her side just in case; she knew her arrows wouldn't last all day.

A knight came at her with a sword and sent her into retreat. She threw her bow around her shoulder and unsheathed her sword. Twirling around, she and the knight met blades. He swung and thrust, but she skillfully deflected. He succeeded in cutting her arm, which made her groan. She pretended to thrust but cut it short just in time to find an opening in his block. She struck him down and took a deep breath.

"You okay?" Max stopped on his way past her.

"I'm good," she nodded and placed her sword back on her belt. She looked down at her arm and winced at the look of it. Oozing blood, she wiped it on the skirt of her dress and read-justed her bow. She looked back up at him, and they nodded at each other before advancing again. *Where was Sir Dolion?*

David advanced toward his next opponent. The fight was quick. The knights were well-trained, but some were less skilled than others.

His heart was beating rapidly, yet he ignored it and used the adrenaline to power his swings. He could see his allies around him in battles of their own. Some had fallen, but they must continue.

A Mizcriean knight came charging at David with sword raised and ready. David caught his swing, and they were im-mediately in combat. Cut, thrust, block, swing, repeat. David ducked under a cut the knight released and returned the favor with a volley of cuts and slices. This knight was more skilled, making David realize he would have to push harder this time. Going back and forth between offense and defense, David finally made a victory thrust that sent his opponent to the ground, holding his shoulder in agony.

Looking to his right, he could see Evelyn and Gavin as they fought the enemy. His father was further in front of him. Koen and Cronin were in a battle together with a larger knight. Alaina was holding her ground well. He spotted Max and Finwick teaming up as several knights tried to take them down. They seemed unstoppable. Harleigh was somewhere, but he didn't know where. Jamie was . . . well, he couldn't see him either.

"David, on your right!"

David laughed. There he was. Jamie ran past him and turned to wink before spinning on his heel again to meet blades with a knight.

"You good?" David called out as he ran past Jamie.

"Better than ever," Jamie said out of breath as he battled his opponent.

Focusing back on the moment, he looked down to go around a knight on the ground. *Onto the next fight,* he thought. As he ran, he never stopped praying.

He was pretty sure they were winning by now—or at least, he hoped so. Koen had lost track of time as the battle raged on. His muscles ached, and his body was tired. It didn't matter, though; he pressed on.

He had lost sight of his friends a while ago, but Azgalian knights still surrounded him. Cronin still stood by him, fighting.

"I haven't seen Uncle this whole time!" Cronin yelled above the clanging of blades.

"Neither have I! Maybe he cowered out and let his army fight for him!" Koen responded in the same way. Almost at the same time, their opponents fell. They moved closer to each other.

"I don't know why, but I feel he still plans on showing up. You know Dolion likes to keep secrets for a big reveal," Cronin reasoned.

Koen nodded, "I'm afraid you might be right."

Then suddenly, they were surrounded by a circle of knights closing in on them. Cronin and Koen raised their swords and readied themselves.

"Koen, we're surrounded!" Cronin said just loud enough for Koen to hear.

"Now we'll be able to attack in any direction," Koen smirked. Cronin gave him a wide-eyed stare and a disapproving head shake. Koen laughed and jumped forward to initiate the first strike.

Harleigh was hidden away from the war, not ready to come out. She was breathing hard, trying to muster the courage to leave her area. She knew she had come because she wanted to help, to fight for her kingdom. She knew she could help, but now, she sat paralyzed by fear and unable to move. Tears slipped down her cheeks as she thought about how weak she must have looked right then.

"Oh, don't look at me like that, Rigel," she said when she met the gaze of her dragon.

Harleigh glared back. He lay in front of her, waiting for her to get up.

A man ran past her toward the fighting, but paused when he noticed her. The man turned toward her and looked from the dragon to her.

"Harleigh!" His eyes widened, and he smiled as if he had just found treasure.

"Yes?" Harleigh sniffed and wiped the tears off her cheeks.

"Harleigh, my name is Aldrich, I'm Alaina and David's father." The man walked over to her and sheathed his sword.

"But I thought Alaina said your name was Koen?" Harleigh looked up through her blurry vision.

Aldrich laughed. "It is. I recently changed it to make things easier for everyone. With there being another Koen and all." Aldrich smiled kindly down at her. "May I ask why you and your magnificent dragon aren't joining us?"

Harleigh smiled at the fact that he described Rigel as "magnificent."

"I don't think I can do it."

"What do you mean? You've come to fight, haven't you? You strike me as a brave young lady." Aldrich tilted his head. "Am I wrong?"

"I like to think I am; I thought I was, but now I'm not so sure." Harleigh looked down at the ground. "I'm so scared."

"Harleigh, my dear, many of us here today are scared. Terrified even. However, we fight confidently knowing our God wins no matter the outcome. And my dear, true bravery and courage come when you are scared, but rise anyway," Aldrich said.

Harleigh had never met anyone like this man.

"Really? I can be scared, but brave?" Harleigh sniffed again and raised her chin.

"Honestly."

Aldrich nodded and stretched out his hand. She took his hand and stood up. "Now what do you say? You and that dragon make a grand entrance?" Aldrich smiled.

Harleigh grinned, "I'd like that."

Cut, slice, strike. Duck, parry, retreat. Advance, slice, thrust.

Alaina planned the moves out in her head as she fought to remain on her feet. A few times, she struggled to take down her opponent, but she had yet to fall. Her brother and grandmother had trained her well, and now it was all paying off.

"Ah!" She ducked under a close call but rose with a cut in an opening the knight had left for her to see.

He fell, clutching his side, and Alaina looked up to see her surroundings. Koen and Cronin were against several knights, and David was moving through the knights with ease. Up ahead in the distance, she noticed something that hadn't been there before. Was it moving? She squinted.

"No." Her heart sank.

Ahead, on a hill, behind the army, Sir. Dolion rode on a horse with another massive army behind him.

She looked over at David, and he met her eyes with the

same look she probably had on her face. It seemed impossible, but she knew they couldn't just give up.

"Fight for victory, Azgalia!" a voice cried above Alaina's head.

Startled, she looked up and to her amazement, a dragon whisked over her. Harleigh yelled from on top of Rigel with her fist in the air. Dragons followed her and crowded the skies. Alaina's hope was renewed, and the other Azgalians felt the same way, because they all began to cheer. They shouted and charged forward again with strength and hope renewed.

Alaina watched Harleigh fly over to Dolion with his army. Once Harleigh reached them, a wave of fire poured down from the dragon's mouth. It blanketed the army, and Alaina knew right then that victory was still in sight.

Alaina met David's eyes again, and they both nodded. They wouldn't give up.

THIRTY-THREE

Koen took a deep breath before his last thrust. The knight fell, and another came at him. "Cronin!" Koen called out to his brother above the clanging of swords.

"Over here!" Cronin answered from somewhere behind him.

"Just making sure you're still alive!" Koen called and ducked under a swing. Suddenly, a knight came from his left with a surprise attack that Koen knew he couldn't thwart. He battled the knight before him to keep the sword from striking him; he hoped the side attack wouldn't be fatal.

"Oh no, you don't." Gavin jumped in just in time to knock the sword from the knight's hands. He was caught off guard, so Gavin's blow sent him backward. Gavin spun around and delivered a volley of cuts beside Koen until the knight fell.

"Thank you," Koen said gratefully. All three men jumped over a fallen tree and crouched to hide behind the trunk.

"I'm not losing my little brother again." Gavin turned to meet Koen's eyes.

Koen realized they both had the same sea-green eyes. He'd always thought it strange that, growing up, he had been the only one with exotic-looking eyes. Gavin's chin was set firmly, and his frame made him the perfect model prince. Now, though, he would be king of Azgalia.

"I appreciate it." Koen smiled.

"I know," Gavin laughed and looked out at the Azgalian soldiers. "It's weird."

Koen shrugged. "I'm just glad I know that I'm not actually the son of Cleatus," he said jokingly.

"Hey now," Cronin said from the other side of Koen.

Koen gave him a playful shove. "Joking."

"No, you're not. I don't blame you," Cronin laughed.

Gavin smiled, "Just sorry I have to meet you under these circumstances."

"I agree," Koen nodded. "But I think you and I agree this is better than walking the flower fields in a castle garden."

"I'd have to agree," Gavin smiled. "Duck."

He dropped down just as Gavin swung his sword to meet the torso of a Mizcriean knight.

"Better just get used to me saving you. I'm your big brother now," Gavin smirked and turned to fight off more.

Koen and Cronin did the same. Pretty soon, they found themselves in the heat of the battle. Koen paused for a moment to look around. He realized he was now in the middle of the Mizcriean army. "Now, I just have to work my way through," Koen muttered as he skillfully thwarted one cut after another. His muscles ached from the constant action.

After knocking down his fifth opponent, he took a few deep breaths to regain strength. He had lost sight of Cronin and Gavin. He was sure he was the only Azgalian fighter this far into the army.

"Glad to see you home."

Koen stiffened. It was the same deep, steely voice that had brought him nothing but pain the last few days. He turned to face his uncle.

Sir Dolion peered down at Koen as if he were a mouse. When a knight came up to take Koen down, Dolion yelled at him to back off.

"He's mine!" he growled.

The knight cowered back and disappeared.

"You don't deserve to set foot in this kingdom. Or any kingdom for that matter," Koen said.

"Oh? You think I care?" Sir Dolion gave an amused laugh and rolled his eyes.

"No, I don't think you do. But as you can see, Azgalia cares very much. That's why you won't be walking away from this battlefield today," Koen spoke sternly.

"Is that a threat to my life I'm hearing? I thought you had joined the faithful? If I'm correct, they don't speak that way," Sir Dolion mocked.

"What you've done deserves death. However, I do not intend to kill you," Koen told him.

"I'd say that's a mistake," Dolion shook his head. "And here I thought I had trained you well."

"You did."

Koen flipped his sword in the air to show he was ready to fight.

Dolion stared him down. "I suppose this has to happen sooner rather than later." He climbed from his horse and threw the reins over the saddle. He unsheathed his sword and looked Koen up and down. "Only because you were my favorite student, will I make this quick," he said.

"Only because I considered you my uncle as a child, will I let you live." Koen glared at him. "I've beaten you before, I can do it again."

They stood, eyes locked, waiting for the other to make the first attack. Koen knew that he would've already attacked just a few weeks ago. Koen used to be impulsive and act before thinking. Now, though, he had learned much. He decided to fight more like David. So, he waited. No matter how much it killed him.

Sir Dolion was patient and a skilled swordsman, but Koen was sure his hate would get the best of him.

He was right. Dolion made the first move.

Dolion launched forward and didn't hold back. Koen parried his swings at first in a struggle, but he quickly poised himself. Their swords clanged together more loudly than Koen thought normal; that's how he knew his uncle was fighting out of rage.

Koen ducked to avoid a thrust. Recovering, he stepped to the left and made a pivot on his foot to bring momentum in for a slash. His uncle fell back and grabbed his side in pain. He fixed his stance, and their swords clashed together again. Koen held onto his sword as his blade vibrated from the impact, took a deep breath, and continued to fight.

He failed to block one move and fell back, jarred from the slash Dolion had delivered, which left him defenseless. He looked up at Dolion, and all he could see was a sword coming down on him. He had failed, and now he would die on the battlefield. He knew, though, that he didn't fear death. Like he had grown to learn from being surrounded by so many believers at the faithful camp, he knew where his soul would go. As the sword inched closer, he prayed for thankfulness and closed his eyes.

"No!" Cronin's voice came loud, and at that very moment,

Koen heard the sword pierce flesh.

Yet, he felt no pain.

It wasn't his.

Koen's eyes shot open, and he saw Dolion looking beside Koen; Cronin was on the ground with the sword through his abdomen.

"Cronin, no!" Koen cried and rolled over beside his brother.

"It's my job to protect my little brother," Cronin managed to speak, but his voice was weak. He breathed deeply but winced at the pain. Tears gathered in Koen's eyes as he watched his brother in agony. Their eyes met, and Koen shook his head in disbelief.

"No, Cronin, no." He wasn't sure how much more his heart could take.

"You have a kingdom to restore," Cronin said, squeezing Koen's hand one last time, and his last breath escaped his lips.

Koen whirled at his uncle. "Look what you've done!" His heart ached like never before, and adrenaline began rushing through his body in an instant.

"Oh, don't act so surprised," Dolion rolled his eyes and bent down to pick up a sword from a fallen knight, "Besides, I was aiming for you." He shrugged, which made Koen's anger burn.

Sir Dolion motioned around them at the vast army. "Give up now, Koen, look around you. I've already won."

Koen glared up at him. "Never." He leaped forward and released a volley of cuts and slices. His eyes kept a sharp eye on Dolion to catch any trickery.

Dolion found an opening, but Koen saw his opportunity and took it. He slid through Dolion's wide stance and ended up on the other side of him. Going in for a stab, Dolion managed to evade it. He spun around in anger.

"I didn't teach you that," Sir Dolion sneered.

"No, you didn't," Koen answered, but left no room to continue the conversation. Swords ringing together again, Koen couldn't explain it, but he felt stronger, more capable this time. He knew it was the opportune moment.

He approached with a thrust but cut it short. After pulling short and going in for the legs, Dolion leaped in the air, thinking he had avoided a fatal blow. Instead, Koen launched forward and sent Dolion tumbling onto his back and sword a few feet away from them.

Koen was over him in the next instant with the tip of his sword at Dolion's throat.

"Congratulations," Dolion growled. "Now finish it."

"That's what you deserve," Koen paused. "But it's already finished," Koen said, peering down at the man he used to consider his uncle. He then removed his sword from Dolion's throat and stepped back.

Dolion quickly rose. "Fool! You should have ended me when you had the—" he was cut off by giant talons. A dragon swooped in and yanked him into the sky, unable to finish his words.

"Chance?" Koen finished his sentence as he watched the dragon fly off.

It was over. It had taken great sacrifice and loss, but they had won. He then fixed his gaze on the sky momentarily and thanked God.

"Only by your strength was I able to defeat him. Thank you." Koen bowed his head and took a deep breath. "It's truly finished."

Looking back up, he caught sight of his friends and family. When they saw him, he lifted his sword in the air and cried out, "Victory is ours!"

The news quickly spread across the battlefield, and the Mizcriean knights dropped their swords one by one. They knew their defeat. Without their ruler behind the army, they had nothing to fight for.

The Azgalian people cheered. They had conquered Mizcriea against all odds. Together, they praised God for His providence.

The cheer seemed to go on forever.

That same night, the people of Azgalia celebrated the victory in Malikai. Those who were hurt had been taken to tents to be tended to so they could heal. The young people and elders decided to return to the Mizcriean castle to set things right. David, Gavin, and Koen found the men around the royal castle and either released the prisoners or found new positions for those who chose to stay. Aldrich and Peter visited the parchment room to find the information they needed to continue with the restoration plan for the kingdom. Alaina and Evelyn visited the maids and told them of the good news. Those who were captured were set free. Those who lived nearby decided to stay and serve whoever would rule next.

"Who will rule next?" Peter looked at Aldrich as they stood in the parchment room. There was much to be discussed, but they agreed the two diverse kingdoms would function better with different rulers, yet God and His Word would be the ultimate authority.

"Well, is there any real question?" Aldrich smiled. "It has to be Koen."

Peter nodded, "Do you think he's up for it?"

"I think he will be. I don't think we need to force it, but I believe his story has prepared him for this moment," Aldrich said.

"I think so, too." Peter smiled. "No doubt God's hand has been on Koen since day one."

The next day, Aldrich and Peter called for a meeting in the great throne room to discuss their new findings and plans for the future. After giving their reports, Aldrich and Peter looked at each other.

"What is it?" Alaina asked, looking from one man to the other. The young people waited expectantly.

"We have both decided that there must still be a king in Mizcriea to establish order under God and continue peace with Azgalia," Peter started the explanation.

"Who will that be?" Evelyn asked, but Alaina already knew, and her eyes went wide.

Aldrich looked over at Koen and looked into his eyes. "Koen, we believe the duty is reserved for you, if you're willing."

"I . . . I don't know what to say." Koen shook his head in disbelief.

"Well, do you accept? What do you think?" Aldrich laughed.

Alaina saw Koen's nerves and emotions swirling. She knew that he knew this duty had been reserved for Cronin as the true bloodline. However, Cronin was no longer with them, as he gave his life to save Koen. Yet, he was not altered by this offer. Alaina believed that God had been preparing Koen for this in small ways. Although surprised, Koen did not seem overwhelmed.

"I would be honored to take on such a responsibility," Koen answered.

Alaina's smile widened, and soon, all hands were on Koen. Together, they prayed over Mizcriea's future and Koen's rule over the kingdom.

"Would you believe it, little brother? We'll be kings together." Gavin smiled and embraced Koen.

This was a moment they would never forget.

In Azgalia, the celebration continued. They had planned to begin preparations to build Mizcriea on a righteous foundation after the celebration.

Alaina watched as the people of Malikai city danced, ate, and smiled in joy. Although they grieved for their fallen king, the royal family encouraged the people to celebrate Azgalia's victory. King Malikai would have wanted it.

There were so many candles everywhere she looked; they twinkled like the night sky. The feast was incredible, with aromas from the food that she thought were the closest she could get to a heavenly feast. Her heart was full of thankfulness as she looked around at her new friends and the family she had found. She adjusted her gaze and saw David standing on the bridge overlooking the castle courts. On her way to join him, she met Koen.

"Alaina, you did it," Koen smiled.

"Couldn't have done it without you," Alaina smiled back.

"True," Koen shrugged jokingly. "But really, you trusted me and convinced David to let me help you. Even if you didn't have the gift, something tells me you still would have shown me grace. Not only did you give me a chance, but you were an example of the love and grace of Christ. I saw it before, but now I see it even more as a believer. Joining you and your brother on this quest was the greatest thing that could have ever happened to me. So, thank you."

Alaina initially didn't know what to say; tears welled up in her eyes. She wiped one escapist away and looked up at Koen. "I'm so thankful you gained so much from it. I also gained so much from it and from having you on it with us."

She paused, remembering all that Koen had done for her. "I need to thank you as well. You were there when David couldn't be; even when he was, you were there for us both. You proved yourself to be a true hero and warrior for Christ. It has been an honor to be a part of your story, Koen. I can only wait anxiously to see what else the Lord does with you."

When she finished, Koen didn't try to fight the tears that fell down his face. It was a joyous yet emotional night. They embraced, and when they separated, Koen's eyes met Alaina's. With a soft smile, Koen reached up to tuck a piece of hair behind her ear, making her heart skip.

Care.

Tenderness.

Admiration.

Love.

Alaina realized what she had just seen in Koen and looked

down, worried she shouldn't have known.

"Alaina, I have nothing to hide," he said, lifting her chin. "My care for you has grown." He moved his hand and reached behind his neck to rub it out of nervousness. "I spoke with your father about it, actually, and if you feel the same, I would like to possibly, uh . . . " While he spoke, Alaina could hardly believe what she was hearing. *Was this really happening?* "I would like to pursue more than a friendship with you."

Alaina smiled. *Yep, this is really happening.* "Koen, I would love that." She met his eyes, and he mirrored her smile.

"Me too." He smiled sweetly at her before taking her hand and kissing the back of it. "I believe you were on your way to see your brother. I'll find you in a moment. I am going to tell Jamie the good news." Koen walked away with the biggest smile she had ever seen on his face.

She walked the cobblestone path and followed the candlelit torches up to her brother.

"It's amazing," David whispered.

Alaina smiled and followed his gaze to the celebration. "It is. You found a good spot."

David smiled, "Sure did." They sat silently before he spoke again, "Can you believe it? What happened? And where are we now?" David looked at her. "I mean, our father is right down there."

"I know." Alaina smiled through yet more tears of happiness. "I can't believe it." Their eyes met briefly, and Alaina knew they both had much to say to each other. She was so proud of David and all he had gone through, and how he had come out of it. She couldn't imagine being on the slave ship and in a slave trade escape! He was shocked to hear that she and Koen had gone through the Mizcriean desert and to hear that Koen had almost died from a snake bite. She thought back to their journey through Azgalia and how the Lord perfectly orchestrated their quest so that they had met certain people at the most perfect moments. Their sibling bond was forever strengthened.

"Alaina?" David said.

"Yeah?" Alaina tilted her head.

"You know what I realized? We started this as a quest to find our father, but it ended up being much more than that," David said.

"I thought the same thing." Alaina nodded.

"It was a quest for the kingdoms," David said.

Alaina thought of her grandmother and knew she would be so proud. Alaina knew that if she were there, she would be overjoyed to see the two kingdoms on the way to restoration and peace. Alaina thought about what her grandmother would call their extraordinary story. She smiled when she knew and fixed her eyes on the celebration below. It would be a story she prayed she could tell her own grandchildren one day. How God gained victory over evil, and used His people to restore peace in the land.

Alaina leaned forward on the ledge in front of her. She rested an arm down, and with the other, she rested her chin on it. Tilting her head to the side with a glimmer in her eye, she said, "I think I'll call it Kingdoms Quest.

ABOUT THE AUTHOR

Faith Culpepper is a wife, mother, and, above all, a daughter of the King of Kings. She considers herself a "multipotential-ite," always diving into new interests. Whether spending time with her family, traveling, sketching, writing, or working on her photography business, Faith thrives in creativity and adventure. She also enjoys action sports, CrossFit, reading, coffee, and running her multiple businesses.

Originally from Southern California, Faith now lives in South Georgia, where she met her husband, Jeremiah. She is the second eldest of eight siblings and has traveled to 11 countries and 45 U.S. states. Among her greatest adventures, she has been blessed to have climbed Mt. Kilimanjaro and dive in the Great Barrier Reef! These experiences have deepened her faith and filled her with an awe of God.

One of her biggest passions is spreading the truth about her Savior, Jesus Christ, and encouraging others in their walk.

Kingdom Quest has been a long time coming, and she prays that it encourages and inspires believers to seek first the Kingdom of God!